About Cheryl Adnams

Cheryl Adnams lives in Adelaide, South Australia. She has published four Australian rural romance novels and this is her second Australian historical novel. Cheryl has a Diploma in Freelance Travel Writing and Photography, has lived and worked in the United States and Canada, and spent two years with a tour company in Switzerland and Austria. Her favourite writing retreats include Positano on the Amalfi Coast and Port Willunga Beach just south of Adelaide. When she's not writing, Cheryl is still creating in her busy full-time job as a learning designer.

If you'd like to know more about Cheryl's books, visit her webpage cheryladnams.com.

The Bushranger's Wife

Cheryl Adnams

First Published 2019
First Australian Paperback Edition 2021
ISBN 9781867208129

Published by
Mira
An imprint of Harlequin Enterprises (Australia) Pty Limited (ABN 47 001 180 918), a subsidiary of
HarperCollins Publishers Australia Pty Limited (ABN 36 009 913 517)
Level 13, 201 Elizabeth St
SYDNEY NSW 2000
AUSTRALIA

® and TM (apart from those relating to FSC®) are trademarks of Harlequin Enterprises (Australia) Pty Limited or its corporate affiliates. Trademarks indicated with ® are registered in Australia, New Zealand and in other countries.

A catalogue record for this book is available from the National Library of Australia
www.librariesaustralia.nla.gov.au

Printed and bound in Australia by McPherson's Printing Group

MIX
Paper from
responsible sources
FSC® C001695

This book is dedicated to my dedicated readers.

One

September 1861—Central Highlands, Victoria

His heart pounded against his ribs. Thrill mixed with nerves to bring on that heady feeling of power. Sweat matted his russet hair and trickled down his jaw into the black kerchief he wore across his nose and mouth. After all these years, he still felt the tiny element of fear that came with the thrill. The day it was no longer there was the day he ought to give it up for good. Fear was what kept him alive.

Beneath him, the horse could sense his emotions. Her hooves shuffled restlessly in the dry gum leaves. Her nostrils flared, snorting with anticipation as the thud and vibration of a carriage, pulled by a team of horses, drew closer.

Leaning forward in the saddle, he patted the twitching shoulder muscles of his trusty bay mare.

'Easy, Persephone,' he soothed. Named for the bride of Hades, she was the perfect horse for Jack the Devil.

The two men beside him sat light in their saddles, primed and ready, awaiting his timely nod. The shake of his head was barely perceptible, but they understood.

1

Not yet.

The rattle of the approaching wheels on the road was now unmistakable in the quiet whisper of the trees, but still they waited. The timing had to be perfect to ensure the carriage was not allowed a last-minute change of course. They'd chosen this particular place on the road for its narrowness and the rocky out-crop that hemmed the left side. No chance of escape once inside the naturally formed bottleneck.

After nearly a decade on the highway, Jack had learned a thing or two. Like how not to get caught. And, more importantly, how not to get shot.

'Stay calm, stay alive,' he told his men.

He'd said this before he'd robbed his first coach with Bobby as a reckless young man, and throughout his long and illustrious career it had become his motto. Like a prayer and an order com-bined, he said it to his men before each encounter.

And then …

'Go!'

Leaping from their hiding place behind the copse of stringy-barks, the three masked men of the highway formed a v-shape as they rode directly into the path of the oncoming carriage.

Startled, the four horses leading the vehicle pulled up despite the coach driver whipping them to keep moving. In vain he tried to urge them onwards, but the highwaymen circled the carriage, forcing it to halt.

Jack lifted his gun and aimed it at the driver.

'Stand and deliver!'

Swearing up a storm, the coach driver resignedly settled the horses.

'Drop the reins.'

With another quiet curse, the man did as instructed, raising his hands in surrender.

Jack edged Persephone closer to the coach, while Bobby kept his eyes and gun aimed on the driver. Huge steamer trunks were strapped to both the rear and the top of the coach.

Jack grinned beneath his kerchief. *So much baggage. And expensive looking.*

'Start checking those trunks on the back,' Jack instructed Garrett. The boy was young, and flighty yet, but he had the makings of a good bushranger. 'See if there's anything of value in them.'

Dismounting with the innate grace of an expert horseman, Jack sidled up to the window of the coach with caution, his gun still at the ready. It wasn't uncommon for passengers to carry arms these days. After all, the highway was a dangerous place.

Carefully peeking into the dark carriage, he counted only two women. He relaxed his stance and tipped his hat to them. 'Good afternoon, ladies.'

'What's good about it?' the older woman shot back at him, her voice elegant and acidic at the same time.

'Madam, I beg you forgive the delay in your travels,' Jack said, unruffled by the lady's irritability. 'You seem to be carrying an awful lot of cargo for only two women. Have you travelled far?'

'All the way from England,' she sniped. 'And what greets us in this wretched outpost of the mother country? Nothing but ill-mannered thieves and these damn flies the size of cattle.' She took a swipe at a large blowfly with her gloved hand.

'Careful now,' Jack said in mock warning. 'It would be a shame to kill the national bird on your first day here in Victoria.'

A small squeak came from the opposite side of the carriage and he wondered if the other woman might have chuckled at his little joke, but it was quickly covered with a delicate cough.

'I promise we shall take but a moment to relieve you of your heavy load and you will be on your way to your destination in no time. Now, do either of you ladies have a weapon on your person?'

'We most certainly do not.'

Ignoring the grouchy old duck, Jack shifted to try to get a better look at her companion. She was a much younger woman, and although her face was slightly obscured by the darkness of the carriage, a pair of large, green eyes, bright as emeralds, stared back at him. Intrigued, he moved behind the carriage to the window on the other side, smiling as he passed Garrett filling his saddlebags with a silver cutlery set from one of the trunks. The grin on the boy's face reminded him of himself as a younger bushranger. Though at twenty-one, Garrett was slightly older than he'd been when he'd started out.

Leaning an elbow on the window ledge, Jack studied the young woman. He was used to the wide-eyed terror he saw on the faces of passengers, and particularly in the eyes of the women he robbed, but in these extraordinary eyes he saw something beneath the fear. Had he been a more whimsical man he may have thought it was fascination or excitement. Surely he'd merely imagined it. Regardless, he would rather deal with her than the old battleaxe shooting daggers at him through her frosty, wrinkled eyes when he turned to look at her.

He turned his attentions back to the young lady but could no longer read her expression. She had to be afraid. Everyone feared the bushranger. Many highwaymen thought nothing of taking lives along with money and jewels. The worst of them took liberties with ladies they came across. Jack had never taken a life in all his years of plundering the roads of Victoria, and had certainly never harmed a woman. It was a point of pride for him.

Tilting his head to peer further into the carriage, he studied her. Early twenties, he guessed, and pretty. Those eyes, large and bright, glowed against the dimness of the carriage. Her long sweep of flame-coloured hair was pulled back from her face and held with intricate combs. Mother-of-pearl, if he wasn't mistaken. He'd be sure to retrieve those before he left.

'Bail up, if you please.' He kept his voice quiet, almost soothing.

'I have nothing of value, sir,' she answered in a stronger voice than he'd expected.

'That is not strictly true, is it?' He glanced down at her décolletage.

The sudden indignant spark in those wide, green eyes thrilled him. He'd always admired spirited women and didn't bother to hide his delighted grin.

'I meant your locket, my lady. Do not fear. Your virtue is completely safe with Jack the Devil.' He shot a quick look at the old lady. 'Yours especially.'

The old woman huffed and began to mumble incoherently to herself.

Jack turned back to the pretty redhead, expecting to see her looking less concerned now that he had guaranteed he would not harm her physically. If anything, she looked more so.

'Please, sir, I beg you.' She spoke in an even tone, but her anxiety was evident to Jack. Her small lace-gloved hand gripped the gold necklace like a vice. 'This locket is precious to me.'

'It's precious to me too.'

She frowned. 'It is not.'

'Is too,' he tossed back, grinning slowly, surprised at her sudden determination.

'Is not!'

'Shall we go another round?' he said with a chuckle as she fumed.

'Oh, Prudence, just give him the damned locket and let's get out of here,' the old woman commanded. Leaning over, she snatched the locket from the girl's neck, ripping the chain roughly from its clasp, making the girl gasp in pain. She shoved it at him. 'Take it! And let us be on our way.'

His amusement disappeared in a heartbeat.

'What is your name, madam?' he asked the old lady, his jaw clenched.

'I am Lady Deidre Stanforth,' she said proudly. 'My late husband was the Earl of Carrington.'

'Well, Deidre,' he said, deliberately slighting her by omitting her title. 'There is no need for violence.'

Slowly, Jack took the locket from her and looked back at Prudence. There were tears pooling in her eyes, but she didn't allow them to fall. He admired her strength, and an emotion he was unused to squeezed tight in his chest.

Shaking it off, he took her hand lightly in his. 'Prudence,' he began softly. 'I apologise. But a lady so beautiful as yourself has no need for expensive baubles.'

'It is not expensive, sir.' Her voice quivered only slightly. 'It will fetch you nothing.'

'We'll see about that.'

The pain that had filled her eyes was replaced quickly by annoyance bordering on anger. The changes of expression on her pretty face captivated him. He'd thought her prudish-looking at first in her high-necked, lace-trimmed dress. The older woman was clearly in charge; not a governess or a chaperone, but a relative most likely, grandmother perhaps, and young Prudence had stayed quiet, leaving all the talking up to the old witch. But when she had something to fight for, she showed her true personality. Not quite fearless, but not completely devoid of courage when it mattered.

He really should let her keep the locket—if only to irritate Grandma—but something made him want to hold on to it. To hold on to a piece of the lovely, emerald-eyed woman with hair the colour of fire and a temper to match.

Hair.

The combs.

He reached into the carriage and Prudence leaned back further against the seat. His hand continued its forward path, slowly so that he wouldn't frighten her, and removed the shiny, mottled pearl comb. Her soft hair swept across his fingers as it fell from its perfect chignon and cascaded down her shoulder, stopping just below her breast.

He stared at the transformation, entranced at the new wild beauty before him. It suited her much more than the prim, staid facade. He wondered what she'd be like out from beneath the oppressive thumb of the crotchety chaperone.

He shook himself. He was romanticising again. If he didn't concentrate, he'd end up with a bullet in his gullet. Looking back at his men, he could see they had finished ransacking the trunks and were waiting for him with the horses.

'Your earrings please, madam,' he said, holding out his hand to the old woman. Squeezing her lips together so hard they disappeared into her wrinkled face, she removed the ruby earrings and thrust them at him.

'We have lightened your load, ladies,' he said, touching a finger to his hat. 'You may continue on your way.'

'Scoundrel,' the old woman shot back. 'You'll be caught and gaoled one day, you can be sure of that.'

'No one's caught Jack the Devil yet.' He grinned, pocketing the earrings.

Stepping back, he kept his eyes on Prudence. She didn't look away, even when he winked at her and said, 'Farewell, milady.'

'Drive on,' he told the coach driver, and stood back as the carriage lurched forward.

'Nice haul,' Garrett said, moving up beside him with a large hessian bag.

Jack just continued to stare after the carriage until it was almost out of sight. When the young woman leaned her head out of the coach and looked back at him, he grinned like a madman. He didn't know why it thrilled him so much, but it did.

Once the coach had crested the hill, he glanced down at the gold locket in his hand, rubbing it lightly between his thumb and forefinger.

'We should move,' Bobby said, leading the horses up to them.

'Mmm,' Jack agreed distractedly, staring again at the dust disappearing over the rise before mounting his horse and following his men back into the bush.

'Prudence, stop doing that.'

At her grandmother's snapped words, Prudence leaned back against the seat and felt the heat rush into her cheeks. He had caught her looking back at him. And so had her grandmother, who immediately proceeded to launch into admonishments. As usual.

She listened to her grandmother rant on about 'that dreadful man' and 'this country full of convicts'. As much as she adored her grandmother, she had learned quickly how to ignore her tirades.

Besides, she was consumed with more exhilarating thoughts.

A bushranger. A real live bushranger! And on her very first day in Victoria.

She should have been terrified at being bailed up by a band of gun-wielding men in the middle of nowhere, but it had quickly become evident that their leader had no intention of hurting them. And at that point, for Prudence anyway, it had become an adventure.

Though his face had been covered by the kerchief, he hadn't looked dangerous or menacing like she'd expected. His eyes were the oddest shade of light brown, honey-coloured almost, and they revealed more mischief than danger. Long dark eyelashes rimmed the eyes she would say were pretty—feminine, even. She didn't know how she knew, but she suspected he was smiling beneath the black kerchief. Hardly the epitome of the frightening scourge of the highwayman depicted in the periodicals she'd read back in London.

Jack the Devil, he'd called himself. He was no devil as far as she could see. He'd not fired one shot from his gun, and had not forced himself upon them, nor threatened them physically in any real way.

The enjoyment he displayed in the situation was devilish, perhaps. Was he devilishly handsome beneath his mask? Possibly, she mused. Those honey-coloured eyes had twinkled when he'd teased her. And then that parting wink when she'd continued to stare at him as the carriage had finally moved away …

He really was a devil, she thought with a tiny smile touching her lips.

Schooling her features, she exhaled a deep breath, bringing her attention once again to her grandmother's ranting to ensure she hadn't been expected to respond to something. The woman was hard as nails and her tongue just as sharp. She hadn't appeared to be frightened of the bushranger either. But then Prudence had seen the strongest of men cower at her grandmother's reproachful demeanour. Though none of them had been holding a gun to her at the time.

The only change in the bushranger's cheery disposition had been when her grandmother had torn her locket from her neck to hand to him. She lifted a hand to stroke the delicate skin that still burned. She had no doubt she would have a red mark, but it hurt more that Gran could so easily hand over her most precious keepsake.

Jack the Devil's eyes had hardened then, and she'd seen the first signs of a man to be reckoned with. He had not been pleased with the vicious way in which her grandmother had treated her, but he had taken the locket just the same, and that broke her heart.

She cared nothing for the mother-of-pearl combs or her grandmother's earrings he'd taken. They were all replaceable.

Her locket was not.

It had belonged to her mother.

Gran had been all too happy to hand over the necklace. She had no sentimental connection to it, or to her only daughter. As far as she was concerned, Olivia Stanforth had never existed.

When the man had requested the locket, any fear Prudence may have felt throughout the robbery was quickly replaced by her desperation to keep it. Her sudden argumentative response had done nothing more than amuse him at first, but when he'd removed the comb from her hair, he had looked at her with the strangest expression. She'd held her breath as his hand swept lightly, gently through the hair that fell across her cheek. His eyes had darkened, closer to whisky than honey, and the sparkle had turned to another type of mischief.

Prudence may not have had a lot of experience with men, but she certainly knew how a man looked when he saw something he liked. He had said her virtue was safe with him, but when she saw the heat that flashed in his eyes as he stared at her, she had to wonder whether he was telling the truth.

The clang and shudder of the carriage moving across a cattle grate snapped her out of her wayward thoughts. They had arrived at the Carrington estate.

Poking her head out of the window, she was surprised to see bright green lawn lining the dirt drive. It was in stark contrast to the dry, brown countryside they had travelled through to get there. Everything she'd read about Australia spoke of the terrible drought gripping the colony, and she had certainly not expected to see such well-maintained gardens as those that greeted them. Clearly water was not a problem on the Carrington estate.

She leaned further out to get a better look at the homestead and gasped audibly. The house was enormous. Not even a house. It was a mansion. Carrington Manor stood three storeys tall with a wide frontage and no conjoined buildings—unless you counted the servants' quarters, which skirted the side of the house. A wide verandah ran the length of the frontage and wrapped around the entire house.

Their home in London had been one of the largest and finest estates in the city. When Grandad George died in 1847, her uncle, Charles, had inherited the title of Earl of Carrington. Prudence and her grandmother had stayed on at Carrington Hall in London but, not happy about living in his brother's shadow, Robert, the younger of the sons, had decided to take his young wife and start a new life in Australia.

Shortly after Uncle Robert and Aunt Alicia emigrated to the new colony of Victoria, Prudence had overheard a heated discussion between her grandmother and Uncle Charles. Apparently, Uncle Robert had settled in Ballarat, having been caught up in the gold rush of 1851. He'd sunk a mine in hopes of finding gold and had struck it rich.

Prudence remembered being fascinated by the stories that had come out of the Victorian goldfields. Gold in abundance, a lawless land, bushrangers and the terrible and fatal incident at the Eureka Stockade all made exciting reading for a young girl, stifled by heritage and breeding. She would squirrel away the newspapers so that she might read all the gory details without Gran finding out.

The carriage came to a halt in front of the main entrance and a servant dressed in black trousers and a white jacket moved quickly to open the door. Deidre stepped out and Prudence followed, still staring with stunned admiration at the great house before her.

Robert had already been well taken care of thanks to his inheritance on his father's death. Striking gold had added a new level of wealth, and he and Alicia had built Carrington Manor from the ground up. Over the past decade, Robert had created one of the most revered and prominent horse studs in the colony, raising horses for the prestigious Victorian racing circuit.

'Welcome to Carrington Manor!'

Prudence spun at the call to see Uncle Robert and Aunt Alicia sweep out of the double doors of the house and onto the verandah with great welcoming fanfare.

'Mother,' Robert said and moved to buss her cheek. 'You're looking well.'

'Robert.'

'Prudence,' he said, examining her as though he had expected her to stay twelve years old forever. 'Haven't you grown into a beauty?'

'Thank you, Uncle Robert.'

'You'll have all the men in the district vying for your hand.'

Pru blushed. Not from the compliment, but out of embarrassment. She hoped she'd have some time as a free woman to explore her new country, before she was sold off to the highest bidder as a wife and baby maker.

Thankfully, Robert turned back to Deidre and the conversation moved on. 'How was your journey?'

'Dreadful,' Deidre grumbled. 'The seas were rough, the train was slow and just now we were robbed on the road from Geelong.'

'Robbed?' Alicia asked, her hand flying to her mouth in shock.

'Highwaymen,' Prudence added.

'Good gracious,' Alicia said. Her aunt was a mousy little thing. Pretty in a plain sort of way, her skin was still pale and translucent, as though she never left the house to enjoy the warmth of the Australian sun. And when Alicia hugged her with thin arms, Prudence thought her aunt might snap. 'Did they hurt you?'

'What did they take?' Robert asked, talking over his wife.

In contrast to Alicia, Robert was tall and broad, taking after Grandad George. He was in excellent shape for a man heading into his fifties. His love of working with the horses in the outdoors was no doubt a contributing factor. He had thick dark hair with only a touch of grey, and his skin showed a healthy-looking tan; the Australian lifestyle obviously agreed with him.

'I'm not certain what they took,' Deidre snapped. 'I was too busy being held at gunpoint to ask.'

'Well, please, come inside out of the heat,' Alicia offered. 'The servants will bring the luggage.'

Prudence followed her family into the house and arrived in a large foyer with parquet flooring that was polished to such a shine she had delicious visions of slipping off her shoes and sliding across it in her stocking feet.

The trunks were unloaded and brought into the foyer, where Robert and his men took stock of the belongings to gauge what had been taken.

'The silver is missing,' Deidre noted. 'And my jewellery box.'

'Mine too,' Prudence agreed, digging through her own trunk. She didn't particularly care about the baubles in her jewellery box, but the box itself had been an intricate wooden chest carved with African animals. Grandad had brought it back for her after one of his visits to the African colonies and she had adored it.

'Wretched bushrangers,' Robert said. 'It's no wonder they've started hanging the devils.'

Prudence stared wide-eyed at Robert's use of the word devil. *Jack the Devil*. Had he heard of him?

Alicia gasped, perhaps mistaking Prudence's response for panic. 'Robert, please.'

'Apologies, Prudence, Mother.'

'It's quite alright, Robert,' Deidre responded. 'Hanging is too good for them. They should not be allowed to go on frightening and harassing good people.'

'How perfectly terrifying for you,' Alicia put in again. 'And you, Prudence, were you frightened?'

'A little,' Prudence lied. 'He took my locket.'

'Oh, forget about that paltry thing,' Deidre chastised. 'We've lost more important things. All of my pearls and gemstones, gifts from George from his many travels abroad. The silver was my mother's.'

'Positively dreadful,' Alicia agreed. 'Cook has tea and scones in the drawing room. No one bakes like Camilla. She's a marvel in the kitchen.' Alicia directed them to a spacious drawing room. As they entered, Robert walked to a large writing desk in the corner.

'I'll inform the local constabulary,' he said and sat down to write the letter.

Alicia and Deidre sat on the sofas as a servant poured the tea. Prudence wandered the large space, stretching her legs after the long journey and trying to rein in her temper. She was irritable from the long trip but more annoyed at Gran's dismissal once again of the loss of her locket. A few moments later Robert called to his butler.

'Gerald,' Robert said, handing the man the sealed note. 'Have young Master Hugh ride out to the constabulary in Ballan with this note for the sergeant. Then please ensure the luggage is delivered to Miss Prudence's and Lady Carrington's suites.'

'At once, sir.' Gerald took the note and disappeared from the room.

'I have set aside the eastern-wing suites on the first floor for you, Mother,' Robert said, taking a seat beside his wife and lifting his teacup. 'And Prudence, you will have rooms in the western wing on the second level. I trust the stairs will not be a problem for you.'

'Not at all, Uncle. Thank you,' Prudence said with a smile. She was thrilled to have almost an entire floor to herself.

'I see you took my advice and built this drawing room north facing,' Deidre said.

'Of course, Mother,' Robert said. 'It was good advice. The sun warms it nicely in winter.'

'Saves on heating costs.'

'It does indeed.'

They shared tea and scones, and once they had finished Prudence thought there had been enough time for the butler to unpack her things into her suite.

'May I be excused?' she asked, standing. 'I'm a little weary from the trip and could perhaps benefit from a lie-down before dinner.'

Deidre waved her hand dismissively. 'Of course.'

'Get settled, niece,' Robert said, standing to kiss her cheeks. 'Dinner is at seven.'

Prudence smiled politely and left the room. She wasn't tired, just bored. She wanted to explore this giant mansion that was now to be her home.

She took her time climbing the red-carpeted grand staircase that led from the foyer to the first level. The ceiling rose high above her, with its intricate stained-glass domed window speckling sunshine down on her in a rainbow of light.

Reaching the first-floor landing, she saw that the long hallways had the same plush red carpet as the staircase, but with the

Carrington coat of arms taking pride of place in the centre. To the east would be her grandmother's rooms; to the west must be the family apartments. Looking out a nearby window, she gained her bearings and headed west, walking slowly along the hallway, their cream-coloured walls dotted with art—family portraits showing years of Stanforth nobility. Turning a corner, she found a less grand staircase and headed up to the second level where she would find her rooms.

She opened the first door she came to and found a comfortable sitting room. Peeking into the room and through another open door, she spotted her luggage. Walking slowly through the sitting room, she gazed with an open mouth at the exquisite furnishings, before stepping into the bedroom where she saw her trunk sitting in the corner of the room.

She stopped and stared, amazed at the luxurious suite. Her room in London had been elegant and comfortable. This was palatial in comparison. Much too large for one person.

At the centre of the far wall stood a large, four-poster double bed. She'd only ever had a single bed in London; she smiled, suddenly feeling very grown up. This was not a child's room but one meant for a woman. The bright cherry wood gleamed on the bedposts that rose up to a canopy. Gauze netting was hooked around the sides, ready to be dropped at night to keep the bugs out. She had heard the size and volume of flies and mosquitos were unimaginable here in the colonies.

Moving to the window, she gazed out over the gardens of the property. As she exhaled a breath, the tension of the day left her body. Her rooms faced west and she was thrilled that she would be able to see the immense Australian sun as it lowered over the distant hills.

Sailing from England, she had formed a habit of watching the sun set every night over foreign lands and wide expanses of ocean.

As they had ventured further south, the sun seemed to grow larger and larger as they left the winter behind.

To the right, she could also see the stables. Not your average wooden stables but an almost brand-new robust stone building with an iron roof. It seemed Uncle Robert's horses were as well housed as she would be.

Relaxed and contented, she smiled and, by habit, reached a hand up to grasp her locket. Her smile faded. It was gone. Gone for good. The only real connection she'd had with the mother she had never known had been taken from her.

She shook herself. It was just a thing. She needed to get past it and look forward.

There's no point to looking behind or you will miss what's in front of you; she heard Grandad's voice in her head. She'd loved him like a father. Because that's what he'd been to her. The only father she'd ever known. He had doled out cuddles and presents without restraint and she'd missed him terribly since he'd died, only a few days before her tenth birthday. Her real father had never been mentioned. At least not to her. She didn't even know his name, had never known her real surname, as she'd become Prudence Stanforth when she'd come to live with her grandparents. She assumed they didn't discuss him or her mother because it was too painful for them to talk about. Only when she begged her grandmother to tell her how they'd died did she discover they'd been killed in a fire in Cornwall. And that was when she had come to live with them. On her sixteenth birthday, Gran had given her the locket and, while it was hard to mourn a woman she'd never met, she had cherished the link with her mother.

And just as her grandmother had given it to her, she'd given it away to a bushranger without so much as a second thought.

She loved her grandmother but the woman could be stifling sometimes. She didn't have the same easy ability as her husband to show affection to those she loved. Prudence hadn't wanted to be cooped up in drawing rooms playing piano, or painting. She longed for adventure. Adventure like she had read about in her books. But she had been the dutiful granddaughter and taken her lessons with grace and poise.

She had never been alone. Not truly alone in her entire life. In London, if she had tried to go anywhere without a chaperone, even just a walk down the street, her grandmother would hear about it before she'd taken ten steps. Too many people knew the Stanforths and all wanted to stay on the good side of Lady Deidre.

Ladies do not go out unaccompanied, her grandmother would say.

But here in this new land so far from town no one knew her, and she wanted some freedom to explore without her grandmother constantly breathing down her neck. And if she had that space maybe she would meet a man. A man suitable for her grandmother, of course. She had no delusions that she would be allowed to make that decision for herself. And she knew that her making a good marriage had been her grandmother's priority ever since Prudence had turned eighteen.

Despite what she read in her novels, she wasn't romantic enough to believe that people actually married for love. At least, women didn't get that luxury. Should a man take a fancy to her—and be agreeable to her grandmother—he would make his case and she would have no say in the matter. It was something she had resigned herself to years ago. It wouldn't hurt if he was a handsome fellow, but above all she hoped that he would not be a silly man. She hoped he would be a man who read, a man who enjoyed the works of Shakespeare and Keats. It would be even better if he liked the fact that she read. For who wanted a silly wife, after all? And her love for books was a huge part of who she was. A man who did not understand that would not understand her.

Currently, the author she was obsessed with was Alexandre Dumas. Oh, how she loved *The Three Musketeers*. It was her favourite novel above all the others. She loved stories of adventure and travel, duels and swordfights, intrigue and betrayal.

She sighed as she watched horses being led in and out of the stables for their evening exercise. She had only just begun a journey of her own. So why did she still feel bound and tied to the same way of life she had left behind in London?

Determined to shake the melancholy that threatened to descend, she decided to go for a walk to stretch her legs. She went back downstairs and out the rear entrance of the house to the gardens. Three gardeners worked diligently, sculpting the hedges along the pathway. With three yardsmen, no wonder the grounds were so immaculate. Looking back at the house to ensure her grandmother couldn't see her from the drawing room, she moved quickly towards the stables.

Stablehands nodded and said a polite hello as she passed by them and entered the huge building. The familiar smells and coolness of the stables hit her at once, the soothing scent of horses and hay. Sidestepping a fresh deposit of manure, she walked slowly along the stalls, marvelling at the horses until she came to a pretty chestnut Arabian. The horse snorted and tossed its head over the gate, just begging for attention.

'Well, hello to you too, beautiful,' she said, leaning over to stroke the horse's nose.

'Hello yourself.'

She jolted back at the voice.

A man stood upright and grinned at her. He'd clearly been checking the horse's feet and she hadn't seen him.

An older man, in his late thirties maybe, with jet-black hair cut close to his head, he was unshaven but not scruffy-looking for it.

She looked warily from man to horse.

'She won't bite,' he said, a strong American drawl rolling through his words. 'Neither will I.'

Prudence chuckled and held out her hand to stroke the horse's cheek again.

'What's her name?' Prudence asked.

'Misha,' he responded. 'What's yours?'

'Prudence.'

'I'm Brock,' he said. 'I'd shake your hand but ...' He held up his hands, skin and nails black from work.

Prudence smiled and offered her hand anyway. After a moment's surprised hesitation, he took her hand lightly.

'I'm not averse to those who do a good day's hard work,' she said as he held her delicate pale hand in his huge tanned one. 'It's nice to meet you, Mr Brock.'

'Prudence? That makes you the boss man's niece then.'

'Yes. My grandmother and I just arrived on the boat from England.'

'Well then, I believe Miss Misha will be your horse.'

'Really?' She was tickled. The mare was exactly the horse she would have chosen for herself, had she been given the opportunity. She desperately wanted to take Misha for a ride across the open plains of the property, but dinner would be served shortly and there was, sadly, no time.

'Thank you, Mr Brock,' she said. 'Perhaps I can take a ride with her tomorrow morning.'

'As you wish, Miss Prudence,' he said easily. 'And it's just Brock.'

Prudence smiled, gave Misha another good scratch and headed out of the stables, crossing quickly back to the house.

Changing out of her travel clothes into a dress suitable for dinner, she checked her appearance in the bevelled mirror. She had hoped she'd be able to relax her standard of dress now that they had arrived in the wilds of Australia. But just because they had left London that didn't mean her grandmother wouldn't expect the same level of proper attire for each occasion. Maybe with some careful plotting, she thought, smoothing the heavy silk skirt of her dress, she could convince her grandmother over time that lighter clothing would be more suitable to the climate. Puffing out a breath at the heat building beneath her lace-covered throat, she eyed her determined expression in the looking glass. Yes, she could be quite persuasive, even quite devious, when she wanted something badly enough.

Two

Jack was shedding his bushranger persona in a rented room in a Ballarat boarding house after he and his men had spent a good portion of the afternoon dealing out the loot from their very lucrative day on the highway.

'What are you going to do now, Jack?' Bobby asked. Their third, Garrett, had already taken his share and headed out to the brothels.

'Thought I would set off to the Duchess of Kent for a pint or a nobbler of whisky,' Jack said, taking a few pieces of the jewellery from his portion of the haul and tossing them up and down in his hand.

'I'll come with you.' Bobby's face lit up. 'I want to see if that Katie girl is working the bar tonight.'

Jack laughed. 'Taken a shine to that sweet Scottish lassy, haven't you?'

'She's alright,' Bobby said, blushing red all the way up to the tips of his ears. At twenty-six years of age, Bobby's experience with women was not limited. But lately he'd had his sights set on one lady only. The barmaid at the Duchess. Love was a danger-ous, tricky business. Not that Bobby realised yet that he was, in fact, in love. And love was certainly not a business Jack was keen to enter into any time soon.

'What about you, Jack? Going to see Miss Parker this evening? If her father finds out, he'll shoot your thing off.'

Jack just grinned. 'He'll have to catch me first. Anyway, I'm not really in the mood. Think I might find a card game and lose some of the jewellery we just appropriated.'

'It was a good catch, wasn't it?' Bobby said. 'Been a long time since we took such a haul now that the gold escorts are doubly armed.'

'It was a good day.' Jack was thinking of flame-red hair and a pair of bright green eyes flaring with anger.

They set off out of the boarding house, and after leaving Bobby at the Duchess of Kent, Jack decided he should drop in on his legitimate business. It had been a while since he'd met face to face with the man who managed the transport company so ably for him. And besides, he had to pay him his share of the takings.

'Mr Jones,' Jack greeted his manager as he entered the building. He glanced around. They'd recently renovated the small office and he was pleased with the space. A new luggage-loading area sat near the door that led to the passenger coaches. All the better to see what travellers were carrying that might entice a visit from Jack the Devil somewhere out on the highway.

'Mr Fairweather,' Alfred Jones said, returning the greeting. 'What a pleasure to have you here. I thought you were still in Melbourne.'

'Just arrived back not an hour ago,' Jack said, smiling and nodding politely at a couple who waited for their luggage to be unloaded from the carriage. 'I trust you had a pleasant journey?' he asked them.

'Yes, thank you, sir,' the lady answered with a flirtatious smile that her husband couldn't see.

Jack grinned back and gave her a wink.

Their luggage was placed on a small cart and he bid them a good evening as they followed it out onto the street, no doubt heading to one of the many hotels in Ballarat.

'That looked to be quite an impressive jewellery case there, Jones,' Jack said now that they were alone. 'Why was I not apprised of this journey?'

Jones just smiled easily and shrugged. 'You were otherwise occupied. And with a much larger haul, as I understand it.'

'Yes, yes, of course,' Jack acquiesced and dug into the satchel he carried. He handed over two silver candlesticks and a pair of ruby earrings, as well as the mother-of-pearl combs. 'This lot should fetch quite a nice price.'

'I should say so.'

The man's wrinkle-lined blue eyes lit up as he studied the ruby earrings and combs. Alfred had to be almost sixty, Jack guessed. He realised he'd never really known how old the man was and wondered why he'd never bothered to ask.

'My Gloria would love these earrings,' Alfred said, speaking of his daughter.

'Then give them to her,' Jack offered, feeling generous. 'If she doesn't like them, she can sell them as always through the pawn shop.'

Alfred's daughter Gloria lived in Melbourne with her husband. They ran a pawnbroker's storefront in Flinders Street. A shop of good repute, despite its less than reputable method of receiving stock. Much of what Jack and his friends stole went directly to the Melbourne pawnbroker via Alfred, and any monies gained for the goods were then sent back to Ballarat via the transport business. Alfred was a valued member of staff and a good friend. But, thinking of Alfred's age again, Jack wondered if he might be looking for a new manager to run his business sooner rather than later.

'How is Gloria?' Jack asked.

'Well enough,' Alfred returned. 'As long as she keeps that rat-bag husband of hers in line. The man likes to gamble too much for my liking.'

'Perhaps you should go to Melbourne for a few weeks,' Jack suggested. 'Spend some time with her and the family.'

Jack felt the piercing blue eyes as the man glared at him. 'Are you suggesting I'm in need of a break? Am I not doing my job to your satisfaction, Mr Fairweather?'

'No, I am absolutely not suggesting that.' Jack backtracked, feeling the wrath of his elder colleague. 'Your work is as exemplary as always.'

'Don't handle me, boy,' the old man sneered. 'I can still knock your block off.'

'No doubt.' Jack lifted his hands in surrender. He'd offered the man a way out, a chance to step back from the stressful work of hocking stolen goods. He'd never make *that* suggestion again.

Alfred nodded once and began stashing the goods into a satchel marked for Melbourne. 'No problems with the heist, I take it?'

Glad to be back on even footing with Alfred, Jack thought again of the pretty Prudence and her battle for the locket.

'Not really,' Jack answered. 'The old lady had a mouthful of complaints, but there were no guns in the purses so it was only my ears that suffered injury.'

Jones wheezed out a laugh. 'You have to watch out for those old ladies. Remember that one who struck you with her umbrella? The lump on your forehead looked like a boulder and Bobby said you forgot your name for about a minute.'

Jack cringed and rubbed his forehead. 'Yes, I remember. Sort of.'

Danger for a bushranger could come in many forms.

'Well, I am off to lose some of my ill-gotten booty in a game of cards,' Jack announced. 'I'll wait to hear from you about any forthcoming carriages.'

'Staying at the boarding house as usual?'

'As usual,' Jack agreed.

'Then I'll find you.'

Jack left the building and walked out into the street. The lamp-lighter was just beginning to ignite the gas lamps that now lined the main street of Ballarat. He remembered when only campfires and torches lit the dirt roads of Ballarat. *How things have changed,* he thought as he followed the man along the road back towards the Duchess of Kent Hotel. He could always find a game of cards there and a nobbler of whisky to sooth the stress of the day.

Stepping into the saloon, he waved to Bobby who sat at the bar chatting with the pretty little Scottish barmaid, Katie, as she came and went with her drink orders. At five foot six, she was no drunkard's pushover. He'd seen her physically toss men twice her size out of the hotel for putting their hands where they shouldn't have. She had a redhead's temper despite her hair being as black as night, and sharp, almond-shaped eyes that shone pale blue. Since she'd arrived in Ballarat two years before, Jack had taken to Katie in a brotherly way. But Bobby—he was a fool for her.

The smell of stale whisky and tobacco smoke hung in the air as he headed for the back room where several card games were in progress. But before he could make it through the door, he was pulled into a dark corner of the corridor where his mouth was suddenly pressed to a pair of warm and luscious lips. An ample bosom squeezed enticingly against him and he enjoyed the surprise attack for a moment before needing to come up for air.

'Melody,' he said, recognising his assailant as he fought to find his breath. 'If your husband sees you devouring me this way, he'll kill us both.'

'When will you come to my bed again, Jack?'

'You're married now,' Jack said while she continued to nibble at his ear. 'To most women that generally means not sleeping with other men.'

'I dare you to stay away from me, Jack Fairweather,' she purred and then went on to tell him what she would do to him if he went with her now. He had to admit her offer was quite tempting. But when he felt her hand creeping down the front of his trousers, sense somehow prevailed.

'Melody.' He lifted her wrists and held them away from him. 'You must forget about me. Go back to your husband.'

'He spends more time playing cards than playing with me,' she sulked, drawing his attention to her full, wet lips again. 'Women have needs too, you know. He's in there right now. Come on, Jack, we can sneak out and be back before he's finished.'

Hell, her husband was in the next room? The room he was about to go into and join a card game?

'That's not a good idea, Melody.'

'But I love you, Jack.' Her eyes welled with unshed tears.

Oh, dear Lord.

'You don't love me, Melody. You love your husband. You know you do. You just need to bail him up the way you did me just now and he will pay you all the attention you want. I'm sure of it.'

'Really?'

'Believe me. Go in there right now and whisper in his ear exactly what you said to me and I guarantee cards will not be looking too interesting to him anymore.'

'Do you think so?' She looked unsure, but at least the tears had dried up.

'I know so. What man could resist such … inventive temptations?'

She giggled and stepped back to tidy herself up, tugging at her bodice to show even more cleavage—if it were possible.

'How do I look?'

'Dangerous.' It wasn't a lie. 'Go forth and seduce your man.'

She giggled again and he leaned against the doorway as she flounced into the room. More than one male head turned to follow her path, and when she leaned down to whisper in her husband's ear, he saw the man's eyes widen momentarily before he licked his lips.

'Gentlemen,' he said, standing quickly to gather his money, shoving it haphazardly into his pockets. 'I think it's time I took my winnings and left while I am still ahead. Goodnight to you.'

Jack passed the happy couple as he entered the room and Melody gave him a beaming smile. He exhaled a relieved breath and decided then and there: no more married women for him. They just weren't worth the chance of a bullet to the back from a jealous husband.

Jack took the position that Melody's husband had vacated and settled in.

An hour later, he'd won some and lost some. He had little cash left, but a few pieces of the old lady's jewellery remained in his pocket ready to bid. The men at this table would not ask questions about him betting such an interesting collection of ladies' baubles.

Betting the gold pin was easy enough and Jack shrugged it off when he lost it in yet another unlucky hand.

The next hand was better and his blood began to race through his body in anticipation. He didn't have any money left but he really wanted to bet big. It was the best hand he'd had all night.

He pulled out the locket and rubbed it absently between his thumb and forefinger while he watched the other players up the ante around the table.

As he was about to drop the locket into the pot it flipped open. Inside was a photograph of a woman. He stared at it. She was striking, beautiful. And looked almost identical to the girl he'd taken it from. But this was not Prudence. A sister perhaps? Or her mother. A rare feeling came over him. The same emotion that had come upon him unexpectedly when he'd taken the locket from the girl. Remorse. She'd said it was priceless to her. Had it been a gift?

'You gonna bet that or just stare at it?' Wendall Crabbe grumbled out of the side of his mouth. Jack had heard that a bullet to the neck at the Eureka Stockade had left him with a face and body partly paralysed.

Jack looked up at the men at the table. He'd been so distracted by the locket he had forgotten they were waiting for him to bet.

'Uh, no,' he said. He dug around in his pocket, pulling out some pearl earrings instead, and tossed them into the pot. Sadly, it was not his night. His three of a kind was not good enough to beat out a straight.

Finally, out of items that he was willing to bet, Jack retired from the game and headed out onto the streets of Ballarat.

Standing on the busy corner, he looked in one direction and then the other. Stone and brick buildings now lined the main streets of the town, where less than a decade earlier the most modern buildings were the timber hotels. Nine years since he'd arrived with the initial gold rush at the small settlement of Ballarat, nothing but a dustbowl of mineshafts and calico tents. Jack was astounded by the small city that had grown into existence before his very eyes. The tents and timber buildings had made way for permanent structures, built by the wealth generated in those early years of gold mining.

His mining days had lasted only a year before he'd discovered the less backbreaking, and more lucrative, profession of thievery.

The early days had been easy. Stealing gold from tents while their owners were passed out drunk had been like taking Raspberry Drops from a baby.

Eventually though, miners had gotten savvy and diggers invested in guns or vicious dogs, or both, to protect their tents and their claims. Claim jumping had been rife in those early days and many a man caught a bullet in the back for his trouble. It had been a lawless time—even more so than now.

Shaking away the old memories, Jack began the walk towards the widow Barnett's boarding house. He could see it up ahead, dwarfed by new brick buildings on either side. It looked dilapidated in comparison. He could afford better. He could afford the Royal if he was so inclined. But Mrs Barnett had taken care of him in the early days and loyalty was Jack's strongest trait. He would continue to lodge with her until she finally made good on the threats she'd been tossing at him for years and kicked him out. He knew that would never happen. Mostly because he saw to it that goods headed for her house were never pilfered on the highway.

Entering the old timber house, he winked at Mrs Barnett, who hovered perpetually between the front door and the drawing room, and headed up to his usual bedchamber. He stripped off his shirt and washed the day's dirt and grime from his body, before laying back on the small bed with a heavy exhale.

Now that he was alone, Jack had time to think on the day's proceedings. He'd stolen from a lot of pretty women over the years and they had all been quite rightly scared of him, even disgusted by him. But the young woman he'd encountered that day had acted more fascinated than fearful. It was as though it was the first time she had come across a man of ill repute. Had the scoundrels of London become so subdued that a woman of her age—he thought back and guessed she was in her early twenties—had had no dealings with a dangerous man such as himself? Then again, she had probably spent her life wrapped in cottonwool by the overbearing chaperone.

The girl had had spirit, that was for sure. And the prettiest green eyes he'd seen in a good long while. He closed his eyes and the vision of her came to him easily. Flame-red hair that fell around her shoulders once he'd pulled the combs out and let it run free. He could feel the softness of it brushing against his hand even now. He imagined those full pink lips of hers pressing against his and felt the familiar stirring in his groin.

He rolled onto his side, restless. Then rolled onto his back again and stared at the ceiling, contemplating heading back out again to find one of his *unmarried* lady friends. Jack Fairweather could always find a willing bed partner. But right now, none of them compared to the vision in his mind of the lovely Prudence.

Groaning, he sat up, reached over to the chair where his waist-coat had been flung and retrieved the locket. It was odd. He just couldn't bring himself to bet it. Lying back on the bed, he opened the locket to look again at the picture of the pretty woman inside. This definitely wasn't Prudence. The eyes didn't hold the same spark. Annoyed with himself, he snapped the gold locket shut and put it on the side table. He was getting soft in his old age. He'd sell the locket the next day for whatever he could get.

The next morning Pru was up before the sun, and in her split riding skirt and boots she headed for the stables. A blue mist hovered, shrouding the stables in wafting strands of spidery clouds and obscuring the hills in the distance. The dampness touched her cheeks, fresh and cool, and she followed the gravel path leading her into the huge stable building. The crisp smell of fresh hay and manure, exacerbated in the frosty temperature, filled her nose and she inhaled deeply.

She was unsurprised to see many of the stablehands at work already, preparing to exercise the horses. Several smaller men, who Pru assumed were the jockeys for Robert's racehorses, were sitting about in their training outfits, drinking tea, the steam rising from their cups as they waited for their mounts to be ready.

'Well, good morning, Miss Prudence.'

Turning on the spot, she came face to face with Brock and his broad grin.

'Good morning, Mr Brock.'

'Just Brock,' he reminded her.

'Just Prudence,' she countered.

He laughed. 'And what brings you out even before the birds have begun to sing?'

'I was hoping to take Misha for a run before breakfast.'

Brock rubbed the back of his neck, looking hesitant. 'Did Mr Robert say you were able to ride alone?'

She could have told him to mind his business, but Prudence was not one to treat servants as lesser humans. She hadn't known she needed her uncle's permission to ride, but it didn't surprise her. Gran would have taken care of that. She decided to play innocent and hope for the best.

'I'll not go far,' she said, smiling coyly. 'Please, Brock, I promise I will stay to the closer paddocks and I won't take her any higher than a trot.'

Brock didn't speak and by the look on his face she was sure he was about to say no.

'Alright then,' he gave in. 'But be back in good time before breakfast or it'll be my neck in the noose.'

She beamed. 'Understood.'

He moved across to the tack room to collect a side-saddle. Following him, she reached out to lay a hand on his arm and pointed to another saddle. She hated the side-saddle. It was too restrictive.

'I promise I can ride better in a real saddle.'

'Ladies don't ride one leg either side of the horse,' Brock said, but she could see he didn't believe it any more than she did.

'Come now, Brock,' she said in her best flirtatious manner. 'I am sure the ladies of Australia have given over the silly rituals of the old country.'

Still he hesitated.

'I won't tell anyone if you don't,' she added, with a wink she hoped was playful and not completely inappropriate.

Whatever it was, he relented with a chuckle and she helped him saddle Misha with a sturdy man's saddle.

Stepping up on the riding block, she mounted the horse easily and took a moment to find her seat. The sky was lightening in the east as Brock followed her out of the stables. He stood by as she got comfortable in the saddle and with Misha's temperament. It had been some time since she'd ridden, and a new horse should always be treated with respect. Turning circles, Prudence marvelled at the elegance and strength of the animal. She urged the horse into an easy trot before waving goodbye to Brock.

'Back before breakfast,' he warned again.

'Yes, sir.' She saluted and, giving Misha a strong kick in the flanks, she took off across the paddocks at a speed that shook out the last of the sleep from her body.

Half an hour later she returned to the stables where Brock was waiting, his face a hard scowl.

'You promised you wouldn't go faster than a trot.'

'Oh, Brock, she's wonderful,' Prudence gushed, out of breath and trying to change the subject.

His frown didn't abate.

'I couldn't help it,' she said, a little more contrite. 'Misha is built to run and so am I. I have so few amusements. Please don't tell Grandmother or Uncle.'

'I won't,' he said, helping her down from the horse. 'But you really must stay inside the estate grounds. There are dangers out in the bush for young well-bred ladies. It's not safe, Miss Prudence. This isn't Hyde Park.'

'We've already encountered bushrangers,' she tossed back lightly. 'Thank you, Brock. I must get in to breakfast.'

Still exhilarated from her ride, she ran all the way back to the house. Passing the kitchen, she could hear Camilla finishing preparations for breakfast. She rushed up the rear stairs and straight into Uncle Robert.

'Oh!'

'Prudence, what on earth …?'

'Sorry, Uncle Robert.'

'Why are you so out of breath?' he asked, his eyes wandering over her attire. 'Did you go riding? Without a chaperone?'

'I just took Misha out for a quick trot. I didn't go far. Just in the home paddock. She's wonderful, Uncle Robert, I adore her. Please don't tell Gran I was riding alone,' she begged, kissing him on the cheek. If he did tell her grandmother, she wouldn't be able to placate her with just a kiss on the cheek.

Moving quickly past Robert, she continued up to her rooms where she washed and dressed. When she returned to the breakfast room, it was obvious that her uncle had not followed her wishes.

'Robert tells me you went out riding alone this morning.'

Not even a 'good morning' before the inquisition, then.

Sagging a little, Prudence graced her uncle with a small frown of disappointment but said nothing.

'I'll be speaking with the stable manager after breakfast to ensure it doesn't happen again,' Robert said, scattering salt on his boiled eggs.

'It wasn't Brock's fault …'

'Brock?' Deidre's face turned ashen. 'Brock?'

'You should not be so informal with the help, Prudence,' Robert said, disapproval creasing his brow.

'You are to stay away from the stables unless Robert or Alicia ride with you.'

'But Grandmother …'

'Where is this sudden wilfulness coming from, Prudence? You used to be so obedient.'

'What is the point of having a horse if I am not allowed to ride her?' Prudence asked, sliding down in her seat.

'You can ride with a chaperone,' Deidre said. 'And don't slouch.'

Prudence sat up straight in her chair, taking a sip of her tea before spreading a slice of bread with jam. But she had lost her appetite. Riding was to have been her one path of escape from the boredom of sewing cushion covers and drinking tea. It wasn't as though they would have any visitors either, being out in the middle of nowhere.

'Uncle Robert is away so much and Aunt Alicia told me last night that she doesn't like to spend too much time out in the sun.' She wasn't ready to give up yet. 'What if I promise to stay only to the grounds? The estate is large enough that I have no real need to leave it. Please, Grandmother?'

'I'll think about it,' Deidre agreed. 'But only if you prove you can behave like the mature lady I raised you to be.'

There was hope. She'd just have to be patient. 'May I be excused?'

'Where are you going?' Deidre asked.

'I thought I might read in the garden,' she said, thinking of the only activity her grandmother might approve of that would allow her to leave the house.

'You've not eaten anything,' Deidre argued.

She shovelled the bread into her mouth, chewing quickly and swallowing it with a mouthful of tea.

'Now may I be excused?'

Her grandmother gave her a look of displeasure but finally gave in. 'Stay in the shade.'

'I left a hat for you in the hallway,' Alicia said, speaking for the first time. 'The sun is very strong on our English skin.'

'Thank you, Aunt Alicia.' Prudence stood and left the room.

She spent a good twenty minutes in Robert and Alicia's library perusing the collection of books. There were plenty of horse-breeding and racing books. All the Jane Austen novels, which she had already read a multitude of times.

'*Wuthering Heights!*'

Prudence was astonished to see the novel her grandmother had deemed unsuitable for a lady in its content and ideals. She'd been dying to read it and, naturally, Gran's opinion had only made her more interested in the controversial book. Perhaps Aunt Alicia was not as buttoned up as she had first thought. With a devious smile, Prudence grabbed the book as if it was a lifeline, and on her way out the door she took a larger book on the history of Australian horse breeding from the shelf, hiding the novel between its covers should she encounter anyone on her way out of the house.

Retrieving the wide-brimmed hat Aunt Alicia had mentioned, she stepped outside into the gardens and, walking as far from the house as she dared, she made herself comfortable on a wooden garden bench beneath a large tree covered in fragrant purple flowers. She opened the larger book on horse breeding and, inside it, she flipped to the first page of *Wuthering Heights*. To the passer-by it would look as though she were studying up on her uncle's business.

By the time Prudence reached chapter nine of the novel, she felt both a kinship and a separation from the female character. Cathy was a girl who started out with all the freedom in the world to run wild across the moors with a man she loved. But then, having had a taste of the good life at Thrushcross Grange, it looked as though she would gladly give up her love for Heathcliff and marry Edgar for luxury and fine possessions. It would degrade her to marry Heathcliff despite how much she loved him.

Disappointed at where the story was going, Prudence closed the book and stared out into the wild, dense bushland just past the fence line of the Carrington estate. She had been brought up with fine possessions and luxury. But what she wouldn't give to have the freedom to roam the wilds of this country, of this world. She knew she was being ungrateful but … freedom was what she craved most. A man she loved? She'd never really thought about it. She'd never met a man she thought she could love. She would never have the freedom to love a man of her choosing anyway, should she meet one. A man like Heathcliff? A dirty orphan with no fortune and from a lesser social class? Her grandmother would pitch a fit. No, she was destined to marry a man like Edgar. And she was resigned to it. Wasn't she?

Three

The weeks dragged by and Pru became lonelier with every passing day. Thankfully, after Pru had spent an interminable amount of time acting on her best behaviour, her grandmother had finally allowed her to ride Misha unchaperoned as long as she promised to stay within sight of the house.

When she wasn't bound to the manor practising the pianoforte or doing needlepoint, she spent as much time as she could in the stables with the horses and Brock. And when her Uncle Robert was away in town and her grandmother was resting, she would defy her grandmother's edict and take Misha to the far edges of the huge property. Upon her return, Brock would inevitably give her one of his looks of disappointment, but he never reprimanded her.

'Why do you never give me up to Grandmother or Uncle Robert?' she asked one morning, after another exhilarating ride along the boundary fence line. 'You know I'm not supposed to ride away from the house.'

He looked up at her from where he'd been sorting feed into each of the horses' stalls.

'A girl needs to rebel now and then,' he said, his deep American drawl unable to hide the mocking tone.

'Did you know many rebellious women back in Kentucky?' she asked, leaning on the edge of the stall as he moved along. America intrigued her. Especially now as it looked as though the country was to go to war once again. Not with the British this time, but against its own countrymen.

Brock smiled his crooked smile. 'Miss Prudence, I knew women of the South that could make your hair curl, just with their language. But I also knew ladies, such as yourself, young, rich and bored—daughters of plantation owners—who were willing and able to get a man to do stupid things just to catch her attention. They would also rebel. But their rebellion, more often than not, led to their ruin.'

The warning didn't go unnoticed, but Prudence chose to ignore it. She was no flighty plantation-owner's daughter. And she certainly had no desire to watch a man do stupid things in the hope of catching her eye.

'I'm not a rebel,' she said, although she did enjoy the idea of it. 'Just a woman trying to make her way in a man's world as best she can.'

'Well, you'll be a sorry woman if your grandmother finds out,' he tossed back as they reached the last stall.

The midnight-black head of a tall stallion popped over the top of the stall, nipping Brock lightly in the ear.

'Blasted animal!' He gave the horse a swipe across the nose and Pru chuckled.

'It's not funny,' Brock argued, rubbing his sore ear. 'Ornery beast takes a bite out of me every chance he gets.'

'Oh, come now,' Pru said, rubbing her hand down the horse's cheek. 'He's meek as a child.'

'Meek is he?' Brock grunted. 'We'll see if you still feel the same when he takes your finger off. Keep your hands back, Miss Prudence. He's a biter, as you can see.'

'What's your name, sweetheart?' she asked the horse.

'His name is Samson,' Brock grumbled. 'He's your uncle's prize racehorse. I've been training him and, despite my consistent advice that he isn't ready yet, your uncle is entering him in the upcoming Spring Carnival in Melbourne.'

'He'll do just fine, won't you, Samson.'

The stallion snorted wetly at Brock before turning back to nuzzle gently into Pru's shoulder.

'Can I ride him?'

Brock's eyes widened. 'Of course you can't. And don't go getting any ideas about sneaking out with him when I'm not here. You do that, and I will definitely tell your grandmother just how far out you ride on your little morning trots.'

She pulled a face at him, already devising ways to get a ride on the powerful stallion.

The smell of the grass and horses lifted Pru's spirits. She'd been cooped up on the Carrington estate for weeks since they'd arrived, with only the company of her grandmother, her Aunt Alicia and the servants. Thanks to the beginning of the spring season, she was thrilled to be able to accompany her family to her first Australian race meeting.

The trip to Melbourne had given her a chance to see more of the countryside and she looked forward to spending a few days exploring the city. Although, now that she was there, standing at Flemington Racecourse dressed in a heavy taffeta gown in the heat of the spring sun, she wondered why she'd been so keen to come.

Following her grandmother, her aunt and uncle into the spectator's area, Prudence craned her neck to see the magnificent animals pacing in the staging area, waiting for their turn to race.

Uncle Robert called to Brock, who led Samson to them at the barrier fencing. The stallion was agitated and Prudence believed the jockey chosen to race him was lacking in his ability to control the horse. Sitting astride in his shiny Carrington colours of blue and green, the jockey looked nervous, and that nervousness would be transmitted directly to the stallion. She moved in to try to pat Samson in the hopes of calming him, but her grandmother called her back.

'All prepared, Brock?' Uncle Robert asked.

'He could do with a few more months, sir,' Brock answered and tipped his hat to Prudence, who smiled back.

'Well, we don't have a few more months,' Robert snapped. 'I've got a lot of money riding on him.'

'Yes, sir,' Brock responded begrudgingly and taking the reins, he walked the horse and jockey out to the track.

Prudence dropped her parasol as she scanned the crowd, fascinated by the interesting mix of people who had come to watch the races. Only a rope separated their small upper-class section from the rest of the spectators and as she watched the fun on the other side of the rope she wished she could join them.

'Prudence, cover yourself,' Deidre instructed.

She sighed. 'Yes, Grandmother.'

She lifted her parasol back into place and surreptitiously scanned the crowds again. Groups of men stood by a bar, drinking and betting, while the women congregated in small groups talking. She would have liked to join them at the bar. She wished she could try a beer. She'd never had beer. Gran had allowed her to drink sherry or wine once she'd turned twenty-one, but she was never to have more than one glass. Prudence wondered what it was like to feel drunk.

All attention turned to the racetrack as the bugle called the horses to the starting line. Prudence moved to the fence to get a better look. She could see Samson shifting restlessly, the jockey struggling to keep the stallion at the line, and when the starter's gun fired and the horses lunged forward, Samson was facing the other way.

'Damn that blasted jockey!' Robert cursed.

'Robert, mind your language,' Deidre reprimanded.

Prudence ignored them and watched as the stallion finally settled into the run.

'Give him his head,' she murmured. Her uncle was right. The horse wasn't the problem. It was the jockey who was incompetent. Even she could have run a better race than that pipsqueak of a man.

Despite the slow start, and the poor control the jockey had, Samson managed to cross the line in fourth place. The cheer went up around her from those with tickets on the winning horses.

'Fourth place is not bad for his first race, Uncle,' Prudence said, trying to console him. 'He'll do better next time.'

'Thank you, Prudence,' he said, but she could see the disappointment in his eyes. 'And yes, he will do better, when I fire that jockey.'

The jockey in question rode Samson back to the barriers. As he took his scolding from Uncle Robert, Prudence leaned out and stroked Samson's cheek, annoyed she'd yet to find a way to get a ride on the stallion herself. She was certain she could get a faster time out of him. Perhaps she could sweet-talk Brock into letting her ride Samson one morning. Although she highly doubted it would work.

'Don't spoil the animal, Prudence,' Gran told her. 'Or he'll not be fit for anything but the knackery.'

Hanging his head low, the jockey led Samson back to the stables to cool off.

One by one, Prudence was introduced to friends of Robert's and she shook hands and made conversation where necessary, but she wished she could go to the stables and spend time with the horses. As Uncle Robert's friends went, the horses were much better company.

Jack couldn't believe his luck. Not in the race. He let the losing ticket flutter to the ground as he stared across at the red-haired beauty snuggling up to the stallion that had lost him money. It had been a month, but he was positive it was her. Prudence. The owner of the gold locket that now resided permanently in his pocket.

He watched her for a while. She talked and smiled at people, the personification of politeness, but when she thought no one was looking, the smile fell and she looked bored. Her gaze would wander across to the rabble by the bar and she almost looked envious of the men and women who gathered around, drinking beer on a warm spring day. And when a man, obviously horrendously drunk, fell and knocked over a table, she didn't look on him with disgust, but instead chuckled into her lace-gloved hand. As the drunk was carted away by the police, Jack recognised Robert Stanforth exchanging words with Prudence. Was she a relation of his? He had a vague recollection that the Stanforths were from nobility.

As he was musing on that, her eyes scanned the crowd and fell on him. He smiled broadly at her and she did a double-take, but she did not smile back. He dipped his head in greeting and a miniscule frown formed between her eyebrows before she looked away again. But as he continued to watch her, every few minutes she would turn her head and peek back in his direction. And each time he would smile again and she would pretend she wasn't looking at him, or dip her parasol to hide her face.

He knew he dared not go over to her. Most people didn't make the connection between Jack Fairweather and Jack the Devil. They would not imagine it possible that a gentleman who walked among them, attended the same parties and balls, could be a fearsome bushranger. There was always the possibility that someone would recognise him, but that just added to the thrill. What did that say about him? He was a twisted man, that's what. He didn't usually lose his mind enough to actually engage with persons from whom he'd stolen. But there was something about this woman, something in her own show of duplicity that intrigued him. He had to speak to her again, even if just for a moment.

Sliding his hand into his pocket, he ran his thumb across the smooth gold of the locket. Why he'd held on to it or why he carried it around with him constantly, he didn't know, but now it was giving him an idea.

He spotted Mr Walter Harris, a councilman in Ballarat with whom he was friendly. He liked the man. As far as councilmen went, he was one of the least annoying of the preening buffoons who thought of themselves as the fathers of the city.

'Walter,' he said, making himself known to the gentleman.

'Fairweather,' the man responded, extending a hand.

Jack took it and shook heartily. 'Good to see you. How are your horses running today?'

'Not well, I'm afraid.' Walter gave a despondent sigh. 'My champion drew up lame just before her race and the new stallion is not working out at all.'

'I'm sorry to hear that,' Jack said, fighting his impatience. He could see Prudence just a few yards away over Walter's shoulder. She was scanning the crowd again. Was it possible she was looking for him?

'How's the transport business?' Walter asked.

'Oh, fine, fine. Walter, I wonder if you might introduce me to Robert Stanforth and his family,' Jack requested. 'I see them over there and I have yet to make their acquaintance.'

'Of course,' Walter agreed. 'You know he owns that grand horse stud just outside of Ballan. Trains racehorses. Although, his stallion didn't do much better than mine today.'

'Is that so?' Jack couldn't give two hoots about Stanforth's business as he followed Walter across the grass to where Prudence stood with her family.

'Robert,' Walter said, interrupting the conversation.

'How do you do, Walter?' Robert asked, shaking the man's hand. 'Sorry to see Apple Blossom pull up lame.'

'Yes, I think my man has overworked her,' Walter went on with annoyance. 'But Samson ran a good race.'

'Not as good as hoped,' Robert said with equal annoyance. 'My trainer says he is just young yet and may take some time to get the hang of it.'

'Brock's a good trainer,' Walter said. 'He worked for Robert Alexander in Kentucky for a few years, I believe.'

'Yes, it's why I hired him.'

Jack had stopped listening to the two men as he stood slightly behind Prudence. She had not yet seen him and he was able to take a good look at her in profile. The lavender dress she wore was simple and modest, with that high neck once again. She must have been sweltering in the hot day under all that taffeta and lace. What he wouldn't give to see her delicate neck free from the confines of such restrictive clothing. Inhaling deeply, he could smell the perfume she used. Not the cheap overpowering scents the women in hotels and brothels wore, it was subtle and sweet.

'Robert, may I introduce Mr Jack Fairweather.'

Walter's introduction broke him out of his reverie and he stepped forward.

'A pleasure, sir,' Jack said with a nod as he shook Robert's hand.

'Fairweather.' Robert eyed him as though studying his worth. 'May I present my mother, the Lady Carrington, Mrs Deidre Stanforth, and this is my wife Alicia and my niece, Miss Prudence Stanforth.'

Jack nodded politely to Deidre, whose face did not alter from her permanent scowl—no recognition there—before turning his gaze upon Prudence.

Her green eyes widened momentarily. She was clearly surprised to see the man she'd been sneaking peeks at for the last fifteen minutes now standing before her.

'Miss Prudence. It's a pleasure.'

He took her hand and raised it to his lips. The miniscule frown returned as she studied him.

'Nice to meet you, Mr Fairweather.'

Deidre and Robert returned to their conversation with Walter about the horses but Jack noticed that Prudence continued to stare up at him with a wary expression. Had she worked it out?

'I beg your pardon, sir, but have we met before?'

Jack shook his head. 'I do not believe so.'

'In London, perhaps?'

'I left London a good many years ago.'

Her perplexed frown was a delight to watch as she tried to muddle it out.

'I could swear we have met before.'

She was tenacious indeed, he thought.

'Do you enjoy the race meetings, Mr Fairweather?'

'I rarely make it to the races. Football is more to my taste.'

'Football?'

'Yes, it's the latest sport,' Jack said. 'Currently it's played mostly in Geelong and Melbourne, but Ballarat and Castlemaine are putting together teams in order to have real matches and to grow a league.'

'I'm afraid I do not know the game, sir.'

'It's a new sport with Australian rules based loosely on the Gaelic football.' He leaned closer to her. 'Very rough and tumble, very manly. Perhaps you should come and watch a match with me one day.'

She did not baulk as he had expected but instead grinned at his graphic explanation of the physicality of the game. 'It sounds exciting.' But her smile dropped when her eyes flicked to her grandmother. 'Although, I doubt my grandmother would allow me to watch such a sport.'

'What a pity. I imagine you would enjoy it.'

His eyes stayed on hers and he didn't know whether it was the colour of the dress she wore or the green of the grass surrounding them, but her eyes looked like two gemstones glowing in the afternoon sun.

'Mr Fairweather, do you have an occupation?'

'Of sorts,' Jack replied to Deidre's question as he turned back to the group. 'I work on the highways.' He took in their blank looks. 'Transport,' he added.

'Oh, like the Cobb and Co?' Robert asked.

'Precisely.'

'And do you use coach drivers brought over from the wild west of America, like the Cobb and Co?' Robert enquired, his distaste for the practice showing in the way he turned up his nose.

'No, I prefer to hire my drivers locally,' Jack said. 'Unlike the Cobb and Co, my business is a small enterprise. But I am always on the lookout for new teams of suitable horses for a good price. I understand you breed good stock.'

'I do.' The man all but puffed up like a peacock at the compliment. 'I concentrate mostly on racehorses, but I have a good selection of Clydesdales if you would care to visit me at the manor sometime.'

'I'll keep it in mind, Mr Stanforth,' Jack said. He was quickly becoming bored with the conversation. Meanwhile, Prudence was still staring at him oddly. Still trying to sort out where she had seen him before. It amused him greatly. She was a perceptive thing, that was for certain.

'The Cobb and Co has become dreadfully expensive,' Robert admonished, bringing Jack's attention back to him. 'It costs a fortune to get transport from Melbourne or Geelong to Ballarat or Bendigo to attend the horse auctions.'

'It's virtually highway robbery,' Jack agreed.

He turned and winked at Prudence. She gasped mid-sip of her drink and immediately entered into a coughing fit, drawing everyone's attention. Jack watched her eyes widen as realisation and recognition crossed her features.

Whether it had been his little highway robbery joke or the wink he'd sent her, she'd figured it out. She knew exactly who he was.

He leaned in as though to pat her on the back and spoke quietly in her ear.

'Clever girl.'

If possible her eyes became larger as she continued to cough, trying to catch her breath, pointing at him as she tried valiantly to get out the words she desperately wanted everyone to hear.

Jack took the hand she pointed at him and put a handkerchief to her mouth to stop the coughing, and to stop her giving him away.

'Prudence, what on earth is wrong with you?' Deidre said with a disapproving frown. 'Get a hold of yourself.'

'Oh dear,' Jack said to the others. 'She seems to be choking. Perhaps she needs some shade and fresh air away from the crowds. I'll escort her to the ladies' room to recover.'

'Thank you, Mr Fairweather,' Deidre said, seemingly more concerned over Prudence embarrassing the family than her granddaughter being unchaperoned.

Prudence shook her head rapidly as he took her arm, not roughly, but with a grip she wouldn't be able to fight, and led her away through the crowd. Not to the ladies' room as he'd told her grandmother but around to the back of the grandstand where they were now very much alone.

Her coughing fit slowly abated and although he let her go, he herded her into the corner of an empty stable where she was unable to escape.

'Now, Miss Prudence, what seems to be the matter?'

She took a deep breath.

'You're him.'

'Who?'

'Him!' she blurted. 'The bushranger!'

'Bushranger?'

'Jack the Devil.'

She'd remembered his name. It was a ridiculous thing to focus on, but it also made him ridiculously happy.

'What on earth makes you think a thing like that?'

'You winked at me,' she said. 'You winked at me today like you winked at me when you robbed us. I would know those eyes anywhere.'

'Really?' He was more than happy now. He was thrilled.

Her eyes narrowed on him. 'That wasn't a compliment.'

'And you're not frightened?' he asked. 'Being alone here, cornered by a dangerous bushranger?'

'No.'

'Really?'

'I'm annoyed. You stole my locket.'

Jack felt that strange twinge of remorse creep up on him again. It was not a sentiment he'd had to deal with often, but somehow she brought it out in him.

'I did,' he agreed solemnly.

Her eyes widened again as he confirmed she was indeed correct. He was a bushranger and he had stolen from her.

But while he waited for the fear to come into her eyes, all he saw was determination.

'Did you get a lot of money for it?' she asked.

'No,' he said. 'You were right. It wasn't worth much to anyone except you.'

She didn't need to know that he had not been able to bring himself to sell it.

He saw her courage slip a little as a look of pain crossed her pretty features at the loss of her locket.

'So,' he began again. 'You recognised me. No one has ever recognised me before. You know what that means, don't you?'

'No. What does it mean?'

Finally some fear showed as a tremor in her voice.

'It means you will need to stay with me now. I can't let you go, knowing what you know about me.'

She gasped. 'You're kidnapping me?'

'Well, I can't have you dobbing me in to the local troopers now, can I?'

'I won't tell anyone,' she promised.

He shrugged. 'No one would believe you anyway.' He rubbed his chin, as though deep in thought. 'How about a negotiation?'

'Negotiation?'

'A compromise.'

'I know what a negotiation is,' she snapped. 'But you are a fool if you believe I will let you have anything else of mine.'

'Then how about if I give you something instead.' Her wary frown drew his attention to the long lashes above her narrowed eyes. 'I'll give you something and let you go if you will guarantee you won't tell a soul that you know who I am.'

'You'll give me something?' she asked, disbelief ringing in her tone. 'I don't want anything you have stolen from someone else.'

'You'll want this thing I've stolen,' he said, and reaching into his coat, he removed the locket and held it up in front of her face.

'My locket!'

She made to grab for it but he lifted it high out of her reach. It was then that he realised how he towered over her. He wasn't the tallest of men but she really was a little thing. Perhaps her courage had made her seem taller to him.

'Uh, uh, uh.' He waved his finger in front of her face.

'I thought you'd sold it.'

'It interested me enough to hold on to it a while. Who is the woman in the photograph?'

She went very still then as her expression softened, and her eyes glistened momentarily with tears before she pulled herself together admirably. 'None of your business.'

'It's not you,' he said, flipping the locket open to look once again at the picture of the pretty young woman. 'But she could be your sister. Your mother.'

She put her hand out. 'Give it to me.'

'Not until you promise that you will tell no one about me and my sordid second life.'

'I promise,' she said quickly and reached for the locket again.

He yanked it away with a laugh. 'Well, that was convincing. I want you to say "Jack, you handsome devil, I promise I will never tell a soul of your real identity".'

She huffed and put her hands on her hips. 'Jack, you ... devil.' He grinned at her deliberate shot at him. 'I promise I will never tell a soul your real identity,' she finished. 'Now give me my locket.'

'Not yet,' he said and she gritted her teeth and growled at him, making him chuckle.

'First, we must seal it with a kiss.'

She met his eyes and took a cautious step back. But there was nowhere to go in the corner of the stable.

'A kiss?'

'A kiss,' he repeated.

'I have to kiss Jack the Devil?'

He gave her a look of censure and she rolled her eyes impatiently.

'I have to kiss Jack Fairweather?'

'Yes.'

'And if I don't?'

He gave an exaggerated and sad sigh. 'Then no locket.'

She seemed to be mulling it over, which surprised him. He'd expected a slap in the face, or at the least a flat refusal. He had never forced himself on a woman in his life and wasn't about to start now. If she refused, he'd accept it and give her the locket anyway.

'Just one tiny, little kiss,' he tried again, feeling hope bloom.

'And then I get my locket?'

'Yes,' he said and stepped closer, bridging the gap between them. He could smell her perfume again and was so close he could see the fleck of gold in one green eye. 'Kiss me, Prudence.'

She still wasn't saying no but he wanted her to kiss him, he wanted her to want to. It surprised him how much he wanted it.

'Have you ever been kissed?' he asked.

'Yes,' she said, her chin going up defiantly.

He was sceptical. 'By someone who wasn't a relative?'

Her chin dropped again but she didn't answer.

'Didn't think so,' he said. 'A kiss is a small price to pay for your locket, wouldn't you say?'

'Fine,' she said, surrendering with a huff. 'If it will get me my locket back, you may kiss me.'

She closed her eyes and firmed her lips. She wasn't going to make it easy for him. He took the opportunity to study her pretty face, her little turned-up nose, the sweep of fiery red hair bundled up. He wanted to see her lips, so full and pink, but they were pressed so tightly together. Closing the gap between them, he placed his lips against the stiff line of hers. At first she didn't move.

Determined little minx, he thought, nipping lightly at the corners of her mouth, coaxing, teasing, hoping she would surrender and let him kiss her properly.

He opened his mouth just a little to envelop both of her lips with his and felt the sigh escape her as she finally relaxed. As her lips parted on her gasp, her little exhale of breath went all the way to his toes. Then he felt her, ever so lightly, begin to kiss him back and his mind went blank of anything but her. He swept his tongue over the fullness of her upper lip, and the spark that ignited was all consuming. One more minute and he would step back, he promised. His hands formed fists at his side as he fought the urge to touch her, to drag her bodily against him. She was an innocent and a lady. He had to remember that.

He pulled back quickly and stared at her, astonished that such an inexperienced kiss from her had strained his control to breaking point.

Slowly she opened her eyes, her expression as startled as his. Her fingers went to her lips, making him want to kiss her all over again.

'There. Was that so hard?' he asked, his voice a little huskier than he'd expected.

He waited for her to answer him, to censure him in some way over his unacceptable behaviour, but she kept staring at him, unblinking, her eyes filled not with disapproval but with wonder.

Determined to save his sanity, he held up the locket.

'All yours. You earned it.'

When she didn't reach for it, he leaned forward and placed it around her neck, his eyes fixed to hers as he fastened the clasp. And when his fingers brushed against the delicate skin high on the back of her neck, he felt her shiver.

'Thank you,' she said in a voice that trembled.

'And you promise to keep my secret?'

She nodded. 'I promise.'

'Then you can go.'

He stepped back, giving her room to pass him, but she didn't move.

Why wasn't she leaving? If she didn't go soon, he'd not be responsible for his actions.

Struggling to resist her large eyes, glassed over with unabashed emotion, staring up at him, he summoned willpower he didn't even know he possessed, turned and walked away from her.

She staggered back against the wall of the stable and watched him disappear around the corner. Her fingers went to her lips again and the hand that had risen to her pounding heart shook. Exhaling long and slow, she told herself it was relief she felt. Relief that he was gone. Relief that he had left her safe and sound … and trembling with a delicious warmth coursing through her body. She had never been kissed before. Putting her mouth to a man's had always seemed so strange to her, so … unsanitary even. How silly she'd been.

Her belly somersaulted as she recalled the sensation of his lips brushing lightly against hers. She closed her eyes and tried to bring back every thought and feeling she'd had while he'd kissed her, and then licked her. Yes, his tongue had touched her lips once, ever so softly, and her knees had turned to water, her pulse had raced in her ears, blocking all sounds other than his quickening breath. And when he'd stepped back, she had very nearly reached for him in a reaction beyond her control.

When she'd opened her eyes, the expression on his face had been so strange. So different from the teasing, arrogant bushranger he'd been until that point. His eyes were softer, darker, touched with what looked like confusion, as though a great battle were taking place within him. She'd been unable to move, even when he'd given her the opportunity to leave. She'd just stood there staring at him, enveloped still in the heat that had radiated from him. And then he was gone. Reaching up, she grasped the locket. Even when he'd offered it to her, she'd been unable to take it, unable to lift her hand to accept it, no matter how much she'd wanted to. He'd had to clasp it around her neck himself, and as he'd leaned in, she'd taken a deep breath of his manly scent. His scent hung in her nostrils even now.

In a trance, Prudence walked back to where her family were situated trackside.

'What have you been doing all this time, Prudence?'

Tucking the locket safely under the high neck of her dress, she turned to face her grandmother and shook her head. 'Nothing, Grandmother. Nothing at all.'

Four

Pru raised her face to the rising sun and revelled in its warmth. The days were getting longer, the sun warmer as summer approached, and there was nowhere she would rather be on such a pretty morning than riding across the vast expanse of the estate. While she enjoyed a good gallop, today she was happy to give Misha her head and let the horse choose where she wanted to go and at what speed. Inevitably, Misha headed for the eastern side of the property. While the fields had begun to dry out with the warmer weather, there were still green mounds of sweet grasses to be found by the little creek that ran through one corner of the estate.

As the horse leaned down to drink at the babbling waters, Pru's mind wandered, not for the first time, to the day at the races. Had it really only been a week earlier that she'd been kissed by a bushranger? She'd never been kissed by a man before, but she had certainly read plenty about it, about kisses and sexual intercourse between a man and a woman. The things she had read had been both romantic and scientific, but she would take the romantic descriptions any day over the mechanical explanations in the biology books she'd studied.

Adventure and romance—romance and adventure. The two so often went together in literature, and while in her mind she had known it was wrong to let him kiss her like that, her curiosity had taken over. Her body had rejoiced in the explosion of new sensations that had overwhelmed her at the soft, wet warmth of his mouth against hers. She didn't swoon, as so many women seemed to in literature, but Jack the Devil could certainly make a girl light-headed.

But with the distance of a week, she was coming to realise that what Jack 'the Devil' Fairweather had done to get her to kiss him was tantamount to blackmail and abuse. He was beyond reproach, incorrigible. Infuriation had gradually replaced her romantic girlish fantasies and she swore that if she ever saw Jack the Devil again, she would indeed tell the world who he was.

Done with being a starry-eyed fool, Pru pulled at Misha's reins and set them off at a cracking pace. Her annoyance spurred her on, and seeing a section of the fence that was lower than the rest, she headed for it.

Jumping Misha over the border fence with ease, Pru grinned broadly at the sense of freedom leaving the estate always gave her, and rode straight across the plains towards the small hill and the rocky outcropping she could see from her bedroom window. There'd be hell to pay if her grandmother found out, but Uncle Robert was in Melbourne and Grandmother had come down with spring allergies and had taken to her bed for the past few days. Knowing she had all the time in the world to explore, she wasn't about to give up this opportunity.

Reaching the dirt road, she slowed a little, unsure how far she should go. It would be imprudent of her to get lost and to have Brock sent to look for her.

Suddenly, Misha startled and reared a little as another horse bolted out of the bush and into their path. She stayed seated thanks

only to the saddle she continued to request from Brock. Had she
been on a side-saddle, she doubted she would have stopped herself
from falling.

Angry with the man who had so carelessly flown out of the
bushes, she was about to reward him with a mouthful of abuse,
but she stopped when she saw the familiar mischievous grin.

'Jack! Mr Devil, Mr Fairweather ...' She stopped before she
could make an even bigger fool of herself.

'I am so glad you remembered me, Miss Prudence.'

'How could I forget?'

She regretted the words the minute they were out of her mouth.
But the moment she'd recognised him her mind had flown back
to the races and that kiss. The thrill that coursed through her was
unexpected and heady.

'It seems I made quite an impression,' he said, his arrogance
reminding her that this was no gentleman suitor but a thief.

'Yes, you left the impression of a rude and uncouth criminal
who takes what he wants, when he wants it.'

She lifted her chin and did her best to appear haughty, despite
her racing heart and traitorous belly, fluttering like the wings of
a thousand butterflies. He didn't need to know that she'd thought
about that kiss more than once since the day she'd discovered Jack
Fairweather was really Jack the Devil. Her lips tingled even now
at the memory and she licked them without thinking.

'Are we talking about my bushranging ways or the kiss you
gave me at the races?' he asked, his gaze firmly resting on her lips.

'I didn't give you a kiss, you took it from me.'

'You got exactly what you wanted.'

Her mouth dropped open but she was so stunned at his accusation that no words came out.

'Your locket,' he said, pointing at the necklace now hanging
around her neck.

She looked down. She had been keeping the locket hidden beneath her clothing, but it had been jolted out during her ride. If her grandmother were to see it, she would demand to know how she came to have it again after it had been stolen.

As though reading her mind, Jack leaned forward and took the locket between his thumb and forefinger before tucking it back beneath her shirt, his fingers brushing against the skin of her throat. Swallowing hard, she felt the heat rush up her body to her face. Eager to hide her reaction, she tried to ride around him, but he manoeuvred his horse to block her path.

'Please, get out of my way.'

His expression changed, the arrogance giving way to a concerned frown. 'I'm sorry. I didn't mean to frighten you. I saw you riding by and just wanted to say hello.'

'You didn't frighten me,' she said. It was true. She hadn't had time to be frightened.

His brow furrowed a little at that. 'It's an interesting coincidence that we happen to be riding on the same road, don't you think?'

'An unhappy one,' she added with a curtness she didn't feel.

She was so muddled. Torn between how she should be behaving and her curiosity. She had so many questions about his life as a bushranger, but she knew she ought to leave; ought to get away from him as fast as her horse could carry her.

She needed to get home in case her grandmother rose and admonished her for going riding out of the estate unchaperoned … again. Decision made, she tightened her grip on the reins and sat up straight.

'I must be getting back to the manor,' she said, finally able to turn Misha on the narrow dirt road.

'Then please allow me to escort you back,' Jack said, moving his horse alongside hers. 'The highway is a dangerous place.'

She rolled her eyes. 'I'm not sure being escorted home by a bushranger is the wisest course of action.'

'You forget,' he said with a conspiratorial wink. 'Your grandmother thinks I am a businessman. Jack Fairweather of Fairweather Transport.'

'And how is business?' Pru asked as they set off at a walk.

'Business does quite well,' Jack said with a nod. 'So well, in fact, I rarely spend any time at the office in Ballarat. My staff are so efficient the transport business runs like a well-oiled machine without me.'

'And what about the other business?

'The other business?'

'Yes. How is the thieving business?' she questioned, allowing a small teasing grin to touch her lips.

He tilted his head as he looked at her. The intensity in his dark stare made her uncomfortable.

'It's alright. As a matter of fact I'm taking a break from bush-ranging just now.'

'Oh? Conscience pricking, is it?'

He shot her a narrow-eyed sidelong glance to which she returned a smug grin.

'No,' he said. 'There's a new police sergeant in town. Sergeant Carmichael is a little overzealous in his duties. It's wise to lay low for a while when the constabulary changes hands. They always seem to want to prove themselves by rounding up all the bush-rangers in the district.'

'Mm, fancy that. A policeman chasing criminals,' Prudence said, the sarcasm dripping from every word.

'Yes, well, it pays to keep one's head down at such times. Besides, the troopers have become quite vigilant since the last gold wagon was held up and soldiers were killed.'

'Do you rob gold wagons?' she asked, suddenly aware again of the dangerous, and fascinating, nature of his work.

'No.' He shook his head. 'No, I know better than to try to steal from the government wagons these days. It's not like it was in the early days. The wagons were easy to rob back then, hardly any protection save a few drunk soldiers. Now they not only use soldiers and troopers to protect the wagons, they have these big bastard ...' he paused and gave her a repentant look. 'Pardon me. They have these big guns mounted on the wagon. It's unlikely a thief would get away with his life, less likely he would get away with any gold.'

They rode in silence for a few moments. Only the magpies and the wind whispering in the trees accompanied the synchronised beat of their horses' hooves on the hard dirt road.

'How do you know which coaches to rob?' she asked. 'I mean, there are many people who travel these roads who have nothing worth stealing. Would they not be a waste of your time?'

She studied him as he stayed unusually quiet. And then the answer came to her in a flash. 'The transport business.'

He gave her a quizzical look.

She grinned with admiration. It was surprisingly clever. 'That's how you do it. Through your transport business.'

He didn't confirm or deny but again stayed oddly silent on the matter.

'Oh, don't be shy now, Mr Fairweather.'

'You are too perceptive, Miss Prudence.'

'Your legitimate business provides the opportunity to peruse the luggage to see whether that coach is worth bailing up or not. It's quite brilliant really. But it's not always how you do it. Our carriage, for instance, came from Geelong and was not a Fairweather coach. Sometimes your heists are planned, other times they are crimes of opportunity. Does it add to the thrill of it? The unknown element?'

Jack laughed. 'You have an inquisitive mind. What brought on this sudden interest in the work of a bushranger?'

She shrugged a shoulder. 'I read. A lot.'

'Always a dangerous thing for a woman,' he murmured. She heard him, and chose to ignore it.

'I read about bushrangers well before we came here from England. The periodicals were full of reports about Bold Jack Donohoe, the Wild Colonial Boy. The escapades of Black Douglas and Mad Dog Morgan.'

'Escapades is it?' Jack said with a sardonic laugh. 'That's a pretty word for what I do. Why would a lady such as yourself enjoy reading about dangerous and corrupt men?'

'I read a lot of things,' she said, proudly. 'My grandfather adored books and he passed that love on to me. One of my favourite stories as a child was the penny series on Robin Hood and his merry men.'

'Interesting considering your heritage.'

'What do you mean?'

'Well, he was a nobleman fighting for the rights of the peasants. He was the Earl of Huntingdon and you are related to the Earl of Carrington.'

'A title means nothing,' Prudence said, miffed at being reminded of the heritage she'd grown to see as a restraint. 'Especially here.'

'It means something alright,' Jack said casually. 'Tell me, Miss Prudence, in all your reading, did you ever read about the Eureka Stockade?'

'Of course. Everyone heard about it. It was in all the papers in London.'

'Well, as little as six years ago, only the gentry, your type, were allowed to own land or vote in this country until the so-called "peasants" stood up to the British government,' Jack went on. 'The battle for that democracy cost the lives of miners and soldiers, but eventually the laws were changed allowing any man to campaign for a position in the legislature and to own land if he could afford to do so.'

'You certainly know a lot on the matter.' She studied him closely. His brow was furrowed and he stared out at the horizon as though lost in memories. It was a rare sight to see his usually jovial mood dulled. 'You were there.'

He met her eyes and she saw the haunted look in them.

'No,' he answered definitively. 'That is to say, I was not at the stockade myself. I was around Ballarat at the time, but … I knew people who were there. I knew people who died there.'

Prudence desperately wanted to ask him all about it. What had he seen? Had the military really murdered all those poor souls as the periodicals had reported? Or was it the miners who were the villains of the piece?

But she could see by his expression that this was not a conversation he wanted to have.

'Anyway, the idea of a band of outlaws with big hearts like Robin and his merry men appealed to me,' she said, returning reluctantly to the original subject. 'When I got older I turned to other adventure books like *The Three Musketeers*. I just adore Alexandre Dumas.'

'And what does your grandmother think of you reading such unladylike literature?'

She shrugged a shoulder. 'She doesn't know everything I do.'

Jack chuckled. 'Clearly. I'd bet she doesn't know you are out here now, riding alone.'

'I'm not alone,' she said, straightening in her saddle. 'I'm with you.'

'Mm, chaperoned by a dangerous outlaw. I'm sure Grandma would be less than thrilled.'

He was right about that.

'You shouldn't romanticise things you know nothing about,' he said. 'Robin Hood gave what he stole to the poor and the

Musketeers were the king's guard. They were good men. Hardly the same as the drunken, murdering Mad Dog Morgan.'

She stopped her horse. It hadn't occurred to her that, as charming as he was, he might also be a dangerous killer, just like those bushrangers who had come before him. When he too stopped and turned back to look at her questioningly, she asked, 'Do you do murder?'

'No, Miss Prudence,' Jack said, his expression serious. 'I have never shot or killed a man in my life. It's not my way. And that is why I was glad to see the back of Mad Dog Morgan when he fled to New South Wales.'

'You knew him?'

'Don't look so thrilled,' he said, concern on his face. 'You shouldn't be so eager to learn about the darker side of bushranging. It's not as adventurous as those periodicals back in London will have you believe. After Morgan left, my partner and I spent more time around the Bendigo area, ran with another gang for a while, til they moved on to New South Wales. Then we joined up with a man named Viktor. Better known as Viktor the Vicious. And he could be. Brutally vicious. One day we were robbing a coach. It should have been an easy bail-up, but Viktor took a liking to a lady's engagement ring. He grabbed for it, wrenching the woman's hand, and her fiancé or husband made the bad decision to fight Viktor for it.'

'Bad decision? To fight for what was his?'

'You were lucky the day I robbed you.'

'Lucky?' She shot out a derisive laugh.

'Yes, lucky,' Jack said. The sudden darkening in his demeanour wiped the smile from her face.

She could see he was struggling with something until he finally spoke up.

'Viktor slit the fiancé's throat with a hunting knife.'

Prudence's hand went to her own throat and then to her mouth. Jack seemed to slump over his horse a little, as though the weight of the world was on his shoulders.

'What happened?'

'I'd already decided I wouldn't work with Viktor again and was going to tell him when the police got there first. He was arrested for murder. The girl in the carriage identified him from the scar across his left eye. Bobby and I decided it was time to leave Bendigo and we headed back to Ballarat. We watched the trial of Viktor closely. He never mentioned us, never said a word about who'd been with him that day.'

'A loyal murdering bushranger?' She couldn't have been more surprised.

Jack nodded. 'So you see. You were lucky that day, that it was I who robbed you. Not all men would have been as generous as to leave such a beautiful woman with her virtue,' he said. 'Or her life.'

She understood his meaning, but the warning in his words got lost in the compliment he had paid her.

'You think I'm beautiful?'

He didn't answer but his expression softened as his eyes moved across her face. Finally looking away, he urged his horse forward again.

She did the same and made a thorough study of him as they walked quietly for a moment. 'I don't believe you are dangerous at all.'

He huffed lightly. 'Do you not?'

'No.'

'Well, don't let that get around, you'll ruin my hard-earned reputation.'

'I doubt another bushranger, especially Viktor the Vicious, would have returned my necklace to me. Why did you?'

She could see his unease at her question, but he recovered quickly and grinned that mischievous grin.

'I returned it because you kissed me, remember?'

'You kissed *me*,' she tossed back, halting her horse once again. 'I simply stood there.'

He stopped too, his leg brushing against hers as the horses sidled up next to each other. 'If it makes you feel better to think that, then please, do go on deluding yourself. But I was not the only person having input into that enjoyable moment.'

Prudence felt the heat rise in her cheeks again and looked away from him to the road ahead, but his finger was under her chin, turning her face towards his.

Her face was a furnace as he studied her with such intensity. 'Such beautiful green eyes.'

Her belly quivered and she found herself hoping he might kiss her again. She even leaned towards him, but he dropped his hand and broke eye contact.

Releasing the breath she'd been holding, she silently reprimanded herself for being so foolish. 'I must get back.'

She kicked her horse into a trot, but instead of letting her go, he followed her.

'You do not need to escort me any further, sir. The estate is just past that collection of trees by the creek.'

'I will see you to the edge of the property,' he said in a voice that brooked no argument.

'I take it you do not have a wife or a lady friend who is missing you,' she said and then wished she hadn't. Why did she care about his marital status?

She saw his lips quirk with a smile. 'Do you think I would kiss you if I had a wife waiting for me at home?'

'I don't know you,' she said with a shrug. 'You are a thief. Would adultery be so inexcusable a sin to Jack the Devil?'

'I am not married and I do not have a lady friend,' he said, the arrogant grin firmly back in place. 'I have many lady friends.'

She rolled her eyes again. 'Of course you do.'

'I am a solitary man, Miss Prudence. No woman will tie me to a house or make an honest man of me.'

Reaching the trees by the creek that separated her uncle's property from Crown land, she stopped her horse and turned to look at him.

'Well, now I feel sorry for you.'

'And why is that, Miss Prudence?'

'You are destined for a very lonely existence, Mr Fairweather,' she said with a heavy sigh. 'Who will you grow old with, who will share the spoils of all your plundering when the bushranging is done?'

She didn't bother to wait for an answer. It had been a rhetorical question anyway.

As Prudence rode away, Jack turned his horse and started down the road towards Ballarat. Looking back once, he could still see her in the distance as she rode across the plains. Panic choked him as she leaped the horse over the high fence. Only once she had safely landed on the other side, and was racing far too quickly across the uneven paddock, did he breathe again. The foolish girl could have killed herself!

She was reckless. Conversations with bushrangers on the road aside, she rode like a crazy woman. Her grandmother ought to keep a better eye on her.

Instead of heading directly back to Ballarat, he decided to take a little diversion and moved the horse onto the road that led to his country home. He had rarely been to the homestead since he'd bought it. But just now he didn't feel like being surrounded by thousands of people in the gold-mining town.

Up ahead the iron gates came into view and he smiled. Passing through the slightly askew gates, he made a note to get them straightened out so they'd close properly. If he didn't, one day he'd come home to find squatters had moved in. Riding beneath a canopy of willow trees some long-ago owner had planted, he could see the house. Not quite Windsor Castle. But a man's home was his castle, was it not? And so he had named it Little Windsor.

The garden looked rough. There'd been no rain for a few months so it was to be expected. But the sandstone facade was in good condition and the iron roof looked as sturdy as when he had purchased it.

He'd only been back there once. He'd bought it three months earlier in readiness for his retirement. That had been the plan. He had stayed only one night before it had felt much too big for just one man. Since then he'd continued to stay in boarding houses and hotels as he ran his transport company, and roamed the highways when the mood took him.

Stepping inside the house, he watched a small rodent dash away into a corner. The front door opened directly into a large living area with enough space for the plain dining table he'd bought at an auction. It could seat six people, should he ever be inclined to invite anyone for a meal. It would more likely be used for games of cards with the lads.

A wide archway connected the living area with the kitchen. Two bedrooms adjoined the space on the right side, and attached to the kitchen was a small utility room that led out onto the back verandah. He had loved that the verandah wrapped all the way around the house, the way he'd seen on much grander mansions. It made him feel the king of his little castle.

But standing in the middle of the spacious living area, he felt the same sense of emptiness. And—dare he say it?—loneliness.

You are destined for a very lonely existence, Mr Fairweather.

Dammit. Her words had gotten to him. Would he end up like Mad Dog Morgan? Damaged? Crazed and forever on the run? Or was he destined to live to be an old man, alone and solitary with only the spoils of his thieving to keep him company in this big empty house?

Backing out of the house, he took one more look before climbing back onto the horse. His thoughts were too loud. Perhaps thousands of people and Ballarat were appealing after all.

Five

A week before Christmas the temperature soared above one hundred degrees. How strange it was to have a hot Christmas, Prudence thought as she wandered the halls of the manor festively adorned with decorations. It would probably be snowing at their house in the English countryside where Stanforth Christmases had been held for generations.

Did she miss the cold and white Christmas? Not particularly. Although, despite having chosen her thinnest dress to try to combat the heat, the high lace neck still made it stifling. Annoyed, she tugged at the material, accidently tearing the lace away. She turned to look in a hallway mirror and gasped at the jagged tear from the seam of the collar down to the décolletage. Oh dear, what would her grandmother say?

A breeze brushed past her and she sighed audibly and closed her eyes. Oh, that felt deliciously, wickedly good. Examining the fabric again, she shrugged at her reflection.

'Well, it's too far gone now.'

With one strong tug, and a rebellious grin, she ripped away the entire lace panel, revealing her throat and collarbones.

Feeling free, and much cooler, she skipped lightly down the hall to the stairs. Pausing at the top of the grand staircase, she ran her hand along the smooth wood of the banister. Listening for a moment to gauge if anyone was coming, she giggled quietly and hopped up onto the banister.

'Prudence! What are you doing?' Her grandmother's voice came up the stairs from the drawing room.

Her head fell back and she groaned at the ceiling. Dear God, it was as if the woman had a sixth sense that she was about to do something fun.

'Nothing, Grandmother!' she called back. Lamenting the slide that could have been, she jumped off and trudged down the steps into the drawing room.

'Prudence, what are you wearing, child?' Deidre asked. 'What happened to your dress?'

She looked down at herself. 'It tore, Grandmother. I think my clothes are literally dissolving in this heat.'

'Then it's just as well,' Deidre said, her expression stern. 'Have the maid pack your trunk.'

Panic flared. 'My trunk, Grandmother?'

Had she finally done her dash with her grandmother? Was she being sent away?

'We are travelling into the city for a few days,' Deidre continued. 'Robert has business, and I believe we deserve to do some shopping in town. I have not had a new dress since we arrived in this country, and clearly you are in need of some new clothing. The stores in Ballarat do not stock the appropriate fabrics. Hardly surprising really, it's such a godforsaken place. All those grubby gold miners and their new money.'

Her grandmother's eyes scanned her from head to toe, her nose screwed up as though she'd tasted sour milk. 'Just because we are now country folk does not mean we should allow ourselves to be reduced to country fashions.'

'No, Grandmother.'

'Robert left early this morning,' Deidre said, sipping her tea. 'Alicia will join us on the train to Melbourne. We shall stay at least a fortnight.'

'Wonderful.' Prudence let loose a genuine smile. A trip to the city! It was just what she needed—an adventure! Two weeks in town, shopping, eating in glamorous dining rooms and mixing with people her own age again. And the busyness of town would take her too-idle mind off a certain handsome bushranger.

Jack Fairweather was a hard man to figure out. A gentleman? Hardly. A complete scoundrel? Possibly. Either way she found him fascinating. Yes, it was improper for a lady of her standing to be interested in such things. But, dammit, she was tired of being nothing but her breeding, her heritage. She was a woman. A woman with a mind, and since the kiss at the races, she had discovered she was a woman who could be incited to passion by a man who knew what he was doing. And Jack 'the Devil' Fairweather knew what he was doing. What did she call him? It was all so confusing. She hoped she wouldn't see him again in public for fear that she would give him, and his double life, away. Beneath it all, though, she found herself hoping she would see him again.

She frowned as she moved back up the stairs to begin packing. This was exactly why she needed to get out and meet some more people and forget all about Jack the Devil.

A few days after arriving in Melbourne, Prudence stood in front of the bevelled mirror in her room studying her green taffeta gown.

It matched her eyes and brightened the red of her hair. Spinning on the spot, she muffled an excited laugh. She would look like Christmas itself at the Lord Mayor's Ball that night.

She liked being in the city again. As much as she adored the country manor, her access to the horses and the freedom of the bush, she missed people. People other than her uncle and aunt, her grandmother and the servants.

Brock was her only true friend and she knew her grandmother would not be happy about their friendship. It was inappropriate to be so familiar with the staff, but he was the only person at the manor she felt she could really talk to. The only person who really understood her need for freedom and adventure. He was a traveller himself, having left America to bring the highly prized American Quarter Horses to her uncle's stud. Robert had made him an offer too good to refuse to stay on as a trainer. He'd fallen in love with Australia, he said, and just never went back to Kentucky.

She looked forward to the ball and hoped she might meet some people her own age with whom she might strike up a friendship. Perhaps she might even meet an eligible bachelor.

Unbidden, she was struck with the memory of a kiss with a certain bushranger behind the grandstand at the races. Shaking her head, she was determined to put the man out of her mind. No good could come of thinking of his pale brown eyes with those long, long lashes, or the smooth, powerful lips that had made her belly quiver. There were plenty of men out there. Surely Jack Fairweather wasn't the only one who could kiss a girl until her knees gave way beneath her. Clipping the sparkling gemstone earrings she'd bought just hours before to her lobes, she wondered if businessman Jack Fairweather attended society balls.

'Stop it!' she scolded her mirror image.

Twenty minutes later, the carriage pulled up outside the hall and she followed her aunt, uncle and grandmother into the ball. The place was filled to exploding with elegantly dressed ladies and gentlemen. She left her thin wrap at the cloakroom and shyly wandered behind her family as they said hello to friends and acquaintances.

Finally, settled in a corner with a glass of champagne in her hand, Prudence was able to survey the room and its inhabitants.

Lamps glowed yellow, flickering muted shadows across the high ceiling, and the room was quickly filling with the pungent smell and smoke of cigars and cigarettes.

'I think I may step outside for some fresh air,' Prudence said.

But as she was about to leave, Robert returned with a man by his side and her grandmother grasped her hand, forcing her to stay put with a terse, 'Robert insists he is a gentleman worth knowing. Be sweet and subservient.'

Prudence blinked, stunned and a little blindsided.

'Frederick Grantham, may I present my mother, Lady Deidre Stanforth, and my niece, Prudence.'

'Ladies, it is indeed a pleasure,' Frederick said and took Deidre's hand, offering her a stately bow. Taking Pru's hand, he bent to kiss it. She was surprised at his blatant study of her. And by the way her grandmother was beaming, she guessed Frederick was not here by accident, but by design.

As the gentlemen spoke about work-related things, Prudence took the opportunity to examine the man. He was at least ten years her senior, she guessed. Tall and slim, he didn't strike her as a man who enjoyed galloping across the meadows in the sunshine as she did. In fact, she doubted he partook in any exercise that required more effort than a gentle stroll. How a man could live in this new sun-drenched colony and still look as pallid as an Englishman fresh off the boat, she would never know. He certainly exercised his jaw enough though, and she was unimpressed with the sport he made of belittling other people in the room in an effort to make himself appear more impressive.

The orchestra began to play and couples moved out onto an area of the floor cleared for dancing.

'Miss Prudence, I wonder if you might care to dance,' Frederick asked her.

She smiled dutifully. 'Thank you, sir. I would.'

Taking the arm he offered, she walked out to the dance floor with him.

Discussion was difficult given the tempo of the dancing and the changing of partners, but Frederick gave it a good shot.

'How do you enjoy Melbourne?'

'I like it immensely.'

She swung on the arm of a portly gentlemen for a few beats before ending up back with Frederick.

'Your uncle and I do business on occasion.'

'Do you?' she responded, trying to muster the appropriate amount of interest before she was passed to another man.

'I believe you enjoy riding,' Frederick tried again when they were back together. 'I'm not an accomplished rider myself, I prefer the carriage, but I would enjoy perhaps …'

She missed the rest of his sentence as she was spun away to yet another partner.

Glancing up at the man she had been passed to, she gasped and stopped dead as she stared into an equally stunned face.

'Jack,' she said breathlessly, before being knocked aside by couples continuing in the dance.

Jack caught her before she fell. 'Are you alright?' he asked, still holding her in his arms.

'Yes.'

Unable to miss the looks of censure from the people around them as she stood in the arms of a man, she struggled against him until he finally let her go.

His trademark crooked smile was soon back in place. 'How lucky I am to have such a beautiful woman simply fall into my arms. I'm sorry if my rugged good looks caused you to swoon just now.'

The ego was back in place too, it seemed.

'Mr Fairweather,' she said, straightening her skirts. 'I was not expecting to see you here amongst polite society.'

She did her best to look bored. Meanwhile her insides were betraying her, fluttering with unbridled excitement. 'Reconnoitring the carriages out the front so you know which you'd like to rob later?'

His grin faded. 'And that's what you consider polite, is it?'

His hurt expression didn't fool her. She could still see the telltale glint of mischief in his eye.

'As a matter of fact, Miss Stanforth, I keep a place in town as well as a house in the country.'

'Then bushranging must pay much more than I had first thought.'

'Prudence?'

'Hmm?' She turned her head to see Frederick standing beside her, glancing questioningly between her and Jack.

'Oh, Frederick.' She had forgotten all about him the minute she'd landed in Jack's arms. 'Mr Jack Fairweather, may I present Mr Frederick Grantham.'

The two men shook hands but neither looked overly thrilled to be meeting the other.

'Grantham,' Jack said in greeting.

'Prudence, may I get you a drink?' Frederick asked.

'Please.'

'Will you meet me out on the terrace?'

She smiled sweetly. 'Of course, Frederick.'

'Frederick Grantham,' Jack said when the man had disappeared into the crowd. 'A solid choice by your grandmother. Good breeding, a man of no occupation. Just perfect for the Lady Carrington's granddaughter.'

'A man of no occupation is better than a man who makes his living by others' loss.'

'Touché.'

'And we only met Mr Grantham tonight. I'm sure my grandmother has more good sense than to align me with a man we know nothing about.'

'I'm sure your grandmother learned all she needs to know about Mr Grantham long before tonight.'

She opened her mouth to argue but had no retort.

Had her grandmother been planning a match between her and Frederick Grantham for weeks without her knowledge? Prudence felt a flicker of concern, but she refused to let Jack bait her.

'Excuse me, I must meet Mr Grantham on the terrace,' she said and began to walk away. But Jack was right there beside her as she moved through the crowd.

'He will bore you to tears.'

Prudence said nothing. She would not let him rile her.

'Do you think he will understand your love of books?' Jack went on as they made it to the rear terrace of the building. 'Do you think that once you're married he will allow you to ride alone? In a man's saddle?'

'I never said I would marry him,' she shot back.

'He will ask. And your grandmother will approve the match. If you believe you have much say in the matter, you are not as clever as I had first thought.'

Happy to be out in the fresh air, Prudence turned to face Jack.

'Why do you care who I marry, Jack the Devil?' she asked, lowering her voice. 'You are a solitary man. Isn't that what you said? No woman will tie you to the house or make an honest man of you.'

'That's right,' Jack said. His humour seemed suddenly less smug.

'So it shouldn't matter to you who I do, or do not, choose to marry.'

'That's my point,' he said. 'You will have no choice.'

With an angry flick of her skirts, she turned and made her way across the terrace.

With teeth grinding together, Jack gazed after Prudence. She tapped Frederick on the shoulder and he turned to face her, a drink in each hand. Jack was filled with the oddest sensation as he watched her fall into conversation with the other man. He didn't have anything against Grantham in particular, but he suddenly felt the overwhelming urge to ram the man's teeth down his throat.

Taking a glass of whisky from a passing waiter, Jack moved to the far end of the terrace where he could stew in his sudden filthy mood alone. But he also made sure that he could still see Prudence. He breathed the fresh night air deeply, and drank as he took in the wide expanse of stars above him.

On more than one occasion over the past month, his mind had floated to Prudence Stanforth. The woman haunted him. She entered his mind far too often, both in daylight hours and in his dreams. It didn't help that everywhere he went he seemed to run into her. Thanks to the gold rush, there had to be hundreds of thousands of people here in the new colony by now. How was it possible that he continued to see the same woman over and over again?

Since that fateful day, when he'd bailed up a carriage and been transfixed by a pair of large green eyes, he'd run into her at the races, on his morning ride and now again here at the Lord Mayor's Christmas Ball.

He wasn't often caught by surprise, but when she'd fallen into his arms on the dance floor just before, he had to admit he'd been overwhelmed with pleasure to see her.

Looking back across the terrace, he saw that she and Grantham had been joined by her aunt and grandmother. Obviously enjoying the party, they were all smiles and laughter. Who knew the old bat could smile? He watched them for a while longer, and although he couldn't hear what they were saying, he could see the smile slowly wane from Prudence's pretty face.

She turned her head and looked directly at him. The resignation in her eyes said everything. He'd been right. Granny had organised the meeting between Frederick and Prudence, and it was a pre-ordained match.

Jack continued to watch the small group, stewing in his bad mood as he tossed back another whisky. When Prudence excused herself and headed indoors again, he ignored his better judgement, and that little voice in his head that told him to stay away, and went after her.

Moving in the direction of the ladies' powder room, he waited outside as she went in. A few moments later she stepped out and with no one around to see, Jack grabbed her arm and pulled her down the corridor and into the nearest empty room, closing the door behind them.

'Mr Fairweather, let me go.'

'I wish I could,' he mumbled, but doing as she asked he let her go and paced away from her.

He spun to face her, but that spelled disaster. The orbs of green now fixed on him, wide with surprise, served to fill him with more lustful thoughts. Why had he dragged her into this room? The absolute last place she should be was alone with him.

'Why do you continue to pursue me, Mr Fairweather?' she asked, sighing. She wore a downtrodden expression as though she were suddenly very weary.

'I find you interesting,' he said, baffled by his own behaviour.

'I find you annoying,' she shot back.

He smiled at that. 'No you don't. You find me fascinating, exciting and handsome.'

She snorted out a laugh. 'You are very impressed with yourself, Mr Fairweather.'

'I'd be happier if you were impressed with me, Miss Stanforth.'

'That will never happen.'

Dammit, he'd never had this much trouble wooing a woman before. Most ladies thought him quite dashing as Jack Fairweather. He rarely allowed the women he associated with to know his other persona. Bed partners could have very loose lips, particularly if slighted or scorned. Hell hath no fury, and all that.

'You asked me to keep your secret and I have,' she said. It was as though she had read his mind.

'I would hope so,' he said, the gruffness in his voice causing her to blink and lean away from him. It sounded angry even to him. He turned away from the apprehension that had come into her eyes. He was not angry with her. He was angry with himself for his lack of control when it came to her. He shouldn't be chasing her down. He should be running as fast as he could go in the other direction. He did not want to scare her, but if he didn't kiss her again soon he would go stark raving mad.

Leaning closer, he braced one hand above her head against the door, but only stared into her eyes. Those eyes, green like a Christmas tree, lit up and sparkling.

'Are you going to kiss me again, Jack?'

Her question floored him. The woman was too perceptive, too bewitching.

Battling his own confusion, he paced away and back, and away again, before he faced her once more. She didn't look frightened. Why did she never look frightened around him? It was almost offensive. People should be scared of bushrangers.

'Why are you never afraid of me?' he asked, snapping out the question he hadn't meant to verbalise. 'I'm a dangerous criminal who has just dragged you away from the safety of a party.'

Her chin went up in that stubborn show of strength he was coming to adore. 'Is that what you want? Do you want me to be frightened of you? Do you want me to think you are big, terrifying criminal? The legend of the Victorian highways, the great Jack the Devil?'

He thought about it. Yes, he wanted people to remember him as the famous bushranger, to cower in his presence. But no, he couldn't bear the thought of her thinking of him that way.

'No, that's not what I want,' he said, his voice quietening as he got lost in her eyes again. Dammit all to hell, he couldn't help it. 'This is what I want.'

In two steps he'd reached her, in two seconds he had grabbed her shoulders and pulled her to him. His lips pressed roughly against hers and he heard her quick cry of shock before she surprised him by leaning into him and kissing him back.

She was kissing him back. Fervently. He hadn't imagined it at the races that day. Her inexperience was unmistakable, but when her head tilted a little to allow him better purchase against her mouth and she opened ever so slightly, he could see she was learning fast.

It was all the encouragement he needed and he pressed his tongue into her mouth, lightly at first, his body sizzling to the bone when his tongue touched hers.

Moving his hands from her shoulders, he slid them down her arms to her torso where he rested them on the soft fabric just below her breasts. Straining against the urge to take the two beautiful mounds and feel the soft weight of them, he glided his hands down and fixed them against her hips instead.

Her sharp intake of breath spurred him on; spurred him on when he should be stepping back.

He shook his head and tried to pull out of the kiss. But suddenly her hands were there, grasping the lapels of his jacket, forceful, holding him closer. She allowed him no escape and pressed her tongue into his mouth, licking and tasting with a new-found skilfulness that erased any intention he had of letting her go from his mind. Oh, she was a fast learner alright.

'God, help me,' he said against her mouth, pressing her back into the door. But it was he who gasped when her hands moved around his neck and she pulled him closer, her fingers combing through the hair at his nape. Sweet Jesus, she was a wildfire, hot and bright and out of control. Control. It was time he found his.

She was a maid. He was sure. It didn't matter how much he wanted her, taking her would be wrong. Her eyes were hooded and her lips were pink and swollen, her chest rising and falling alluringly with the depth of her breaths. She was the very definition of the unwitting temptress. A special breed of woman who did not know her own power of seduction, but could tempt a man with only a smile. She had bewitched him. He thought of her more than any man should think about an innocent woman. And he was almost certain that she would be engaged to Frederick Grantham before the night was out.

A bushranger had no chance with a lady of Prudence's standing. She deserved better than the likes of him. Even if it weren't Frederick Grantham, knowing she would marry some well-bred gentleman one day tore at him. He couldn't do this to himself any longer. Pulling her away from the door, he tore it open and without looking back he dashed from the room.

Her face was scorched with heat. Her blood felt like warm molasses, thick and heavy. Her mind whirled and sparks sizzled across her skin as though his hands and mouth were still on her.

While he'd kissed her, she'd felt a clenching sensation low in her belly and a heat building lower still. Her nipples had hardened when his hands had slid down her bodice. She'd thought he was going to take her breasts in his hands and believed she would have liked that very much. She hadn't been the stiff, resisting girl this time. When he'd pressed his lips to hers, something inside her revelled in the glorious sensation and she'd gone willingly into his arms, into his mouth.

And then he'd torn himself from her and run. She sighed. Body and mind were scattered, confused by emotions she didn't quite understand. A heady thrill mixed with frustration at the loss of him. She leaned back against the door and closed her eyes, committing every touch, every kiss, every exquisite reaction he had incited from her to memory. And what he could do with his tongue? She licked her lips, still tasting him there.

Straightening her dress, she checked her appearance in a mirror to ensure her hair was in place. Her lips were swollen, her cheeks were a little flushed, but there wasn't much she could do about that. Taking a deep breath, she left the room and made her way back out to Frederick and her grandmother.

People moved about the ballroom in a golden haze and she had the sensation of floating on air as she moved through the crowd.

'Prudence,' Frederick greeted her but then frowned. 'Are you alright? You were away so long.'

'I'm fine.'

'Why are you so flushed?' her grandmother asked, ever observant.

'Oh, am I?' Prudence put her hands to her cheeks. 'It's very warm inside.'

Frederick took her hand in both of his. It was bold in such a public setting and her eyes flitted to her grandmother, waiting for her to admonish him. But Gran only smiled and respectfully turned her face from the intimate moment. Despite the innocence of the touch it felt … wrong, compared with having Jack hold her only moments earlier.

'Sweet Prudence, I have wonderful news,' Frederick began. 'Your grandmother believes we will make a suitable match and I must say I am inclined to agree.'

'A suitable match?' Her head was still reeling from Jack's kisses and she struggled to comprehend him.

'Yes, she has proposed a marriage between us.'

Prudence felt her mouth drop open, but she could find no words.

'Don't look so astonished,' he chided. 'I'm known as quite a catch, you know.'

'I'm sure you are,' she answered in a small voice. Jack had been right. Her grandmother had secured Grantham for her. Without her knowledge. Her shock began to give way to irritation, but she held her temper in check. She'd always known this day would come, but now that it had, she felt impotent, like a chess piece moved about a board with no say in her own life. Of course Grantham would want to marry her. She was the granddaughter of an earl. His importance would rise upon their union.

'I have told her, of course, that I need to get to know you better first and for you to get to know me better,' he went on. 'But it's all for appearances as I already believe we're going to make the perfect couple. I will come to Carrington Manor the day after Christmas and shall stay until the new year at the least. There is quite an age difference between us, but I hope the time we spend together will allow you to feel more comfortable around me. Are you thrilled?'

Prudence tried to smile, but knew she was failing dismally. 'I am beyond words.'

'When our week together is finished we will announce our engagement to the world.'

She felt her dress tightening around her ribs. Was she still breathing? She couldn't tell anymore. Marriage? To Frederick Grantham? The dress was strangling her.

'It is allowable for you to show your pleasure,' Frederick said in a gentle tone, as though he was imparting some great social wisdom upon her.

'Oh, I know,' she said. 'I think I'm just …'

'Surprised and overjoyed? Consumed with happiness?'

'Um.'

Her mind was still shattered and scattered by the kiss of another man and she couldn't think straight. Surprised? Yes. Overjoyed? That probably wouldn't have been the first word that entered her mind. But she was sure once she had time to digest the idea of marriage she'd realise it was a good match. Wouldn't she? It was so fast. But at least there would be no announcement until the new year. She would take the week of his visit to decide if she could endure being married to Frederick Grantham for the rest of her life. And if she couldn't?

As Grantham moved away to speak with a friend, Prudence recalled the look in Jack's eyes after he'd kissed her. She'd been unable to interpret the look then, but now she realised what it was she had seen in his pale brown eyes. Defeat. Defeat and resignation. He had guessed that Gran was negotiating with Frederick for her hand. Defeat. Under it all, Jack Fairweather was an honourable man. He would not kiss another man's wife. And yet, the thought of Jack never kissing her again sent a wave of unexpected desolation through her.

'Are you alright, Prudence?' Alicia asked, ever the sympathetic observer. 'You've gone pale.'

'I do feel a little out of sorts.'

'Perhaps you've had enough excitement for one evening,' Alicia said with an understanding smile.

She has no idea.

'Yes, perhaps.'

'I'll tell the others you are ready to leave.' She laid a hand on Prudence's arm before moving away to speak with Deidre.

'Thank you.'

It wasn't much cooler outside than it had been in the busy dance hall, but the air was definitely fresher and Prudence inhaled deeply to calm her addled emotions.

Frederick took her hand to help her into the carriage, and as she sat he lifted her hand to his lips and kissed it lightly.

'Goodnight, Prudence,' he said. 'I look forward to seeing you again after Christmas at Carrington Manor.'

She could only muster a weak smile as he stepped back and the carriage pulled away into the night.

Leaving Melbourne was bittersweet for Prudence. She was happy to be getting back to the countryside she had come to adore. She looked forward to riding Misha out into the fields and working with the other horses in the stables—when Gran wasn't watching of course. But she was also sorry to leave Melbourne without seeing Jack Fairweather again. No matter how thoroughly, albeit surreptitiously, she had searched the assembly rooms on their way out, she had not seen him again at the ball once he'd fled after their kiss. He seemed to have simply vanished, and she had left for Carrington Manor the following day with her aunt and grandmother. Uncle Robert remained in town to complete some business, but after the attack on their carriage by Jack the Devil, he always sent an armed man along with the ladies.

Even if Prudence had wanted to seek out Jack in town, she didn't have the first idea where to look. She knew he kept an apartment in Melbourne and that he had a home in the bush. Since the main centre of operations for his legitimate business was in Ballarat, she assumed he lived somewhere near there. Ballarat was also, no doubt, the centre of operations for Jack the Devil.

She'd spent a lovely Christmas day with her family, enjoying roast pork with all the trimmings, and the day after Christmas, as arranged, Frederick Grantham arrived at Carrington Manor. Prudence was in the stables when she saw the carriage pull up in front of the house.

'So this is the man you're going to marry?' Brock asked over her shoulder.

She turned and gave him a glare.

'No secrets around here, Miss Prudence,' he said with a shrug. 'The workers hear things. I hear things.'

'I've not said I'll marry him yet.'

Brock gave her a sympathetic look. 'I'm not sure that matters, Miss.'

Prudence rubbed at the headache forming between her eyes. She knew he was right.

'You'd better get on inside,' he added. 'Can't meet your beau dressed like a boy and smelling of horse manure.'

Prudence huffed defiantly. 'Maybe that's exactly what I should do. He might decide I'm not marriage material after all.'

He seemed genuinely surprised. 'Don't you want to be married, Miss Prudence? I thought all women wanted to find a husband to settle down and have babies with.'

'I have no objection to marriage in general,' she said, handing him the curry comb she'd been using on Misha. 'I am, however, beginning to have a small problem with arranged marriage. Especially mine.'

His rich chuckle followed her as she wandered down the path to the rear of the house. Did she dare meet Frederick looking like one of the horsemen? Her grandmother would throttle her. She wasn't completely averse to Frederick. If she had to marry, well … it could be worse, she supposed.

She rushed up the rear stairs to the second level, and once in her rooms she washed quickly and changed in preparation for dinner.

Before she could enter the drawing room for pre-dinner drinks, the butler handed her a large envelope.

'I thought the post had already been collected,' Prudence said, frowning at the envelope as she took it from him.

'It came with a rider just now, Miss,' Gerald explained.

'Prudence, is that you?' Her grandmother's voice rang out from the drawing room.

'I'll have to look at it later. Please take it to my room, Gerald,' Prudence instructed, handing the envelope back to him.

She steeled herself and entered the drawing room.

'Mr Grantham, you've arrived,' she said, smiling as he took her hand and kissed it.

'And wouldn't it have been nice for you to be here to greet him,' Deidre said, the censure in her voice unmistakable.

'I apologise. I was working with the horses,' she said quite deliberately to gauge his response.

'That is what we have stablemen for.'

She refused to let Deidre's narrowed glare worry her. She knew her grandmother would never make a scene in front of their guest.

'I like to groom my own horse after a ride.'

'Ladies do love their horses,' Frederick said with an almost pitying smile for her. 'Men understand that horses are for work, they're not pets.'

At least she could be thankful that he didn't seem perturbed either by her not being there to greet him or by the fact that she enjoyed working with the horses.

When dinner was announced, Prudence sat beside Frederick and made a good study of him as he ate and conversed. She was happy to see that he treated their staff with respect and not just as lowly servants. Through discussion, she discovered he was well read and that they shared an enjoyment of the poems of Keats.

'I found a book of poems recently by an American named Walt Whitman,' Prudence said, happy to have someone she could talk with about her love of the written word. She didn't let on that it was Brock who'd given her the book.

'The only good poets are English poets,' Frederick responded, receiving a nod of agreement from Deidre. 'One mustn't be confused by modern ideas coming out of the Americas. Tradition is tradition for a reason.'

And just like that, the happy bubble burst.

After dinner, Frederick asked Prudence to take a walk outside in the garden. The sun was just beginning to set but the evening was still warm.

'The days are so hot out here in the bush,' Frederick said.

'Perhaps you should remove your coat,' Prudence suggested. 'We are a little more relaxed in the country.'

'No matter the temperature, there is no need for a lapse in decorum.'

'It's hot in the city too,' Prudence said, turning away from him so he couldn't see the irritation on her face.

'Yes, but my home in Altona is near the seafront and we get such a lovely evening breeze. It cools things down dramatically. You'll enjoy Altona. It's a wonderful place and we'll be so near to town.'

'Will there be somewhere for me to stable Misha?'

'No, my dear,' he said, using his hat to fan away the night bugs that had begun to gather. 'Besides, when we are married you won't have time to ride horses. You will be running a household. It will keep you occupied, I can assure you. My home is quite large and I have many staff.'

They walked the gardens quietly for a while and stopped beneath a large eucalypt. She examined Frederick as he stood so straight and still in the twilight. He was slim, but not bad looking. His lips were not as full as Jack's but she found herself wondering what they would feel like against hers.

'Frederick.'

'Yes, my dear?'

'If we are to be married,' she began, unsure of the wisdom of making her next statement. 'Do you think perhaps we should …'

'Should what?'

'Perhaps we ought to, you know, try a kiss.'

He blinked, obviously stunned at her suggestion.

'It is not improper for a man to kiss the woman he is betrothed to,' Frederick said, a small frown between his brows as he thought it over. 'I suppose we could try it. Are you so keen to enjoy the physical allowances of marriage to me, Prudence?'

The thought of *enjoying physical allowances* with Frederick did take the shine off her little experiment. 'I just think that it would be another way to confirm that we are compatible.'

'Very well.'

She watched him place his hat on the wooden bench beneath the tree and stepping up to her, he leaned down to her height and put his lips to hers. Flat, wooden, unmoving and uninspiring. He stood upright again and smiled.

'How was that?'

She smiled politely. 'Lovely. Perhaps just one more time.'

He hesitated a moment, appearing a little confused, but gave in and leaned forward again. This time, Prudence put her hands to his shoulders to hold him closer to her and she moved her mouth over his lips, the way Jack had done with her. When his lips parted on a surprised gasp, she pressed her tongue in between.

He pulled away quickly and stared at her in appalled shock.

'Prudence, what was that?'

'A kiss.'

'Young ladies don't usually kiss like that.'

'Really?' she asked. It had been how she'd kissed, and been kissed by, Jack. Was that not the normal way of kissing between men and women?

Whoops.

'I'm sorry, Frederick,' she said. 'I suppose I have no frame of reference, having never been kissed before. Was it so bad?'

Flustered, he frowned down at her. 'Never mind, my dear. You are young and inexperienced. I should not forget that. Come, let's go back inside for a brandy before bed.'

Prudence sighed and followed him into the house.

'I think I will pass on the brandy, thank you, Frederick,' she said at the foot of the stairs. 'I'm tired. But thank you for a lovely evening.'

'Sleep well,' he said, taking her hand and kissing it.

She nodded and headed up the stairs to her rooms.

Kissing Frederick had been nothing like kissing Jack. Where was the passion? If she was going to marry Frederick, she needed to know there would be passion. Jack had more passion in his left thumb than Frederick had in his entire being. Jack could excite her with only a look. His lips and hands could incite wildfires in her body. Frederick could barely strike a match. She knew it was foolish and futile to compare Jack to Frederick but she couldn't help it. How could she marry Frederick, knowing what she would be missing out on?

The warbling song of the morning birds nudged Prudence from sleep. Magpies. A pretty song, but the birds were to be avoided during nesting season. Brock said they could swoop down and cause a man to bleed with their sharp beaks if you got too close to their nests, the devils.

Devil.

Jack.

Her sleep over the past few nights had been filled with dreams of Jack. Hardly appropriate with her soon-to-be fiancé just down the corridor.

Growling in her frustration, Prudence threw back the covers and climbed out of bed. Washing the sleep from her eyes in the water basin, she reached for the towel and huffed, annoyed when she knocked her hairbrush to the floor with a clatter.

Bending down to retrieve it, she noticed something beneath the chair. Picking it up, along with her hairbrush, she realised it was the large envelope Gerald had shown her on the day of Frederick's arrival. She'd forgotten about it, and somehow it must have ended up falling from the armoire where Gerald had left it, and lain beneath the chair for several days.

Moving across to the window seat, she could see mist rising outside as the early sun warmed the ground. Reaching into the envelope, she pulled out several formal documents.

Reading the cover letter, she was baffled. It made no sense to her. But as she read on her heart leaped into her throat. It was from lawyers in London stating that her mother had left her some things in her Last Will and Testament.

'Oh.' Her fingers went to her lips and her eyes welled. Both her parents had been killed in a fire in Cornwall when she'd been only a few months old. Had it taken twenty-two years for them to find her mother's will? She read on and flicked through the pages, stopping when she came to a copy of a death certificate notarised and dated …

Her breath caught. She read the date again. Read it a third time. There had to be some mistake.

Moving quickly, battling her impatience, Prudence washed and dressed and inside twenty minutes she was rushing downstairs to the breakfast room.

'Grandmother,' she blurted as she entered the room, puffing and out of breath.

'Good morning, Prudence. I trust you slept well.'

She gave Frederick a quick look, so intent on her mission that she hadn't registered him sitting at the dining table.

'Uh, good morning, Frederick. Yes, thank you.'

'Don't you look lovely this morning.'

'Thank you,' she answered again, impatiently walking across to her grandmother at the head of the table.

'Good Lord, Prudence, why do you always look as though you've run a mile?'

Ignoring her grandmother's criticism, she placed the papers on the table.

'I received these documents from London,' she said without preamble.

'What are they?' Deidre asked, barely sparing them a glance as she sipped her tea.

'The Last Will and Testament of Olivia Stanforth.'

The teacup froze at Deidre's mouth and her steely eyes moved again to the papers. The cup shook a little as she lowered it to the saucer, and she slowly raised the linen napkin to delicately dab at her thin lips.

'Odd.'

'Odd?' Prudence was stunned and irritated at her grandmother's calmness. 'It's more than odd, grandmother. After twenty-two years someone finally miraculously finds my mother's Last Will and Testament?'

'Papers go missing all the time, child.'

She remembered the death certificate. 'But Grandmother, it doesn't make sense. These other papers include a certificate of death for Olivia Stanforth.'

'That's no surprise, child, you know your mother died.'

'This certificate is dated only twelve months ago.'

Like a statue in a museum, Deidre sat, her back straight as a ruler. Only her eyes moved and Prudence noticed they could not move in her direction.

'A mistake,' Deidre said, lifting her teacup again. 'A disgraceful error by one of those dreadful officials.'

'A mistake, Grandmother?' She could tell when she was being lied to.

'Mr Grantham,' Deidre said, looking to their guest who watched on with bewildered interest. 'Would you mind excusing us? My granddaughter and I have some family business to discuss.'

'Of course, Lady Deidre.' Frederick wiped his mouth and stood, nodding at them both before he left the room.

Finally, her grandmother looked her in the eye. 'I suppose it is time you knew.'

'Knew what?'

'Your mother didn't die when you were young.'

'I don't understand.'

'When she fell pregnant with you, she was unmarried,' Deidre explained. 'A liaison with a boy she met during her coming-out season. But he was to marry someone else. Olivia was sent to Cornwall to see out the pregnancy and, when you were born, we decided it would be better for everyone if your grandfather and I were to raise you ourselves.'

A horrified numbness washed over Prudence and she sank into the nearest chair, only half listening as her grandmother told the whole sordid story of her mother's reckless youth, and the web of lies that had been created to hide the shame she'd brought upon the family.

'You mean ... she's been alive all this time?'

'Yes. I believe she married a baker and had other children.'

A gasp escaped Pru's mouth. She had brothers or sisters or both?

'You believe ...? You mean ... all this time ... and you never contacted her? Did she ever contact you? Or did she let you just take me and then tell herself that I no longer existed?'

Her grandmother's expression said it all. 'She came to London once, during your debut. She wanted to see you, but so much time had gone by, there was no point in upsetting you before you went to court.'

'No point in upsetting me?' She was appalled. 'You kept me from my own mother. Grandmother, please, help me understand.'

'It was for the best,' Deidre said, not giving an inch. 'She had shamed the family. We survived it only because the young man's family agreed it was in everyone's best interests that neither Olivia nor the gentleman owned to having a child out of wedlock.'

'You mean a bastard,' Prudence spat. Her numbness was now replaced by a raging fury that heated her cheeks.

Deidre's expression darkened. 'Prudence, I understand you're upset, but you will not use such foul words in my presence.'

'But that's what I am, isn't it? A bastard. You won't put up with the word, I'm surprised you put up with me for twenty-two years. You created a lie to ensure people didn't know you were harbouring a bastard. I guess that's how you lived with it yourself.'

'Prudence—'

'No!' Prudence cried, standing so quickly that the chair tipped backwards and hit the hardwood floor with a clatter. 'Grandmother, how could you? How could you let me believe that my own mother was dead, when all along I could have known her? I could have known half brothers and sisters. And now she's dead. She is *actually* dead, and we live half a world away, which was no doubt part of your plan. And now I will never know her or my half siblings.'

Prudence turned and ran from the room. She could hear her grandmother calling after her as she raced through the foyer.

'Prudence, what is it?' Aunt Alicia called as she descended the stairs. 'What's happened?'

But she couldn't stop. The tears began to fall as she reached the rear of the house, but as she was about to step out the door she spotted the housekeeping purse on the bench inside the kitchen. Without hesitating, she grabbed the little purse, and her riding coat that hung on a peg, and pushed open the back door of the house.

Running as fast as she could, she found the sanctuary of the stables. She wiped her face and slowed her gait, not wishing any of the stablehands to see her distress. She was furious and upset and she had to get away as quickly as she could, and she didn't want anyone trying to stop her.

Without even bothering to saddle Misha, she tossed on a bridle, climbed onto her beloved mare and bolted out of the stables. Men scattered, trying to get out of her way as she sped out of the building and into the morning sunshine. Fleeing across the fields, she leaped the boundary fence and did her best to put as much distance as possible between herself and Carrington Manor and all the lies of her life.

Six

Jack rode at a leisurely pace along the narrow path. There was no particular place he needed to be and it was pleasant to simply amble the countryside. The rhythmic clap of the horse's feet on the hard dirt path lulled him, and the warm morning sun dappled across his face as they passed beneath the thin canopy of gum trees.

He might have been happy to amble along, but the colt he rode danced beneath him, frustrated and impatient. He clearly wanted to have his head, to run free and fast. Jack deliberately held him back, knowing he had to show the young animal who was boss.

Overall, he was pleased with how the new colt was working out. He'd managed to wrangle a good price for the young buckskin stockhorse at auction a few weeks earlier, despite the bidding war with Lionel Bridgewater. The battle had caused great excitement at the auction yards that day, drawing in a huge crowd. Jack had enjoyed himself immensely, watching his opponent, red faced and sweating, as he challenged each bid. Eventually, old Lionel had backed down and Jack had taken the colt, to the crowd's enthusiastic cheers.

Handing over the pounds, Jack had led the colt away from the auction house and to the holding yard behind the Fairweather Transport office.

He'd spent some time acquainting himself with the animal, choosing to groom the horse himself instead of letting one of the stableboys handle it. Nothing cemented the relationship between man and horse better than a good brush down.

'What shall we call you then, eh?' he'd asked, running the brush across the colt's flanks.

The horse had let out a snort and stepped back, directly onto Jack's foot.

'Ouch! You little terror.'

Jack had removed his booted foot from beneath the horse's hoof and scrunched his toes to release the pain.

'You're a feisty young thing, aren't you?'

For some reason, Prudence had jumped into his head at that moment. More than a little feisty herself, he knew she would adore this beauty, with his dark mane and tail and the distinctive tan hide.

Jack remembered Prudence singing the praises of Alexandre Dumas and his story *The Three Musketeers*. He'd picked up a copy at the book exchange in the city and had been about halfway through it. Despite his elementary reading skills, he had been enjoying the story, and could see how Prudence had drawn comparisons between the unconventional king's guards and bushrangers.

'D'Artagnan,' he'd said out loud.

The colt had turned his head to look at him. If Jack had been a fanciful man, he might have said the colt had smiled at him.

'D'Artagnan, hey?' Jack had said again. 'Well, I guess it fits.'

Now as he rode D'Artagnan alongside the grassy plains, he thought of Prudence again. Would she ever get the chance to meet D'Artagnan? Of course not. Frowning at the direction his

thoughts had taken, he recalled their interaction at the Christmas
Ball. He was quite sure that by the end of the ball she would have
been promised to Frederick Grantham, especially if her grandmother had had anything to do with it. Even now, she might
already be engaged to the man. She was a beautiful and vivacious
woman. Her love of adventure stories, and the sparkle that came
into her green eyes whenever she spoke of them, was intoxicating. The idea of Frederick Grantham smothering that spark was
indigestible. His remorse that she was forever out of his reach
was deep and unnerving. He had to shake this fascination he
had with her. No good would come of it. He needed to go to
town and find a willing woman—a willing, available woman—
to clear his mind of Prudence Stanforth.

The colt's ears pricked up and Jack's own senses went on high
alert. Hoof beats. Fast, and coming closer by the second. He
turned in the saddle to see a horse racing across the open paddock
at an incredible speed. As it neared, he recognised the chestnut
Arabian mare and its rider.

Prudence.

'Prudence!' he called. But she didn't stop. She just kept riding,
dangerously fast across the plains and into the craggy bushland,
dodging trees and jumping the horse over rocks and downed logs.
As he kicked the colt with his heels, the flighty young animal happily leaped into action. They did their best to match Prudence's
speed, but damn, she was a skilled rider, and fast considering she
rode without a saddle. Terrified she'd fall and break her neck, he
urged the colt to go faster.

Finally, as they both broke through the scrub and out into open
fields again, he was able to ride up alongside her. She only seemed
to notice him when he reached for her reins and slowed both their
horses expertly.

Puffing with his exertions, he grinned, impressed by her ability on the horse. 'You're a hard woman to catch, Miss Prudence.' But his pleasure at seeing her again gave way to concern as he saw that tears tracked down her cheeks.

'Prudence? What is it? What's wrong?'

Holding onto the reins, he dismounted his horse and reached up to pull her from hers. She fell into his arms as her legs buckled beneath her. His concern took a rapid turn to panic at her near collapse and he held her against him. Her head fell against his chest and he heard the sobs, felt her shuddering breaths.

'Please, talk to me. Are you injured? Did someone hurt you?' he demanded fiercely. He'd never killed a man in his life but he would gladly kill whoever had caused Prudence such obvious pain and grief.

'Prudence, please, what's happened? At least tell me if you're injured.'

He felt the shake of her head against his chest, but she sobbed again.

Taking her under his arm, he led her away from the horses to sit on a downed tree log in the shade of a large eucalypt. When he would have moved away, she clutched at him, held him close to her.

'Prudence, sweetheart, talk to me.' Her sobs were clawing at his heart, but he decided she needed to cry it out before she could be coherent enough to speak to him. He asked no more questions, his imagination running wild as he waited. When he'd left the ball in Melbourne, he had no doubt that Prudence would be engaged to Frederick Grantham by the end of the evening. Had Grantham said something, done something to hurt her? The thought of the man laying hands on her had his fury rising once again.

Stroking her hair with one hand and her back with the other, he tried his best to comfort her. Having her warm body pressed to his was delicious torture. The soft strands of her hair tickled his nose, the perfume of it intoxicating.

His protective instincts, usually reserved for himself and his bushranging cohort, were now on high alert for this exquisite creature in his arms. Whoever had made such a sweet lady sob so heartbrokenly would pay for it.

After a time, he felt her hitching breaths decrease and then finally subside on one last heavy exhale.

Pulling away, she looked up into his eyes for a moment before she stood, turning her back on him. He felt the loss immeasurably. She wiped her wet face on the sleeve of her dress, prompting him to stand and hand her his handkerchief.

'Don't you need this to cover your face?' she asked and he smiled, marvelling at her ability to make jokes in her upset state.

'I have others,' he said with shrug. 'Besides, I'm having a day off.'

'Thank you,' she said, mopping at her tears. 'I'm sorry.'

'Don't be. I'm only glad I found you and was able to assist.'

She made a move to mount her horse, but he reached her first, took her hand and led her back to the downed tree trunk. Then he removed his water canister from his saddlebag and handed it to her.

She took a sip.

'That's water.'

He frowned, confused. 'Yes.'

'Don't you have anything stronger?'

He chuckled and lifted the canister to her lips. 'Drink.'

She did so and heaved a large sigh.

'You have a new horse.'

He looked across at the colt, nibbling contentedly at grass beneath a wattle tree.

'He's young,' he said. 'But he's learning. The gelding was getting too old.'

'Your other horse?'

'The one I was riding the day we ran into each other along the roadside,' he said. 'Zeus. He's enjoying a quieter life now. I ride Persephone when I am … on the highway. But I can't exactly be seen on the same horse as Jack Fairweather that I ride as Jack the Devil.'

He hoped that his light conversation would give her time to pull herself together, but he was impatient to know what was wrong, to put his wild imaginings to rest.

'He's pretty. What's his name?'

She was doing her best to not talk about whatever had upset her and he humoured her a while longer.

'D'Artagnan.'

She blinked at him through still damp eyes. 'From the Musketeers?'

'Yes.' He brushed at a strand of hair that had fallen across her forehead. 'You inspired me. It seemed a good name for him.'

She managed a weak smile before her face crumbled again as whatever upset her returned.

'Pru, what happened? Are you alright?' It was a pointless question. It was obvious she was not alright.

'No. I'm not.'

She said it so honestly and it hurt him physically to see her looking so forlorn.

'Did someone harm you?' he asked again.

'Yes.'

The anger rising in his chest was fit to burst. 'Was it Grantham? Did he … assault you? Did he …?' He didn't want to put words to his fears.

'No, no. Frederick has been nothing but a gentleman since he arrived at the manor.' She waved it off, reaching out to touch him, to comfort *him*. Her hand was warm against his forearm and he had to struggle to concentrate on her words as the truth sunk in. Grantham was staying at the manor. That could only mean one thing. She was engaged. Lost to him for good. And the thought was agony.

'I am not injured physically,' she went on. 'Although it feels as though someone reached into my chest and ripped out my heart.'

He exhaled a relieved but shaky breath and gathered his out-of-control emotions. She needed him. His own pain could be dealt with later.

'It was my grandmother.'

Jack was so surprised at her admission he was momentarily lost for words.

'The woman who raised me,' she continued. 'The one person in this world I thought loved me unconditionally, the one person I thought could never hurt me, just destroyed my idea of what it is to have family. My life is a lie.'

'Do you want to tell me about it?'

She took a deep unsteady breath, looking as though she might start crying again, but she exhaled slowly and began.

'My grandmother always told me that she and my grandfather took me in when my mother, her daughter, died when I was just a baby.'

The devastation of having been abandoned as a child. Jack knew it only too well.

'But now I find out that it's all a big fabrication,' she said.

'What do you mean a fabrication?'

'A lie,' she said, and pulling a letter from her coat pocket, she held it out to him.

He looked at the letter but didn't take it from her.

'Sorry,' she said. 'I'll read it to you.'

Mildly offended, he snatched the letter from her hand.

'I may be but a lowly thief, Miss Prudence, but I am also a businessman. I can read,' he said, and was relieved when she smiled a little. He'd let her insult him all day long if it turned her frown into a smile.

Opening the letter, he began to scan the words quickly.

'This says your mother left you some personal belongings upon her death that are being shipped to you,' he paraphrased. 'It's taken a long time for this letter to reach you.'

'No it hasn't,' she said. 'Look at the documents attached. Look at the date of her death.'

Jack read on. 'December twenty-eight … 1860?'

'My mother didn't die in a fire when I was a baby,' Prudence said, the tears coming again. 'She died last year.'

'I don't understand,' Jack admitted.

'Neither did I,' Prudence said, her voice raised. 'And when I asked my grandmother what it meant, she told me it was a mistake at first, an error. But the letter has been notarised.'

She pointed to the signatures on the letter and the documents.

'That's when Gran gave in and told me the truth.'

Prudence stood and Jack watched her pace the ground before him.

'My mother met a man when she was sixteen. It was during her coming-out season in London. She fell in love with him and she went to bed with him. Discovering she was pregnant, and being naive and young, she believed the man would marry her. But he'd been betrothed to another woman since childhood. He and his parents refused the marriage that my grandmother proposed.

'Apparently, to save face, my mother was sent to the country to hide her pregnancy and wait out the birth. And when I was born my grandmother removed me from her. To avoid scandal, Gran told everyone that my mother had been married when she had me but that both my mother and my pretend father had perished in a fire. Only I survived and she had decided to bring me to London and to raise me herself.'

Jack listened intently as Prudence continued with the story of her life. A story she had only just discovered. How close she had come to meeting her mother when she'd turned sixteen and how her grandmother had so callously stolen that opportunity from her. She was putting a lot of trust in him, and it made him want to be a man worthy of her trust.

She was crying again, so he stood and walked towards her, taking his handkerchief from where she was twisting it in her hands so he could wipe her cheeks gently. She looked up at him through sorrow-filled eyes. The brightness that usually put emeralds to shame had been dulled, snuffed out by her pain. Seeing that light gone from her eyes, the colour drained from her pretty face, increased his dislike for her grandmother. Regardless of what she thought she was doing to protect a grandchild, he had no doubt the old battleaxe had been less than sympathetic or sensitive when she'd finally told Prudence the truth about her mother.

'Thank you,' she said quietly.

'For what?'

'For listening to a silly girl and her sad story.'

He shrugged and lifted a red tendril of hair that had fallen across her cheek, tucking it back behind her ear. 'You've had a shock. It's not silly to be upset. Your grandmother is a formidable woman. Frightening even.'

Prudence laughed a little and his heart soared at the sound.

'Jack the Devil is frightened of a seventy-year-old woman?'

'It's my one Achilles heel in life,' he said, with a faux grimace. 'Seventy-year-old ladies, and the beautiful women they make cry. And you are a beautiful woman, Prudence. And strong. So much stronger than you think you are. Despite your current distress, you will rise above it and come out on top. I have no doubt about it.'

She smiled shyly at his words and again his heart jumped about as if a plague of grasshoppers were bashing at his ribcage to get out. He had to be sensible. She was promised to another man.

'No doubt your grandmother thought she was doing the right thing,' he said, putting some distance between them.

Prudence huffed. 'She did it to save the family's reputation.'

'But you've had a good life, haven't you?'

'Whose side are you on?'

'I didn't know I was supposed to choose a side.'

Shaking her head, she walked away from him. But she didn't leave. He was grateful for that.

'Now you're being silly,' he said.

She spun back, her face a picture of anger and shock.

'Prudence, I didn't know my parents either.'

The fury in her expression softened a little.

'I was dumped at a home for the poor in Surrey, where I lived until I was fifteen,' he explained easily, as though it had all happened to someone else. 'Terrible conditions. Not Kensington or Belgrave Square, I can tell you. At fifteen, I ran away to London after having been sold to work at a piggery.'

'And that's how you became a thief?'

He winced. His past was his past, and he would normally not give a damn about it. But just now he didn't like being reminded of the fact that she was a lady, and he was just a common thief. Well, not common perhaps. Jack the Devil was not your average bushranger.

He moved to her, took her trembling hands in his. She tried to pull away, her face wary, but he held tight.

'I do not deny your pain, or that learning about your mother being alive all this time is heartbreaking and a definite betrayal by your grandmother. All I'm saying is that you had a comfortable life regardless. It's not all bad. And you have grown into a kind and beautiful woman. Your grandmother must take some credit for that.'

'I suppose,' she agreed reluctantly, relaxing her hands in his. 'You really think I'm beautiful?'

She'd asked him that once before, and he had dodged the question for fear that he would give in to feelings he had no right having. But stripped of all his armour in the wake of her distress, his hand went to her cheek.

'Devastatingly,' he said, marvelling at the softness of her skin.

'Will you kiss me, Jack? Please?'

Every fibre of his body screamed *Yes*. But he had to be sensible.

'You are promised to another man. It's not right.'

'Since when do you do what is right?'

She had a point there. He lifted his hand to her other cheek and held her face between his palms. The crackle of tension between them intensified.

He searched her eyes. There was no fear, no hint that she would fight him off if he tried to kiss her. He dipped his head and pressed a chaste kiss to her mouth before leaning back, just the tiniest distance, to gauge her reaction.

Her eyes were glassy, affected. And the emotions swirling in them gave him all the encouragement he needed. But still he held himself in check.

The kiss he had given her at the ball had been forceful and reckless, fierce and passionate. This time he wanted to savour her lips, drink in every moment as though it was his last. He kept his kisses light. He tasted, teased, and promised himself that after this kiss he would convince her to go back to Carrington Manor.

She didn't pull away. Didn't want to. Out here in the bush, there was no one to see them, to judge her. His mouth was pure magic against hers. His lips feathered lightly across hers. Soft, but powerful. Her body leaned into his like a magnet drawn by powers unexplainable. She wanted him to touch her, but his hands stayed resolutely on her cheeks. It was obvious he was trying to be gentle with her, but she didn't want gentle. His kisses had opened up a new world to her and she wanted the mind-blowing, thought-exploding passion he had displayed at the ball.

As he took the kiss deeper, she gasped at the exquisite wet warmth when his tongue brushed against hers. His hands slid down to her shoulders, down the side of her body, brushing past her breasts, which were aching to be held. Had her gasp forced him to touch her? She tried it again, this time with a little moan of pleasure, and his arms wrapped around her, crushing her against him. He may have been a big, strong bushranger, but she had power too, and she was learning quickly how to wield it in her favour.

She'd read about love and lust in her books and had marvelled at how her body had warmed, how her belly had tightened and quivered at the sensual scenes in the stories. Now she was living her own sensual story and she felt those same quivers, those same head-spinning waves of—well, she supposed what she was feeling was lust.

It wasn't like the last time they had kissed though. It wasn't a shock, pleasure and panic warring for space in her mind. This was a slow heating of her blood, a liquefying of her bones and then the unfamiliar but delicious tickle deep down in her intimate places.

And it was a terrible loss when he stopped the kiss and leaned away from her.

She opened her eyes slowly to see him staring at her with the oddest expression on his handsome features. She tilted her head and studied him. He really was handsome. Boyish features and pretty eyes would give him an advantage on the highways, she imagined. And still he stared at her in silence.

'Why did you stop?' she asked, suddenly self-conscious. 'Am I not a good kisser?'

She heard a little laugh bubble up from his chest, felt it too as she realised just how closely she had pressed herself against him.

'Miss Prudence, your kisses would undo even the saintliest of men.'

She couldn't help the smile of pride that formed on her lips at his compliment. 'Frederick said young ladies don't kiss like that.'

He blinked at her, before pushing out of her arms and stalking away to the log again, putting his back to her. 'You should probably go home.'

His statement wiped the smile from her face and killed the pure joy she'd been flying on since the kiss. She probably shouldn't have mentioned the kiss with Mr Grantham. Was Jack jealous? Was it wrong of her to hope that he was? Regardless, there was a bigger issue at stake.

'I can't go back there,' she said, softly. 'Ever.'

'Your grandmother will be worried.'

'I don't care,' she responded, feeling her anger return. 'She deserves to worry for what she's done. I'll not slink back and forgive her so easily simply because she'll be worried.'

'They'll have people out looking for you,' he said. 'You shouldn't be here with me alone.'

She stepped to him, putting a hand to his stubble-roughened jaw, and turning his face to hers. 'I want to be here, with you, alone.'

'Prudence—'

'I can come home with you,' she said, cutting him off.

She would have found the look of shock on his face comical if she hadn't been so desperate.

'No.'

'Why not?'

'Because.'

'That's not a reason.'

'You're being silly again,' he said and brushed past her. 'Come on, I'll escort you home.'

Rejection burned, too close to the still-raw pain her grand-mother had inflicted on her just that afternoon.

'I know you want me, Jack,' she said, staying where she was as he readied the horses. 'You want me as I want you.'

He didn't look back at her but the stiffness in his broad shoulders told her he was conflicted.

She moved in and placed a kiss to his neck. His hands tightened on the reins of the horse until his knuckles turned white.

'I've had enough lies in my life, Jack,' she whispered against his ear. 'Please, be honest with me.'

He spun so quickly she had to take a step back.

'Honest? You want me to be honest? Of course I want you.'

Her heart swelled.

'But you are engaged to another man. A good man, by all accounts. A man who can take care of you and continue to provide you with the life you are accustomed to.'

She huffed and shook her head. 'A man whose kisses are as staid and as lifeless as his personality. I do not want to marry Frederick Grantham. And you just said you want me.'

'Yes, I want you. But I can't have you. I'm a bushranger, an outlaw.'

'I may not be able to make an honest man out of you, Jack. But you can make an honest woman out of me.'

He went very still. 'Did you just propose marriage to me?'

A moment of uncertainty washed over her, but the more she thought about it, the more appealing her impulsive proposal sounded. She was desperate to stay away from Carrington Manor and if she had to marry the Devil to do it, then so be it.

'Yes,' she said, straightening her shoulders. 'I did. Marry me, Jack Fairweather.'

He stared open-mouthed at her for the longest time until he finally found his voice. 'Prudence, you should marry someone you love. You don't love me.'

'What a romantic you are, Jack,' she said with a derisive laugh. 'I was going to marry Frederick Grantham. A man I do not love, a man I could never love. How many women do you know of who get to marry for love? At least I *like* you.'

'High praise,' he murmured, and pushing past her he sat heavily on the log again, staring at his boots with a scowl so deep his caramel eyes darkened. She didn't understand his strange mood, so taking a deep breath and smoothing her skirts, she moved to sit beside him.

'Jack, think of it as a marriage of convenience. We both need something. I need somewhere to live and someone to take care of me. And you need someone who can throw the troopers off thinking that Jack Fairweather has anything to do with Jack the Devil.'

He looked surprised that she knew so much.

'I read the papers,' she explained with a shrug. 'I know Sergeant Carmichael has arrested several bushrangers in the last months. And, by all accounts, he's closing in on Jack the Devil.'

She continued despite his looking at her as if she'd lost her mind. 'I am the perfect cover for you. Who would ever believe the granddaughter of an earl would marry a bushranger?' Her heart raced, her hope dwindling with every moment that passed with not a word or a twitch of movement from him. 'But she may marry a prominent businessman. It wouldn't be all that bad to have a woman about, would it? I'm not experienced at keeping house but I learn quickly.'

He closed his eyes as though a great battle were going on inside his head. When he opened them again, she saw a different look. Not denial but acceptance.

'I won't give up bushranging,' he declared.

'I didn't ask you to.'

'I'm serious, Prudence. You won't change a man like me. It's pointless to try.'

'Is that a challenge?' she asked, her eyes narrow and daring. 'You think I can't make you see the error of your ways should I decide to? Well, lucky for you, that's not what I want anyway. I'm tired of living my adventures through books.'

'Be careful of what you think you want, little girl,' Jack warned. 'It may seem exciting and adventurous like your books, but my life is not a fairy tale.'

'I don't want a fairy tale, Jack. I want a life. I want a life of freedom. I believe I can have that with you. I certainly won't have that with Mr Grantham.'

Jack stared at her again, still weighing up the pros and cons. Then he smiled and simply lifted a hand to gently caress her face. Leaning in slowly, he kissed her softly, soundly, until she felt her toes curl and her limbs melt. This marriage of convenience may indeed have some benefits. She knew for a fact that Frederick Grantham's thin, emotionless kisses would never be able to melt her limbs.

Her head spun, even before she felt him lift her off the log and into the saddle of his horse. He climbed up behind her and, leading Misha by the reins, they rode gently in silence. Not in the direction of Carrington Manor, Prudence was thrilled to discover, but away from it. Away from all she knew, towards a new beginning.

Seven

Back and forth he argued with himself, nearly turning the horse around to head back to Carrington Manor. But each time he resolved to do so, she would turn her head and smile at him, or lean back against his chest and he'd smell the perfume of her hair, feel the warmth of her body pressed to his.

Did he dare to believe this would have a good outcome?

He'd battled against his growing feelings for her since that day at the races. It was easy to tell himself back then that she was too good for him, and so it had been fun to play with her. And then when they'd met again by accident on the road, he'd enjoyed talking to her, enjoyed her company, her intelligence—a rare occurrence for him with women. But at the Christmas Ball, he'd had to admit to himself that what he'd begun to feel for Prudence Stanforth was not just some fleeting attraction. And he'd run. Knowing she was promised to Grantham had provided a sort of closure for him. She was not only out of his league, but very much out of his grasp.

Yet, here she was. Not with Grantham, but with him. She'd talked him into taking her home with him. Home? What home? His house was a shambles. He barely lived there himself. How could he take a woman like Prudence there? How could he take any woman home to live with Jack the Devil? He'd never lived with a woman in his life. What made him think he could start now? What made her think it?

She was a determined little minx when she set her mind to something. But despite all her bravado and her love of adventure stories, would she be strong enough to survive such adventures out in the real world? She might have been the one to suggest a marriage of convenience, but did he have any right to take a lady from her safe and comfortable home and force her into a life less worthy of her and, more importantly, one which put her in the path of danger?

The sun was high in the sky as they passed through the gates of his estate. He stopped the horse at the turn in the driveway where the house came into view.

He dismounted and helped Pru down, his hands gripping her waist as she dropped lightly to the ground. He wanted to kiss her again, desperately wanted it, but he needed to give her the time and space to change her mind.

She walked towards the house and he held his breath, waiting for her to realise she had made a huge mistake. His house was pleasant and well appointed, if currently filthy, and a great deal more impressive than many homes in the district, yet it was no Carrington Manor.

'Welcome to Little Windsor.'

She turned and smiled at the name and he shrugged a shoulder at his little castle joke.

His palms were sweating and his heart was pounding in his chest with nervous anticipation. Would she come to her senses? Would she panic that she had allowed herself to be led astray, into a man's home—not just any man's home but that of an outlaw. The lair of Jack the Devil.

She stared at the house with her back to him for a long time. He wanted her to love it, but the battle raged inside him—she shouldn't be here, and he should take her home. Her silence spoke volumes and he decided to let her off the hook.

'Pru …'

'I love it, Jack,' she said, turning her beautiful face to him again. Her smile pleased him, but he still needed to be sure.

'I'll understand if you've changed your mind,' he said, taking hold of her hands. He'd understand, but it would likely kill him to have come so close to having what he'd never thought possible. 'I can still take you home.'

She snaked an arm around his waist and they stood looking at the house together before she said, 'I am home.'

As they walked inside the house, Jack wished he'd tidied up a little. It wasn't too bad but it needed a good sweep, and dust had collected on the dining-room table and surfaces about the sitting room. At least he could be thankful no rodents had appeared as yet.

'I don't come here much,' he said by way of an apology. 'I stay in hotels and rent rooms around the towns. It's just easier. And I don't cook for myself so there isn't much to eat—well, nothing to eat actually. But at least there are no dirty pots and pans.'

He was rambling and he knew it. He couldn't keep his eyes off her as she wandered around the large house, opening every door and looking into every one of the three bedrooms.

'It's perfect. Just needs a woman's touch, that's all.' She turned back to face him and rolled her eyes. 'Stop looking at me as though I'm about to throw myself to the floor in a fit of tears and ask you to take me back. It's not going to happen. It will never happen. You're stuck with me, Jack.'

Relief flooded through him at her words, but he still held reservations.

'You take this room,' he said, opening the main bedroom door. A double bed sat in the middle of the room; a relatively good mattress lay between the intricate iron-lace foot and head of the bed. 'We'll need to get some new linen. I'll use the room across the hall.' He would set himself up in the little cot that had occasionally been used by Bobby or Garrett.

'I wasn't expecting company, so if we are going to eat, I'd best go into town and buy some provisions,' Jack said, wiping his damp hands on his trousers. A tough bushranger he might be, but Prudence could reduce him to a nervous wreck with just a smile. She was smiling at him now and stepped forward to kiss his cheek. Her eyes told him she wanted him to kiss her again, kiss her properly. He stepped away. Now wasn't the time.

They spent the next hour making a list of items Jack would have to buy in Ballarat. Not only food, but pots and pans and other kitchen utensils. New linen would have to be purchased from the Criterion store as well.

'It's a lot to carry,' Prudence said. 'Are you sure you don't want me to come with you?'

Jack knew they could not be seen together in public as people would ask too many questions. Who was she? Where had she come from? Why was she living with him? And he had no idea how to answer them. He only knew that her reputation had to be protected. But that wasn't the only reason. Her family would be searching for her and, if they found her, he would no doubt be accused of kidnapping. Christ almighty, what had he done?

'No, please, make yourself at home,' Jack insisted. 'I'll be back before dinnertime.'

'A good thing since there's no food,' she teased.

And with that he climbed back up onto D'Artagnan and headed off at pace, out of the grounds of Little Windsor.

He looked back once to see her waving at him and his world tilted. Having her there to wave him off and welcome him home was like a miracle. And it would be a miracle if she was still there when he got home. No one would find her out here in his secluded part of the world. But if she changed her mind, all she had to do was take Misha and head back to Carrington Manor.

He shook off his elation as she continued to wave him out of the gates. No. He had to stay smart about this. She could still change her mind. After a week or two of living rough with him, she would come to her senses and ask him to let her out of their agreement. He would help her by delaying the marriage she was so insistent on having. And he resolved not to lay a hand on her during that time. It would be a battle of epic proportions, but he was determined.

When he returned to Little Windsor, poor D'Artagnan was laden with all the food and supplies he could carry. Jack had made arrangements for larger items to be delivered to Little Windsor the next day. Unloading what he could, he stepped into the house. Prudence had been hard at work. He hardly recognised the living area when he walked in. The dust was gone, and lighted candles were spread about the house now that darkness had set in. He hadn't even known he'd had candles in the house. As the sun had dropped lower to the horizon, he'd rushed the last few miles, pushing himself and the horse, not wanting Prudence to be alone in the house after dark.

'I don't think it's ever looked so clean,' he said, unloading the first armful of supplies onto the kitchen table.

'I didn't have much to work with,' she said, squeezing filthy water out of the old rag she'd been using. 'I don't suppose you picked up a broom while you were in town.'

'Didn't think of it, sorry,' he said, staring at her delicate hands, red from the hot water. But she didn't seem concerned as she wiped them on her skirts. Skirts! 'Oh, I borrowed a few things from a friend.'

Rushing out to unload the last of the saddlebags, he returned with a package. Opening it, he pulled out a dress. It was plain as dresses went, much plainer than the granddaughter of Lady Carrington would be used to, he was sure. 'I thought you'd need more than the dress you're wearing.'

Her eyebrows went up, suspicion in the green orbs below them. 'And which *lady friend* did you borrow this from?'

'She's the daughter of Mrs Barnett, the boarding-house owner,' he explained, wary of the narrowed gaze she was sending him.

'And she was happy to part with her dresses for another woman?'

'She's a good Christian lady,' Jack said. Prudence's apparent jealousy of another woman surprised him. 'Hilda married recently and her husband bought her several new gowns when they moved to Melbourne. She left these behind. I told Mrs Barnett the dresses were for a homeless woman. They aren't very fashionable or glamorous but ...'

She dropped the dress on the kitchen table and turned to stare out the window. 'I'm homeless. Destitute, I suppose.'

'You are not homeless,' he said, moving to put his hands on her shoulders. He turned her to face him. 'You have a home here, for as long as you want it.'

'But I left with nothing. No other clothes. Just the coat I was wearing and ...'

Her demeanour lightened as she seemed to remember something. Reaching into her coat pocket, she pulled out a purse. 'The housekeeping money from the manor.' She handed it to him.

He didn't take it. 'Why are you giving it to me?'

'For the supplies,' she said. 'The food, the linens.'

He was appalled. 'I don't need your money and I don't want it. If you are to be my wife, you will be kept comfortable. Do not worry about that, Miss Stanforth.'

She winced as though he had slapped her and he felt bad for it instantly. His pride had made him lash out.

Walking to her, he took the purse and put it back in her pocket. 'Save it. I have plenty of money. And yes, I stole most of it,' he added before she could say anything. 'But some is earned legitimately too. That is the money I will spend on you, if it makes you feel better.'

'You've misunderstood me,' she said. 'This is an agreement of convenience, a partnership. I don't expect you to keep me in the manner to which I was accustomed at the manor. I expect to live as you do and earn my keep.'

'You're going to start bailing up coaches on the highway?' he joked.

'Wouldn't that be fun,' she said, with a slow devious smile he didn't like the look of.

'Don't be ridiculous. I said I would marry you, and if you wish to keep that agreement then I will treat you as my wife and provide for you.'

'Of course, Jack,' she said, looking meek. He hated that. Meek didn't suit her.

He watched a moment as she began unpacking things from the bags he'd carted in.

'I'll get the rest of the supplies and deal with D'Artagnan—he needs a brush down before I settle him back in the stables,' he mumbled and left her in the house, closing the door behind him.

Scrubbing his hands over his face, he looked back in at her through the front window. Great. They'd had their first fight. And they weren't even married yet. This was going to take some getting used to. Having a woman in the house. Having a wife.

Having someone who relied on him for everything but expected to do her part. Navigating a relationship for the first time in his life was going to be akin to walking through Ballarat at night without falling down a mineshaft.

The next morning, Jack half expected her to be gone. And as the days passed he kept waiting for her to realise the insanity of the situation. He figured once her anger wore off, she would forgive her family and miss them and her luxurious mansion, then ask to be taken home. As much as he wanted her with him, if she wanted to leave, he knew he'd never force her to stay.

One warm afternoon, less than a week after Pru had arrived at his house, Jack prepared to meet Bobby and Garrett. Alfred had given them the details about a coach arriving from Melbourne carrying a wealthy gentleman and his son who'd just arrived from France. Just because Prudence was living with him now didn't mean he would stop working. He'd been very clear about that part of their arrangement. A man didn't change who he was simply because a woman came into his life.

It was impossible to ignore her as she stood at the door of the stables and watched him saddle Persephone. She wore one of the dresses he'd borrowed from Mrs Barnett's daughter, the deep purple one, and it made her green eyes glow like the eyes of the cats that ran wild around Ballarat. He kept expecting her to tell him not to go, to give him that frighteningly judgemental eye of hers. So when she spoke, he couldn't have been more surprised.

'I'd like to come.'

He sent her a dismissive look but said nothing.

'Just once. To see how you do it.'

'You've seen how I do it,' he tossed back with a cheeky grin. 'Firsthand.'

'I wouldn't get in the way. I'd just stay on the sidelines and watch.'

'A highway robbery is no place for a lady.'

'Unless she's the one being robbed, is that it?'

He didn't answer, just kept working on preparing the horse.

'So who is the unlucky soul who gets to meet Jack the Devil today?' she questioned, stepping up to pat Persephone's nose. 'Another silly man trying his luck at gold mining? Honestly, I don't know why people keep coming over to try their luck at finding gold. Most of the mines duffered out years ago, at least in this district.'

'What do you know about duffered-out mines?' he asked with a chuckle.

She gave a light shrug. 'They'd be better off heading for South Australia. I read they've just found copper in the west of the state.'

'Ah, yes, but then we wouldn't have the pleasure of robbing them,' Jack said with a wink. 'But I believe today's lucky marks are a French gentleman and his son. Here to set up a dress shop.'

'Really? Perhaps you can steal me some French couture.'

'Couture?'

'Dresses, Jack. Clothing. The French are very fashionable.'

'What's wrong with the dresses I got you?'

'Nothing at all,' she said. 'But I don't feel right taking them from such a good Christian woman.'

That sting of jealousy was in her tone once again. Erring on the side of caution, Jack ignored it and mounted Persephone. 'I'll be home before dinnertime. What will you do to amuse yourself today?'

'Can't I come with you?' she tried again, a little pout touching her lips this time.

'I said no.'

She huffed with annoyance. 'Fine. Then I had best do some clothes washing. My undergarments will be standing on their own soon.'

Jack shifted uncomfortably in the saddle. He didn't want to think about her without her undergarments on as she washed them in the big outdoor basin. Best to stay away from that tempting image. She'd been with him for five days now, having run from Carrington Manor with only the dress she had on. The dresses he'd borrowed from Hilda Barnett were old and worn. He made a mental note to have some new dresses—and some new undergarments—delivered to her as soon as possible.

'Well.' He stared at her for a moment, wondering whether he should lean down and give her a kiss goodbye. He wanted to. Really wanted to. It wouldn't be unheard of. They'd kissed several times now. But since she'd come to live with him, he didn't want her to think he was going to force himself on her, so he thought it wise to keep a distance between them for now. She looked up at him with a gentle smile, before running a hand down his shin, sending tingles up his leg directly to his groin.

'I'll see you tonight,' he said, and rode out of the stables.

The robbery took place on the main road to Melbourne. A little too close to Ballarat for Jack's liking. He'd left the planning of the heist to Garrett. The boy was still a little green and he'd have to have a word with him about not pulling heists so close to where they all lived. But because it was close to town, the job was done in record time, which meant Jack could stop at the store in Ballarat before he headed back to the house. The French dressmaker they'd bailed up did have plenty of fabrics, including silks and satins. But Prudence could hardly wear dresses made from stolen fabric so easily identifiable, so he'd left them behind and taken only the cash and other valuables.

'Got yourself a lady friend, Mr Fairweather?' Mrs Bowie, the manager of the store, said as she wrapped his purchases in brown paper.

What had he been thinking, buying dress fabric in Ballarat? He should have gone to Melbourne where no one knew him.

'Uh, no, these are for my sister,' he lied.

She tapped the undergarments Jack had picked out. 'Sister?' The coquettish smile said she didn't believe him. 'I didn't know you had a sister, Mr Fairweather.'

'She lives in Geelong.'

Mrs Bowie's smile didn't waver as she tied string around the parcel. 'The city would have a much nicer selection than we do. Should you wish to impress your *sister*, that is.'

'I like to support the local economy.'

That pleased Mrs Bowie no end. 'Bless you, Mr Fairweather. Wish more folks had the same idea.'

He gave her a weak smile, took the parcel and headed out of the store and straight into the path of Sergeant Carmichael.

'Fairweather.'

'Sergeant,' Jack said in return.

'I hear one of your coaches was robbed today,' the sergeant said, removing his hat to wipe the sweat from his nearly bald head. 'A gentleman by the name of ...' he consulted his notebook, 'Pierre Rochelon spent the last hour in my office listing all the goods stolen from him and his son.'

'Indeed?' Jack showed the appropriate level of shock. 'I had not been made aware as yet. I'd better head down to the office and check with my manager.'

But the sergeant wasn't done, it seemed, as he turned to walk with Jack towards the main street offices of Fairweather Transport. 'I noticed you haven't been around town much this last week.'

'Been watching out for me, Sergeant?'

'I like to get to know the people in my town. It seems you don't spend much time working in your own business, Mr Fairweather.'

'As I just said, I have an office manager,' Jack replied easily. 'He is much better at running things. I'm just the money behind the business.'

'I see. So what do you do with your time?' the sergeant asked as they arrived at the office.

'What all men of no occupation do,' Jack said, raising his eyebrows. 'Play cards, ride my horses, and at night? It's all wine, women and song.'

Jack tipped his hat and stepped into the office, leaving the sergeant to wander back down the street alone.

'Nosy bastard, isn't he?'

Jack turned to see his manager, Alfred, leaning on the counter.

'Mmm, a little too nosy.'

'He was in here this morning, doing the rounds of town. Apparently a girl's gone missing from her home, not far out of Ballan. Wanted to know if she'd taken a coach to Melbourne perhaps. Family thinks she was kidnapped. Sergeant believes it's more likely she ran away to the city.'

'Really?' It wasn't a surprise that the police had been contacted, but it still gave Jack a moment's concern. 'Did the sergeant say who she was?'

'Some nobleman's niece.'

'Mmm.'

'Beggin' your pardon for saying so,' Alfred began. 'But you seem ... distracted.'

Distracted. He couldn't deny it. Prudence was a distraction. His mind hadn't been on the job that morning. If it had, he would have suggested moving the robbery further up the road to the other side of Creswick, or cancelling it altogether. His mind had been on Prudence. His mind was constantly on Prudence. He was wound up so tight, he couldn't think of anything else and it was becoming detrimental to his job. Going this long without laying with a woman was a rarity for him. Stepping to the window, he glanced down towards the Duchess of Kent Hotel. There was any number of willing women there who would help him let the steam out of the kettle, so to speak. He wasn't married yet.

But none of them were Prudence. She was the only one he wanted. And he wanted her badly.

'Jack.'

'Mmm?' Jack broke out of his thoughts and glanced at Alfred again. 'Oh, distracted, yes. I've been spending more time at Little Windsor. Finally getting her up to liveable.'

'Are you thinking of retiring?'

'Good God, no.' Jack shot out a laugh. 'You can't get rid of me that easily, old man.'

And with that he headed out the back to the stables where he'd hidden Persephone.

Prudence was asleep in the chair by the fire when he arrived at Little Windsor. A delicious-smelling stew bubbled in a pot hanging over the fireplace. Placing his purchases on the other armchair, he approached her. The firelight played on her face and in her hair, sparking the orange highlights. Unable to resist, he leaned down and kissed her lips lightly.

She stirred and her eyes fluttered open.

'Jack, you're home,' she said sitting upright, before stretching in a way that made his eyes fall upon her bosom, straining against her dress. 'Oh, I fell asleep. The bourguignon, is it ruined?'

'Bourguignon?' Jack asked. 'Looks like stew.'

Pru chuckled. 'By any other name …'

'Smells wonderful.' He moved to dip a spoon into the stew to give it a taste test. 'It tastes wonderful, too. You made this?'

'I may not know which end of a broom to use,' she joked, letting out a delicate yawn. 'But I had a wonderful culinary tutor in London. Are you hungry?'

'Starving,' he said, taking her hand and helping her from the chair. 'But, before we eat, I have a surprise for you.'

'I can come with you on your next robbery?' she asked, wide-eyed with excitement.

'No, that will never happen.'

'But Jack—'

'I said no, Prudence. I won't talk about this again.'

The mood took a rapid shift from happy and relaxed to tense and irritated.

He shook it off and moved to where he'd left the parcels. He handed the brown paper package to her.

'What is it?'

'Well, open it and find out,' he instructed.

Nervously, he waited until she untied the string, and tore through the brown paper. The green cotton unfolded and he caught it before it hit the floor.

He helped her to drape the pale green fabric over the chair. 'You said you didn't feel right wearing the borrowed dresses. We can donate those to the church if you wish. I know of a dressmaker in the city. My tailor tells me she's more than adequate. I'll take the fabrics to her next time I go to Melbourne but I wanted to see if you liked the colours first. There's some blue in there too.

I didn't purchase anything for formal wear. It may be some time before we're attending balls.' He was babbling. And she stayed so quiet, he wondered desperately what she was thinking. 'We can take them back if you don't like them—'

'I love them, Jack.' She stepped forward and, laying her hand against his chest, she reached up and kissed him. 'This was so sweet of you.'

Her chaste kiss sent shockwaves of lust through his body and he moved away, putting the armchair between them. 'Of course, if you decide to stay, we'll need to get you a winter coat before it gets too cold. I also got you some ...'

She opened the other package and pulled out the undergarments. *Oh God, he didn't need to see those right now.*

She smiled coyly as she held the thin chemise up against her body. The heat of the fire had nothing on him as she peered up at him through her lashes.

'Perhaps you should put those things away for now.' *Dear God, please.*

Moving to him, she ran her hands across his stubbled jaw, leaned in slowly and kissed him again. 'Thank you.' Another kiss, and her lips lingered longer on his this time, before she pulled back. 'But we'll need one more dress.'

'One more?' He tried to make his voice sound light and unaffected. It wasn't working. 'You can have as many as you want.'

'I think I need to choose the fabric for this one myself. My wedding dress.'

Hope and lust were a confused ball in his stomach. 'You still want to marry me?'

'I proposed to you, didn't I?'

'You were upset and frightened. I didn't want to hold you to that.'

His groin tightened when she pressed her body against his. 'Hold me to it, Jack. Hold me.'

His arms went automatically around her tiny waist while her hands feathered in his hair, and holding her to him, he kissed her, strongly, soundly. God, he wanted her. He was used to being able to take the women he wanted to bed without a second thought or guilt. But this was Prudence, she was a lady, and he had no doubt she was a virgin. He couldn't take what he wanted. Not yet.

Pulling away, he took in the rosiness in her cheeks, the passion in her eyes.

'You've cooked a delicious dinner,' he said, putting some distance between them. 'I'm starved. Let's eat.'

Holding a hot pot of stew between them would force him to rein in his out-of-control desires. So he picked it up carefully and placed it down on the metal plate next to the fire.

He grabbed one of the bowls she had nearby and the ladle. 'One spoonful or two?'

They ate at the large dining-room table, candlelight flickering between them along with unspoken wants and desires.

'Pru, you should know, your family have reported you missing. The police are involved.' She put down her spoon and sat back, a sad expression marring her pretty features. 'If they find you, they'll take you away and probably have me arrested.'

'Then the sooner we marry, the better,' she said, lifting her eyes to meet his. 'I proposed to you, Jack, and I meant it. I'll be happy to be your wife, in every sense of the word.'

He averted his eyes. 'But if you ever feel differently …'

'I won't,' she said, standing from her chair and moving around to his side of the table. 'I won't.'

'I will not pressure you to do anything you're not ready for.'

She leaned down and whispered in his ear. 'I think it's me who is pressuring you.'

'You have no experience with men.'

'None,' she admitted, sitting down in his lap and playing with the hair at the nape of his neck.

He swallowed hard. 'You're doing fine so far.'

Oh, the smell of her, the softness of her. He certainly felt the pressure. 'Perhaps you need to think about it a bit longer.'

'If we're going to be married, don't you think we should … test the waters?'

Lord, she was testing him alright.

Her lips were on his ear and he began to harden beneath her round bottom.

'Pru …'

'I love it when you call me Pru.'

His whole body went rigid when her mouth closed over his earlobe and sucked.

Groaning, he let himself be feasted upon by her for a moment before he could stand it no longer. He pulled her mouth to his, licking, tasting and biting, and everything he did to her she did in return, like the good little student she was.

And then he was up. Standing upright and holding onto her arms as she struggled to regain her footing from his sudden move-ment. Her surprise and disappointment was evident in the wide green of her eyes.

'Er, I have to … um, feed the horses.'

Closing the door behind him, he moved quickly across to the stables. Fresh air. Outside. Outside was good. Outside was breathing. Breathing without the heady scent of her filling his nostrils and his mind with lascivious thoughts. D'Artagnan let out a whinny that sounded not unlike a laugh.

'Oh, you think it's funny, do you?' he asked his horse. 'I'd like to see you show as much restraint when faced with such an incredible, alluring girl.'

Persephone joined D'Artagnan with a very unladylike snort.

'Just whose side are you two on anyway?'

He delivered their feed and checked their water. 'Now eat and keep your opinions to yourself.'

His chores completed, Jack still couldn't bring himself to go inside just yet. He needed time to cool down. Standing at the stable door, he could see Pru wandering back and forth in front of the windows. Light from the lanterns made her glow and she sang as she cleared the dinner table. His promise—to keep his hands to himself, and give her the space she needed—was going to be harder than he'd expected.

He was driving her crazy.

Frustrated, Pru tossed and turned in the big bed. It was obvious he was still waiting for her to change her mind and run home, but she thought she had made it abundantly clear that she was never going back to Carrington Manor. Even if the police found her and tried to drag her kicking and screaming, she would not go back. Ever.

And since when had Jack become such a gentleman? He had stolen kisses from her several times before she'd come to live with him. Now it seemed he didn't want to touch her at all. She had managed to lure him into a few kisses, but then, before she'd been able to take the kisses further, he would find something he had to do out in the stables. Or he'd say he was tired and run off to his room.

And she was bored. She couldn't go to town with him for fear someone would recognise her. She wasn't allowed to go riding alone. She may as well be back at Carrington Manor for all the freedom she had here. And worst of all, he wouldn't let her come along and watch him on a robbery. She desperately wanted to see him work. Wanted to experience the thrill of the bail-up, from the other side.

Well, she was having none of it. He would marry her—and soon. She'd make sure of it. As for him letting her watch him work? Well, he didn't need to know she was watching, did he?

Eight

'Why are you up so early?'

The sun hadn't even risen when Pru, clad in a thick blanket, wandered into the stables as Jack prepared for a dawn robbery.

'I wanted to say goodbye and good luck.'

His smile was slow, and despite his determination the night before to keep her at a distance, he went to her. Smoothing a hand over her hair, he grasped the back of her neck, leaned in and kissed her forehead.

Back to the forehead, she thought with some annoyance as he mounted Persephone.

'I'll be back for breakfast.'

Watching him ride out the gates of Little Windsor, Pru tossed off the blanket she wore. Little did Jack know that she'd been up and putting her plan into action before he'd even woken. She checked her attire once more. Over the past few days, she'd been stealing some of his clothes and hiding them in her room. That morning she'd risen early, pulled on her manly costume and, covering herself in the blanket so he wouldn't know, she went out to say goodbye. The clothes were far too big for her, but the belt helped cinch in the trousers so they wouldn't fall down, and the shirt, which went down to her knees, was tied at the waist. She thanked God that her breasts were small enough to hide beneath the loose shirt. Her riding boots were a little too feminine, but that couldn't be helped. Jack had feet the size of railway sleepers.

Shoving her long, bright hair up under the floppy hat she'd found, she opened Misha's stall and led her out of the stables. She'd already saddled her before Jack had gotten out of bed, knowing he'd never spare her a glance in her end stall.

Using the nearby fence, Pru hoisted herself aboard Misha and, as quietly as she could, followed Jack down the driveway and out into the darkness of the pre-dawn.

She followed him for miles, doing her best to keep enough distance that he wouldn't hear her horse over his own but staying close enough not to lose him in the darkness. She was relieved when the horizon began to pale and her path was easier to see. But she became caught up in the beauty of the sunrise, and when she looked back at the road ahead she could no longer see Jack.

'Damn,' she murmured, pulling on the reins to slow Misha down. The road forked and she had no way of knowing which direction he had taken. Deciding to go left, she passed into the shade of an outcropping of rocks. Misha startled as a horse rode out in front of them.

'Who are you and why do you follow me?' he demanded, his pistol aimed at her as he edged closer.

The rising sun breached the rocks, and tilting her head back to peek up at him from beneath her hat, she saw the realisation cross his face.

'Pru?' The shock was evident on his features. 'I could have shot you. What the bloody hell are you doing here?'

'I want to come with you.'

He just stared at her. 'Are you mad? You can't be a part of this. I'm not taking a woman into a highway robbery.'

'That's why I dressed as a man,' she told him. 'I'll keep my hat on and I'll wear a mask.' She pulled out one of the white linen and lace napkins he'd purchased for the house. 'Who will know I'm a woman?'

'I'll know,' he said, then shook himself. 'Why am I discussing this with you? You're not coming. It's too dangerous. Now go home.'

Annoyed and determined, she tried a different tack. 'I thought Jack the Devil had more guts.'

'Is that a dare? Are you daring me to take you along?'

'Perhaps. Are you man enough to take my dare?'

Frustrated, he swore in a way he'd never done in front of her before. Obviously having a hard time turning down a dare, Jack shook his head.

'I won't be a bother,' she said, hating the pleading tone in her voice.

'I said no.'

Temper threaded through her at his definitive tone.

'You don't own me, Jack,' she said. 'You can't force me to do anything. I'll just follow you.'

'You test a man's patience.'

She gave him her pleading pout. 'I swear I'll keep my distance.'

He made a groaning sound deep in his throat and she was sure he was going to send her away.

'God save me from independent women,' he muttered, and turning his horse he set off at a canter down the left fork in the road.

Proud of her flirtatious negotiation skills, she gave Misha a good strong kick and took off after him.

The sun was still low and flickered through the trees that lined the road when Jack and Pru came upon two men on horseback.

'Jack,' one of them said, greeting him with a handshake.

None of them dismounted, but Pru could see the shock on the two men's faces as she rode up behind Jack. One of the men looked to be about Jack's age, with short, dirty blond hair and a pleasant face. The other was younger, tall and lanky, and had long, scraggly hair as dark as midnight.

'Who's this?' the blond man asked.

'This is Pru.' She loved the ease with which he used her shortened name. 'Pru, this is Bobby and Garrett.'

'What's she doin' 'ere?' Garrett gave her a look of distaste.

'She followed me.'

'From where? Buckingham Palace?' he growled. 'Who wears pearl earrings to a hold-up?'

Heat rushed into her cheeks as she quickly removed the tiny pearl drops from her ears and shoved them into the pockets of her corduroy trousers. *Blast and damnation!* She must have put them on by habit while she'd been dressing.

'Jack, we can't have a girl come along on a robbery,' Bobby said.

'And why not?' she asked prissily.

'Because it's bad luck, that's why,' Garrett shot back. 'Now bugger off home, little girl, and leave the bushranging to the men.'

Finger raised, eyes firing, Jack glared at Garrett. 'Don't speak to her like that.'

'You bring your bit of skirt along to a robbery?' Garrett replied. 'You've gone bleedin' mad.'

'You don't seriously expect her to be a part of this?' Bobby asked, a little less antagonistic than Garrett. 'Sorry, miss, but bushranging is no place for a lady.'

'She'll be observing only,' Jack said and moved his horse closer to Garrett and Bobby, trying to ensure she wouldn't hear him. But in the quiet of the morning she heard every word.

'Just let her watch. Once she sees it's no place for a woman, she'll be done with this lunacy and we'll have only had to deal with it for a day. She doesn't even have a weapon—'

'Yes, I do,' she interrupted and pulled out the little percussion pistol she'd stashed in her trousers.

'Where did you get that?' Jack snapped, his tone caught between irritated and horrified.

'I found it in the house.'

'Stop waving it about before you shoot one of us,' he told her. He grabbed for the pistol but she was quicker and pulled it out of reach. 'You do not get to have a gun.'

'And why not?'

'Christ, you ask so many questions.'

'I need to protect myself, don't I?'

'That old thing hasn't been fired in years,' he said. 'Besides that, do you even know how to fire a gun?'

'How hard can it be?' she asked, aiming the little pistol at a nearby tree and pulling the trigger. The sound reverberated through the forest. Birds took flight, the horses spooked and before she knew what had happened, Jack had relieved her of her gun.

'She's gonna end up shooting one of us!' Garrett called out, dusting his coat of the tree bark that had flown when the ball had struck.

'Time's wasting,' Bobby tossed in, checking his pocket watch. 'The carriage will be here any minute.'

Jack exhaled a whoosh of frustrated breath. 'It's too late to send her home now.'

He turned to her. 'Pru, you have to stay out of the way, do you understand? No matter what you see or hear, do not speak, do not move.'

She nodded, excitement overtaking her displeasure at being scolded.

'Be it on your head then, Jack, if she gets hurt,' Garrett tossed back with a shake of his head and a look of disgust aimed at her.

They rode together to the dry riverbed Bobby had scouted as the best place for an ambush. The carriage would have to slow down to traverse the small gulch, Pru realised, making it easy for the bushrangers to block.

'Get behind those rocks and stay there,' Jack instructed her.

As the carriage came closer, her heart began to pound in her chest, the pulse of it in her head matching the hoof beats of the team of horses. Crossing glances with Jack as he pulled the kerchief into place across his nose and mouth, there was a powerful tug in her lower belly. The thrill she felt was mirrored back at her in his gold eyes. Thrill mixed with something else, something more primal. She held there, fixed in his gaze for a second and then it was all movement. With Jack in the lead, they rode their horses into the path of an oncoming carriage.

'Stand and deliver!'

A shiver ran down her spine at the deep and authoritative command in Jack's voice, as he pointed his gun at the coach driver. She knew she shouldn't be so fascinated with this display of thievery, but she couldn't help it. Wide-eyed, she watched the three men bail up the carriage and its occupants with the expert precision and timing of men who had worked together for years.

They went for the obvious prizes: the gentleman's billfold, the earrings and necklace the lady wore. Jack was the picture of politeness and his suave, devilish conversation took her back to the day he'd robbed her and her grandmother, the day she'd first met Jack the Devil. What she had begun to recognise as arousal ran through her at his smooth voice, and her belly lurched again when he turned and winked at her. She licked her lips beneath the linen napkin she wore across her mouth.

Looking away to save her sanity, she noticed Garrett was almost done with the trunk but had very little to show for it. He'd claimed a few baubles, but one look at the finery the lady seated in the carriage wore, and Pru knew she had more expensive adornments than what Garrett had found in that velvet jewellery case.

Realisation struck. They didn't know. They weren't aware of the secret places women hid their most valued possessions.

Almost bouncing with excitement, Prudence cleared her throat loudly. Garrett turned to glare at her, getting set to close the trunk.

'Got a furball there, kitty cat?' he shot at her.

She shook her head vigorously. She knew she couldn't speak out loud. A woman's voice would not easily be forgotten by those who were being held up.

Garrett glowered. 'What's your problem?'

She pointed at her shoes, trying to make him understand.

'Jack, I think … er … our guest robber,' Garrett didn't know what else to call her, it seemed, 'has a question. Maybe you can figure out what, er … *he* wants.'

Impatiently, Jack turned to look at her. 'What is it?'

She waved him over.

Rolling his eyes, he went to her. 'What? Can't you see we're a little busy here?'

She leaned down from her seat on the horse to whisper in his ear. 'Look in the lady's shoes.'

He frowned at her like she'd gone mad, but she nodded fervently.

'Open that trunk again,' he called out to Garrett.

'What in blazes for?' Garrett argued. 'We looked in that trunk. There's nothin' there!'

'Just do it,' Jack insisted.

Swearing and grumbling, Garrett opened the trunk. Jack walked across and, digging through the trunk, he pulled out one of the fancy satin slippers. Pushing his fingers into the shoe, he froze before glancing across to where she was grinning like a cat that got the cream beneath her lace-edged mask. She could see it in his eyes that his grin matched hers when he pulled out his hand, opening it to show diamond earrings, a ruby necklace and a choker of pearls with one of the largest sapphires she had ever seen.

'Sweet Mary and Joseph,' Bobby said, his eyes as wide as saucers as he stared at the gems in Jack's hands.

'How dare you?' The gentleman in the carriage was leaning out now. 'Put those back. Haven't you taken enough?'

'You are correct, sir, we have taken enough of your time and your goods,' Jack agreed. 'Be on your way and have a safe journey.'

'Safe journey? Safe journey!'

The man was still blustering as the coach driver pulled away but Bobby and Garrett were laughing and whooping as they examined their loot.

Jack walked back to where Pru sat on her horse. She'd behaved. She hadn't moved from where he'd told her to stay. But she had contributed to the haul and felt a heady sort of power in it.

'My, my,' Jack said, removing his kerchief now that the coach was at a far enough distance. 'Quite the clever little bushranger aren't you, Miss Prudence.'

She couldn't help the smug smile when she removed her own mask.

'That was incredible!' she laughed, throwing her arms in the air before she threw herself from her horse and into Jack's arms. He caught her easily and held her for a moment, cradled against his body. The look in his eye told her he was about to kiss her before he seemed to remember Bobby and Garrett, who were now watching with interest, and he let her feet fall to the ground.

'How'd you know to look in the shoes?' Garrett asked, eyes narrowed.

Her smug smile returned as she addressed them. 'My dear gentlemen, women have been hiding their most precious items in their shoes for years. Travelling by boat, there were plenty of opportunists who liked to help themselves to what was easily available in cabins and trunks. But no man would ever think to look at a lady's shoes.'

When she glanced back at Jack, his expression held amusement and pride.

'Take the goods back to town and see Jones,' Jack instructed his men as they all remounted their horses.

'We're not going to town?' Pru asked, looking disappointed.

'No, I'm taking you home,' Jack said, waving Bobby and Garrett off.

Pru was practically bouncing in the wake of the thrilling encounter and Jack couldn't help but chuckle.

'Is it always like this?' she asked.

'Like what?'

'This ... I have all this energy.'

'Your blood is up,' he explained. 'You'll calm down eventually. It's a combination of the thrill and the fear. It makes one feel intoxicated for a while.'

'Intoxicated,' she repeated. 'Let's get drunk. I've never really been drunk, but if this is what it feels like ...'

He chuckled some more as she repeated every step of the heist from her point of view. They rode at a relaxed pace through the bush and Pru continued to ask questions at such a rapid-fire rate that Jack didn't feel the need to attempt to answer, even if he could have got a word in edgewise. She was positively buzzing and it amused him.

'Oh, I feel like I'll explode if I don't expend some of this,' she said, a gleam coming into her eye.

Jack always felt a little sexually aroused after a bail-up, and seeing the flush in Pru's cheeks, and the fact that she couldn't sit still on her horse, he wondered if she was a little aroused as well. Considering she was a virgin, he doubted she'd understand the warmth that rushed through the body to settle in the lowest parts of a woman's anatomy, or the tightening of her nipples that he could now see straining against the man's shirt she wore. His shirt. The cotton pressed tight against her lovely bosom. Realising he was staring at the outline of her body in his borrowed clothes, suddenly it was he who was unable to sit still in his saddle.

'Let's race,' she said, snapping him out of his lustful thoughts.

'What?'

'I'll race you back to the house.'

'Pru, I don't think that's a good …'

'Go!'

She'd kicked Misha into action before he'd finished his sentence, and he watched her race across the plains ahead of him. He had no choice but to chase after her and urged Persephone up to speed.

Damn, she's fast.

She leaped her horse over a fallen log and Jack's heart leaped into his throat.

And reckless.

'Blast it. Pru, slow down!'

'*Wahoo!*' she screamed like a banshee.

He'd almost caught up with her by the time they reached the gates of Little Windsor and they were neck and neck as they pulled their tired horses to a halt near the home paddock.

'I win!'

'It was a draw,' he insisted, highly entertained by her childlike behaviour. 'And you cheated.'

'I still feel so energised, so …'

'What?' he asked, dismounting and tossing Persephone's reins over the fence.

'Alive!' she yelled.

Letting go of the reins, she threw her leg over the horse's neck in a most unladylike fashion, and slid from the saddle into his waiting arms.

Since there was no one around to see this time, without hesitation he took her mouth with his. Each time he kissed her she became more and more a willing participant. She'd learned fast what excited him, and was no longer demure, no longer waiting for him to take charge.

Had she been wearing one of her flouncy dresses she may have missed it, but wearing the man's corduroy trousers she'd donned for the robbery, he had no doubt she would feel his arousal pressing against her. He tried to lean away but her hands grasped his hips and pulled him closer still. His control, already paper thin, snapped, and he lifted his head to catch the breath she'd stolen from him. But the want he saw in her eyes just served to take his arousal up one more notch.

Walking her backwards, he leaned her against the fence, his hands gripping the top rung of the wooden railing behind her head. Keeping his eyes on the ground, he fought his basic urges. He needed to slow down. He needed to slow down before he dragged her into the house and took her like a caveman. He felt her finger beneath his chin as she lifted his face to hers. Her green eyes open wide, watching him, she lightly flicked her tongue across his lips, teasing, coaxing until he gave in. His tongue entwined with hers and the moan that escaped her was like a red flag.

His fingernails dug into wood. He couldn't touch her. He couldn't give in to the desire that was like a racing wildfire in his blood. She was an innocent, regardless of the way she was currently kissing him. And they were unmarried. He still had enough sense in his skull to know he had to pull back.

Abruptly, he pushed off the fence and tore himself from her grasp, taking a good five paces away before he felt strong enough to turn back and face her.

Big mistake.

Her hooded eyes, her swollen lips, her breasts, lifting with her breath, straining against the thin cotton of the shirt, all enticed him, screamed at him, to walk the five paces back to her and take … and take.

'Jack …?'

The breathless way she said his name tugged at him, but he had to stay strong. 'I have to go to town.'

'Now?'

He took in the hurt that melded with the want on her perfect face. 'Yes, now. I have to work out the shares with the boys.'

He mounted Persephone in one quick movement, using the horse like a lifeline.

'If I don't go now, Garrett will spend my share.'

'Our share,' she added with a lust-filled, confused smile.

He ran a hand across her cheek. A dangerous angel sent to tempt him.

'Our share,' he said with a nod.

She stepped back and clasped her hands in front of her. 'Will you be home tonight?'

'I … I don't know.' Her smile faded and he hated himself for it. But he had a big decision to make and he needed time to think things through. He couldn't trust himself alone in the house with her anymore. Time was running out. 'You are the most incredible woman I have ever known.'

Her smile came out again and he felt the power of it in his chest.

'I'm not leaving because I don't want you. I'm leaving because I do. And I can't have you like this.'

'You can have me any way you want, Jack.'

'I've never been honourable about anything in my life. Will you at least let me be honourable about this?'

'Jack …'

He turned and rode out of the gates. Yes, he had some serious thinking to do.

When Jack returned to Little Windsor, it was almost midnight. The house was quiet, and one lamp burned on the dining-room table.

He stepped up to the door of the room Pru was occupying. It was closed but he couldn't stop himself from checking on her. He hated leaving her in the house alone at night.

As quietly as he could, he opened the door a slit. The light, pale as it was, washed across her face. Eyes closed, mouth parted slightly, Pru slept. He stared, longer than he should have, at her cream complexion, touched with pink from her morning in the sun. Every time he saw her face, her beautiful face … the revelation came as a shock to him. He'd fallen in love with her. When exactly, he couldn't say, but there was no denying it now. And she deserved better than a dirty, uneducated bushranger, despite his alter ego as a prominent businessman. Yes, she deserved better, but there was no sending her away now. He couldn't bear the thought of her leaving. Still, he had to remember it was a marriage of convenience. She had no more love for him than she had for Grantham. But at least she *liked* him; he recalled her words during her proposal a month earlier. Had it really been a month?

She bewildered him. Not once had she shown any sign that she was even thinking of giving in and begging to be taken back to Carrington Manor. He thought by now she would be tired of living rough with him. But she'd taken everything in her stride. Even doing housework seemed to make her happy—useful, she'd said. And she often sang as she worked. Her voice was angelic. She'd managed to shock him with a rather bawdy tune when she'd thought he wasn't about. That's what he loved about her. She could still surprise him. So gentle and vulnerable one minute, and so strong and adventurous the next.

And today … well, today, she had been magnificent. Dressed in ugly male clothes—his clothes—and battling against her nature to keep quiet during the robbery, and then that tip-off about the hiding places in the shoes! She'd looked so proud and exhilarated. And she'd never been so irresistible to him.

Pru sighed in her sleep and shifted so that the covers dropped a little. He groaned quietly. She still wore his old shirt. It gave him a thrill to know that some part of him, something that belonged to him at least, was pressed against her warm, firm body. What would it smell like? He liked the idea of wearing that shirt again, being able to smell her fresh scent wherever he wore it. He was losing his mind. To preserve what was left of his sanity, he backed out of the room.

Four weeks they had been cohabitating. He'd given her the time she needed—the time he needed—to be sure that she belonged with him. But he could put it off no longer. Moving back out to the stables, he mounted D'Artagnan. Leaving in the middle of the night was a cowardly move, but it was the only move he had left.

Nine

Pru spent a fitful night and was up earlier than usual. She'd tossed and turned in her bed, having worked herself up to a state she knew would only be sated by Jack's kisses and hands. Hands that he still refused to lay on her, damn him. It was romantic, and she admired him for his patience and his strength, but didn't he know how much she wanted him to make love to her?

Having dressed and made breakfast, she went to the little spare room to see if Jack was awake. He must have returned very late from town, as she hadn't heard him come home. The door was slightly ajar and she pushed it a little to see if he was there. No Jack. The bed was made, just as she had left it the day before.

She followed her instincts out to the barn, where Persephone and Misha stood chomping on their morning feed. They lifted their heads to look at her momentarily before digging back into their chaff. He must have come back at some point in the night, or early that morning, and had taken the time to feed the horses. But why had he gone out again?

'He's run away again, has he?' she asked Misha, giving her a good scratch.

A few hours later Pru heard a horse and wagon coming up the driveway, and opening the front door she stepped out onto the wide wooden porch to see Jack pulling a small dray to a halt at the bottom of the steps. When he grinned at her before jumping down off the wagon, she smiled and placed a hand over her belly. It never failed to amaze her how the sight of him caused butterflies to wake in her stomach.

'Where have you been?' she asked. 'And where did you get the dray?'

'I'm sorry I was gone so long,' Jack responded. 'I needed to go a little further afield for this particular delivery, and required something larger to carry it in.'

'Another present? For me?' she asked, clapping her hands in delight.

Taking a step forward to help him unload the dray of whatever he'd bought, she stopped dead when instead he unloaded a man, bound and gagged.

Jack walked his prisoner towards the house and her eyes widened as she saw the man's distinctive clothing.

'What's this?'

'It's a priest.'

'I can see that,' she said. 'Why is he bound and gagged and standing on our doorstep?'

'He wouldn't come of his own accord.'

'So ... you kidnapped him? You kidnapped a priest?'

'He said we had to come to church on Sunday,' Jack said, as though it ought to make sense to her. 'But I needed him to marry us today. He refused. So I talked him into it.'

Pru struggled against the smile that threatened. 'How romantic.'

Jack removed the gag from the old priest's mouth. The man coughed and spluttered. 'He dragged me out of my bed before dawn. Made me get dressed. Dragged me all the way here from Daylesford.'

'Daylesford?' Pru shot another angry look at Jack.

'Well, I couldn't use a priest from Ballarat. They all know me.'

'Really?' Pru raised an eyebrow. 'Priests know you?'

Jack rolled his eyes. 'Fine, so I've never set foot inside a church in my life. But I couldn't risk anyone recognising me from town. This was the only way.'

'Untie his hands too,' Pru ordered.

'But …' Jack started, rubbing his chin as he hesitated. 'He already hit me once.'

'I'd say you deserved at least one, wouldn't you?'

'What happened to "how romantic"?' Jack huffed.

She stepped down the wooden steps and kissed him. Then she slapped him across the back of the head.

'Ow!'

'I was being sarcastic, you madman.' Pru shook her head and turned to the priest.

'Father, I apologise for my wayward, romantic husband to be. You are free to go.'

'Now hold on,' Jack complained. 'I brought him here to marry us and that's exactly what he's going to do.'

'I'll not be married by a man of God who is being held against his will.'

'I do not know why you agreed to marry this reprobate, child,' the priest said, rubbing his rope-burned wrists.

'She proposed to me,' Jack grumbled.

Pru ignored him. 'Can I at least offer you a cup of tea before you go, Father?'

The priest looked from Jack to Prudence with some remaining suspicion before he yielded. 'The name is Father Flaherty. Your friend here did not even bother to ask.'

'You were too busy taking swings at me,' Jack threw in.

'You were dragging me out of my bed!'

'Jack, enough!' Pru ordered.

'A cup of tea, you say?' the priest said, ignoring Jack and stepping up onto the porch. 'Don't mind if I do.'

Both of them turned their backs on Jack and walked into the house.

Jack stood on the doorstep for a good minute trying to figure out just what Pru was up to. She had been angry, that was certain enough, but there was something in the manner of the last grin she'd shot him before she headed inside. She was up to something. She got that same look in her eye right before she tormented him in some way with her feminine wiles. He'd always known women to be a devious species, but none came close to the pure calculating intelligence of his Prudence. Her smarts could make her a dangerous adversary.

Curious, and not a little wary, he stepped into the house. Prudence was just setting the teapot on the table to steep while Father Flaherty washed his hands. Jack opened his mouth to speak but Pru shot him a look of censure that had him closing it quick smart.

'You live here with this morally corrupt man?' Father Flaherty asked, eyeing Jack. 'Alone?'

'I do,' she answered easily. 'He's not so bad, kidnapping aside.'

'Surely you have a family somewhere who are worried about you,' the priest continued as Prudence poured the tea. 'A mother and father who would be distressed to know you are living with such a depraved ruffian?'

Jack saw a moment of pain flicker over Pru's face as the priest mentioned her mother. With hands that shook, she put the teapot down. Jack made a move towards her but she stopped him with a raised hand. Her chin went up and she steeled herself before speaking.

'My parents are dead, Father,' she said with a strength that he admired. 'I have no family but Jack.'

She crossed glances with him and his heart flew at the frail smile she gave him. God, how he loved her in that moment. He was her family. Neither of them had known their parents, but they were each other's family now.

If Jack had been concerned the priest would persuade Pru she was better off going home to her grandmother, he'd been mistaken. She was a determined woman—he knew it only too well—and she seemed determined to be with him. God knew why. And only God knew what he had done to deserve her.

'I'm sorry to hear that,' the priest said, softening, and he spent a long time looking between Jack and Pru as they finally came to stand together. United.

'But you *are* unmarried,' Father Flaherty said, giving them both a look of disapproval.

'And that's why I went to find a priest,' Jack tossed in. Pru cleared her throat and silenced him with a hard look.

'It is true,' Pru said, sitting down at the table across from Father Flaherty. 'Jack went about things the wrong way, but he only wished to make an honest woman of me before we ...' she blushed on cue, 'before we consummate our love.'

The priest studied her, as though he could tell whether her maidenhead had been compromised just by looking at her face.

'And do you love him?' Father Flaherty asked.

Jack tensed. They hadn't made any declarations of love. He'd believed all along that she only thought of it as a marriage of convenience, as she had stated when she'd proposed. But over the past few weeks, her actions had led him to hope that she might actually care about him. Just because he'd loved her since the kiss they'd shared at the ball didn't mean she loved him back. She looked up at Jack in such a way to make his heart turn over in his chest and his pulse quicken.

'Yes,' she said softly, keeping her eyes on his. 'Yes, I love him.'

Jack exhaled, relieved, not even realising he had been holding his breath for her answer.

'And you, kidnapper,' the priest asked in a less approving voice. 'Do you love her?'

'Yes,' he said quickly, not taking his eyes from hers. 'Yes, I love her.'

Her smile lit him up.

'Well then.' The priest stood. 'I can see there is love between you. Even if I think you can do better, Miss Prudence.'

Jack scowled, but he really couldn't argue. She could do better than him.

'If you will follow me outside, I shall marry you here and now as you so impatiently insist, and then you can drive me back to town, Master Jack.'

Jack stared at the priest surprised, and exchanged looks with Pru, who was grinning from ear to ear. Her cunning plan had worked. She'd been making sure the priest would marry them before he left.

She stood to follow the priest outside.

'Wait!'

Father Flaherty and Pru stopped, surprised at Jack's outburst. He walked to her and took her hands.

'Pru, my love,' he started. 'If you would prefer a proper ceremony with a dress and a cake, we can wait. I can wait. If that's what you want.'

'After you stole a priest for me?' she asked, kissing his cheek. 'I want to marry you, Jack Fairweather. Now.'

He grinned, relieved. He'd lied. He couldn't wait, and was thrilled that she didn't seem to want to wait either.

'Lead on, Father,' he said, and followed them out onto the porch.

He picked a few wildflowers for Pru to hold as the priest gave the marriage rites. They exchanged rudimentary vows and Pru eyed him suspiciously when he presented her with a stunning gold wedding ring.

'Where did you get that?'

'At a jewellery store.'

'You mean you bought it?'

He huffed, offended as he realised she thought he had stolen the ring. 'Of course I bought it! I bought it two days after you came to live with me.'

He saw the purse of her lips as she tried not to laugh when she held out her hand. He slipped the ring on her finger and shook his head at her mistrust.

'I now pronounce you man and wife,' Father Flaherty said. 'You may kiss the—'

But Jack was already kissing his wife. His hands were on her cheeks and his mouth melded with hers with such fervour the priest had to finally interrupt.

'Right.' Father Flaherty closed his Bible with a loud snap. 'Can I go home now?'

'Of course,' Pru said with a giggle as she and Jack parted reluctantly. 'Jack, take the man home.'

He hated to leave his new bride to take the long journey to Daylesford and back. But when the priest had moved away to the dray and out of earshot, Pru grabbed Jack and kissed him again.

'Hurry back,' she said in a low voice. 'I'll be waiting.'

His blood heated at the unmistakable desire glowing in her eyes. A month of pent-up frustration between them was bordering on incendiary. Oh, he would hurry alright.

Rushing to the wagon, he helped the priest into the back before climbing aboard and taking the reins. As he turned them out towards the road, he looked back. The last thing he saw was Pru standing on the porch in her shabby day dress, looking like the most beautiful bride in the world.

Jack had never moved the dray so fast in his life, with D'Artagnan pushed to his limits in the rush to get home. On arrival in Daylesford, he'd practically pushed the priest out of the dray while it was still moving.

With his heart pounding in his ears, he'd had to slow down at Dead Man's Bend when the tilt of the dray nearly saw him ending up another of the sharp corner's namesakes.

Barely a hint of sun remained on his arrival at the house. The night bugs were already beginning to take over the symphony from the birds of the day. With record speed, he unhitched the horse and set him to roam in the home paddock.

He gave himself a quick wash in the water barrel beside the porch steps. Then, taking a few deep breaths, he stepped up onto the porch. But as he reached for the door handle, his hand shook. He couldn't go rushing in to Pru like this. He wasn't a boy anymore, jumping into his first foray at sex. He was a grown man, for Christ's sake. Then why did he feel just like a boy? Maybe because the past month of living with Pru had him as worked up as an eighteen-year-old being treated by his mates to one of the girls at Miss Margaret's house of ill repute.

His anticipation had him aroused and impatient. His wife was a virgin and she would need him to be calm and patient with her. More than that, he wanted to be gentle with her, not run at her like a stallion in heat. Breathing deeply, he paced the porch until his heart rate slowed.

At the sound of the front door opening, he spun back, only to have his heart leap like that damned stallion at steeplechase. Pru stood in the doorway dressed only in a thin, filmy chemise. The same one he'd bought her when she'd first come to live with him.

'Welcome home, Mr Fairweather,' she said, her voice a low purr.

Sailors had been called to their peril by sirens with less song in their voices.

He opened his mouth to speak but nothing came out.

His eyes tracked down the ivory-coloured sheath. The lanterns inside the house cast a backlight, making the dress appear translucent so he could see the outline of her body beneath the thin fabric.

She turned slightly and the curve of one shapely breast caught his eye. As he stepped closer, he could see a pointed nipple pressing into the cloth.

Again, he opened his mouth but only a croak came out.

He cleared his throat. 'Good evening, Mrs Fairweather.'

She giggled, momentarily losing that sensuality and reminding him just how innocent she really was. 'I like the sound of that. Mrs Prudence Fairweather.'

She reached out a hand and after a moment of staring at the soft delicate skin of her palm, he took it and let her lead him into the house.

Walking slowly behind her, he marvelled at the thick lustrous waterfall of her sunset-coloured hair, sparking each time she leaned down to blow out a candle. He could get his hands lost for days in all that hair.

The roundness of her backside beneath the nightdress as they walked towards the bedroom made him want to reach out and touch, but he felt as though he were in a dream, being led by the siren song.

Finally inside the bedroom, he closed the door behind them. She'd gone to some trouble setting the mood. Candles burned low, casting shadows in the warm yellow glow. Fresh roses scented the air from the vase on the bureau, and the bedsheets had been turned down. It was his bedroom, but he hadn't slept there since Pru had arrived. He barely recognised it with all its feminine touches.

But it all faded when she turned to face him. His lovely, beautiful, exquisite wife, his virgin bride. He needed to remember that. He didn't want to frighten her so that she would never want to sleep with him again.

Carefully, he stepped towards her. Lifting his hand, he touched her cheek, rubbing his thumb across her full pink lips. His breath caught when she opened her mouth and sucked lightly on the end of his thumb. Undone, he removed his thumb and crushed his mouth to hers, pulling her against him. He couldn't get close enough. His hands sought her soft arse and squeezed, grinding her against his hardness.

At her surprised gasp he eased back.

Calmly, he told himself.

'Pru,' he said, softening the kiss.

'Mmm?' she murmured between his light kisses.

'I'm glad you're here.' He took his lips on a journey down her jaw, her throat, to her ear. 'But this last month has nearly killed me.'

He heard her soft chuckle and lifted his eyes to hers again.

'Jack, I thought of us as married the minute I started living with you. You could have had me in your bed from the first day.'

'You were worth the wait.'

Lowering his hands, he grasped the filmy chemise and gathered it, lifted it up her body, revealing first her long slender legs. His body tightened as he lifted higher, now able to see the dark red curls between her legs, her flat belly, and then, as the dress was lifted off and tossed away behind him, he got his first full look at his Pru in all her naked glory.

She didn't shy away, made no attempt to cover herself.

'Beautiful,' was all he said, before pulling her against him and kissing her until they were both panting heavily with their desire.

Then her hands were at his waistband. 'Let me undress my husband.'

'By all means.'

She had his shirt up and over his head quickly. Her fingers blazed a path across his chest and down his stomach, making him gasp and his muscles contract with the incredible sensation of having her hands move lower and lower.

Her hands shook as she worked the buttons on his trousers. There was no way she could mistake his want. He was pressed so hard against his trousers that when she finally removed the last button, his erection released itself with urgency.

She bit her lips to stop the smile, but he saw it. If he'd been worried about her being afraid of him, or his male parts, he needn't have been. Ever the adventurous student, she was fascinated, running her fingers along its length before reaching out to grasp him in her warm hand.

'Careful,' he warned, his voice gruff with his barely restrained desire.

'Did I hurt you?'

Her eyes were wide and worried, and he had to resist the urge to shove her down on the bed and take her straight away.

'No, you didn't hurt me,' he said, his breath coming fast and deep. 'We need to take this slow. And if you don't stop pawing at me like that, I will either lose my ability to control myself, turn you over and take you like a mare being serviced, or you will unman me as I stand here.'

Carefully, he removed her hand and stripping himself of the last of his clothes, he slowly lowered her to the bed. She opened her legs and reached a hand to him.

He shook his head. 'I said, we're going to take this slow.'

He proceeded to lie beside her instead of on top of her as she had so obviously expected. Biting back on his desperate urge to mount her and take what he needed, he ran his hand across her décolletage, watching one pink nipple rise as he squeezed it between his thumb and forefinger.

She jerked a little with the pleasure–pain of it. He did it again, with the nipple closest to him, following the pinch with a wet and warm sweep of his tongue. She cried out and he knew he had her. He would take her to such heights of arousal—the likes of which she would never have had with Frederick Grantham—before he took his own pleasure.

Jack lay beside her, his fingers combing in slow movements through her hair. It was such a sweet and tender feeling and Pru turned her face to his.

'You have the most beautiful hair,' he said. 'Golden like the sunset. Soft as new grass in the field.'

'Jack, you're a poet.'

'Being lucky enough to be with you would make a poet out of any man.'

She ran her hand lovingly across his cheek. Was this her big, tough bushranger?

'How did I get so lucky? How does Jack the Devil deserve such an angel?'

Her throat closed. No words would pass. So instead she kissed him. Softly at first, but then she found herself wrapped around him again, like a vine to a tree. He did things to her. With just a kiss, her body responded to his and she felt the warming of her blood, the liquefying where he'd pressed into her and taken her virginity. She took her kisses across his cheeks, down his jaw and to his chest. The light smattering of pale brown hair made her smile. He couldn't grow a decent beard. It was no surprise his chest struggled to show more than a few lonely curls.

He had groaned when her hand grasped around his manhood. She couldn't help it. The thing fascinated her. It wasn't as if she hadn't seen the male reproductive parts on animals. But they were animals. Jack was a man. And his manhood was impressive. It had hurt at first. That first slow plunge had stretched her until she began to worry that she'd never enjoy sexual intercourse with her husband. But then he'd held still, stared down into her eyes with such emotion, such a look of desire just for her that she'd relaxed, and her whole body warmed and welcomed him as though they'd always been meant to fit together. As he'd begun to move, slowly, gently inside her, the pain had subsided and a strange and wonderful sensation built and swelled until she found his rhythm and moved with him. Like a fever they'd risen together, melded together and as he'd ground his teeth and groaned she'd felt him release. She'd been so close to some sort of release herself, but hadn't quite got there. She wondered what that release would feel like. Would she have the same powerful reaction Jack had experienced? Now, just thinking about it, she wanted to do it all over again, to feel that building inside her, to see where it would lead her. Keeping him in hand, she moved to situate herself over the top of him.

'I need a break, woman,' he told her with a low chuckle.

Reluctantly, she rolled to lie beside him again, the opposite way to him now with her feet near his head.

A flicker of rising sun permeated the room, but it was still night as far as she was concerned. It could stay night for a month if that meant she would never have to leave this bed, so she would never have to leave Jack, and he would never have to leave her.

'Did you enjoy making love with me?' he asked, taking one of her feet and tickling her.

She squirmed until he stopped tickling, and when he looked down at her with sleepy, hooded eyes, she was lost again in the honey brown.

'I have nothing to compare it to,' she said with a little shrug.

He nodded, a small frown forming between his eyes.

She was being terribly mean teasing him this way. Chuckling lightly, she ran her hand down his bare thigh.

'Yes, I enjoyed it, Jack. It was wonderful. Is this what it's like for everyone? I wonder how people stay out of bed.'

'Many don't,' he said with a laugh. 'It's not like this for everyone, with everyone.'

'Was it like this for you with other women?'

His brow furrowed again. 'I don't want to talk about other women with you. You are my wife. There will never be another woman for me.'

His words made her happy, but at the same time she couldn't help but wonder how many women she would come across whose sly, knowing look she might catch. Would she always wonder whether Jack had had relations with this woman or that one? He'd led a colourful life before she met him. She imagined he'd been with many women. It didn't mean she had to like it.

His fingers ran small lines from her toes, across the pads of her feet and her instep, all the way up her calf muscles to the soft space behind her knees.

She giggled and shifted. 'Stop that, Jack. It tickles.'

'You know,' he said, continuing his feather-light ministrations on her skin. 'I may need to rest, but there are other things a man can do to make a woman feel good while he is replenishing his stores of energy.'

He tickled the back of her knee again.

'Tickling is not pleasurable, Jack,' she said, flicking his hand away yet again.

He grinned, slowly and deviously. 'Oh, tickling can be very pleasurable.'

This time he slowly ran his fingers up, past her knee, to the inside of her thigh. 'You just have to know how and where to do the tickling.'

Pru gasped when his fingers didn't stop but continued up to the apex of her thighs and into the soft mound of hair.

'Just relax, my love.'

She did as she was told and after a few moments of nervousness, she found she couldn't concentrate on anything but the sparks of electricity Jack was sending through her body with the gentleness of his fingers and his mouth.

She could hear sighs and moans of pleasure and realised they were coming from her. She'd never made those sounds before in her life but she'd happily make them again and again if Jack wanted to do this to her on a regular basis.

She was twenty-two years old, and thank God she was married. Because she didn't think she could go another day of her life without knowing the wonders of sex with a man like Jack.

The climax rolled through her and her cries sounded loud in the quiet room. The last thing she remembered was feeling Jack's weight fall to the bed beside her, his arm across her naked breasts and his lips against her neck. Exhausted from a full night of love-making, she drifted off to a heavenly sleep.

Ten

'Right, boys, let's hit the pub.'

Garrett rubbed his hands together before sweeping his share of the loot from their latest successful robbery into a sack. They were in an upstairs room at the Duchess of Kent, sorting out what they could keep and what had to go to Alfred to be sold on the black market.

'There's a hot game of cards and an even hotter woman waiting for a man such as I.'

'Stick with the woman,' Jack advised. 'You're shite at the cards.'

'He's shite with the women, too,' Bobby tossed in.

Garrett took Bobby under his elbow in a stranglehold. 'Take it back!'

'Never!'

'I'm a better lover than you, Bobby boy.'

'That's not what I hear.'

Jack sat back amused as they played about at fighting like children until they wore themselves out. When they were upright again, Jack laughed at their scruffy hair, their red faces. 'Oh, the ladies will adore you now.'

'You coming downstairs for a pint, Jack?' Bobby asked, straightening his waistcoat and doing his best to flatten down his hair. 'That Arabella woman has been asking after you for weeks now.'

Jack thought about it. He would have enjoyed a quiet pint with his mates. But he was a married man now. He could no longer spend his nights in boarding houses or hotels after a robbery, while his wife was at home waiting for him, hoping that he was safe. The shock of it was he not only *needed* to get home to see Pru, he *wanted* to. He'd missed her that day. And only Pru could satisfy the wants that coursed through his system after a good bail-up.

Since she'd discovered the joys of sex, she was more than happy to welcome him home from bushranging with open arms and fervent kisses that often led them to making love in interesting places.

When she'd come out to welcome him home one evening not long after they were married, they scared the horses in the barn as they'd ended up rolling in the hay like a pair of animals themselves. They'd made good use of the kitchen table a few times as well, until the legs had snapped under the weight of them and they'd had to break it up to use for firewood. Easy come, easy go. He'd never liked the table much anyway. Then he'd surprised her a few weeks later with another, much sturdier, shining cedar dining table he'd had delivered from the city. Sadly, it had backfired on him as she'd loved it far too much to besmirch with naked bodies leaving sweat on the immaculately polished wood. His groin tightened as he thought of his lovely Pru and their wild lovemaking.

'Jack?' Bobby's voice broke into his rampant thoughts. 'I asked if you're coming for a drink.'

'Ah, no, I'm heading back to Little Windsor,' Jack said, taking his time to pack his share of the loot safely into his saddlebag.

'It's late,' Bobby said, checking the time on the silver-plated pocket watch he'd scored that day. 'And Windsor's a good forty-five-minute ride away. You may as well stay in town and find a cosy bed and a warm body to keep you company in it.'

Jack remained silent, but Bobby must have seen the smile that had crept across his face as he'd mentioned a warm body in his bed. He'd immediately thought of Pru, naked and waiting.

Bobby shared a quizzical look with Garrett before they both looked inquisitorially at Jack.

'Unless there's a warm body at the house waiting for you.' Garrett narrowed his eyes.

Again, Jack said nothing, just kept loading his saddlebags.

'Jack the Devil, do you have a woman living with you?' Bobby asked.

'That woman.' Garrett stabbed a finger in Jack's direction as realisation struck. 'That tart that came out on the road that day. The shoe lady. She's living with you?'

Jack's jaw tightened but he kept his voice low and calm. 'Garrett, call her a tart again and I'll shoot you where you stand.'

Garrett made a snorting sound but Bobby was undeterred. 'Why is she living with you? Did you knock her up or something?'

'No, I did not get her pregnant.'

Bobby looked perplexed. 'Then what, Jack? What else are you hiding from us?'

'I'm not hiding anything.' Well, that wasn't strictly true. Their unerring stares of disbelief finally broke him. 'I got married, lads.'

Bobby continued to stare at him, unblinking. 'I don't believe I heard you right.'

'I said, "I got married".'

'Fool,' was all Garrett added, before he tossed his bag over his shoulder and left the room.

'And you didn't think to invite us?' Bobby asked, shock still evident in his pale blue eyes. 'Or to tell us, even? I'm your best mate, Jack. You don't think I would have wanted to be there when you got married?'

Jack didn't know what to say. Bobby's hurt expression cut him to the bone. In his rush to get married, he hadn't thought that his best friend in the world may have wanted to be there, to stand up as his best man.

Realisation registered on Bobby's face. 'You didn't trust us.'

He could have lied but deep down, somewhere in the pit of his stomach, Jack knew it was the truth. Despite the fact that they had already met Pru that day on the road—it wasn't his fault she'd followed him—fear and overprotectiveness had made him want to keep her as far away from this part of his life as possible; and if that meant keeping his friends away from her too, he would do it. He loved Bobby like a brother, and it wasn't as though he thought of him as competition—the boy was mad in love with Katie the waitress, even if he didn't know it yet.

'It all happened so fast. I'm sorry.'

Eventually, a slow smile touched Bobby's handsome features. 'Jack the Devil, the old married man.'

'Not so much of the old, thanks,' Jack tossed back with annoyance.

'Is that why you got married? You think you're getting old? Time to settle down?'

Jack exhaled a breath and sat heavily in a chair.

'I don't know how it happened,' he said, honestly a little shocked at how quickly his life had changed. 'One minute I was a single and carefree outlaw, the next I'm a married man.'

'It's one thing to live with a woman, but to marry her?' Bobby asked. 'How much whisky had you had?'

'None.'

'None? You got married plain and sober? She really must be somethin'.'

Jack's face lit up. He felt it, and it was obvious that Bobby could see it by his own returning grin. Concern crept in, and his smile retreated. He didn't know how much he wanted to tell people about Pru and her background. Her family were still looking for her. He'd seen the poster out the front of the police station in Ballarat. There was no reward for her return, he'd noticed. Granny was too cheap for that. Regardless, Pru had already made it very clear she no longer wanted anything to do with her family.

'And she knows about your slightly less than legal occupation. Is that a good idea?'

'That's how we met,' he mumbled.

'What?'

'I said, it's how we met.'

Bobby frowned at him thoughtfully for a moment, but finally the penny dropped.

'You robbed her?' He burst out laughing.

Jack couldn't help but smile along with him, until Bobby finally got a grip on his mirth and his expression changed as he put it together. 'The locket! It's her! The girl with the old bag for a grandma. You stole her locket and were carrying it around with you for weeks. Do you still have it?'

Bobby had known he'd held onto the locket? His friend saw more than he realised.

'No, I gave it back to her,' Jack said. 'But let's not tell Garrett that, he'll be more than put out that he missed his cut. Actually, I'd prefer if you kept as much of this from him as possible.'

'So, does this mean Jack the Devil is giving up the road?'

'Are you mad?' Jack said, snorting out a laugh. 'She married me knowing who I am and what I do. In fact, sometimes I think she is a bit too thrilled with it.'

'She did seem to get a kick out of it that day on the road.'

Bobby had no idea just how much of a kick she got out of it. She'd all but thrown herself at him when they'd got home.

'No, she won't ask me to give it up,' Jack said with certainty. 'She actually enjoys it.'

'We'll see,' Bobby warned, shaking his head in disbelief. 'At least let me buy you a celebratory drink before you head home to the little woman.'

Jack thought about it for a moment. He owed Bobby that, he supposed. What harm could it do?

'One drink. And then I must go.'

Pru decided that the house Jack called 'Little Windsor' needed a lot of love before it could really be called a castle. And by love, she meant work.

Raised a lady in a house full of servants, she'd never so much as dusted a table or made a bed, but she soon got the hang of it. At least she could be thankful that her grandmother had insisted she take cooking lessons from a French chef in London. Gran said the only way a lady could truly know how to set a menu for a formal dinner party was if she knew and understood which courses would complement one another, which cuts of meat to request the cook purchase, and how to present food in a fashionable way.

Washing the clothes was her most hated chore, but Jack had surprised her with one of the latest washboards and a hand-wound wringing machine. It was a trade-off, considering he'd really wanted to hire a housekeeper to do the hard work. But Pru wouldn't hear of it. It was less that she was concerned about a housekeeper querying his second life that had him coming and going at all hours of the day and night, and more that she wanted to be a proper wife to him. She'd never liked being waited on hand and foot, with servants always around every corner, no privacy to be found. And so, she worked. She cleaned and tidied and she dealt with the animals, which consisted of a goat that required milking, and four chickens that laid wonderful fresh eggs. With milk and eggs she was well equipped to cook almost anything and to bake the pies Jack was so fond of. She fed and groomed the horses and occasionally mucked out the stables, despite Jack's insistence that she was doing too much.

When Jack was home, they worked together as a team, fixing broken planks on the porch, and building a fence in order to keep the kangaroos out of the vegetable patch Pru had planted.

And when Jack returned from the highway, she always greeted him enthusiastically. It still excited her to see what he'd managed to pilfer from poor unsuspecting souls making the journey to or from Melbourne or Geelong. She knew her acceptance of his illegal business made her a terrible person, and she didn't know what sort of person it made her that she became aroused when Jack returned, loaded with money and expensive trinkets. Their lovemaking was always more vigorous and thrilling after a heist.

She wondered if he knew that he radiated pure sexual energy after a successful bail-up. His brown eyes would sparkle with mischief, as if he'd reverted back to the years when he'd first started ranging the highways. That look he got in his eye had a direct line to the deepest parts of her womanhood, and they inevitably ended up having sex wherever they landed, very rarely making it to the bedroom.

But on nights like this, nights when the sun had gone down and her beautifully prepared dinner sat on the table, with no husband there to share it with her, she felt the sharp stab of loneliness. If only he'd let her go with him more often on bail-ups, she wouldn't be left wondering where he was. The planned heist had been set for the late afternoon. The lowering sun could make a great mask if you used it at the right angle, Jack had told her once.

Looking at the clock on the wall she did the mental calculation. It was a two-hour ride to the choke point, and two hours return. The men would stop in at Ballarat to drop the acquired goods—she never had become comfortable with using the word stolen—with Alfred. Even with the travel time from Ballarat, he still should have been home by now. Perhaps he had decided to stay in town overnight instead. It had been a long day and he may well have been exhausted. She recalled he often used to stay at the boarding house before she'd come along. Blocking out the fear that he may have been shot or captured, she placed his dinner by the fire in case he did come home, blew out the candles and made her way to bed.

Just before dawn, Pru woke to a racket coming from the front of the house. She'd finally drifted off to sleep just before midnight, but hadn't slept particularly well, still keeping an ear tuned in case Jack came home. The voices grew louder, and then she heard the front door bang open and something smashed on the floor.

Terrified, she stayed in bed, grasping one of the tall, brass candlesticks for a weapon. When the bedroom door flew open, she let out a little scream, before Bobby all but dragged Jack into the room.

'Don't squeal like that, woman,' Jack reprimanded in a groggy voice. 'You'll break a man's head.'

'Christ, Jack, you stink,' Pru said, climbing out of the bed as Jack fell into it. 'Did you fall into a vat of whisky?'

'Aye,' he slurred. 'Was playing cards and there was a bottle, and then another bottle and then …'

He looked about him, eyes glassy and unfocussed.

'How did I get here?'

'Bobby brought you home,' she said, sighing with exasperation and examining Bobby. 'At least he looks like he had the good sense to know when to stop drinking.'

'I tried to get him to stay in town,' Bobby said. 'But he insisted I bring him home to you.'

'Wonderful.'

'I'll go now.' Bobby looked tired and a little worse for wear, but nowhere near as bad as Jack. 'My congratulations on your nuptials, Miss Prudence, I mean, Mrs Fairweather.'

'You think so?' Pru huffed, standing with fists on hips and scowling at her prize of a husband.

Knowing what was good for him, Bobby disappeared quickly.

Pru pulled on her dressing gown before she turned back to face Jack, who lay blinking at the ceiling. 'Was there some special event that had you out all night drinking?'

'We were toasting my marriage,' Jack said, trying to sit up. 'Come 'ere, my darling wife, and gimme a kiss.'

Pru remained at a distance as he reached for her. 'And you didn't think to wonder that your darling wife would worry when you didn't come home?'

'You'll not change me, Prudence,' he slurred again with drunken anger.

She blinked. Where the hell had that come from?

'I'm not trying to change you, Jack, I just …'

'You just need to remember that I am the man and you are the wife, and that means I can do whatever I want without you lecturing me.'

Pru expelled a long calming breath. 'Is that so? Well then, Jack the Devil, you great bloody bushranger, since you are so experienced in the ways of marriage, you may do whatever you wish for the next however long it takes you to apologise to me for that pathetic demonstration of manliness. But you'll be sleeping alone and you'll be doing your own cooking and cleaning, for I am no man's servant and no wife to be ordered about. I may not be able to change you, not that it ever crossed my mind to try, but you knew I was not the meek and obeying type when you married me, Jack Fairweather, and you'll not change me either.'

She stormed out the bedroom door, slamming it hard for good measure.

'Ow! Prudence!'

'I hope his bloody head falls off,' she mumbled, and set about pacing the living room.

Outside, dawn began to pale the sky and Pru stepped out into the cool morning, taking a deep breath to try to cleanse the fury coursing through her system. As the sun rose, it dappled through the trees, its warmth weak yet, the beauty of it not enough to mellow her temper.

Weeds had begun to poke their heads out in her newly planted vegetable garden and as she dug in, the manual labour was just what she needed to work off her righteous anger. But as time went on, and the exercise of ripping weeds out by the roots wore her down, she began to feel the prickle of tears behind her eyes. Wiping them away with the backs of her dirt-covered hands, she shook her head. No. She would not cry. She would not let him turn her into a blubbering mess.

Eventually, the emotions won out and she sat back on her bottom in the garden and wept. Had she made a mistake? She'd wanted freedom and had thought that by marrying Jack she would be free of all the things that tied and bound a woman of circumstance. All she'd found after only a few weeks of wedded bliss were shackles of a different kind. She hadn't forced him into marriage, but he seemed to know less about relations between a man and woman than she did. Although she was sure he knew plenty about affairs of a sexual nature, the emotional relationship between a man and woman was definitely a mystery to him.

It would do her no good to think about Jack's sexual history, and it took a huge effort to push back the fears that he had spent the previous night with one of his lady friends.

One night with the boys and they had no doubt filled his head full of rubbish about wives changing their husbands and turning into nagging shrews. Her grandmother had all but nagged her grandfather to death, and Pru had been determined never to become like that. But nor would she sit around and worry herself to death over a man who couldn't care less that she was left alone overnight while he went out and got three sheets to the wind.

Hunger and thirst had Pru returning to the house. Opening the bedroom door, she saw Jack, still sprawled on the bed exactly as he'd fallen, unconscious and snoring so loudly it was a wonder he didn't wake himself up.

Closing the door, she left him to his sleep. He'd have one hell of a hangover when he woke and, she thought smiling, she would enjoy that immensely. It might even be a good time to hang those pictures Jack had bought to liven up the walls of the house. A good, well-placed and loud—very loud—nail in the wall ought to do the trick.

Four hours later, Pru was grinding ingredients to make a pie when Jack emerged from the bedroom. He grunted. Twice. Groaned a few more times and then sat down at the dining table where Pru worked the handle on the mincer. With his head in his hands, he looked up at her through the hair that had fallen across his face.

'What are you making?'

'Pie,' she said, her tone curt. 'Beef.'

'Sounds wonderful.'

'And kidneys.'

And with that she tossed the bowl in front of him. He went green and gagged a little before making a quick exit out the back door.

Revenge was a dish best served with a bowl of slimy-looking raw kidneys.

Pru kept grinding and smiled smugly as she listened to him heaving over the porch railing. He stayed outside for a while and when he returned, she'd set about hammering nails into the wall.

'Christ, woman, give over,' he grumbled. 'Can't you see I'm in pain?'

Ignoring him, she set another nail in place and slammed it half-way into the wall before hanging a pretty tapestry of an English meadow.

He stepped up and took the hammer from her.

She graced him with a glare.

'Look, Pru, I'm sorry, alright,' he started. 'I felt bad for not having Bobby at the wedding, so I let him buy me a drink.'

'You could have brought him back here,' she said. 'We could have celebrated together.'

'I need to keep you separate from that life.'

'It's a bit late for that, isn't it?' she huffed. 'I've already met Bobby and Garrett. We've robbed a carriage together, for heaven's sake.' She suddenly felt very worn out. Her anger now depleted, her lack of sleep was catching up with her. 'Are you embarrassed to be married to me?'

'No!'

'Jack, have I asked you to give up anything since we've been married?'

'No.'

'Do I not make you happy?'

'Of course you do—'

'I don't understand any of this, Jack.'

His hands went to her shoulders, but still she couldn't let him touch her. The anger might be gone but the pain was still raw. She moved away, out of his grasp, and sat at the dining table.

'Pru, I never meant to hurt you,' he said, sitting beside her. 'It will never happen again.'

Lifting her chin, she met his eyes for the first time. The golden brown eyes she loved so much. The sincerity in them was real, even if they were battling the effects of alcohol and lack of sleep.

'Will you forgive me?'

Before she could speak, the sound of horses plodding up to the front of the house disrupted them. Not expecting company, they both headed out to see who it was.

A dray had arrived with a very large delivery on the back.

'More furniture, Jack?'

He looked as perplexed as she did at first, but then realisation crossed his features.

'Oh, of course.' His face brightened as he rushed down the steps to deal with the driver.

Pru watched, fascinated, as he climbed aboard the dray, undid the ropes and, with dramatic flair, ripped off the protective tarpaulin.

'A piano?'

'A piano,' Jack concurred, looking much more lively than he had only a few minutes before. 'I almost forgot. Before I went and got stupid drunk, I saw this in the music shop in Ballarat and decided you just had to have it. You said you play piano.'

'Yes, but—'

'It's probably not as nice as the one you had at the manor, but I believe it plays quite well.' He put out a hand to her and she rushed down the steps to the back of the dray where he helped her up onto the wagon.

Lifting the protective lid, she ran her fingers lightly across the smooth ivory of the keys of the upright piano.

'It's in good condition,' she said, pressing her right hand on the keys to play a chord. 'The tone is quite good but it might need a retune after having travelled the road from Ballarat.'

She turned and grinned at Jack. 'I love it.'

'Enough to forgive me?'

'That will depend on how quickly you can get a piano tuner out here,' she tossed back with a sidelong glance. 'And I'm not kissing you. Not until you've had a bath and no longer stink of day-old whisky.'

'Done and done,' he agreed. 'It's so good to see you smile again. I'm such a fool.'

'Yes,' she said. 'But you're my fool.'

Jumping from the wagon, he helped Pru down. She supervised while Jack and the two delivery men struggled to slide the piano down to the ground so they could carry it into the house.

Jack was looking so completely worn out by the time the piano was in place in the living room and the delivery men were on their way back to Ballarat, she decided to take pity on him.

'Why don't I heat you that bathwater now?'

'Will you play the piano for me while I bathe?'

'I'll try, but it may be a little off-key from the shift.'

He lifted her hand to kiss it. 'I'll take what I can get.'

Jack stripped off his clothes in the bedroom and cringed. Pru was right. They reeked. How could she bear to be near him? She should never forgive him after what he'd said and done. Granted, he'd been under the influence of liquor, but still.

His hand was on the doorknob just as he heard the piano. It was a soft, lulling tune and he stood where he was, mesmerised by the sweetness of it. Whenever he'd stayed at the Barnett boarding house, there had always been some woman tinkering about on the piano in the parlour. He recognised the melody, even if he didn't know the name of it or the composer, but he liked it.

Soundlessly, he opened the door and in a beam of afternoon sunlight, filtering through the window, Pru sat at the piano, running her long, beautiful fingers over the keys. A gentle smile touched her lips and her cheeks glowed in the warmth of the room. She had no sheet music, but was clearly playing by memory. She was magnificent. And he was an imbecile. What had his pride nearly cost him that day? And his childish behaviour. He was a man. A husband. He had to start acting like one.

He wanted to go to her. To kiss her. To take her in his arms, take her to bed and make love to her. But he'd promised he wouldn't do any of that until he no longer smelled like the floor of a seedy taproom.

So instead he crept across the room and stepped into the hot water of the tub she had set up. She cast her eyes across at him but never strayed from the tune. He marvelled at the calming meditation that overcame her; the softness in her beautiful face replaced her previous anger as she became lost, became one, with the music. He thought he knew every one of her expressions by now. He'd seen the despair cross her delicate features when she'd discovered the betrayal by her grandmother. He adored the way her smile came from her eyes as well as her mouth when she laughed, usually at him. And he knew the expression—his favourite, naturally—she wore when in the throes of passion, when they made love. But this new look of peace and contentment, as she filled the house with sweet music, had him falling in love with her all over again.

When the piece ended, she simply sat there in reverent silence, the last note fading from the room.

'You play beautifully,' he said. 'What was it?'

She turned on the piano stool to face him.

'Chopin,' she responded. 'Prelude number fifteen in D flat.'

Her gaze lowered to his naked chest. And there was that look of passion he adored. Her green eyes shone in the low light, and sparks flickered in them, reflecting the various flames about the room.

She unfolded herself gracefully from the piano stool and toed off her shoes. Barefoot, she walked slowly towards him, undoing the buttons on the front of her dress.

'Is there room in there for two?'

The seductiveness in her question had him hardening beneath the surface of the bathwater. He thanked God he'd let the smithy talk him into buying the large copper bathtub rather than the smaller, cheaper tin variety.

'I think I can make room,' he said, just as her dress hit the floor in a pool of fabric around her feet.

She stepped out of her many complicated undergarments before climbing into the tub, and he was treated to a quick view of her pretty, pale arse as she lowered herself into the water in front of him. Reaching an arm around her, he pulled her back against him. She felt amazing, her backside pressed into him, and his manhood twitched in response.

With her head back, her long golden-red hair tickling his chest, he nipped her earlobe lightly before taking his hands on a journey across her body.

'Does this mean you've forgiven me?'

She sighed. 'I took you for better or worse. Maybe this was your worst.'

He placed a hand over her heart, taking the opportunity to close his hand over her small breast. 'You're a tolerant woman, Pru. I'll try harder to be a better husband.'

'I'll try harder not to be a nagging wife.'

'You don't nag. Mrs Cromwell—the baker's wife—now there's a nagger.'

Pru chuckled, and taking his hand, she began to kiss his fingers.

'You still smell of whisky.'

'Then we'll just have to stay like this so you can't smell me so much,' Jack said, sliding his free hand down, down until he could cup the apex between her thighs. 'And I'll gladly spend the night pleasuring you, until you forgive me.'

'You'd do that for me?' she asked, her voice breathy and affected as his fingers began to tease.

'Oh, it'll be a dreadful burden to watch you in the throes of passion, my love,' he whispered against her hair. 'You make the best sounds.'

In confirmation, she moaned at his expert ministrations.

His thumb grazed across her hard pink nipple as she arched against him.

'You're the most seductive woman I have ever known,' he said quietly, continuing to rub her sensitive places until she was mewling like a kitten. 'I love watching you discover your sensuality, and … I love you.'

'Jack …'

He smiled as she lost the battle with her thoughts, and her body gave way to his demanding fingers as he took her up and over the crest.

Relaxed and satiated, Pru stayed silent for a while as Jack ran his fingers lazily up and down her neck.

'Jack?'

'Mm?'

She turned in the bath, sloshing water over the floor.

He looked down into hooded green eyes.

'I love you, too.'

He smiled and brushed the hair from her forehead, then kissed her there. No kisses on the lips until he no longer stank of day-old whisky. He knew the rules.

But she had other ideas.

She leaned up and fixed her mouth to his. His erection was standing at full attention now with his lovely wife kissing him, her warm tongue crossing with his, her centre lined up perfectly with his.

'The water's getting cold,' he said, using every last bit of restraint he had left. 'Shall we move into the bedroom?'

She nodded, kissed him again and then as elegantly as possible, she climbed out of the bath before him. He watched her slim naked body in the pale orange light of evening as she headed for the bedroom.

Eleven

On the rare occasion Pru coerced Jack into letting her join them on the highway, she kept her mouth closed throughout the heist, knowing that a woman's voice would give too much away. It irked Garrett all the same that she was there, and it confused Bobby. Bushranging wasn't traditionally a woman's profession, but she didn't care. There was no way she was going to be left sitting at home sewing and cleaning while the boys had all the fun. If she were honest though, she really couldn't comprehend why Jack gave in and allowed her to travel with them. Not that she would ever bring it up, in fear that he'd begin to agree with his colleagues.

She was fascinated with the precision and expertise the three men showed in bailing up fast-moving coaches. They knew exactly where and when to meet the coach for the best opportunity at halting them without resistance and wasted very little time relieving their marks of their belongings, before Jack sent the coach on its merry way again. They never injured—or even threatened injury to—any of the passengers or coach driver. Pru didn't delude herself that the same could be said for other bush-rangers who roamed the highways.

Occasionally, they came across those other types of bushrang-ers. It could be an amiable exchange of pleasantries between men of the same profession, a quick suspicious 'hello' in passing or even a friendly chat about the condition of the roads or a conversation where they compared business. Sometimes an agreement about territory needed to be reached, and that was always a tense dis-cussion fraught with danger. But Pru quickly learned that most other bushrangers deferred to Jack's gang. Jack the Devil had run with the likes of Mad Dog Morgan and Viktor the Vicious; he was not a man to cross. He was a patriarch of the industry, had been around since before the Eureka Stockade, and was to be feared as well as respected. To Pru, Jack was simply marvellous. A gentle-man, and a mastermind. And the most exciting man she had ever laid eyes on.

She may have kept her face covered and her mouth closed, but she was rarely just an observer. Ever since she'd helped them on that first heist, the men had agreed that she knew more about where a lady might hide her valuables than they did, and she often helped them to uncover a stash of jewels hidden in an odd place, or recognised the worth of a silver pillbox that the men may have overlooked as junk.

Astride Misha, by the side of the road during their latest bail-up, something about the coach driver bothered Pru. The young man was fidgeting in his seat, nervous or uncomfortable, she couldn't tell. All the coach drivers were smart enough to be afraid when bailed up by Jack the Devil, but this gentleman appeared even more agitated than usual. Did he have a gun hid-den somewhere? Was he just waiting for the perfect time to take it out and shoot one of them? But why hadn't he pulled the gun already?

The man wriggled on his seat constantly. Maybe he just had piles. But she began to wonder if he was perhaps uneasy on his cushioned seat for another reason.

Catching Jack's eye, she waved him over. He knew better than to question her these days, and went right to her.

'The driver looks nervous,' she said, keeping her voice low.

'Of course he's nervous,' Jack responded cockily. 'He is being robbed by Jack the Devil. He's terrified.'

'No,' she argued. 'He's squirming on his bottom like a dog with worms.'

Jack grimaced. 'Lovely image, darling.'

She ignored him. 'Look. Either he has a gun he's about to pull or ...'

'Or ...?' Jack urged, his jovial mood disappearing as he, too, noticed the man's inability to sit still.

'The cushion,' she said. 'Look how he sits on it. It certainly can't be comfortable, it's a very odd shape.'

Jack caught on quickly. 'He's hiding something under his arse. Smart bastard.'

Jack made for the driver, gun drawn in case it was a weapon and not what he hoped was hiding in the cotton pillow.

'Stand up,' he instructed the driver, pointing his gun at his head.

The man reluctantly did so, his hands in the air.

'Toss that pillow down to me.'

His hesitation said it all. Pru had been right. Something was stashed away in his cushion.

Jack cocked the gun. 'It's not worth your life, sir.'

The man tossed the pillow to Jack, who caught it awkwardly. Undoing the buttons that kept the pillowcase closed, he looked in.

Then his eyes met Pru's and a heartbeat pulsed between them, before he grinned like a madman.

'Thank you, gentlemen.' Jack addressed the passengers. 'You may continue on your way.'

'You'll be hanged, bushranger,' one of the men called from the carriage window. 'And I'll be there to watch your neck snap. I'll drink to your demise.'

'And I'll drink to your money.' Jack bowed as the carriage moved off.

Garrett and Bobby practically fell over each other to get to Jack, and when he opened the pillowcase, Bobby nearly choked as he dragged in a gasp.

'There's gotta be hundreds of pounds in here.'

'It's like a sixth sense,' Garrett said, aiming a suspicious frown at Pru. 'She's like a witch or somethin'.'

'I'll thank you not to call my wife names, Garrett,' Jack reprimanded lightly.

'Sorry, Mrs,' Garrett said, appearing almost worshipful of Pru for the first time. 'Don't mean no disrespect. It's just … she's diabolical. How did you know?'

'Human nature, Garrett,' she told him. 'He looked nervous. Like he was sitting on hundreds of pounds in cash.'

'He *was* sitting on hundreds of pounds of cash,' Garrett said, still shaking his head in wonder. 'You'd best watch yourself, Jack. She's too smart for the likes of you.'

Jack was leaning back against a rock, his arms crossed, grinning broadly up at her.

'Don't I know it.'

As they headed back to town, just before the fork at the Melbourne road, where Jack and Pru would part ways with Garrett and Bobby, they could see a group of gentlemen riding towards them.

'Dammit!' Jack cursed under his breath.

'Is that McAuley?' Bobby asked.

'It is,' Jack confirmed. 'Pru, put your mask on.'

'Why?'

'Just do it,' he demanded. 'And stay quiet.'

The unusual tenseness in Jack's demeanour had her doing as she was told, as the group of five men halted their horses at a distance from them.

'Jack the Devil.'

Pru made a study of the man who'd spoken. He was beefy and tall, and when he removed his hat to wipe the sweat from his brow, she saw a dark scar running across his forehead. He was obviously the leader of the gang, as the four other men appeared to hang back a little. Another gang of bushrangers, she surmised. Not the amiable type, not even the wary type. This was a gang that had even Jack on edge.

'McAuley.' Jack returned the greeting with a curt nod. 'You and your boys are a long way from your usual hunting ground.'

'Don't worry, Jack,' McAuley said, in an easygoing tone that had Pru's arm hair standing on end. 'I'm not here to take your territory. We're just passing through. Young Liam's mother died. We went back to Geelong for the funeral.'

'Sorry to hear that, Liam.' Jack looked across at the boy, who Pru guessed was sixteen if he were a day. 'Our condolences.'

The boy nodded but didn't speak.

McAuley flipped his coat open, revealing the revolver tucked into his belt. 'Of course, if I wanted your territory, Jack, I'd just take it.'

Garrett and Bobby flanked Jack and Pru as the two gangs stood in silence, eyeing each other off. Pru began to search the trees for a way out, in case they had to make a run for it. She could feel McAuley's eyes on her throughout the exchange and her heart began to bang against her ribs.

'Who's the new feller?' he asked.

Jack looked at Pru. In all the time she'd known him, she had never seen the fear in his eyes that she saw now.

'The one who won't take off his mask,' McAuley continued.

Jack turned back to McAuley and grinned. He was a good actor when he wanted to be, Pru thought.

'My nephew Peter. His ma would kill me, and him, if she knew I'd brought him out on the road, but he wanted a crack at the life. It's safer no one sees his face til he's old enough to drink at least.'

'Ah, I recall your sister.' McAuley laughed, loud and bellowing. 'Met her at the Eureka protests on the goldfields in fifty-four. She scared the shite out of me.'

'Aye, she'll do that. So, if you don't mind, we'd best be getting him home before she sends out the troopers and we all find ourselves guests of Her Majesty.'

McAuley nodded. 'We've a long ride back to New South Wales. Good to see you, Jack. Let's go, lads.'

The four other men, who had stayed quiet throughout the exchange, followed their leader, riding past them while Pru held her breath and kept her eyes down.

Only once there was some distance between them did Jack relax his seat on Persephone.

'Hell, Jack,' Garrett said. 'I near pissed my pants. Roarke McAuley! In Victoria?'

'Let's just get going before he changes his mind and turns around,' Jack urged, and they pushed on at a faster pace towards the fork at the Melbourne road.

After they separated from Bobby and Garrett, Pru and Jack rode in silence towards Little Windsor until Pru's curiosity got the better of her.

'I didn't know you had a sister.'

'I don't. McAuley met a friend of mine. He was a little too amorous with her, so I told him she was my sister. When that didn't stop him, she kicked him in the balls. He wasn't so amorous with her after that.'

'Is that why you had me cover my face?'

'If he knew you were a woman, we would have had a fight,' Jack said quietly. 'He would have seen me as weak. Would have challenged me to fight for my territory, and for you.'

Pru swallowed hard. Jack, Bobby and Garrett would have fought for her, and probably died for her. And she shuddered to think what would have happened to her after they'd lost.

'Blast it!' Jack finally blurted out. 'You cannot come out on the road with us anymore. What was I thinking?'

'But Jack …'

'I said no! You could have been killed today, do you realise that? We could have all been killed today.'

Seeing how furious Jack was, for once Pru kept her tongue. But it was more the look of fear he'd given her out on the road that stopped her from arguing with him.

Lying together in bed that night, Pru could feel the distance between them. Jack was on the other side of the bed, barely touching her, and it was the first time they hadn't dived into bed and made love immediately after a robbery. Meeting the McAuley gang had taken the thrill right out of it, for both of them. Determined to break that distance, Pru curled into Jack's side, tugging gently at the light spattering of hair on his chest.

'I'm sorry I yelled at you.' Jack's voice broke into the darkness.

'It's alright. You were worried. I understand that my being there was dangerous for you. Particularly today. They aren't like most of the bushrangers I've met so far. Most of them respect you, admire you even. McAuley sees you as a challenge, as competition.'

'Always has,' he said. 'Even when we ran together for a month or so, he would do his best to undermine me. He knew I hated violence, that I'd stand up for the women he tried to assault, and he played on it.'

'You ran with him?'

'That was in the early days.'

'You never told me how you got started.'

'I didn't?' he asked, running his fingers up and down her bare back. 'I was gold mining at Ballarat. It was hot, backbreaking work and, like many others who'd come looking for their easy payday, I'd found bugger all gold. It was easier to steal it from others. After all, I was a thief from way back. What did I know about working hard for a living?'

He stared at the ceiling, a gentle smile on his handsome features, lost in memories.

'One night I met a man in the Eureka Hotel, and after a few drinks he let it slip that he was part of the infamous Black Douglas gang. A group of up to sixteen men, it was rumoured, who terrorised the roads between Melbourne and Bendigo. I listened to his stories, asking questions and taking it all in like an avid student at lessons. Not that I'd ever been an avid student. But the drunker he got, the more he talked. I paid attention and a few days later, on the Ballarat to Melbourne road, Bobby and I robbed our first carriage.'

'How old were you?'

'Nineteen.'

'Nineteen?' Pru exclaimed. 'You were barely older than a child.'

'You're not much older than that now.' He raised his eyebrows suggestively. 'And think of what you've done and with an old man of twenty-eight. Nineteen is not so young.'

'It must have been a hard life,' she mused, thinking of him as a young man trying to make his way in the world. 'So why set up the transport company? Was it just a convenient front for the robbery?'

'Not completely,' Jack said. 'I saw a demand to compete with the Cobb and Co. It made sense. I had the idea, and I had some money saved. But I didn't have the brains to put it all together. I'd done some dealings with Alfred Jones. He'd fenced a few items for me now and then, and we talked about the possibilities of a legitimate business. He'd run the business and feed me opportunities for a cut of the takings. He was the brains. I was just the money.'

'You had the ambition and the acumen to get it all set up in the first place, and now the intelligence to continue to run both sides of the business. A man who robs his own transport company. It's genius really.'

'Genius!' he repeated, laughing uproariously. 'I've never been called *that* before. Genius you say?'

She pulled at his chest hair a little harder than was necessary. 'Don't let it go to your head. If you get caught, it would be both your livelihoods that disappear.'

He shrugged. 'It wouldn't much matter since I would be languishing in Pentridge for twenty to life.'

'Oh Lord, don't say that.' She rolled away from him. She'd never seriously considered the consequences of his illegal actions—the idea that he might go to prison. It lit a spark of fear within her.

'You don't need the money from bushranging, so why do you still do it?'

He lifted up on one elbow and met her eyes. 'You've been there, you've seen it. Why do you think I still do it?'

'The thrill?'

He nodded. 'Because I can. Because even though I own the business, I'm just a brainless bushranger.'

'Stop saying that, Jack,' she scolded, lifting a hand to feather through his hair. 'It's not true. You are smart and resourceful. You can be anything you want to be if you put your mind to it.'

'I thought you enjoyed what I do,' he asked, suddenly serious. 'It used to excite you.'

'It did, it does,' she told him. 'I just wonder how many lives you have, Jack. What happens if you get caught? What happens to you? What happens to me?'

He sat up and leaned back against the headboard. 'I said when we first got together, that you wouldn't change me.'

The distance he'd put between them again was telling. He'd said that once before, when he was drunk. She wouldn't change him. She wondered if he remembered. She wondered if he realised it was his armour whenever she suggested he try and better himself in some way. Moving up onto her knees, she laid her hands against his cheeks.

'I'm not trying to change you, Jack. I will stick by you no matter what you do for a living. I just want you to know that I think you are so much more than you let yourself believe.'

Leaning forward, she kissed him. His mouth remained tight. She'd upset him. She hadn't meant to. It was a sore topic, she realised. It was easy to forget how sensitive he could be sometimes. He'd been brought up in a boys' workhouse, no doubt with limited schooling. He'd turned to stealing to survive. She had no right to lecture him, considering the man he'd made of himself despite it all. But the legitimate transport business had her clever brain wondering. It was only a front, but what if they could make it into a seriously lucrative venture? Jack could give up bushranging and she wouldn't have to worry about him not coming home at the end of the day. It was something to think about. Later. Determined to change the subject, she kept kissing him until he relaxed again and his hands moved to caress her bare back.

All coherent thought left her mind when Jack rolled her over and positioned himself between her thighs.

'I'm going to explore every soft, warm, delicious corner of your body.'

She smiled up at him. The tired, contented smile of a woman— a wife—completely satisfied by her husband, the man she loved. And she did love him. It had been a marriage of convenience to begin with, but she had tripped quickly into love with Jack. It had surprised her just how quickly and how deeply. And he loved her too. And as he made love to her, and took her to heights of plea- sure she'd never thought possible, she heard the morning song of birds outside the window greeting the day.

Leaving the transport office, and Alfred with a nice silver dinner service, Jack stepped out into the twilight. And the first person he saw was Pru.

She was just stepping down from the dray and he rushed for- ward to help her.

'What are you doing here?'

'Oh, Jack, it's you.'

'Who else did you think was grabbing you about the waist?' he snapped.

'Never can tell when a girl might get lucky,' she tossed back saucily.

'What do you think you're doing travelling the roads alone?'

'Well, I thought I'd come into town and meet my lovely husband for dinner,' she shot back, her happy smile replaced by an exasperated glower. 'If you see him, can you tell him I'm looking for him.'

'What?'

'Why are you in such foul mood?'

'Sorry,' Jack said, calming down a little. He probably was over-reacting. 'I just worry about you being alone out on the highway.'

'But the most dangerous man on the highway is you,' she said, her smile returning as she leaned forward to kiss his nose. 'So I have nothing to worry about, do I?'

'Still, I would prefer that if you are going to ride alone that you take this.' He handed her a small pearl-handled pistol.

'I thought you said I wasn't to have a gun.'

'I'll be teaching you how to use it later. But for now, just don't shoot yourself in the foot, or me in my arse.'

'And what elegant lady did you steal that from?' she asked with one eyebrow raised.

He rolled his eyes. 'That doesn't matter. Just take it, put it in your purse.'

She did as she was told. 'So. Dinner? I haven't met many of your friends.'

'There's a reason for that.'

'I've met Bobby and Garrett,' she said. 'Who could be worse than Garrett?'

'You'd be surprised,' he mumbled. But her pleading expression could not be denied. 'Ah, fine. We'll go to the Bath Hotel.'

There were hundreds of hotels and taprooms in Ballarat to choose from. Some respectable, some not so respectable, and all too many of them downright seedy and dangerous. He wasn't about to take her into the Duchess of Kent, where he often used to drink with the lads and several other less reputable gentlemen— and ladies—of his acquaintance.

'The Bath does a nice dinner and the clientele is a little more palatable as well.'

She hooked her arm through his. 'Lead on, Mr Fairweather.'

'Very well, Mrs Fairweather.'

Entering the Bath Hotel, they discovered it would be a one-hour wait for a table for dinner.

'We'll wait in the front bar,' Pru told the dining-room hostess.

'Ah, no,' Jack said as she headed for the front bar. 'The Salon, I think.'

Pru thought Jack was acting very oddly, but when she saw Bobby walking through the glass swinging doors into the front bar she took her chance. 'Oh look, there's Bobby. Who's the girl he's with? Is that his lady friend?'

'Katie,' Jack agreed. 'And he's not really made a proper move on her yet.'

'How long has he been in love with her?'

'About a year.'

'A year?' She was gobsmacked. 'Oh, he needs my help.' And with that she took Jack's hand and dragged him, against his will, into the front bar.

Standing just inside the door, she gazed around. Her eyes watered from the haze of tobacco smoke that hung from the ceiling like a grey mist. She'd never seen inside a real front bar before. Her grandmother would never have allowed it. Tearooms were about as daring a venture as her grandmother would permit.

Men in mining garb of corduroy pants and blue chambray shirts mixed at the long walnut bar with gentlemen in brown and blue suits and waistcoats. Only a few women were present, several of them wearing dresses cut low enough in front to show plenty of milky white bosom. Working ladies, she assumed. She spotted Bobby and left Jack to cross the room.

'Bobby.'

He couldn't have looked more surprised as she leaned forward to kiss his cheek. She loved that he blushed the sweetest shade of crimson.

'Ah, hello, Prudence … Miss … Mrs Fairweather?'

'I convinced Jack to come in for a drink before dinner.' She turned her attentions to the pretty woman beside him. 'This must be Katie.'

The woman, who'd been sizing her up since she'd kissed Bobby, held out a hand to Pru. 'Oh, aye. How do you do?' Her Scottish accent was like a song. 'It's lovely to finally meet the woman who tamed Jack Fairweather.'

'I'm not sure I've tamed him, have I, Jack?' She laughed, but when she turned back to look at him, he wasn't there.

Scanning the pub, her eyes finally fell on him. He was trying to remove himself from a woman's very determined embrace.

Stalking across the room, she stopped in front of them, her eyebrows raised in question.

'Wait your turn, lovey,' the woman said.

'Actually, since he's my husband, I'd say it's always my turn, *lovey*. So if you don't mind …'

'Husband?' The woman snorted out a very unladylike laugh that jiggled the flesh above the bodice of her dress.

Jack carefully extricated himself from the woman to take Pru's hand, leaving the woman staring open-mouthed between Jack and Pru and their linked hands.

'You're married?' she asked Jack, fire igniting in her eyes. 'You bastard!'

The slap connected hard and attracted the attention of all patrons, who cheered or jeered before the woman stormed from the pub.

'Your first wife?' Pru teased.

'Very funny.' He looked so uncomfortable it was almost amusing.

Kissing his offended cheek, she examined the red handprint. 'I know you had a colourful love life before me, Jack. Should I be forewarned about any of the other ladies in the room?'

He scowled at her, but glanced around the room all the same. 'No. My face should be safe from further assault for now.'

She couldn't help but chuckle as they returned to Bobby and Katie.

'Shannon was unhappy about your recent nuptials, eh, Jack?' Katie teased.

'Shannon?' Pru asked. 'Was that the woman who slapped Jack, or one of the other four ladies who looked like they wanted to stab me to death as I dragged Jack away?'

'I wasn't dragged, I came willingly.'

'Your fans are legion, my sweet husband,' Pru continued to mock. 'I hope I don't end up with a dinner fork in my throat or arsenic in my meal this evening.'

'Pru ...' Jack sighed, long and suffering. Definitely weary of being the object of everyone's hilarious jokes, he steered conversation elsewhere. 'Not working tonight, Katie?'

'No, I've the night off,' she replied. 'The boys at the Duchess of Kent will have to make do with old Joe McLeary behind the bar this evening. Let's see how many times he gets his arse pinched.'

'I don't like you working there,' Bobby grumbled.

'You've no say in it, love,' she returned with a pat to his cheek. 'Besides, if it's good enough for the likes of you two to drink there, then it's good enough for me to work there.'

She turned to Pru. 'Bobby tells me you've been going out on the highway with the lads. They never let me join them on one of their adventures.'

Jack glared at Bobby. 'You promised not to tell anyone that.'

'Katie's not anyone,' Bobby shot back.

'Thanks so much,' Katie huffed. 'Just what every girl likes to hear.'

Bobby's eyes widened, his face turning red. 'No, that's not what I—'

'Come on, Pru,' Katie interrupted him. 'We'll get you a drink and let these boys alone to wonder what they did wrong. Give me some money, Bobby.'

He did as he was told and Pru followed Katie to the bar.

Pru studied the older woman as she ordered a whisky for them both. And not cheap whisky, mind you, but top shelf. A Scottish woman aged somewhere in her mid-twenties, Katie had thick, black hair that curled in big, natural loops down her back. She had the pale skin of a Scot and the temperament of her heritage, Pru would bet. She was pretty and confident, and strong enough to handle any of the ruffians that frequented the Duchess of Kent.

And Bobby adored her. That was evident in the looks he kept sending across the room. Watching out for her, watching her. It was sweet really. She only hoped Katie had the best of intentions. She was clearly very aware of what Bobby did for money. Was she with him for his money? Or did she actually have a fondness, or perhaps even love, for him?

'Sláinte,' Katie toasted and tossed back the drink.

Pru did the same and followed up with a huge inhale of breath as the whisky burned her throat. She wasn't much of a drinker, but she thought she might get used to the tasty liquor, slowly.

Katie's smile fell as she glanced back to where Bobby and Jack had now been joined by Garrett.

'Ugh, I don't like that man,' Katie said, a scowl marring her pretty features.

'What do you suppose they're talking about?'

'Don't know, but if Garrett's involved it'll be nothin' good. He's got a mean streak, and a good dose of stupid to go with it. If you want to know what'll get Jack killed, it'll be Garrett.'

Pru winced. 'Katie, please!' She didn't like Garrett much either, but to think he was a loose cannon that might get them all in trouble …

She kept her eyes on Jack as he talked with Garrett. Whatever the man was telling him, Jack's face was a mask. She couldn't read whether the news was good or bad.

Katie ordered them another drink and tossed it down with ease, while Pru chose to sip hers this time. 'Perhaps you can tell me why men are so stupid that they cannot read signs that are as clear as glass. I don't know what else I can do to show Bobby I love him and force him to finally make his move on me.'

'Then don't wait for him,' Pru said with a shrug. 'I proposed to Jack. It seemed to work for me.'

'Aye? You proposed to *him*?' Katie was intrigued. 'Tell me more about this proposal.'

Pru chuckled. Poor Bobby. He'd wasted so much time.

The four of them sat down to dinner together, once Garrett had left to head to Miss Lola's establishment, and Pru enjoyed Katie and Bobby's company immensely. She'd missed having another woman to talk with. Not that she'd ever really talked to her grandmother. But even having the company of women servants had been a pleasure. She hadn't realised just how much she'd missed the unique conversation of women until now.

As the hour grew late, Jack and Pru said their farewells and were about to leave the hotel when a dark-skinned man dressed in the blue woollen uniform and cap of the local constabulary pushed through the door at the same time.

'G'day, Jack.'

The two men smiled and shook hands like old friends.

'Bandi. It's been a while. How are you?'

'Pretty good, eh.' Bandi nodded and eyed Pru, confusion crossing his features.

'Oh, Bandi, this is Pru.'

'Nice to meet you, Mrs,' Bandi said, tipping his hat. He glanced over their shoulders and lowered his voice. 'Hey, you better watch yourself, Jack. New sergeant's looking into the robberies on the highway.'

'I know,' Jack said, lowering his voice, too. 'He's been asking questions around the office again.'

'You didn't tell me that,' Pru said, concern filling her.

'Don't worry, darling,' Jack said easily. 'There's nothing to find.'

Pru studied the constable. It seemed as though he might know Jack's true identity. But before she could ask, another policeman wandered across the bar towards them. Bandi moved aside as the senior officer stepped up to Jack.

'Good evening, Sergeant.'

'Mr Fairweather,' Sergeant Carmichael greeted him. 'And who do we have here?' He looked Pru up and down, licking his lips. 'Miss Lola's girls are getting prettier and more refined.'

Feeling him tense beside her, she put a hand on Jack's arm to steady him.

'Pleasure to meet you, Sergeant,' she said calmly, holding her hand out for him to shake.

He took it and, with lustful admiration in his wandering eyes, he bent to kiss her hand.

'The pleasure is all mine ...'

'Prudence,' she told him.

'Prudence,' the sergeant repeated, still holding her hand in his sweaty one. 'The pleasure could be all yours.'

'I'll thank you to take your hands off my wife,' Jack intervened, his jaw clenched so tightly Pru worried he might break some teeth.

'Your wife?' Sergeant Carmichael laughed. But when neither Jack nor Pru laughed with him, he coughed awkwardly, turning an odd shade of grey before heat flushed his face.

'Begging your pardon, Mrs Fairweather,' he said. 'My sincerest apologies. I didn't realise Mr Fairweather had married.'

Pru smiled and changed tack. 'Is it common for gentlemen of the constabulary to be so familiar with the ladies at Miss Lola's?'

'Um ...'

'I would have thought it improper for men of the law to be seen cavorting with ladies of the night. I wonder what your superiors would think?'

She heard Jack's quiet chuckle beside her.

'Never mind, Sergeant. We'll keep it our little secret,' she said in a faux whisper. 'But perhaps you could do me a little favour.'

'Whatever I can do to make amends, Mrs Fairweather.'

'I'd be ever so pleased if you would stop harassing my husband,' she said, her tone demanding respect. 'He is a legitimate businessman. Do you think it possible a woman like me should marry a criminal?'

'No, I suppose not,' the sergeant murmured.

'Whomever you believe to be the perpetrator of these highway robberies, my husband has nothing whatsoever to do with it,' she went on. 'I suggest you direct your investigations elsewhere.'

Eager to be gone, the sergeant dipped his head and left the hotel. Bandi just gave Jack a wink and followed his superior officer out the door, chuckling to himself.

Pru gave Jack a hard look. 'Why didn't you tell me the police were looking into you?'

'It wasn't anything to worry about.'

'Nothing to worry about? Jack, they must have enough information to believe you could be involved in the robberies.'

'They don't have anything but the ramblings of a disgruntled customer. A judge with an overactive imagination when it comes to criminals.'

'A judge?' Pru squeaked, a little too loudly. Jack grabbed her arm and led her out of the hotel to a less inhabited space. They walked in silence to the dray and, checking that they were finally alone, Pru launched out. 'You robbed a judge on the highway?'

'I didn't know he was a judge,' Jack said, still keeping his voice low. 'All I knew was what Alfred told us, that he and his wife were a wealthy couple moving out of Melbourne to the goldfields. How was I to know James Collins was the new criminal court judge?'

'Jack,' Pru groaned, leaning her forehead on the dray beside her.

'If Judge Collins has any suspicions that the business he was using was corrupt, he has no evidence to prove it. I'm careful. You know I am.'

She let go of a heavy breath and some of the tension.

'You were wonderful in there, by the way,' Jack said, moving in to put his hands against the dray, trapping her between his arms. When she turned into him, he kissed her nose. 'Imposing.' Kissed her cheek. 'Imperious.' Kissed her lips. Slowly her anger ebbed as his mouth teased hers. 'You sounded so much like your grandmother, even I was frightened.'

She froze and met his eyes, before pushing him back.

'That's a horrible thing to say.'

'Why?' Jack asked, blocking her escape. 'I won't begrudge your grandmother for giving you a spine, for teaching you strength.'

'Don't ever compare me with her, Jack. I never want to think I could be anywhere near as heartless as her.'

'You may have inherited her spine. But your heart is your own. And mine.'

Leaning forward, he kissed her softly, his warm full lips igniting tiny lightning strikes across her skin. Despite her best efforts to stay mad at him, she calmed and yielded, as she always did in his arms. He was impossible. Even after all these months, he still had the power to tame her temper, to turn her to liquid with nothing more than a kiss.

'Now, let's go home,' he said, his voice affected with his desire. 'I want to make love to my wife.'

'Well, it will cost you. Being with one of Miss Lola's girls doesn't come cheap, you know.'

She chuckled when he slapped her backside as she climbed into the dray.

Twelve

'Tell me again how you heard about this transport?' Jack queried Garrett.

It was late afternoon and the three bushrangers were hiding in a cluster of trees on the side of the highway.

'One of the O'Banyon boys said he saw the old man loading a lock box full of rare coins and some gold he'd picked up in Castle-maine. They're on their way to Adelaide.'

Jack hadn't been all that keen to let Garrett organise the robbery. The man could barely organise himself out of bed in the morning. But he'd made one good point. Robbing more coaches that weren't run by Fairweather Transport would throw off the new, tenacious police sergeant.

The pounding of hooves alerted them and there was no more time for talk. Covering their faces with the dark kerchiefs, they waited until the perfect moment, before darting out of the bush and into the path of the oncoming coach.

'Stand and deliver, if you please.' Garrett yelled.

That's my line, Jack thought, a little disgruntled. Swallowing his pride, he reminded himself that this was Garrett's endeavour.

Gun poised, Bobby held the coach driver under control, while Jack moved to the interior of the coach. Garrett, he noticed, went straight for the rear of the carriage, no doubt looking for the lock box he'd been told of.

'Gentlemen, we will not hold you but a minute.' Jack began his usual spiel. 'If you could remove your pocket watches and bill-folds, and any other valuables you may have on your person, and place them into this sack, we will get along just fine.'

The three men inside the coach cursed and grumbled as they did as Jack said.

'Dammit.'

Jack turned his head to look back at what had Garrett so annoyed.

'What is it? What's wrong?' he asked.

'Not a lock box.'

'What?'

'I said, it's not a lock box,' Garrett called back. 'It's an iron chest.'

Keeping one eye on the passengers, Jack stepped to the back of the carriage and stared at the heavy-duty safe strapped to the back of the coach. His heart sank. It must have weighed a ton, and a giant metal padlock secured the chest. There was no way they were cracking into it. What a total waste.

Garrett stalked around the coach. 'Where's the key?' he demanded, pointing his gun at the men inside.

'It was sent on to Adelaide ahead of us, for just this reason,' one of the gentlemen told him with a smirk.

Garrett lifted his gun, ready to whip the man.

'Stop!' Jack yelled.

'But …'

'Forget it,' Jack said, shaking his head as he stared at the iron chest. 'We don't have time, let's go.'

Irritated at Garrett for sending them on a wild-goose chase, Jack walked back to his horse. The air split with the crack of a gunshot. His own gun at the ready, he spun to see what had happened.

'What are you doing?' he yelled at Garrett.

'I can shoot the lock off.'

'Christ, you moron. I said, we don't have time, just leave it.'

'I can crack it.' Garrett was insistent. 'I can.'

'I said leave it.' The man was out of control and they were quickly running out of time. He glanced down the highway. If another carriage came along, they'd be caught.

'This was my heist,' Garrett demanded.

Jack stormed back to Garrett and got up very close to his face, keeping his voice low and commanding. 'I still run this outfit and if you have a problem with it, you know what you can do.'

'G, let it go,' Bobby called, trying to defuse the situation. 'We've got plenty.'

Turning back to the coach, Jack caught the glint of the gun as it came out the window. While he'd been distracted with Garrett, one of the men inside the carriage had taken the opportunity to reach for a hidden weapon. Lurching forward, Jack grabbed for it. It didn't take much of a struggle as the elderly gentleman was weak, but suddenly the gun discharged, the noise of it making them all jump.

'I'll kindly ask you to stay seated, sir, and hand over any other weapons you may be hiding,' Jack instructed.

'Jack,' Bobby called. 'You're bleeding.'

The adrenaline must have masked the initial pain, but as he looked down at his thigh and saw the spread of the thick, dark blood through his pale brown trousers, the agony flared immediately. 'Get everything you can and send them on their way.'

Garrett finished taking what he could manage from the cargo, before instructing the coach driver to move on.

As the coach rolled away down the road, Bobby quickly wrapped his shirt around Jack's leg, tightening it to stop the flow of blood. 'He needs a doctor.'

'No,' Jack insisted, gritting his teeth through the pain. 'No doctors. Just get me home.'

They helped get Jack into the saddle. The wound throbbed, and he swore as he tried to find a comfortable position.

Trying to move as fast as they could, they set off for Little Windsor. After only a few miles, as the pain in his leg became unbearable, he had to slow his pace.

'Go on ahead,' he told them, sweat pouring down his jaw. 'I'll get there.'

'Don't be a fool,' Bobby shot back. 'You won't make it on your own.'

'We're not leaving you,' Garrett added.

Jack's eyesight began to blur and he swayed in the saddle. He just had to get home. Had to get home to Pru.

Bobby reached out to steady him as he swayed again, but by the time they'd gone five miles, Jack was unconscious, slung over the back of Persephone like a sack of wheat.

It was always hard waiting for Jack to come home from a job. She knew she shouldn't be so excited about her husband's unlawful ways but it was as though she were living one of her beloved stories. Instead of escaping into the novels depicting swashbuckling pirates and Robin Hood, she was living her own real-life adventure. It was also wrong that she enjoyed seeing what Jack brought home from whatever coach he had robbed. The jewels, the silver, the expensive trinkets—even if they didn't keep any of it. That would be dangerous and stupid. It was always sold for cash by Jack's man, Alfred, either to a buyer on the black market or through his daughter's pawnbroking store.

Pru had had a large allowance, thanks to her grandmother, but she had never been able to access it herself. Which was why she had left Carrington Manor with nothing but the bag of coins she'd found in the kitchen.

Hearing the horses coming up the driveway, her relief was palpable. Jack was home. When she stepped out onto the porch, she was all smiles. Until she saw Jack slumped over his horse.

'Jack?' she called, confusion melding with concern.

Garrett and Bobby dismounted and lifted Jack from his horse, carrying him towards her. She felt dizzy at the sight of her limp and unconscious husband, and had to grab hold of the porch post.

'Bobby, what …?'

'He's been shot.'

'Oh, God.' She looked at Jack's lifeless body slung between Bobby and Garrett like a side of beef.

'Is he … dead?' Her heart pounded in her ears as she waited for the answer.

'No,' Bobby said, struggling to lift Jack up the porch stairs. 'But it's bad. He's lost a lot of blood.'

The men carried Jack inside and through to the bedroom where they laid him gently on the bed. Pru had to take a few deep breaths before she could move her legs and follow the men inside.

Staring down at her beloved husband, she gaped wide-eyed at the blood now seeping from the sloppily bandaged wound on his upper thigh.

'Go get the doctor,' Pru demanded, snapping into action. She slowly removed the shirt Bobby had used to try to stop the bleeding.

'Jack said no doctor,' Garrett grumbled.

'I don't care,' Pru shot back. 'I can't remove a bullet.'

'What about Doc Blackmore?' Bobby offered.

Pru shook her head. 'He's a drunk. He's no use to anyone.'

'He keeps his mouth shut,' Bobby said. 'He won't report the gunshot wound to the police.'

'I'll go.' Garrett nodded reluctantly and disappeared out the door.

Two hours later it was dark, and Garrett still hadn't returned from town.

'He's not coming back,' Pru said, leaning over to wipe Jack's sweaty brow.

'He will.' It was more for reassurance than because he believed it, she was sure. 'He probably had to sober old Blackmore up before he could travel.'

That didn't fill Pru with any confidence as she gazed worriedly at the man she loved, lying in bed, pale as death already, his wound still bleeding through the latest bandage.

'He'll be okay, Pru.' Bobby tried to console her. 'Jack's tough.'

'He's never been shot before, Bobby,' she replied, swiping a rogue tear from her cheek before it could roll down. 'What happened out there?'

Bobby took a deep breath. 'It was all so fast. Garrett was trying to get into a safe that was on the back of the coach. He was wasting precious time and Jack called him on it.' He stood up to pace the floor as he thought back. 'I guess the distraction was enough for a passenger to pull out a hidden gun and in the scuffle Jack was hit. If he hadn't turned back in time, the bullet might have been in the chest and he'd be dead. If Garrett hadn't been such a greedy bastard, none of this would have happened.'

Pru covered her face. Katie had warned her that Garrett would be the cause of Jack's death. He was stupid and reckless—a bad combination.

Just then the man himself burst into the bedroom with Doc Blackmore. Pru studied the doctor carefully. Despite being a little shaky and having bloodshot eyes, he seemed to be sober enough as he moved quickly to examine Jack's wound.

'That bullet has to come out now,' the doc said. 'Been in there too long already.'

'So do it,' Garrett demanded. 'And keep your mouth shut about it.'

'Alright, alright, settle down,' the doc tossed back. 'I need light, heat and whisky.'

'You'll not get a drink til that bullet is out of my husband,' Pru insisted, moving the lantern closer to the foot of the bed.

'The whisky is for him,' the doc told her calmly. 'Removing the bullet is going to hurt like the blazes. If he wakes, he's going to need it to dull the pain.'

Bobby left the room and returned a moment later with a bottle.

'Outside,' the doc instructed them all.

'I'm not going anywhere.' Pru sat on the edge of the bed.

'Do you faint at the sight of blood, my dear?' Doc Blackmore asked. 'Because this is going to bleed a lot more before I'm done.'

'He's already bled a lot and if he wakes you'll need someone to hold him down,' she said determinedly. 'I'm not leaving.'

'Me either,' Bobby said, just as determined.

Garrett just sat down in the corner chair.

The doctor poured whisky over the bullet hole, took a quick shot for himself despite the angry glare of Pru, then, heating the scalpel against the lantern's flame, he widened the wound before using his fingers to dig into the leg to remove the bullet. Pru did have to take a lot of deep breaths to keep from fainting. She'd never seen so much blood before and the metallic smell churned her stomach. Jack never opened his eyes, but his weak groans cut at Pru as much as if he had screamed.

'He's lost too much blood,' Pru said, once the bullet had been removed. The sheets she'd torn up for bandages were soaked in the dark red that had seeped from Jack over the last hours. The doctor was stitching him up, somewhat unsteadily Pru thought, but better than she could have done.

'Yes, he's lost a lot,' the doctor agreed, wiping the blood from his hands.

She watched the doctor walk over to where the bottle of whisky had been left. He took a long swig and, closing his eyes, sighed in relief.

'Keep the wound clean,' he instructed. 'Change the covering regularly. Are you a praying lady, Mrs Fairweather?'

'I used to be,' Pru answered sullenly.

'Well, I suggest you resurrect it,' the doctor said, placing a hand gently on her arm. 'For he's in God's hands now.'

He lifted the bottle to his mouth again, then pointed it at Garrett. 'You, smiley, I believe you can take me back to town now. There is a woman at a saloon waiting for me to satisfy her.'

'She'll be waiting a while,' Bobby murmured to Pru as Garrett led the already tipsy doctor from the house.

'Mmm, and sorely disappointed, I would say,' Pru added, sitting back down beside Jack. They both laughed tiredly, and it felt good, but inappropriate under the circumstances.

'Pru, you need some sleep.'

She shook her head. 'I need to watch him.'

'He'll be sleeping, too. For a good while yet.'

She didn't answer him.

'You're quite amazing, Miss Prudence,' Bobby said, and then frowned. 'Sorry, I mean, Mrs Fairweather. I admit, I thought Jack was mad to bring you out here.'

'He didn't have a lot of choice in the matter,' she said with a wistful smile as she remembered the day she had proposed to Jack.

'You were so dainty and delicate. Even dressed as a man, you were swallowed up by his clothes.' Bobby chuckled. 'I couldn't understand why he'd allowed you to travel with us, or what he saw in you. But I see it now. You are stronger than any woman I have ever met. And you don't judge us, as so many would.'

'I was raised to be delicate and dainty,' she said. 'But it's not what's in my nature. I love Jack, despite his many flaws. I found the adventure I was seeking with him. Although, now I am worried that the adventure is becoming just a little too real for both of us.'

Bobby laid a hand on her shoulder. 'He'll come out of this.'

'This time maybe,' she said, pulling the blankets up to keep Jack warm. 'But what about next time?'

When Bobby didn't answer her, she looked up at him. 'I can't lose him.'

'You won't.'

Pru turned her exhausted gaze back to Jack. His breathing was uneven, and sweat matted his dark hair, pasting it to his forehead.

'Try and get some rest,' Bobby said, and left the room, closing the door behind him.

Jack didn't stay still for long. He writhed with the pain and the fever. He became delirious, calling out strange things that she didn't understand half the time. Pru passed a tense night, watching him move in and out of consciousness. The fever he ran was scalding, even to her touch, and she spent half the night using wet, cool cloths to try to bring it down.

In the morning, Bobby came into the room with Katie at his side.

'Garrett came to the pub, told me what happened,' Katie said, tossing her hat aside. 'Pru, you look exhausted. Why don't you let me take over for a while?'

Pru shook her head. 'I can't leave him.'

'You need to sleep and you need to eat,' Katie instructed. 'You're no good to him like this.'

Finally, with her stomach growling, Pru had no choice but to give in. She nodded and stood up to leave, but took one last look at Jack before she went out to the living area. Garrett was nowhere to be seen and she was glad. He probably hadn't returned from town after dropping the doctor back. She hoped he felt the weight of what he'd caused, but she doubted it.

She made a pot of tea and sat down to drink it, but after a few sips she had to rush out the back door to heave it up into the garden. It was the stress, she was sure. It had been a very traumatic night and her system just couldn't cope with anything yet. With a cool cup of water, she rinsed her mouth, drank another cupful, and took a piece of bread to try to get something into her stomach. She felt hollowed out. But Katie was right. She was no good to Jack if she got sick too. She nibbled on the bread carefully and her stomach seemed to accept it, so she continued eating. She tried the tea again and found it stayed put this time.

Feeling better, she went back into the bedroom. Katie was looking at the wound beneath the bandage and Pru gasped at the swelling and redness around the bullet hole.

Katie looked up at her solemnly. 'It's inflamed.'

Pru nodded. 'The doctor said it would be.'

As Katie prodded at the wound, a foul-smelling pus seeped from the haphazardly sewn-together skin. Pru retched, and even Katie had to turn her head away from the stench.

'Blood poisoning. I've seen this before.'

'Do you have nursing experience?'

Katie's face was bleak. 'When miners ran from the Eureka Stockade, many of them hid for weeks with bullet wounds. They couldn't see real doctors because the police and the army were watching for fugitives. I helped a few men who'd made it as far as Geelong. I was able to save some, but most had left it too late to seek help, and succumbed to the poison in their blood.' She shook herself, as though she were shaking off the bad memories, and studied Jack's leg. 'I can clean out the wound, but it's going to be painful and not pretty. But Pru, if it's got too far into his blood … you'd best prepare yourself.'

Pru nodded numbly. She wanted to help but her stomach revolted at the sight of the badly infected leg. Her eyes filled with tears and she rushed from the room, again losing what was in her stomach to the rose bushes in the backyard. Jack was knocking at death's door, and she couldn't help him.

She heard Jack's weak groan and assumed Katie had decided to get to work immediately. At least a groan meant he was conscious enough to feel pain, and he was not dead yet. But all the same, she sat on the porch steps in the cool morning sun and prayed like she had never prayed before.

Katie's cleaning of the wound seemed to help bring down the fever a little and Jack finally fell into a deep and calm sleep. There was no change by nightfall and finally, giving in to her exhaustion, Pru climbed up on the bed on Jack's good side and lay beside him. If he was going to die, she wanted her arms around him to be the last thing he felt.

The light tickling on Pru's cheek brought her back to the surface from a deep and heavy slumber. Her body ached, her eyes didn't want to open and her stomach was doing horrible somersaults.

But the tickling continued and she finally had to open her eyes. Eyes the colour of warm honey stared back at her from a close distance. The usual spark and lustre was missing but she recognised those eyes. Her love. Her Jack.

'Jack,' she said, sitting upright, suddenly very awake. 'Oh, Jack,' she cried with relief, leaning over to kiss him, thrilled to feel his skin was no longer hot to the touch. 'I was so scared.'

'My sweet angel,' he said, his voice raspy. He coughed. 'Drink?'

She leaned behind her to take the beaker of water by her bedside table and lifted his head to give him a little sip.

'Not too much now,' she said, as he tried to gulp it thirstily.

He rested his head back down and she got up from the bed to check his wound.

Katie and Bobby must have heard them talking, because they were in the room moments later.

'Jack,' Bobby said, grinning like a madman. 'You gave us all a scare.'

Katie took a look at the wound too, and her smile was enough to lift Pru's spirits.

'I think he'll be fine,' Katie said, nodding to Pru and then sending a wink at Jack. 'You've got nine lives, Jackie boy.'

'Excuse me,' Pru said, as her somersaulting stomach revolted against her and she rushed out to the backyard. She fell to her knees, but with nothing in her stomach to begin with, she only retched. Lifting her face to the warmth of the rising sun, she closed her eyes, said a little prayer of thanks, and burst into tears again. Tears of release, racking, violent sobs that she had held on to throughout Jack's ordeal, that she could not hold on to anymore. She muffled her sobs with the skirt of her dress, and only when she'd got it all out did she stand and turn back to the house.

Katie stood at the door watching and gave her a huge hug when she stepped back up to the porch.

'He's going to live, Katie.'

Katie nodded. 'He's going to live.'

Pru took a deep breath, wiped the tears from her face and straightened her spine determinedly. 'If he goes back out on the road after this, I'll kill him myself.'

Thirteen

It was a slow road to recovery for Jack. He slept a lot, but Pru stayed by his side, barely sleeping herself in those first few days, until finally she became so fatigued that Katie banished her to the spare bedroom and ordered her to get a solid night's sleep.

And she did. For ten hours straight she slept without waking. But when she did wake and went in to check on Jack, Katie stared at her with the oddest expression.

'Pru, you look terrible.'

'I slept well,' Pru said quickly, worried Katie would send her straight back to bed.

'How do you feel?' Katie stood and placed a hand over her forehead, checking her temperature.

'Tired. I have a headache and it's making me nauseated,' Pru answered, looking down at Jack. He looked better. 'How is he?'

'Fever's gone completely now,' Katie answered, a smile touching her lips. 'He woke once and asked for you.'

'Why didn't you wake me?' Pru asked, a little irritated.

'He was only conscious for a moment. Pru, you really do look awful. Perhaps I should call Doc Blackmore again.'

'No, no, I'm fine.' Pru waved her off, but leaned against the doorframe to fight another wave of dizziness.

'Right, that's it.' Katie grabbed her by the arm and practically carried her across to the other bedroom. 'You Fairweathers are an obstinate pair. Now get into that bed and stay there. I'll be back in a while with some soup.'

'Oh, I'm not really—'

'You haven't eaten a solid meal in days,' Katie said. 'Don't think I haven't noticed.'

Pru lay back on the bed and didn't wake again until Katie returned with a tray of soup and bread. It smelled divine and her stomach growled loudly.

'How's Jack?'

'He's fine, sleeping. Which is exactly what you are going to do after I've seen you eat at least half of this food.'

Pru pushed herself up in bed and let Katie feed her.

'You need to get strong, Pru,' Katie said, blowing on the hot broth before lifting the spoon to her mouth as though she were a child. 'Jack needs you now, and he'll need you for the next few months while he recovers.'

The soup was delicious and she finished the bread as well. It all seemed to settle alright in her stomach, for which she was grateful.

'Thank you, Katie,' she said, taking her friend's hand. 'I don't know what I would have done without you here.'

Katie put the empty dishes on the bureau beside the door and sat down beside Pru again, examining her closely.

'So is it just exhaustion? A sympathy sickness for Jack, perhaps? Or is there some other reason you've been throwing up your food every morning?'

'What do you mean?'

'Are you pregnant, Pru?'

She sighed wearily. With everything that had happened in the past week, she hadn't paid much attention to her own body, her worry for Jack being paramount. And she had to admit she'd been in a little bit of denial since her first suspicions had arisen.

'I think I might be.'

'Then you certainly need to start taking better care of yourself,' Katie said, squeezing her hand sympathetically. 'I'll stay here at Little Windsor with you until Jack is mobile again.'

'I can't ask you—'

'You didn't ask, I offered,' Katie said in a tone that brooked no argument. 'Jack needs around-the-clock care, and you need to take care of baby Jack in there so that when his daddy wakes fully, he has something to spur him back to health.'

'Please keep the baby between us for now,' Pru begged. 'I'll tell Jack when he's well enough. I'm not completely sure he'll be pleased about it.'

'Why shouldn't he be? He's going to be a father. He'll be proud as a peacock.'

'Please, Katie.'

'Of course, 'tis not my place to be telling anyone anything.'

'Not even Bobby,' Pru checked.

Katie crossed her heart and spat on her shoe for emphasis, and Pru wondered if the woman had spent far too much time in pubs.

Over the next weeks, Jack slept a lot, regaining strength every day until Doc Blackmore gave him the go-ahead to move out of the bedroom for short periods of time. And none too soon as far as Pru was concerned.

Jack was not a good patient. He was grumpy—to be expected after having been bedridden for almost a month—but he was belligerent too, acting like a sulky child one minute and throwing things in a fit of anger and frustration the next.

Pru took his mood swings in her stride, just happy and relieved that he was going to be alright, that he was going to live. Refusing to leave him alone in the house now that Katie had gone back to town, she set up an order with the stores in Ballarat to deliver all their food and supplies to Little Windsor. And she wore herself out regularly, working the vegetable patch and dealing with the animals.

The first day Jack stood up out of bed, he passed out cold. Luckily Bobby and Doc Blackmore had been there to catch him before his head hit the bedside table.

'Too fast, boyo,' Doc Blackmore said when Jack regained consciousness. 'You lost a lot of blood and, now that you've built your stores back up, you have to give it a chance to circulate again. It's all sitting in your arse right now, since you've been on it for a month. It has to work harder to get up into that thick skull of yours.'

'Just shut up and help me stand.' Jack was determined.

The second attempt wasn't much better. But as days went by, with Pru's help, he was able to move as far as the chair in the living room, where he could sit by the fire. The winter cold made his leg ache and Pru waited on him, feeding him hearty meals to get his strength up. She'd help him work the leg to get some movement back, as even when he walked it was as though he had a wooden leg.

It hurt him to do the exercises, but he never complained, just gritted his teeth and sweated until he'd had enough, and would fall into an exhausted sleep. By the middle of winter, Jack was up and about every day, walking around the perimeter of the house when the weather allowed, determined to get back to his former agile self. Climbing aboard Persephone was more challenging even though he used the fence to mount the horse. But once he was on, it wasn't too taxing and Persephone was so in tune with Jack that she knew exactly what he needed before he even made a signal to move. When the heavy winter rains set in, he would sit in his chair by the fire and lay a bag of flour across his shin, using it as weight to strengthen his thigh muscles.

While Jack improved each day, Pru struggled with her morning sickness in silence. Despite being exhausted, most nights her sleep was erratic. Nightmares plagued her. Horrible dreams tormented her with images of Jack lying dead on the highway, bleeding and cold. And she'd wake in a cold sweat, breathless and crying, scrambling up in the bed to check that Jack was there. She didn't settle again until she could see the rise and fall of his chest with his breaths, and knew he was still with her.

Throughout his convalescence, Jack had lost interest in sex. And Pru had been thankful, considering she was so exhausted all the time with the first few months of pregnancy. She'd put him to bed first usually, then tidy the house a little before settling in front of the fire with a book for a few moments of peace and pleasure. Occasionally, she would think about her grandmother and what her life would have been like had she married Frederick Grantham instead of a bushranger. Then she'd chuckle and think of dull days spent drinking tea and listening to inane conversation with well-bred ladies, and she thanked God she was where she was and that she had fallen in love with that crazy bushranger.

While helping him bathe one evening, she ran her hand across the prickly growth of his beard.

'Seems I finally have enough beard to be called a man,' he joked.

It had always been a dent in his pride that he could not grow a full and bushy beard like many of his counterparts on the highways. Before he'd become Jack the Devil, he'd been known as the 'Boy Bushranger', for his lack of beard and his baby-faced good looks.

Pru smiled, 'I quite like it,' she said, and ran her hand across the light scruff.

'Do you?'

She took a mirror from the table near the doorway and brought it to him. At first he seemed thrilled, but moving his head left and right, his smile faded.

'What is it?' she asked. 'What's wrong?'

'I hadn't realised how grey it was becoming,' he said, handing the mirror back to her.

'You've had a rough time of it,' she told him, placing the mirror on the floor beside her. 'It makes you appear dignified, worldly.'

'It makes me appear old,' he said, sighing. 'Older than my years.'

'You're still a young man, Jack.'

When he only grunted, she asked, 'Would you like me to shave it for you?'

He met her eyes. 'Please.'

She collected the razor and the shaving soap he used and returned to sit by his side as he wallowed in his bath.

Slowly, she lathered the soap across his hairy jaw. His beard wasn't long enough to need trimming with the shears first, so she carefully began to scrape at the scruff of a beard, removing soap and hair as Jack sat still, his eyes steady on hers as she made every slow sweep of the razor. His concentration on her was unsettling.

'Stop staring at me,' she said finally. 'You're making me nervous. I'll cut you.'

His eyes flicked away momentarily, but it wasn't long before they were back on her again, studying her eyes, her mouth, her neck. She felt a long-forgotten pull, low in her belly. Not morning sickness this time; the pleasing ache was not due to the baby that grew inside her. Beads of perspiration popped out on her brow and décolletage that had nothing to do with the hot bath water, and everything to do with the naked man sitting in it. Thankfully, she finished the last sweep of the razor, doing her best to remove his beard and not cut his throat. Taking the wet towel, she wiped the remaining soap from his jaw. He took her hand, halting her actions and again his warm, honey-coloured eyes studied her face.

'Thank you.'

She smiled, shy all of a sudden, as though she looked at a potential suitor and not her husband of four months. 'You're welcome.'

Since he insisted on getting himself back into the bedroom without her help, she cleaned up the bath and stoked the fire, as the night had a chill on it, before blowing out the candles. When she joined Jack in the bedroom, she was surprised to see him still awake.

'Is something wrong?' she asked, unbuttoning her dress as he lay propped up on his elbow on the bed. His clean, bare chest appeared golden in the lamplight, even though neither of them had seen any real sunlight in a while.

'Nothing's wrong.' His voice was quiet, his eyes firmly on her as she slipped the dress down her body and tossed it over the chair. The familiar ache that had begun to pulse in her again as he'd bathed grew stronger—a growing, desperate need to have her husband touch her again.

Slowly, she untied the ribbons at the bodice of her undergarments, before slipping one shoulder strap down, and then the other.

'I've missed you, Pru.'

She smiled. 'I've been right here.'

He nodded and held out his hand. 'I know you have. And I am more grateful than I can say for what you have done for me.'

She took his hand and let him pull her onto the bed. He kissed her bare shoulder, traced his tongue across her exposed cleavage.

'I know I have been hard to deal with, and you have put up with more than any woman ever should.'

He sat up and dragged her chemise down, exposing her breasts fully to him. Sitting back, he looked, a small frown marring his features. Her breasts were larger than he would remember, and his expression said he'd noticed. Was now the time to tell him about the baby? But when he leaned in and took a nipple into his mouth, she sighed as pleasure shot through her system like a fever, and she decided that telling him about the baby could wait until the next day. Let them have this night, let them reconnect before she hit him with the news that would again send their lives on another course.

He moved his attentions to the other breast, while his hands got busy removing the rest of her undergarments. She ran her fingers across his clean-shaven face, so smooth and handsome. He'd lost some weight during his recuperation, lost some muscle definition, but he was still her beautiful Jack, and she wanted him, desperately. The desire that burned through her body was unlike anything she'd ever known. Everything felt so tender, so sensitive. Everywhere he touched or kissed took her ever closer to release, and when his hand found the soft warmth between her thighs, she cried out and white light exploded behind her eyes as the unexpectedly quick orgasm ripped through her.

He sat up and grinned at her. 'You have missed me.'

She sighed and fought to catch her breath, even as the desire began to build again. What was making her this aroused? Had she missed his touch that much? She had, but perhaps she had been too tired to notice, or to think about their wonderful lovemaking.

Rolling him over, she pressed her mouth to his. Kissing him, devouring him, while his hands streaked lightning sparks across her skin. She straddled him, and positioning herself she took him over. She needed him like she needed water. She needed to feel that connection with him and he let her take control. She rode him like a woman possessed, yet it still didn't feel like enough.

His hands gripped her hips and met her thrust for thrust until she screamed out at the climax and rode the wave to the end, before falling against his chest, depleted, breathless and very, very satisfied.

'My darling, what has come over you?' Jack panted heavily. 'Don't get me wrong, I'm not complaining. Although, you test my strength. I'm not yet fully recovered.'

She sat up again so she could look at him. 'Did I hurt you?'

In her out-of-control need to have him she'd all but forgotten he had been injured. Now she tried to shift from sitting on his damaged leg, but he held her to him.

'No, you didn't hurt me,' he said, once again taking his eyes on a journey across her naked body. 'Something is different. Your body is different. You've always been beautiful, but ... I don't know what it is. You're radiant, voluptuous. These breasts ...' He stopped talking and took her breasts in his hands, smiling broadly. 'Amazing.'

'While you have lost weight, I seem to have gained some,' she told him, a little self-conscious.

'I like it,' he said. 'And I like how wild you were for me just then. I'm sorry I have not been able to fulfil my husbandly duties.'

'Oh, Jack,' she said, and promptly burst into tears.

'Hey,' he said, pulling her to him again and rolling her so that she lay beside him.

His fingers brushed her hair and it felt so sweet, so calming, she closed her eyes.

'It's okay,' he said. 'I'm here. I'm safe. And I love you more than ever for taking care of me.'

They cuddled in close, his arms around her, her hand against his damaged thigh. Was now the time? Should she tell him he was going to be a father?

'Jack?'

'Mmm?' His reply was more a sigh than a word.

'I have something I need to tell you.'

'Mm-hm.'

'Jack.' She opened her eyes. His eyes were closed, his face relaxed, his breathing light and even.

Already asleep, she thought. Typical after sex, even before the injury.

'Tomorrow,' she whispered and kissed him lightly, before dropping into a heavy and dreamless sleep.

The next day Bobby and Katie joined them for lunch at the house. The sun was finally shining and, after a wonderful night of sex and solid sleep, Pru and Jack were back to their cheerful and frisky selves. The ladies did the lunch dishes while Jack and Bobby took their tea out onto the porch to enjoy the sunshine. Looking out the window as she washed dishes and Katie dried, Pru couldn't help but smile at the bright blue sky and the shiny green grass. A trio of kangaroos bounced along the far boundary of the yard and Millie the goat bleated her displeasure at the nearby intruders.

'Alright, what's got that smile back on your face?' Katie asked, breaking into her daydreams. 'I haven't seen it in so long, I thought it was permanently gone.'

Pru felt herself blush a little as she thought back to her overactive desires the night before.

'You haven't told Jack about the baby, so that can't be it.'

'I was going to tell him last night but ...'

'But?' Katie asked and then smiled herself when Pru grinned and blushed again. 'Ah, so the two of you put the Devil back into Jack last night, hey?'

'The two of us? You mean me and Jack?'

'I mean you and the baby,' Katie replied. 'It's a little-known fact that pregnancy makes women … itchy, let's say.'

'Itchy?' Pru chuckled. 'I don't know the word for it, but itchy? Insane, delirious, out of control perhaps.'

She shivered with delight at the memories and it was Katie's turn to chuckle. 'Gave the Devil a run for his money, hey? Good for you. But you have to tell him, Pru. Do it while he's in you, if that's what it takes.'

'Katie!'

'What? You can tell a man damn near anything when you're riding him to glory.'

'I'm not sure he's ready for this,' Pru said, sighing.

'Ready or not, Pru, you've got a bairn on board. He, or she, will not wait for either of you to be ready.'

Pru nodded and wiped her hands on a towel. 'I'll tell him tonight, when you and Bobby have gone.'

Her mind whirled with exactly how she was going to broach the subject with Jack as she headed out to the front porch to collect dirty teacups from the men. But as she neared the open door, their voices carried in on the breeze and she stopped in her tracks.

'Alfred said the gentleman paid double to ensure the carriage made it to Castlemaine safely,' Bobby spoke, barely louder than a whisper. 'He said the cargo was very precious and was to be delivered directly to the Castlemaine Bank.'

'Straight to a stronghold.' Jack's voice was full of excitement and it set Pru's nerves on edge. She knew that tone. 'But what if it's in an iron safe like the last one. I'd rather not throw effort after something we can't carry or open. When does it travel?'

'That's the thing,' Bobby said. 'It goes tomorrow, before dawn. I figured we'd take them when we cross their path in Daylesford.

But we'd have to leave tonight if we were to reach the choke point before them.'

'We can camp out at Sailors Falls. There's fresh water there and we can cut them off in the morning and be back again by lunchtime.'

'Right.'

Pru had heard enough. She stormed out onto the porch, tore the teacups from Jack's and Bobby's hands and stormed back into the house. She dumped the crockery into the sink with such force a handle broke, before heading to the bedroom, slamming the door behind her.

Bobby and Jack exchanged glances before Bobby wiped the drops of tea from his trousers where Pru had spilled it.

Exhaling a breath and a frustrated groan, Jack stood from his chair.

'Dammit.'

Katie met him at the door, her face red with fury. 'She told you? What the hell did you say to her?'

'Nothing, she didn't say a word,' Jack argued, heading for the bedroom. He turned back to give Katie a puzzled frown. 'Told me what?'

'Nothing,' Katie spat. 'Bobby, we're leaving.'

'Uh, okay. I guess I'll see you later, Jack.' Just as confused, Bobby followed Katie out the door.

Not quite sure what to do, Jack knocked on the bedroom door. 'Pru?'

'Go away!'

It was obvious she'd overheard him and Bobby talking about the robbery they were planning for the next day. He didn't think she'd be thrilled about him going out again so soon but, refusing to be banished from his own bedroom, he pushed the door open and ducked just in time for the bronze candlestick to miss the side of his head.

He stepped in, rushing to restrain her before she could find another projectile.

'How could you, Jack?'

She was mad, but there was also hurt behind the anger.

'You're going out there again?' she asked. 'You're barely recovered.'

'I'm fine,' he insisted. 'Fit as a bull.'

'And just as stupid,' she shot back, sitting on the bed with her arms crossed over her chest.

Moving slowly, as though approaching a wild animal, he sat beside her.

'I am completely recovered, as you yourself discovered last night,' he said, trying to sweeten her up.

'Don't use our lovemaking against me,' she demanded, pushing up from the bed.

'It's one easy heist,' he said with a shrug.

'Please don't go, Jack.'

'You used to love it when I went out on the hunt,' he said with a smirk, pulling her between his legs and squeezing her bottom. 'It used to get you excited.'

'Things are different now,' she said, tearing herself from his grasp.

'How are they different?'

'They just are.'

She wasn't making any sense and he was getting annoyed with it.

'Why, Prudence? Why now? It never bothered you before.'

'You've never been shot before!'

She moved back to him, taking his face between her palms. 'You nearly died, Jack. In my arms. I had to sit by your bedside and watch you go through the pain of having a bullet removed from your thigh. I had to watch you sweat and writhe with delirium as the wound became inflamed. I thought I was going to lose you. Don't make me go through that again, Jack. Other men live perfectly happy lives working perfectly normal jobs and come home to their wives and families at the end of the day.'

'So, what you're saying is that what I am, what I do, isn't good enough anymore,' Jack said, his face now a stony mask.

She dropped her hands. 'No, I'm not saying that at all. Why do you think your worth is relative to being a bushranger?'

'I don't, but you obviously do. When you came here to live with me, I told you I would not give up being a bushranger. It's all I know, Prudence.'

'It's not all you know, Jack,' she insisted. 'You have the transport business. There are profits to be made as the colony grows. We can expand. Make it bigger and better.'

'Oh, can *we*?'

'Yes,' she said, taking his hands in hers. 'You already make plenty of money from the legitimate side of the business, and I wouldn't have to worry about you coming home bleeding and unconscious at the end of the day.'

'I'm a bushranger,' he said, his voice quiet but stern. 'I am Jack the Devil and have been one of the best, most respected highway-men on these roads for almost a decade. And if that's not good enough for Lady Stanforth's granddaughter then maybe Lady Stanforth's granddaughter should go back to the manor.'

Pru's mouth dropped open. He could see his words had not only shocked her, they'd hurt. He had never been deliberately cruel to her before, and it didn't sit well with him. But he was the man and she was his wife and he deserved more respect. Didn't he?

'Now, I'm going to meet Bobby at Black Swamp,' he explained, grabbing his jacket out of the cupboard and taking his bag of bushranging gear he kept stored in a secret compartment in the back of the wardrobe. 'I won't be back until tomorrow. If you want to yell at me some more, you can do it then.'

At the door, he turned to look at her but she wouldn't meet his eyes. He hated to see her looking so forlorn, but he was too angry and disillusioned to bring himself to comfort her.

'I'm disappointed, Pru,' he said, truly flummoxed. 'I thought we understood each other.'

The sun was already high in the sky as Jack rode up to the house. The heist had been successful, but the night, sleeping rough at Sailors Falls, had left his leg aching and stiff. He was so tired, he didn't even bother to unsaddle Persephone. He simply tethered her to the railing nearest the water trough where she drank thirstily. He wanted to see Pru. He needed to. He'd said some awful things to her, things he regretted. Not that she hadn't baited him into it. What had gotten into her head suddenly about him becoming a full-time businessman? A law-abiding office worker? Not him. Not Jack the Devil.

'You did good, girl,' he said, giving Persephone's flanks a light slap.

The horse looked up, gave a snort of thanks, and buried her mouth in the water trough again.

Inside the house, Jack tossed his hat on the coat rack by the door.

'Pru!' he called out.

He wandered through the house and into their bedroom first. She wasn't there and the bed was made. Perhaps she was out in the back garden working in her vegetable patch. She was so proud of it. He'd certainly never eaten so well since they'd planted the garden.

Pushing open the back door, he gazed around the empty yard. The goat bleated, standing at the gate of its pen waiting expectantly to be milked. Jack frowned. Millie hadn't been milked. It was the first job Pru did in the morning. What was going on?

Yes, she was angry with him for refusing to give up bushranging and settle down, but he figured she'd cool off overnight. He thought back over their argument. It was fear rather than anger he'd seen in her eyes.

She'd always been so excited by it all. The tales of his bushranging, going through the loot together when he returned home. Then there was their extraordinarily wild lovemaking after a bail-up. She couldn't deny it was arousing to her.

His getting shot must have been frightening for her. It had been no picnic for him either. But he'd recovered well, and with no remaining ailments, save a small limp. He'd been bushranging for almost eight years. Why wouldn't he return to what he knew best?

Back in the house, he went to their room and sat on the bed trying to remember his last words to her.

And if that's not good enough for Lady Stanforth's granddaughter then maybe Lady Stanforth's granddaughter should go back to the manor.

Dread moved slowly through his body and he closed his eyes, dropping his head in his hands. It had been said in anger, in the heat of the moment, but he hadn't meant it. Had she thought he'd meant it?

He frowned. It wasn't possible. There was no way she would go back to her grandmother. Especially after all this time had passed. Especially since she was now married to him.

Looking around, he realised something was amiss. A few of her items were gone from her dressing table. Slowly, he stood from the bed and walked to the wardrobe. With a shaking hand, he opened the door. A groan escaped his lips. Half her dresses were gone.

He whirled around and moved back out to the living room. Pru was gone.

She'd left him. He sank into the upholstered chair and stared about the room. The house suddenly seemed so large, so empty. At this moment he didn't understand why he'd gotten so defensive. Had he seriously chosen his life on the highway over her?

Before he'd met Pru he'd been happy with his life, content. He'd been free. He'd had women when he wanted them, all the money he needed to buy what he needed, and often things he didn't. Thinking about going back to life on the road without her to come home to left him feeling hollowed out. He loved her. He needed her with him.

Anger began to replace his melancholy and he stood. She was his wife, dammit. How could she leave him like that? Just like that? No word, no note. She belonged by his side, no matter what he did for a living. Was she going to run every time they had an argument? And how dare she run back to that old woman who had treated her so abominably?

'I'm not having it,' he said out loud.

Grabbing his hat from the coat rack again, he stormed out the house, glad he had left Persephone saddled because he was in a rage and he needed to get moving as quickly as possible. He was going to get his wife back—whether she liked it or not.

Rolling over in soft, expensive sheets, Pru stared at the bright light coming through the window. She had barely slept a wink, tossing and turning and reliving the fight with Jack over and over again.

Jack didn't want a wife. He was a man who liked his freedom, the freedom to roam the highways stealing from honest hard-working people. He didn't want a woman who told him what to do and what not to do.

If he couldn't deal with a wife, how would he feel about a baby? A child was an even bigger burden. She admitted she was a coward for not having told him about the baby. But he was already so angry with her—'disappointed' was the word he'd used—because she had expected him to give up his dangerous life on the road.

Sitting up in the huge bed, she put her hand to her stomach as it roiled with the morning nausea that still plagued her. She couldn't think about herself anymore. She had to think about the baby growing inside her. A child needed a stable environment. What if Jack was shot again? What if he was arrested? Their child needed its father but, more importantly, Pru needed to know that they would be safe and secure from Jack's less-than-salubrious friends and enemies, and from the lawman that would no doubt catch up with him one day.

After Jack had left to meet Bobby, she'd paced the house, trying to decide what to do. She had no real money of her own. A pregnant woman on her own would be shunned by all polite society, no matter where she went. And that had made her think of her mother.

Olivia had been a lot younger than her when she'd found herself pregnant and unmarried. Pru understood a little more now how frightened her mother must have been, how she could have agreed to give up her child. She had been sixteen, barely more than a child herself. Pru was twenty-three, and she knew she would never give up her baby. Without Jack, without anywhere to live, she had no choice but to go back. Back to Carrington Manor.

Upon her arrival at the manor the night before, surprise had soon given way to stern lectures and admonishment. She'd been less than twelve hours in her grandmother's company before she knew she'd made a terrible mistake leaving Little Windsor.

In a sort of daze, she stood and walked to the giant mahogany wardrobe in her old bedroom. Opening it, Pru chose one of her old day dresses. Washed and properly attired for breakfast, she wandered down the stairs to the dining room.

'Good morning, Prudence,' Alicia said sweetly. 'I hope you slept well.'

Thank goodness for Alicia. She was the only person who cared how she felt and did not lecture her at every turn.

'Good morning, Alicia, good morning, Grandmother,' she said, sighing at the hard glare in her grandmother's small grey eyes.

'I'm not going to ask you where you've been all this time, Prudence, as I do not care to know.'

'Good,' Pru responded, sipping her tea. 'As I do not care to tell you where I have been, we can leave the matter at that.'

Her grandmother's teaspoon clattered against the saucer. 'Insolent girl.'

'I am no longer a girl, Grandmother.'

If only she knew, Pru thought. Married, pregnant. No, she was no longer a girl, no longer a child to be bullied by a mean-spirited, dishonest old woman. The old feelings of anger and betrayal began to rise. How could she have so easily forgotten what her grandmother had done?

Yes, Deidre had helped Olivia. She'd helped her mother to have the baby in secret, to keep Pru, an illegitimate child, from the cruelty of the world by taking her from her mother and raising her. But they were different times, and London, with all its high society, was a different place. If Pru decided to stay at Carrington Manor, she knew that no matter how hard her grandmother tried to persuade her, she would never let anyone take her baby.

Picking up the silver spoon, Pru cracked the hard-boiled egg with shaking hands and a heavy heart. She was trapped. Without Jack—she fought the tears that threatened again—without Jack, she had no home, no money.

'You are a silly girl,' Deidre started again, making Pru sigh and put down her spoon. She had no appetite. 'What did you think would happen? You run from the only home you know, the only family you have?'

'This isn't the only home I know.' Certainly wasn't the only family, she thought, rubbing a hand softly across her stomach.

'So where did you live for the last six months?'

'I thought you didn't want to know.'

'Answer me, Prudence. I deserve an honest answer.'

'What would you know about honesty?' Pru shot back. She might be trapped at Carrington Manor, but it didn't mean she had to like it. 'Were you so honest? You stole my mother from me!'

'Lower your voice. It was for your own good; Olivia's too.'

'Who are you to decide that?'

'If you intend to live in this house again, Prudence, you will treat me with respect.'

Prudence bit her tongue. Trapped.

'Yes,' Deidre said, a gleam coming into her eye. 'You have nowhere else to go, do you?'

Pru stared at her hands in her lap.

'Now,' Deidre began again. 'I shall ask you again. Where did you go when you left here?'

Pru stayed quiet.

'Some boarding house somewhere, I'd wager,' Deidre went on, regardless of Pru's silence. 'Fell for a man, didn't you. Thought he would take care of you, didn't you. You were always too wild for your own good. You tossed away a perfectly good proposal from a respectable man like Frederick Grantham. He's engaged, you know. Will be marrying the mayor's daughter come spring. You've thrown your life away. Just like your mother.'

Pru finally looked up, horrified at the things coming out of her grandmother's mouth. Taking a deep breath, she prepared to let fly with a few home truths of her own. It would be a pleasure to see the look on her grandmother's face when she told her she was pregnant. But before she could get out a word, a ruckus from the hallway interrupted her.

'Where is she?'

Jack's voice echoed in the grand foyer, his loud baritone reaching her easily.

'Sir, you cannot just barge in here.' Gerald's voice shot back insistently.

'Like hell I can't.'

A moment later, Jack burst into the breakfast room.

'Jack!' she exclaimed, staggered by how thrilled she was that he had come for her.

He started towards her. 'Pru …'

'Just what in God's name do you think you are doing?' Deidre demanded, standing with the help of her walking stick. 'Who are you?'

'I've come to get Pru.'

'Come to get her? Get her for what?' Her beady eyes narrowed on Jack as recognition registered. 'Aren't you that Fairweather person from the races?'

Ignoring Deidre, he took Pru's hands. 'I'm sorry. Please, Pru, you have to come back with me.'

'Why, Jack? Nothing has changed, has it? You're still …' She hesitated, glancing warily at her grandmother and Alicia, who were looking on in astonishment. 'You're still not ready to give up that other life.'

'Let's go home and talk about it,' Jack said.

Pru sighed. He still wasn't willing to say that he would give up bushranging. How could she go back, when she had a much more pressing responsibility growing inside her? Staying here wasn't an option either though. She belonged with Jack, and he deserved to know about the baby.

'Prudence!' Deidre demanded attention. 'What is he talking about? You cannot possibly be having a relationship with this man!'

'Why not?' Jack asked, clearly insulted.

'He may be a successful businessman here in Victoria, but he is not an appropriate sort of man to enter into an arrangement with the granddaughter of the Earl of Carrington.'

Jack opened his mouth to speak but Pru got in first.

'I am sorry you feel that way, Grandmother,' she said calmly. 'Because Jack is my husband.'

Pru saw the colour drain from her face. 'What did you say?'

'Jack and I were married five months ago,' Pru said proudly. 'And I have been living with him.'

'Living …?' Deidre fell back into her chair in horror.

'Yes,' Pru responded, feeling her strength returning. 'Sleeping in the same bed and everything, like a real married couple.' Oh, how she ached to tell her about the baby now. But considering Jack didn't know yet, she held her tongue.

'Don't you speak to me that way, Prudence Stanforth.'

'Uh, it's Prudence Fairweather actually,' Jack piped in with a grin. Pru gave a chuckle and took his hand.

'So this is why you showed up on our doorstep so late last night,' Deidre said. 'Running from a husband. You married a man so obviously beneath you, threw your life away and then wondered why it didn't work out.'

'Now hang on—' Jack began to argue, but Pru stopped him with a hand on his arm.

She walked across to stand in front of her grandmother.

'You're right. I came back because Jack and I had a fight,' she said. 'But I was naive, Grandmother, to think you and I could mend the rift between us. You've just reminded me of why that is not possible. And if you will not accept my husband ...'

'Of course I will not accept him.'

'Then we have nothing more to talk about,' Pru said, answering Deidre's flustered admission. 'Goodbye, Grandmother.'

She turned her back and, taking Jack's hand, she walked to the door.

'You will never be welcome in this house again!' Deidre called after her. 'You have brought shame to this family.'

Pru stopped, turning slowly to take one last look at the woman who'd raised her.

'Then I guess I take after my mother.'

She left the room.

'Bravo, wife,' Jack said, beaming proudly at her.

She didn't smile in return. 'Wait here while I gather my belongings,' she told him as she headed up the stairs to her room to pack not only the belongings she had brought with her, but anything else she deemed hers. Two of her favourite books made it into the small bag she could carry on her horse, as did her favourite dress from her wardrobe.

She wasn't running this time. She was going home. Standing up for her family; her husband and the tiny person they had created together. She was no longer a child. She was a wife, and about to be a mother, and she was taking control of her life.

At the bottom of the stairs, Jack took the heavy bags from her. 'Let's go home, Jack.'

'I'm so proud of you,' Jack said with a grin, as they headed out to the stables to get Pru's horse. 'You stood up to her.'

'Just get on your horse and take me home,' she said, overcome by weariness all of a sudden. They had things to talk about. She was still angry and hurt by the things he had said, but all the drama of the last twenty-four hours had worn her out. She'd barely slept the night before and she needed to get home to rest.

Jack took the reins of his horse from a stableman just as Brock walked Misha out for Pru.

'I'm sorry to say goodbye to her again,' Brock said, patting Misha's nose and handing the reins to Pru. 'She's a great horse. Take care of her.'

'I will,' Pru promised.

'I'm sorry to say goodbye to you too, Prudence,' Brock said.

'I belong with my husband, Brock.'

'I know. That's not what I meant,' he said, smiling. 'I leave for America tomorrow.'

'America?'

'Yes, back home,' he said.

'But you don't have any family left in Kentucky, you said.'

'No ma'am, but if war indeed does break out between the states then I don't feel right being all the way over here while good men fight and die for the South.'

Pru stared at her friend, surprised and concerned. She wished she could tell him not to go. She hated the thought of someone else she loved possibly taking a bullet.

'I'm glad I got to say goodbye, but I'll worry about you, Brock,' she said. 'Please take care and try not to get yourself shot or killed.'

'I'll do my best, ma'am,' he said. 'The war will probably only last a few months. I'm sure it will all be over before you can say "succession".'

Pru tried to smile but her heart ached.

Brock turned hard eyes on Jack. 'You'd best take better care of her this time.'

She caught Jack's quick look of offence and stepped in before his temper could flare.

'Don't worry about me, Brock, I can take care of myself and him,' she said with a reassuring smile.

Brock chuckled richly. 'I have no doubt about you, Miss Prudence.'

She kissed his cheek and mounted the horse. Jack was still glaring at Brock even as he mounted and turned his horse away from the stables.

'That man takes too much liberty with you,' Jack grumbled.

'Brock is a friend,' Pru said. 'He saved me from going slowly mad living here. Kept quiet when I took long morning rides off the property.'

Jack just grunted. 'At least he's leaving the country.'

'Yes, he is going into battle, into war. And if he gets shot it will be for something he believes in and not just because he got distracted while he was stealing from others.'

Jack grunted again.

Pru sighed heavily. God, she was exhausted. 'Jack, we need to talk.'

'Always a frightening prospect,' he said with a sigh. 'You know you outwit me. I haven't the intellect to win any argument with you.'

'Then don't argue,' she shot back.

'You said you would take me as I am,' Jack reminded her. 'When we married, you said …'

'I said I would accept the challenge of trying to make you see the error of your ways.'

'God, woman, you have the memory of a card counter.'

'Jack, I need a husband who will be around for his child.'

'There's time for that yet,' he tossed back with a laugh. 'We've barely been married more than a minute.'

'Actually, Jack, there isn't time. You only have about five months.'

'Five months for what?' he asked, confused.

'To give up the highway and make the transport company a reputable business that your child can be proud of and perhaps even take over one day.'

Jack shook his head as he studied her.

'Why do you keep referring to a child we don't even …'

Pru watched as realisation struck like a plank of wood across the back of his head.

'Or do we? A baby?' he asked hoarsely. 'Pru, are you pregnant?'

'Yes.'

He stopped his horse and she halted hers to stand beside him. After a moment spent staring open-mouthed like a fish, he frowned. 'Is that why you ran from me?'

She fiddled with the horse's reins.

'Why didn't you just tell me?'

'When you were shot I begged you to stop bushranging and you didn't. You know that I had no problem with what you did for a living until you were injured. I can't live without you, Jack, and I can't bring a baby into a world where his father is a criminal who may end up in prison or dead.'

'A son?' he asked excitedly, latching on to her use of the word 'his'.

'I don't know. You're missing the point,' Pru said, her exhaustion making her impatient. 'We have a baby on the way, Jack. You have to stop now. Can you do that? You couldn't stop for me, but will you do it for your child?'

Jack nodded quickly. 'I will stop, Pru. I will go to work like a normal man. A normal family man with a wife and a son waiting for him to come home to at the end of the day.'

Pru smiled. 'It could be a girl, you know.'

'A tiny little Prudence?' he asked, beaming like a madman. 'Even better.'

He leaned over and placed a hand over her belly.

'I will do my best for you,' he said talking to her stomach, before he gazed up at her in awe. Drawing her head towards his, he kissed her strongly before looking into her tear-filled eyes. 'For you both.'

Then throwing his hands in the air he yelled, 'I'm going to be a father!'

Pru laughed and together they rode back to their house to prepare for this new chapter in their lives.

Fourteen

It wasn't easy for a career criminal to suddenly become a fully law-abiding citizen.

While Bobby had been supportive of Jack's decision, Garrett didn't give a damn, almost as though he'd been waiting for the day he could take over Jack's role on the highway. But without the transport business feeding them information, the two men found it increasingly difficult over the next few months to know when and where to bail up a coach.

After a few near misses, Bobby decided it was too much like hard work now that their honey-pot had been taken from them, and he gave up the road as well, taking a job at the Duchess of Kent to be closer to Katie. Garrett finally hightailed it to New South Wales, looking for more fertile roads to plunder.

Since Jack was now a full-time employee of his own business, Alfred Jones took the opportunity to retire to Melbourne to live with his daughter and her husband. And so Jack was left to run a business he really had no clue about.

Pru went into the office with him before Alfred left, and the old man handed over as much information about the legitimate running of the transport company as he could before he left for

Melbourne. Pru had been well educated, and she did her best to teach Jack all he needed to know. Sadly, he was about as good a student as he'd been a patient, but eventually they had the inner workings of the company sorted out, and new roles and responsibilities were divided between them.

As the months passed, they worked side by side, doing their best to increase business, in order to cover for the loss of the income they would have made had Jack still been ranging the highways.

For the most part, Jack settled in and was happy with the work. But occasionally, that familiar thrill would come across him when a particularly wealthy passenger retained his services. Nothing got past Pru though, and she would recognise the glint in his eye when he spied a prospect, shutting him down before the spark could ignite.

One warm December afternoon the coach arrived from Melbourne, its passengers in an uproar.

'We were robbed!' the gentleman announced as he climbed out of the coach.

'Robbed?' Pru asked, shocked, and looked immediately at Jack. He shook his head quickly.

'How awful for you.' Pru went on placating the gentleman and his wife as they took inventory of the losses.

Jack took the coach driver aside. Sam Carruthers was a good man who had been with the company since the beginning and had been complicit in all robberies staged by Jack the Devil and his crew.

'Did you recognise the thief, Sam?'

The man looked shaken. Being bailed up was obviously a more frightening prospect when you didn't know the assailant.

'I couldn't see his face clearly,' Sam said. 'My eyesight isn't so good anymore. He wore a hat low across his eyes, and a kerchief across his face. Fancy-looking gun, one of those newfangled things, and he had a foreign accent. Mean bastard too, struck me bung knee with the handle of his whip. Not gentlemanly like Jack the Devil used to be.'

'Where did it happen?'

'Not far out of Bacchus Marsh,' Sam said. 'Other side of the ravine.'

It could have been anyone, Jack thought. Garrett was long gone, and it didn't sound like him anyway. While Jack had been going straight, more and more gangs of bushrangers were popping up all over the district. Young guns with bad tempers and itchy trigger fingers. There was no art to it anymore, no manners. He suddenly felt like a very old man.

When the couple had retrieved what was left of their belongings, Pru saw to it that they were delivered immediately to the Bath Hotel. But once they were gone, she turned on him and Sam, anger firing in her eyes.

'I swear I had nothing to do with it,' Jack insisted before she could say anything, holding his hands up in surrender. 'Tell her, Sam.'

'T'wasn't him, Mrs,' Sam promised. 'I didn't know this was coming. I didn't know the chap. But he ain't someone I want to come across again. I think it's time I retired, Mr Fairweather. I don't see so well anymore, and the roads are getting busier and more dangerous.'

'We understand,' Pru told him, and taking out the wages tin, she paid him his due, and a little more, Jack noticed. 'Thank you for your service, Sam.'

'You've been a good friend, old man,' Jack said, shaking his hand. 'Let's go have a nobbler of whisky for old times.'

'Don't mind if I do,' Sam agreed, relaxing a little more.

Jack gave Pru a wink. 'Let's lock up early today. We have no more carriages coming in. That's the joy of being the boss, right?'

'Do you miss it?'

Jack pushed up onto his elbow, his lean muscular body stretched out beside Pru in bed, naked and glorious in the warm December evening.

'I swear to you, I had nothing to do with that robbery today.'

'That's not what I asked,' she said. 'I asked if you miss it. The bushranging.'

He walked his fingers lightly across her naked, swollen belly, igniting little fires once again as though they hadn't made love only minutes before. 'My fingers get a little itchy when I see something of value. Once a thief, always a thief, hey?'

'But you don't take,' she said, running her hands through his thick brown hair.

'It's not even the value of the thing,' he said, rolling back to stare at the exposed wooden beams of the ceiling. 'It's the challenge, the thrill. I've been picking pockets and taking what wasn't mine for as long as I can remember. It's what comes naturally to me. Back in England, it was steal or go hungry. I told you I was fifteen when I left the boys' workhouse, and the manager sold me to work at a piggery outside of London.'

She remembered, nodded.

'A group of us older boys were transported and once we were close enough to the city, we escaped. Lived on the streets, stole food to survive. I was good at it too. We worked the docks a lot. People left their luggage lying about, it was easy pickings. Plenty of people were heading out to the new colony of Victoria by then, and I could hear them talking about gold. Gold that just sat on the ground, waiting to be picked up and carted away so a man could make his fortune. I kept offering myself up to ships as unpaid labour and eventually one took me on. Bloody horrible trip that was. I'd never been on a ship before, what the hell did I know about the ocean?'

Pru smiled. She could feel the baby kicking away under her hands as Jack talked. He, or she, knew the sound of daddy's voice.

'It was hard work,' Jack went on. 'I was seasick for the whole first week and still had to work through it. But I made it to Melbourne and joined the masses heading up to Ballarat to find my fortune. All I found was more squalor, more poverty. Ballarat was a hellhole in those days. You'd scarcely believe it, to look at it now. I dug and dug and found a few bits of gold, enough to buy food to eat and some more equipment to keep digging. I had no education when I arrived, but I met another digger, a girl.'

His face softened as he mentioned her. She was intrigued. 'A girl?'

Jack nodded. 'She was a digger too, if you can believe it. A girl digger! Who'd ever heard of such a thing? She was tough and spirited. Often got into more trouble than I did. I met her gambling on dice behind one of the pubs. She skinned me, and everyone else there. We became fast friends after that. And the little amount of education I have is thanks to her. She taught me to read and write—did so with lots of people in the camps. She was a hell of a girl.'

'Sounds as though you were in love with her. What happened to her?'

His wistful smile said it all. 'She loved another. Married a deserting soldier after the Eureka Stockade massacre—nice bloke—and they headed north, I believe. I never saw, never heard from her again. I was already bushranging by then. I became very, very good at it. It came naturally to me.' He sighed heavily. 'Doing additions in a book and paying wages and taxes does not.'

Pru studied his face closely. 'Are you unhappy, my love?'

His eyes met hers quickly and he pushed up once again. 'No.'

He said it so definitively she couldn't argue that he was being dishonest.

'No,' he repeated. 'My child will never know the pain of an empty stomach, the loneliness of living on the streets, the biting cold of a hard winter. When we met, you accepted me for who I am, but you've made me into a better man than I ever thought I could be. I am so happy I could burst with it.'

He kissed her and his hand joined hers across her belly, just as the baby kicked again.

'Ha!' he said with a laugh. 'He's a tough little thing.'

'He liked hearing his daddy's story,' she said, putting her other hand to his cheek. 'So did I. Thank you for telling me. You prefer to forget your past, but it's what made you the strong man you are today. You're a survivor, Jack. And I know you better now. And I still love you whether you are Jack the Devil or Jack Fairweather.'

'We're both survivors,' Jack said, kissing her belly. She sighed as contentment turned to arousal when his kisses continued their journey to places of pleasure.

Rolling dough for bread, Prudence had to stop and rub her aching back.

'What's the matter?'

She turned to see Jack frowning at her.

'Nothing, just a bit sore,' she said smiling. 'And he or she is kicking up a storm.'

Jack moved to her and placed one hand on her belly while he massaged her lower back.

'Can you not work sitting down?'

'Yes, I suppose,' she said. 'But then my arse gets sore. It doesn't matter what position I'm in these days, I'm always uncomfortable.'

'It can't be much longer to go, can it?'

She smiled. He'd been like a little boy waiting for Christmas the past week. And Christmas itself was not far off.

'Not much longer,' she agreed, and let him lead her to the table to sit down.

She watched him move the dough and the rolling pin and all the other implements she had been using from the counter to the kitchen table.

'I feel like such a fat cow,' she said sulkily.

He leaned down to kiss the top of her head. 'You look beautiful.'

'You just like the size of my breasts.'

He chuckled. 'Aye, there is that.'

A knocking at the door broke into their conversation. Jack gave her a wink and went to see who it was.

'Sergeant Carmichael,' she heard Jack say. A wave of worry rushed through her. Why would the sergeant be here? She stood and went to the living room to see Jack welcoming the sergeant and young Constable Mickey Doyle into the house.

'Mrs.' The constable touched his hat with a finger.

'Sergeant Carmichael, Constable Doyle,' Pru said, greeting them with a nod. They all sat; the sergeant in an armchair, the constable on the loveseat by the window and Pru beside Jack on the sofa, her hand in his. 'To what do we owe the pleasure?'

'There has been an accusation made, Mr Fairweather,' the sergeant began, taking out his little notebook.

'An accusation?' Pru asked, her heart rate increasing a little. She suddenly felt a little nauseated. 'Against whom?'

'Against Mr Fairweather.'

'And what is the accusation?' Jack asked.

'A gentleman says he rode in one of your transport carriages only to be held at gunpoint by a bushranger,' Sergeant Carmichael began. 'He was robbed on the Melbourne to Ballarat road around Bacchus Marsh, and lost more than forty pounds worth of gold as well as some of his personal belongings.'

'I'm aware of the case,' Jack said. 'But the highway is a dangerous place.'

'What is the accusation, sir?' Pru cut in.

'The gentleman believes the coach driver may have been involved in the robbery.' The sergeant again flicked through his notepad. 'One Sam Carruthers.'

Jack laughed. 'Sam is seventy years old if he's a day. There is no way he could be or would be involved in a robbery.'

'Oh? The gentleman said the driver was too quick to stop the carriage and allow the robbery to take place.'

'He probably didn't wish to be shot,' Pru tossed in, annoyed. The baby was annoyed too, clearly, judging by the harsh jab she received. She rubbed her belly, trying to calm the baby down.

'What was he supposed to do?' Jack joined in. 'Try to outrun bushrangers?'

'No, I suppose not,' the sergeant acquiesced.

'It doesn't matter now anyway. Sam Carruthers doesn't work for me anymore,' Jack said. 'He retired after that robbery. I think it frightened him.'

Sergeant Carmichael flipped his notebook closed. 'Still, we had to look into the business.'

'I thought we had agreed you would no longer harass my husband, Sergeant.'

'And I have not harassed him, Mrs Fairweather. Although, in the course of my investigations, I did discover that Fairweather Transport seems to have had more than its fair share of highway robberies over the years,' Sergeant Carmichael said. 'Three times more, it seems. This is not the only suspicion raised, not the only accusation.'

'Really?' Pru asked. What did he know? What other information had he gleaned from other victims of Jack the Devil?

'Surprisingly, the robberies appear to have lessened lately.' The sergeant looked at Prudence's belly then. 'I wonder why that is.'

'I couldn't possibly say,' Pru answered, doing her best to hide her nerves and discomfort under the unwavering and suspicious stare of the sergeant. This man was much smarter than she had given him credit for. He wasn't only investigating Sam Carruthers, he was still investigating Fairweather Transport, and Jack along with it.

But before she could think on it any further, a strong cramp gripped her belly and she tightened her own grip on Jack's hand, bringing his attention to her.

'Pru, what is it?'

'Jack,' she said breathlessly, and awkwardly levered herself up off the couch. 'I think my waters just broke.'

All the men in the room leaped to their feet at once and took at least two paces each away from her. Their shocked faces were a sight to behold, and if she hadn't currently been fighting the pain of what she was sure was a contraction, she would have laughed.

Instead she took a deep, cleansing breath and straightened her posture.

'Gentlemen, my husband and I have a more pressing matter to deal with at this moment. Might we talk about these ridiculous accusations some other time?'

'Of course,' the sergeant said, looking a little anxious, as though she may drop the baby right then and there on the floor. 'If we can be of any assistance—'

'Sergeant, unless you've squeezed a walnut out of your nostril recently, I'd say you have no idea what I need right now.'

'Of course, Mrs Fairweather,' he said again, his face going crimson.

It didn't take any more prodding to get the men to leave, and they did so in haste.

'My wife,' Jack said with pride as he leaned in to kiss her warm and sweaty forehead.

'Jack, we are going to talk about these other accusations, but right now I need you to go into town and get the midwife,' she said, trying to keep the fear from her voice. If she let Jack know just how scared she was, he would never be able to do what she needed him to do.

'Will you be alright alone?'

Just as he asked, they heard more horses arriving. Jack rushed to the window and seeing Katie and Bobby, he threw open the front door.

'What in the hell were Sergeant Carmichael and Mickey doing here?' Bobby called out before he'd even dismounted. 'We passed them on their way out the gates.'

'I'll explain on the way,' Jack said. 'The baby is coming, I have to fetch the midwife in town.'

Katie leaped from her horse and handed Jack the reins.

'Go,' she said, looking at Pru standing in the doorway. 'I've dealt with birthing mothers before. I'll take care of things til the midwife gets here.'

'Thank you,' Jack said and swiftly mounted. With one last look back at Pru, he bolted with Bobby out the gates of Little Windsor and onto the road to Ballarat.

An hour later, the men returned and Jack barged into the house in a panic.

'Pru!' he called.

'Bedroom!' she yelled back before letting out a loud groan.

He walked into the room to find her in her nightdress, on her hands and knees on the bed with Katie rubbing her back.

'Where's the midwife?' Katie asked, snapping him out of his stupor.

'Oh, she wasn't there,' Jack answered, fidgeting as though he wanted to do something. 'She went to Castlemaine to deliver twins or something.'

'Oh God.' Pru groaned as another contraction hit.

'Don't worry, Pru,' Katie told her. 'Mothers have babies without the help of midwives all the time. You'll be just fine. I'll be with you.'

Pru climbed from the bed and kissed Jack's cheeks.

'Katie's right,' she said, rubbing her belly. 'We'll be just fine. Now go outside. I have a feeling you are about to hear some very indelicate words come out of my mouth and I really would rather you didn't think your wife the foul-mouthed sailor.'

'Aye, aye, captain.' He kissed her again before stepping to the bedroom door and closing it behind him.

It was hours.

Agonising hours.

Jack paced the front porch of the house with Bobby.

It was agonising for him and, considering the promised interesting expletives he could hear coming from the bedroom, he had no illusions that the agony Pru felt was well beyond his imagining. But the colourful language was not what worried him—her vocabulary was rather inventive, he thought—it was that he'd never heard a woman shriek like that before.

He hadn't lived in the camps at Ballarat for long during the gold rush. And when he had first started out ranging, he'd always preferred to set up camp between towns, or to make use of the boarding houses in towns. Therefore, he had never heard the screams of women in labour as they fought to bring their children into existence.

And there had been a lot of babies brought into existence in those first years. The gold rush had seen Victoria's population explode unlike anywhere else in the world at the time.

Another strangled cry reached out from the house and tugged at his chest.

'How do they do it?' Bobby asked.

Jack studied his friend. He looked a little wide-eyed and green around the gills.

'One of nature's mysteries, I guess,' Jack said, wishing he had an answer. He knew plenty about a woman's anatomy. But he could scarcely imagine what nature's mysteries were doing to his wife's petite body right this second.

'You've seen animals born though, right?' Bobby went on. 'I mean, how do women do ... that?'

'Bobby, I really don't need to have visions of my wife giving birth to a horse, if you don't mind,' Jack shot back, his agitation finally getting the better of him. 'So will you shut your pie hole and ... go for a walk or something.'

Bobby didn't need any more encouragement. He stepped down off the porch and wandered across towards the creek.

Sitting down on the porch steps, Jack scrubbed his hands across his face, hoping to erase images of horses and cattle giving birth in barns. His poor Prudence. What had he done to her? His part had been easy—not to mention enjoyable. She'd had to carry the baby for nine long months. Dealing with the nausea, the aches and pains, the constant fatigue and now this. Childbirth.

He didn't want to think about how many women died in childbirth, or how often the child didn't make it. He didn't want to think about it. But now that he had started, it was all he could think about.

Dammit!

Unable to sit still, he stood and paced the porch, listening to the screams and groans of his beloved wife. He could stand it no more. He needed an update. It was his house too, blast it, and he wouldn't be shut out of it while his wife fought to give him a son or daughter.

Pushing open the front door, he pounded into the house. He was about to open the door to their bedroom, but stopped dead in his tracks when he heard another cry. A strange cry of higher pitch. The cry cut straight to his core and he would swear he had never heard a sweeter sound in his life.

Laying his palm flat against the door, he closed his eyes and thanked God for maybe the third time in his life. A moment later the door swung open and he fell forward into the room.

Katie stepped back, startled at first, but then grinned like a madwoman.

'I was just coming to get you,' she said, but Jack heard nothing.

His eyes had landed on Pru, her nightgown slick to her body with the sweat of hard work over so many hours. Her face was pale and she looked beyond exhausted, but her smile was as bright as a summer morning, and she held a little squirming, blood-smeared creature, wailing like a banshee.

'Jack,' she said, tears filling her eyes as she looked up from the bundle she held. 'Come and meet your son.'

He didn't think he could contain the explosion of joy in his chest at that moment. The swell of emotion, the pride, the happiness, the sadness, the thrill, his love for Pru, all mixed together into one knotted ball in his chest that was fit to burst up his throat if he didn't breathe again soon.

He inhaled a huge gulp of breath, and when feeling returned to his legs, he moved towards the bed, leaning over carefully to peek at the tiny baby in his wife's arms.

'My son?' he whispered in awe. 'We have a son?'

'We have a son,' she repeated and he looked into her eyes, tired and full of tears.

Jack sat carefully on the bed beside her and leaned over to kiss her forehead, then her lips …

'I was so worried,' he said. 'I love you so much. You fought for so long, I was afraid …'

'Sshhh,' she said through tears. 'I'm fine. He's fine.'

'He's more than fine,' Jack said, taking a closer look at the boy. 'He's a Fairweather lad.'

Pru laughed wearily. 'That he is.'

'Let's get him cleaned up a little, shall we?' Katie said and leaned over them to take the boy.

'Wait!' Jack said suddenly. 'What do we name him?'

'I thought perhaps Henry.'

'Henry.' Jack tried it out. 'Henry Jonathan Fairweather.'

'Jonathan?' Pru asked.

'My real name,' Jack said.

'Alright then,' Katie said and took the boy. 'Henry, let's get you cleaned up. And Jack, you need to let Pru rest a while.'

'Of course,' he said, his eyes following the boy as Katie took him to the basin of warm water to give him his first bath.

Jack turned back to Pru in awe. 'I didn't think it was possible to love you any more than I did.' He kissed her cheeks and rubbed the matted, sweaty hair from her face. 'Can I help you get cleaned up?'

He grabbed a cloth from the bowl beside the bed and wiped her red face lovingly.

She closed her eyes. 'Ah, that feels nice. Thank you, my love. But please, give me a few minutes to wash up properly.'

'As you wish, my darling Pru.'

He kissed her forehead lovingly and stepped towards the door, peering over Katie's shoulder as she washed his son. His son.

He pulled the door closed behind him and walked out to the porch again.

Bobby returned from the creek and one look at Jack's face had him rushing up the porch steps.

'Jack, what is it? What's happened? Is Pru alright? Is the baby alright?'

'I have a son.'

'What?'

'I have a son,' Jack repeated, the shock still swirling through his body. 'His name is Henry.'

Bobby's whooping cheer and laughter broke Jack out of his stunned reverie.

'A son! Congratulations, Jack!' Bobby said, taking his friend in a bone-crunching hug and then slapping him heartily on the back. 'This calls for a drink!'

Bobby rushed into the house and emerged again moments later with a bottle of whisky and two glasses. Putting the glasses on the porch railing, he poured two shots, handing one to Jack. 'To Henry Fairweather!'

Jack raised his glass and grinned. 'To my son, Henry.'

They drank and Bobby poured another drink for them both.

'To Prudence!' Bobby offered.

'The most amazingly strong woman I have ever known,' Jack said and, lifting his glass, he drank again. The warm liquid zapped the last of his shock and like a madman he danced around the front yard, allowing Bobby to top up his drink as he passed by.

'Jack!'

Katie's voice cut into his celebrations. He looked up at her expectantly.

'Pru wants to see you again,' Katie said, sculling the whisky Bobby handed her. Jack took the porch steps two at a time, and twirling Katie so fast she almost overbalanced, he raced back into the house.

Pru marvelled at how quickly Henry was able to latch on to her breast and feed. Katie had said that sometimes it took a while to get the feeding all sorted, and that if it didn't happen then she could hire a wet nurse.

She knew it was common for mothers of the upper classes in London to employ the services of a wet nurse. It was often considered odd and unsocial behaviour to want to feed one's own baby. Had her grandmother been involved in her life, she felt sure she would have been pressured to hire a woman to breastfeed Henry. But Pru thought those women to be genteel ninnies, who cared more about their social standing than their children. There was no way she was going to miss this incredible bonding moment with her son.

It was the strangest sensation and she couldn't take her eyes off him as he suckled mightily for one so little. He already had a thin crown of russet hair. She wondered if he would grow up to have brown hair like his father or be more auburn like her. It was so hard to tell this early. His newborn blue eyes opened every now and again to look up at her and she melted every time.

Running a finger lightly over his peaches-and-cream complexion, she could scarcely believe what she'd done. Whether it was the exhaustion or all the emotions muddled and churning inside her, Pru had a fleeting moment of wishing her grandmother could see him. But then she wished her own mother could have seen him too, and it killed any guilt she had over keeping Henry away from his great-grandmother.

She looked up when the bedroom door opened and Jack stumbled in.

'Been drinking, Mr Fairweather?' she asked without any censure.

'Just a few to celebrate,' he answered with a little slur.

He stood awkwardly at the door, holding on to it for support.

'Come,' she said, reaching out a hand to him. 'Just don't breathe on him too hard or he'll be drunk before he's even walking.'

Warily, he moved closer to the bed, looking down at the now-swaddled child at her breast.

'Lord, he's really gnawing on that thing, isn't he?'

She chuckled. 'He is his father's son after all.'

Jack sat beside her and watched intently. 'Does that hurt?'

'It feels odd.'

'How do you know what to do?' he asked. 'Have you been around babies before?'

'Not really,' she said, exhaling heavily. 'I'm just as scared as you are, Jack. But Katie has dealt with babies a lot. Birthing obviously, bless her.'

'I'll be buying her a year's worth of pretty dresses, you can be sure of that.'

Pru smiled. 'She has given me some instructions, but other than that, she said we will figure it all out as we go along.'

'We?' Jack asked.

'Yes, Jack, we,' she said strongly. 'You will be as much a part of your son's upbringing as I will.'

'I can't do that,' he said, pointing at where Henry was feeding.

She rolled her eyes and hoped it was the drink that was making Jack so dull headed.

'There are plenty of other things a man can do for his child.'

'I don't know ...' he said, and Pru thought he looked more nervous than she had ever seen him before.

'We'll figure it out, Jack,' she said. 'And you are going to be a wonderful father.'

'You think so?'

'I know so,' she said, and when Henry detached she lifted him and held him towards Jack. 'Now take him while I switch sides.'

'Take him?'

She'd been wrong. *Now* Jack looked more nervous than she'd ever seen him.

'Just hold his head and bottom and you'll be fine,' she said, laying the boy in his father's arms for the first time.

At first Jack looked awkward, but then he readjusted himself and cradled Henry quite comfortably in his big arms.

'He's heavier than he looks,' Jack commented.

'He's full of milk just now. No, don't jiggle him about like that ...'

Too late.

The projectile vomit was quite impressive for one so small and caught Jack fair on the chin.

Pru couldn't smother the laugh that burst forth. Surprisingly though, Jack dealt quite admirably with being covered in milky sick. She took Henry back from him and cleaned him up while Jack stood to do the same.

'Suppose I should be used to that,' Jack said, taking a nearby cloth to wipe his chin and shirt. 'It was years before Bobby could hold his liquor.'

'You're a soldier, Jack Fairweather,' she said, allowing the admiration into her voice. She fixed Henry to the other breast, once he was all cleaned up, and felt the glow inside her as Jack continued to stay and watch.

When the feeding was done, and the baby winded, Katie took Henry to put him down for a sleep and Jack left Pru to get some much-earned rest of her own.

'Pru says you are to wet the baby's head,' Katie instructed, as the men climbed aboard their horses. 'But don't go getting into any trouble and be home before dawn.'

'As ordered.' Jack saluted. 'Take care of my family, Katie girl.'

She nodded and laughed as Bobby and Jack rode off in a chorus of cheers and whoops.

Every day Henry seemed to grow noticeably, like a sprout that pokes its head out in winter and is suddenly a blooming plant two days into spring. His features changed so quickly, it was hard to keep up. It was also hard to keep up with how much the boy pooped and threw up after each meal. No sooner had Jack changed a nappy then Henry had soiled it once again. Pru told him it was normal, but Jack didn't know how it was possible for Henry to continue to grow at such a rapid rate when everything he ate was expelled from his tiny body. But grow he did, and Jack's life was a never-ending revolution of work and doting on his son.

He didn't enjoy running the business now that Pru wasn't there with him. Tasks took longer to do without her and his days became a mundane waiting game until he could get home to his boy. Luckily, Pru still did the books, otherwise they would have been out of business before Henry had reached three months old.

He often found himself stuck in the office, dreaming of being out on the open road again, in the sunshine, riding Persephone with the wind in his face and a bag full of stolen goods. Shaking off the discontentment he knew he had no right to feel, he stepped out to greet the coach from Geelong.

At the end of the day, Jack saw Bobby wandering up the street towards him.

'Hey, Jack,' Bobby called out with a wave. 'How's business?'

'Can't complain'.

'It's been a while since I've seen you. How's Pru? Henry?'

'Good, great. You should come by with Katie for dinner again one night.'

Bobby smiled. 'Can you believe us? The settled family men.'

'No,' Jack sighed. 'I can't.'

Bobby laughed. 'Come get a drink with me before you head home.'

Jack checked his pocket watch. 'It will have to be a quick one.'

'Absolutely. Katie's cooking me dinner.'

They walked to the George Hotel, bypassing the Duchess of Kent as they went. It had been months since Jack had set foot in the place. And while Bobby and Katie still worked there, they rarely socialised there anymore.

'Times have changed, hey,' Bobby said as they settled at the bar at the George.

'They have indeed.' Jack lifted his drink in toast before taking a sip.

'I'm asking Katie to marry me.'

Jack spat his drink across the bar.

'Is that such a shock?' Bobby asked. He looked anxious, Jack thought.

'Not a shock, you just could have waited until I didn't have a mouthful of whisky,' Jack said, wiping his face with his handkerchief. Then he grinned from ear to ear.

'Don't you approve, Jack?'

Why Bobby felt he needed Jack's approval was beyond him, but he couldn't resist teasing his oldest friend. His expression turned serious and he shook his head. 'I have only one thing to say to you, Bobby.'

Bobby frowned. 'What?'

Jack let the smile come in slowly. 'It's about time.'

The worry left Bobby's face and Jack called to the barman. 'Another drink for my friend! He's getting married.'

When they both had top ups, Jack raised his again. 'To old married men.'

'Old married men.' Bobby tapped his glass to Jack's and they drank. 'Will you be my best man, Jack?'

'Of course.'

'I'm only sorry I didn't get to be yours,' Bobby said. 'But if Katie and I have a marriage half as good and solid as yours and Pru's, I'll be happy.'

'That's a damn nice thing to say, old friend.'

On a cool but sunny day in August, Bobby and Katie were married in a simple ceremony performed by the new young Catholic priest. Close friends gathered in the large front yard of the little cottage Bobby had purchased that overlooked Lake Wendouree. Once the vows had been spoken, Bobby dipped his lovely bride and kissed her to the cheers and jeers of the revellers and a grand reception got underway.

Like Jack, Bobby had saved much of his takings from their previous occupation, and no expense had been spared to give Katie the day she deserved.

The bride was stunning in an ivory lace gown and lace veil. Music, played by a small band, entertained and allowed for dancing. A huge table was spread with food, and drinks flowed in celebration of the happy union.

'Do you regret not having a day like this?' Jack asked Pru as they watched Katie and Bobby dance, wrapped in each other's arms.

'It is beautiful,' Pru sighed. 'But no.' She turned to him. 'I've no regrets, my love. I wanted to marry you as quickly as possible. You're the one who made me wait.'

'My impatient little Prudence,' he said with a chuckle. 'You tormented me to within an inch of my life. But I wish I could have given this to you.'

'I couldn't be happier,' she assured him with a kiss.

They gazed lovingly across to where Henry played happily with other babies and toddlers on a blanket laid out on the grass.

Katie joined them, her smile as wide and as bright as a bride's should be on her wedding day. 'Jack, Bobby requests you join him and Bandi for a drink while I catch my breath.'

Jack saluted Katie, kissed Pru and headed over to join Bandi and Bobby at the table set up as a bar.

Grabbing the nearest bottle of whisky, he poured a large glass. 'I am under orders to get the groom drunk.'

'Katie said that?' Bobby asked, his eyes narrowed.

'No.' Jack winked, but noted Bobby's less than cheerful expression. 'Smile, boyo, marriage isn't so bad.'

'Tell him,' Bobby urged Bandi, who looked unusually grim.

'Viktor's out of prison.'

Jack halted, the glass of whisky halfway to his mouth. Taking a deep breath, he threw the whole drink down.

'They released him?'

'It's not possible. The murdering son-of-a-bitch got life in prison,' Bobby said in disbelief. 'There's no way they would let him out.'

'Then he escaped,' Jack said, more to himself than the others. It was hard to believe. No one escaped the Melbourne Gaol. 'Are you sure? It's not just some meritless gossip or rumour?'

'Sure as I'm standing here,' Bandi said in a low voice. 'Viktor escaped. A telegraph came across the desk at the station. Sergeant called us all in, said to be on the lookout for him.'

'Well, I doubt he'll come here. This'll be the first place the troopers'll look,' Bobby said. 'He'll be long gone to Queensland if he knows what's good for him.'

When Bandi went to pile his plate with more food, Jack and Bobby stood in silent retrospection for a moment.

'You think he's coming after us?'

Jack frowned deeply and scanned the crowd for Pru and Henry. 'Maybe we should have left the district after Viktor was caught.'

'We had no reason to,' Jack said. 'He was in prison, he didn't tell anyone we were with him. It'll be fine. Just keep your eyes open in case he does decide to come to town.'

'Hopefully, the police will recapture him before he makes it this far.'

Jack didn't feel so sure. Viktor had never been the sharpest tool at the blacksmith's. He'd have one thing on his mind before he left the district. Money. Jack owed him his cut from the last heist they ran before Viktor was caught. He'd be happy to give it to him if he knew Viktor would take it and go away, and stay away for good.

Again, he cast his eyes across the party to where Pru was talking with Mrs O'Callaghan. She looked up and waved at him. He forced a smile on his face and waved back, just as a carriage trundled by along the main road into town. Jack checked his pocket watch. It was four o'clock. The last Cobb and Co from Melbourne. It gave him an idea. A holiday. He'd take Pru and Henry away to Melbourne until Viktor was caught again, or until he was well away from Ballarat.

He wasn't afraid of Viktor. But he would do anything to keep him away from his family.

Fifteen

'This was such a wonderful idea, Jack.' Pru lifted her glass to his. 'We haven't been to the city for such a long time.'

'You deserved a holiday.' Jack touched his crystal glass to hers.

'And a dinner out? Alone.' Pru beamed, gazing around at the lavishly appointed Melbourne restaurant. 'I love Henry to pieces, but it's nice to have a special treat together, just us. I am often so tired, I don't feel as though I give you the time, or the love, you need.'

'You give me plenty of loving,' he said, a simmering, sensual look in his eye, as he took her other hand and kissed it. 'But if you think you need help, we can hire a nanny full time. Young Clara seems to handle Henry well.'

She smiled at his sweet suggestion. The nanny they had hired for the evening so that they could have this time together was a treasure. Henry was not used to strangers, but he had taken to Clara the moment she sat on the floor and played with him.

'No. I don't need help at home. Just treat me to little holidays like this occasionally and I will be blissfully happy forever.'

'Whatever makes you blissfully happy, my sweet.'

Back at the apartment, Jack paid Clara the amount due, plus a little bonus, which sent her on her way with a giant smile on her face and a promise to be available whenever they needed someone during their stay.

He checked on Henry, sleeping soundly, and then returned to the bedroom.

'Darling, I was thinking …'

Closing the door behind him, he turned to see Prudence, standing at the end of the bed, wearing a revealing ivory-coloured silk and lace nightgown. The yellow glow of the single lantern behind her illuminated her red hair, long and flowing and brushed to a shine.

The sight of her had him instantly hard.

Since Henry had been born, their lovemaking had been infrequent. At first, Jack had been worried about the strain giving birth had put on her poor, slight body. Then Henry had been their priority, as they struggled to learn how to be good parents. They were often tired, and stressed whenever Henry had a little sniffle and when he'd had colic.

This trip to the city had mostly been to get them away from the district in case Viktor made his way there. But it had also allowed them to relax, and it had been important for them to spend time alone to remind them that Henry had come from a place of real love, and they needed to find that again.

Now, as he stood staring at his beautiful wife, he knew that nothing had changed his love for her, his desire for her.

'What were you thinking, Jack?' She urged him to continue his sentence.

No idea. He had no idea what he had been thinking before he'd walked into the room and seen her.

'I was thinking, how lovely you looked tonight,' he said, walking slowly towards her. He lifted his hand to her cheek, looking her up and down. 'How beautiful you look now. My angel.'

'My devil,' she returned, with a wink, and leaned forward to kiss him softly on the mouth. 'But you have entirely too many clothes on.'

She began to undress him. Peeling his jacket from his arms first, dropping it to the floor. He helped by kicking off his shoes, as she undid his tie and his shirt buttons, before her hands lowered to the waist of his trousers, undoing the buttons there, pushing his trousers to the floor so he could step out of them.

He stood before her, naked, and revelled in the long, slow, sensual study she gave him, one eyebrow rising as she reached out and took hold of him.

'I've missed you, Jack.'

'I didn't go anywhere,' he said, his voice affected by his arousal.

'You've been so gentle with me these last months, and I have appreciated it. You've been so sweet. But I've missed the devil, Jack.'

'He's always been here, waiting.'

'No more waiting,' she said. Roughly, she pulled him against her and locked her mouth with his. His mind and body exploded with the raw passion between them. He devoured her; she enveloped him. Her scent, the feeling of her soft skin against his, wrapped around him like a hot blanket. The silk and lace of her nightdress scraped against his sensitive skin, igniting and inciting wildfires. He was a goner. And he was the luckiest man on earth.

He tossed her to the bed, none too gently he realised, but when he checked her expression she showed no signs of being hurt or upset.

'Take me, Jack,' she said. 'Love me like you used to.'

Leaning back, he shimmied the silky sheath up and over her head, leaving her bare and beautiful before him.

'So exquisite.'

Her eyes glowed in the light from the lantern, her pale skin shone, and when he ran his hand from the length of her neck, down across the small mound of her breast, along her belly, the belly that had carried his son to him, love exploded inside of him.

'I love you, Pru.'

'I know, Jack. I love you, too.'

He caressed and tasted her body, feasting in all the places he remembered would light her up, and when she arched her back on the bed, he lay his body down on hers and filled her. They made love, not softly or quietly, but with a sort of fevered frenzy, until they both fell exhausted against the sheets, sweat matting their hair and slicking their bodies together.

Taking his weight from her, he pulled the sheet up so she wouldn't get a chill, and hooking his arm around her, he fitted her back against him.

'No one will ever hurt you, my Pru,' he said softly, although the change in her breathing suggested she was already asleep. 'I will protect you and Henry with my last breath.'

Pru smothered her smile as Jack pushed a now eight-month-old Henry down the street in the elegant baby carriage. She'd never seen him look so proud, or be so friendly to everyone they came across. He usually kept a low profile, not wanting anyone to recognise him as Jack the Devil. The way she had. He nodded at people and said hello, stopping whenever a woman wanted to take a look at Henry happily sleeping beneath his warm, pale blue knitted blanket.

'The proud daddy,' she said with a chuckle as they began to walk again. At this rate it would take them hours to make it to the beach and back to the hotel again.

'And why shouldn't I be?'

'I'm the one who went through hours of painful labour to bring him into the world,' Pru argued, good-naturedly.

He leaned over and kissed her. 'Of course, my darling. I am proud of you, too.'

Pru just snorted out a laugh and rolled her eyes.

'I was thinking,' Jack said in a lowered voice.

He'd been looking very pleased with himself since they'd risen that morning. Their lovemaking had been wild and exhausting, and had rekindled their sense of fun and adventure that had been on hold since Henry had been born.

'Always a dangerous thing when Jack gets to thinking.'

He slapped her backside, and she chuckled at the horrified gasps from the pair of women who witnessed it as they passed by. She didn't care. She loved to see Jack in a playful mood.

'How would you feel about having another baby?'

She stopped walking, such was the shock of his suggestion. But she didn't say anything. Didn't know what to say. Remembering how to move her legs, she began walking again to catch up with him and Henry.

'It's a bit soon to be talking more children,' she said, finally finding her voice.

'Not right this minute. But would you consider it?'

Would she? Did she want to go through all of that again? Jack was a wonderful father and he loved Henry dearly, as did she. Would another child be a second blessing on their family? Of course it would.

'I would consider it,' she said, suddenly liking the idea. 'But not yet. Let's wait til Henry is a little older.'

'And we've had more time to "reconnect", as you say.' He leaned down to nibble on her ear, and she felt it in the lowest depths of her abdomen.

'I suggest we go home and put Henry to bed,' she said, keeping her voice low. 'And then you can put me to bed, Mr Fairweather.'

It was his turn to stop walking, and she grinned saucily back at him.

'Prudence?'

She was still smiling when natural reaction had her turning at the call of her name. Her smile fell quickly though, and a cold dread ran through her body as she recognised the woman standing before her.

'Grandmother.'

If she was surprised to see Lady Deidre Stanforth, then her grandmother appeared doubly so to see her.

Slowly, the woman's eyes tracked across Jack and then to the baby carriage. Pru held her breath as Deidre stepped forward and, with narrowed eyes, peered into the perambulator.

She said nothing for a long moment. Then her eyes lifted again to look at Jack. Deidre turned a strange puce colour, and Pru thought her grandmother looked ready to pitch a fit right there in the street. But, being the consummate Lady Carrington, she gathered herself.

'Handsome child. A boy?'

'Yes,' Jack said, more pleased than wary, Pru noticed. 'His name is Henry.'

'A good name,' Deidre said, not taking her eyes off Jack. 'I wish I could say it was good to see you again, Mr Fairweather.'

Pru watched her grandmother's calculating eyes move slowly from Jack to her and then back to her baby, still sleeping soundly.

'Where do you reside?' Deidre asked. 'I should like to send a gift of congratulations.'

Fear struck like a hard fist to her chest. There was no way in hell she was letting her grandmother know where they were living.

'We have to be going,' she said and, shoving Jack out of the way, she took over carriage duty and began to walk briskly down the street, back in the direction of the hotel.

'Pru?' She heard Jack call after her but didn't stop. 'Prudence! Wait!'

She kept walking, as quickly as she could. She had to put as much distance between Henry and her grandmother as she could. She felt a hand clasp down firmly on her arm and had no choice but to stop.

'My darling, you'd give the horses at Flemington a run for their money,' Jack said with a breathless laugh.

'We have to go,' she told him, her heart racing and not just from the brisk walk. 'We have to leave Melbourne. Now.'

'What? Why?'

'Because now she knows I have a son,' Pru said, her eyes filling with tears. Panicked, she began to push the baby carriage again, not stopping even when he called after her.

'Wait, Pru! I don't understand.' Catching up to her again, he forced her to stop. 'Pru, what are you so afraid of? She's an old lady. She doesn't run your life anymore.'

'Don't you see? Henry is a future Earl of Carrington,' Pru said, putting her hand up to stop an oncoming carriage as she crossed the road. Jack tried desperately to keep up with her. 'My uncles don't have sons. She will do anything in her power to take Henry from me. From us.'

'Don't be silly,' Jack said, looking at her as though she'd gone crazy. 'We're Henry's parents. She can't just take him away from us for no good reason.'

'She'll find a good reason.'

'You're being ridiculous. She seemed surprisingly pleasant.'

'That in itself should tell you to be wary,' Pru said. 'When has she ever been pleasant to you?'

Jack looked thoughtful but had no answer.

'She'll be pleasant right up to the point when she serves us papers saying that I am an unfit mother, and she will take custody of Henry.'

'Pru, I think you're overreacting.'

'Do you remember the story I told you?' she tossed back. 'She took me away from her own daughter and kept us apart for twenty-two years.'

Jack looked down at Henry and then back at her. His expression was more serious, as he seemed to suddenly understand that her fear was possibly quite rational. Deidre had done it before; Pru couldn't be entirely sure she wouldn't do it again.

'Alright,' Jack said finally. 'Let's go.'

She exhaled with relief and kissed him quickly before they dashed back along the street and into the hotel. Inside an hour, Jack had their belongings packed and loaded into a carriage to take them to the train station at Spencer Street.

On the journey to Geelong, Pru barely let Henry out of her sight. She held him most of the train trip until Jack finally took him.

'It will be okay,' Jack said. 'Try to relax. You're safe. Henry's safe. She'll never take him from you. I'll never let that happen, you know that, don't you?'

She nodded and leaned her head against his shoulder, suddenly extremely tired.

'At least she doesn't know where we live,' Pru said, but deep down she knew that if her grandmother wanted to know, there would be nothing she wouldn't do to find out. She had the money and resources to do anything she needed to, to get what she wanted.

'Pru, she looked stricken when you ran off with Henry.'

She met his eyes but said nothing.

'She wasn't angry,' he added, 'just disappointed and … a little sad, I think.'

What could she say to that? Staring out the window at the passing fields, she did feel some measure of guilt over her behaviour both that day and on the day she'd left. Not to mention during the twelve hours she had returned to the manor when she'd left Jack. No matter what Gran had done, keeping her real mother from her, Pru had to admit she had been given a comfortable and happy home.

But when she imagined Henry growing up without his mother, being taken from her, panic overrode the guilt tenfold.

'She'll not get her hands on my boy, Jack. Not ever.'

On arrival back in Ballarat, the sun was already setting and dark rain clouds were rolling in. Jack left Pru and Henry in the warmth and comfort of the Bath Hotel while he headed back to the transport office to collect their dray to take them the rest of the way home.

Hearing a noise behind him as he hooked up the horses, he turned and found himself staring straight into the face of Viktor Petrovic.

'Jack the Devil.'

'Viktor,' Jack said, looking around to ensure no one was within hearing distance. The office was closed, the lights out, but he could hear traffic on the street and people walking by. 'I'd heard you'd escaped,' he said. 'I thought you'd be long gone by now.'

'Then you know why I'm here and not running to New South Wales yet,' Viktor said, lighting a cigarette. 'You took off to Melbourne before I could speak to you. That was rude. You owe me the money, Jack. The money from the robbery that saw me go to prison while you and Bobby stayed free. You owe me.'

'Don't know what you're talking about.' Jack shrugged. 'I'm an honest businessman.'

'Ha! Jack the Devil? An honest businessman?'

Laughter from the street reminded Jack he had to be careful.

'Keep your voice down,' he hissed, moving Viktor further into the stables.

Viktor released himself from Jack's grip. 'You have made a good life for yourself here. I'd hate to have to ruin it for you. I've been watching you. I saw you settling your pretty wife at the Bath with your son. Nice family. Would be a shame if something happened to them.'

'Don't threaten me.' All thought of trying to solve the issue with Viktor politely and easily fled the moment Viktor brought Pru and Henry into it. 'You go anywhere near them and you will never see your money. All you'll see is me waving as the police drag you back to prison.'

Viktor's expression hardened. 'You will have to kill me first.'

'That's also a possibility.'

Viktor shot out a sardonic laugh. 'You don't have what it takes to kill. Never did. You will get me the money, and then you will set me up in one of your shiny coaches and take me to Wangaratta. I hear Dan Morgan is there. He also owes me money.'

'You're going to try to get money out of Mad Dog Morgan?' Jack asked with a snorting laugh. 'Do you have a death wish? He's a crazed murderer. Even more so than you.'

'Gaol has mellowed me.' Viktor smiled through rotten teeth. 'I have never told the police who was with me that day. Told them I couldn't remember names, that my English is not so good. But suddenly I am recalling the events more clearly. I can take you down with me, should you decide to turn me in.'

Jack shrugged. 'Who would believe the word of a convict over a man who runs a reputable business?'

'Not so reputable, I hear.' Viktor chuckled. 'Why just the other day, I overheard a gentleman telling someone in the bar that his coach from Melbourne had been held up by bushrangers and he'd lost his favourite pistol.'

Jack shrugged easily. 'Wasn't me.'

'It is clever,' Viktor went on. 'Owning a transport company and robbing yourself. Who would ever guess? And I imagine you have taken quite a good haul over the years.'

Out of patience, Jack hissed quietly. 'Fine, I will get you your money, Viktor. Give me a few days.'

'You have until Sunday.'

'It's Saturday tomorrow. The banks are closed. How do you expect me to get your money by Sunday?'

Viktor tossed his cigarette to the ground and extinguished the burning end with the heel of his boot. 'Don't treat me like a fool, Jack. I know you have a stash somewhere, hidden, so that when you have to run, you can move fast. I want what you owe me from that heist eight years ago. Get it for me by Sunday night, meet me back here at five o'clock, or I will come and take it from you. And whatever else I feel like taking.'

He'd gone over the matter a hundred times in his head. There was nothing left to do but pay Viktor and hope he'd get out of their lives, forever. So when Sunday arrived, he waited until Pru was out of the house and, removing the loose floorboard in the bedroom, he retrieved the canvas bag he'd stashed away for safekeeping. Counting out the money he owed Viktor, he returned the rest to the hiding place and refitted the floorboard, flicking the rug back where it belonged. He needed to head into town, and he needed to leave soon or he'd miss Viktor's deadline. It was already getting late. Checking that everything was set to rights, he walked through the house and out onto the back porch.

Seeing him come out, Pru looked up and smiled. 'Jack, look at Henry.'

He stepped down off the porch to where his wife and son were playing on a blanket in the backyard. Taking his hand, she pulled him down to sit with them.

'Watch,' she said and turned back to their son. 'Come on, Henry, show Daddy.'

Giggling, Henry crawled over to Jack and grabbing hold of the material of Jack's shirt, he pulled himself up onto his pudgy little legs.

'He's standing?' Jack asked in awe, as Henry let go and clapped his hands together.

Pru clapped along with him until Henry fell back on his bottom again, letting out another gurgling giggle.

'Isn't he wonderful?' Pru gushed.

Jack's heart was so full of love for them he thought he would burst. What wouldn't he do to protect his family? He may never have killed a man before, but he would gladly kill anyone who even attempted to harm his beautiful wife and son.

'He is wonderful,' Jack said, pulling her against his side and kissing her. He rolled her onto her back on the blanket.

'Jack! Henry ...' Pru tried to argue and squirm away from him, but he only held on tighter and kissed her more fervently.

'He doesn't mind his mummy and daddy kissing, do you, son?'

Henry crawled across the blanket and joined in the cuddle, making them all laugh.

'Da!'

And the laughter stopped.

Jack sat up and stared at Henry, who had plopped back to his bottom again.

'Did he just …?'

Pru sat up, too, smiling broadly.

'Did he just say "Da"?'

'Oh, Jack, I think it's too early for him to know actual words.'

'For other kids maybe, but my boy is a genius!' Jack scooped Henry up and tossed him in the air, catching him easily. The giggles coming out of his child had him higher than any shot of whisky could ever achieve.

'Say it again, son. Da. Da.'

'Da,' Henry repeated and squealed with laughter when Jack tossed him in the air again.

'My son is a genius!' Jack announced proudly.

'I hardly think one word makes him a genius,' Pru teased, ruffling Henry's soft hair. 'And it's barely a word.'

'Are you joking? Standing and speaking in the same day? We should enrol him in the new school.'

Pru took Henry from Jack. 'It's a few years too soon for that.'

'Not for my boy.'

Pru laughed again. 'Are you going somewhere?'

'Huh?'

She lifted his new bowler hat from the grass where he'd dropped it. He'd seen it in the newspaper. It was the latest fashion statement and he'd ordered it from London. The thing had cost him a fortune. It was his downfall, his addiction to the latest fashion trends. A man in business had to look good though.

'Oh, yes.' His mood soured when he remembered his meeting with Viktor. He glanced at his pocket watch.

Damn, he was running late.

'I have to go into the office for a while.'

'But it's Sunday,' Pru complained.

'Coaches still run on weekends, my love,' he said. 'You wanted me to be a businessman. If I'd stuck with bushranging I would run my own schedule and I would be able to spend my Sundays with my darling wife and genius son.'

'Until you ended up with a bullet in you, again,' Pru sighed. 'Very well. Will you be home for dinner?'

'I shall do my utmost.'

He kissed her deeply. He hated the thought of leaving her, or of handing over so much of his hard-earned—well, hard-stolen—cash to a man as vicious and corrupt at Viktor. But, he reminded himself again, he was doing this for her. For her, and for Henry. They wouldn't be safe until Viktor had been paid, and was gone from the district.

As he reached the side of the house, heading to the stables, he turned back once more and smiled at his little family, a picture of love and innocence in the late-afternoon sunshine. Yes, he would do anything it took to keep them safe.

When the sun began to set, the evening cooled and it was time to get Henry fed and ready for bed. Jack had said he would only be a short while, and as she prepared dinner she wondered what could be keeping him. A drink with Bobby most likely. Sharing the good news of his genius son. She chuckled. She couldn't begrudge him that pleasure.

The knock at the door surprised her. She'd been expecting Jack, but why was he knocking at the door?

'It's about time.' She opened the door and immediately wished that she hadn't when she saw the man standing there. Tall and slim, with unkempt hair and a growth of beard, he looked to her like a drifter.

'Can I help you?' she asked, keeping the door only slightly ajar.

'Where's Jack?'

'Are you a friend of his?'

He snorted derisively. 'You could say that.'

She was sure she had never seen this man before and she really didn't like the way he looked at her. 'And you are?'

'Viktor.'

Viktor? How did she know that name? Her mind rolled back through all the conversations she'd ever had with Jack. A vague recollection came to mind, a long distant memory of the name. Then she noticed the scar across his left eye, and it hit her like a cold wind coursing through her body. Viktor the Vicious.

'Jack's not here,' she told him, and tried to close the door on him.

But the door wouldn't close and she looked down to see that he had stuck his foot in to keep it open. Being stronger than her, he easily pushed the door wide open again and she had to step back as he walked in.

'I'll wait,' he said.

'You can't just push your way into my home.'

Her son took that moment to gurgle and Viktor wandered across to the little bassinet on the floor next to the rocking chair.

'Cute little bugger,' Viktor said and Henry let out a cry when he leaned down to rub his belly.

'What's wrong with him?' he asked, scowling further, if that was possible.

She wanted to say that Henry didn't like Viktor any more than she did, but she felt it was safer to hold her tongue.

'He's hungry.' She leaned down to pick up her beloved baby. 'I need to feed him. So if you don't mind, you should come back later, or wait outside til Jack gets home.'

Pru ground her teeth with frustration when Viktor ignored her and simply sat at the dining-room table. 'I'll wait right here.'

'Why are you here?' she questioned, hoping she'd find some way of getting him to leave.

'Jack owes me money.'

'Why would he owe you money?' she asked. The arrogant smirk on Viktor's face did nothing to calm her nerves.

'You and I both know what he is. What he does for a living.'

'What he did,' she corrected him.

Viktor huffed out a laugh. 'You thought he'd quit?'

Pru didn't answer. Was Viktor lying or had Jack started bush-ranging again?

'A man of the highway can slow down but he's never gonna be anything other than a highwayman. He'll keep on thieving til he's caught or taking the long dirt nap.'

Pru felt the betrayal deeply. She couldn't believe it. Jack was still bushranging? When Henry was born, he had promised her it would stop. She steeled her gaze. Whatever anger she felt over the possibility of Jack's continuing bushranger ways, she wasn't about to discuss it with this revolting man.

Henry cried again.

'I have to feed Henry,' she said, moving to the bedroom.

She could be a polite host and offer the man a cup of tea while he waited but she didn't want to encourage him to stay.

She pulled the door closed behind her and unlaced the bodice of her dress to provide Henry with her breast.

He latched on hungrily and she let out the nervous breath she'd been holding. But that breath was hastily dragged back in on a gasp when the door opened.

Viktor stood there staring at her unashamedly as he leaned against the door. His eyes went to her breast and she used a cloth to cover herself and Henry's head.

'What do you think you're doing?' she demanded, trying to keep her voice calm for Henry, but she was livid. 'Get out of here!'

He didn't make a move. Just continued to stand there staring at her, a lascivious smile on his ugly face.

'Jack won't be happy, Viktor,' she tried. 'Leave now and I won't tell him about this.'

'He owes me money,' Victor said slowly. 'And he's been dodging me. I'm not going anywhere until I get it. And if I don't get it soon, maybe I will take what's owed to me some other way.'

He stepped further into the room. Pru pulled Henry from her breast and covered herself. Henry screamed in protest at having his dinner interrupted. She stood to move towards the door but Viktor blocked her path. Her anger was quickly replaced with fear, for Henry and for herself.

'If you so much as harm one hair on my boy's head, I'll kill you,' she said, trembling with the combination of rage and fear. 'Jack will kill you.'

'Jack doesn't have what it takes to kill another man,' he said with a snort. 'Never has. I always did the dirty work. I am good at the dirty work.'

'Jack may not have what it takes to kill a man,' Pru said. 'But I do.'

Viktor laughed loudly, setting Henry crying again. 'Yeah, I'd bet you fight like a wildcat. I bet you do other things like a wildcat, too.'

Henry stopped crying long enough to spit up some of his dinner and Pru moved towards the armoire. But as she opened the top drawer to retrieve another cloth for him her eyes fell on the revolver that lay there. She'd hated it when Jack had shown her all the guns he'd hidden around the house. Now she blessed him silently for teaching her how to shoot one.

When Viktor took another step towards her, she put her hand in the drawer and pulled out the gun, aiming it at him. He looked stunned for a moment before he smiled again.

'Well, well. You're a feisty one, aren't ya? Now I see why Jack likes you.'

'Get out,' she demanded quietly. She wished her voice and her hand were steadier, but she was doing alright considering the panic she felt.

'Do you know how to use one of those things?' Viktor asked. 'Don't shoot your hand off, little lady.'

She lowered the weapon a little and he laughed.

'You see, it is too heavy for a woman to hold,' Viktor said. 'You can't even lift it to my chest.'

'I'm not aiming for your chest.'

He looked down at where she was pointing the gun and frowned, clearly horrified to see she was aiming at his nether regions. He did take a step back then.

'You might not die, but it will sure as hell hurt and you'll bleed like a stuck pig,' she told him. She could see in his eyes that he was thinking over his options. 'Now move.'

He backed out of the bedroom and she followed him cautiously, a screaming Henry in one arm and the revolver in the other hand still pointed at the mass of his belly. She was careful to stay at a safe distance from him. It would be easy for him to overpower her if she got too close.

When they had made their way across the house to the front door, Viktor stopped.

'Tell Jack I'll find him.'

'Out!' she said, motioning with the gun.

He gave her one last filthy look before turning and stomping out onto the porch, down the stairs and back to his waiting horse. She didn't move until she'd seen him go more than a mile down the road.

As the panic fled her body, she let out a whimpering breath, and allowed herself a moment to cry with Henry, who was still wailing. Then she rushed back into the house, put Henry down in his play area, while she ran around locking every possible door and window and moving heavy furniture up against the doors so that no one could break their way in. For the windows that wouldn't lock, she had to get a little inventive.

When she was convinced that she and Henry were locked up tight and safe, she dragged the rocking chair to the middle of the room and sat with Henry happily back at her breast and the gun in her hand pointed at the door.

Sixteen

Annoyed and exhausted, Jack rode quickly back to the house. He'd missed Viktor by minutes. The son-of-a-bitch hadn't waited. And now he'd have to find another way to get him the money without Pru knowing. He needed to keep her and Henry well out of it. And he needed to make sure Viktor had no idea where he lived.

D'Artagnan snorted as the house came into sight.

'Nearly there, boy,' he said, giving him a good pat on the shoulder.

After settling the horse in the stable with oats and water, Jack dragged himself up to the porch. Lifting the latch, he pushed at the front door. It didn't budge. Baffled, he went to the window. Peering in through the glass, he could see Pru asleep in the rocking chair with Henry asleep in the bassinet beside her.

He smiled. His little family. Not wanting to wake her, he carefully slid the window frame up as quietly as he could. It wouldn't have mattered how quiet he was, because when he put one foot inside, he stepped on something that made a God-almighty racket. Once his second foot was inside the room, he looked down to see a collection of pots and pans and even the chamber-pot collected beneath the window.

When he looked up again, Pru was standing in the middle of the room with a gun pointed right at him.

'Pru?'

'Oh, Jack,' she said, exhaling a heavy relieved breath as she lowered the gun, rubbing at her sleepy eyes.

Jack looked around the house. Both doors had been barricaded from the inside with whatever furniture she could shift by herself, every window had something either in front of it or was set up as a noisy trap like the one Jack had come across.

'What in blazes is going on here?'

She rushed forward and he caught her as she crushed herself to him.

'Pru, you're shaking,' he said, concern filling him. He took the gun from her hand, scared it would go off considering the violence of her tremors.

'Pru, please tell me what happened,' he said again, but she just continued to hold him tightly.

When Henry cried, she seemed to recover a little of her strength. She stepped away from him and went to Henry. Jack laid the gun on the bureau beside him and went to take Henry from Pru as she picked him up.

'What's going on? What happened here tonight?' he asked. 'Why is the house barricaded up like the Eureka Stockade?'

She looked weary, but there was still fear in the deep forest of her eyes. He sat her down at the table and, juggling Henry in one arm, poured himself a glass of brandy. Before he could take a sip, she took the glass from his hand and drank the entire contents in one belt. She rarely drank since she'd been breastfeeding Henry, but saying nothing he poured another glass for himself and sat beside her.

'Tell me what happened.'

'Viktor happened,' she said.

Fear and fury warred within him. 'Viktor was here?'

'He said you owe him money.'

The tone of her voice alerted him. The panic had gone from her eyes and the irritated expression she wore said it all. What lies had Viktor told her? The bastard must have headed straight here when Jack had only been a few minutes late. How the hell had he even known where he lived? He must have asked around. Jack had kept this place a secret when he'd been bushranging, before he'd met Pru. But he had to admit that plenty of people in town now knew that Jack Fairweather and his wife lived in the little homestead between Ballarat and Ballan.

'I'm not bushranging again, if that's what he told you.' He shook his head furiously. 'He didn't believe me when I said I'd gone straight. Anyway, that doesn't matter. What did he say? What did he do?'

'After barging his way in here, I told him to wait for you in the sitting room, but he followed me into the bedroom where I was feeding Henry.'

It took him a moment to realise what that meant as she took Henry and held him close, as if she needed to know he was protected.

Jack went very still.

'He saw you … he watched you …' Jack began but couldn't finish the sentence. Viktor had leered at his wife while she was half dressed. She'd been doing something so natural for a mother and had been made to feel uncomfortable by a lecherous criminal. Viktor had a reputation for being the lowest of men with very little respect for women, and Jack wouldn't put it past him to stoop so low as to threaten a woman and her child. But Pru was his woman. And Viktor would pay for that.

He stood up and paced the floor, the fury rolling through him like a freight train.

'Are you still bushranging, Jack?'

'No!'

'Then why does he think you owe him money?'

'That was from years ago,' Jack assured her. 'Before he went into prison. I owed him his share from that heist. He came to collect.' She stared him down, as though she could make him confess his lies with a look. Had he been a lesser man, had he actually been lying, that look would have broken him.

'Just when exactly do you think I would have time to go back out on the road?' he asked, taking Henry back from her again. He hoped to remind her that he was her loving husband and the father of his child.

'Very well.'

She stood and took Henry from him again. There went his shield. As she disappeared into the bedroom, Jack turned his thoughts to Viktor. He stilled owed Viktor money and the man would come calling again.

Pru returned a moment later, having put Henry in his little bed, and began to make tea.

'Pru …' he tried.

'Viktor isn't going to stop looking for you, is he?'

'Oh, yes, he will.'

'What does that mean?' Pru spun around, a small frown of concern crinkling between her eyebrows. 'Are you going to pay him?'

He didn't answer her. He was thinking, planning.

'Jack? What does that mean?'

'It means I'd kill him before he tried to come back here again,' he said, his voice low and dangerous.

'No, Jack, you will do no such thing,' she said, moving towards him. 'You've already been shot once. I won't go through that again. Henry's fine. I'm fine. We had the gun and we protected ourselves. It was good that you left it and showed me how to use it.'

'You're a good shot,' he said, calming a little. 'Better than me.'

She smiled. 'I know. I managed to convince Viktor of that, too. Scared him enough that he left.'

Jack's teeth ground together again and he couldn't stop imagining all the possibilities of what might have happened.

'Come on,' she said softly, leaning in to kiss his tense mouth. 'It's after midnight. Let's go to bed and forget this whole day.'

'Alright, my love.' He gave in, kissing her forehead and then her lips again.

'And you'll forget about going after Viktor, right?'

He didn't answer, just moved her towards the bedroom.

'Jack?'

He had no intention of promising her that Viktor would not end up face down in a gully with a bullet in his chest.

'Let's just go to sleep.'

Her beautiful brow was still rippled with worry, but she said no more and let him take her to bed.

He made love to his wife, filled with relief that the woman he adored and loved was safe, that his child was safe. He turned his anger into passion and exhausted them both. But when Pru fell into a deep sleep, he lay wide awake, working through the plan that had begun to form. He hoped Viktor slept well. Because it would be his last night on earth.

Prudence woke to Henry's crying. It was a normal morning, but she was exhausted from the late night, the altercation with Viktor and then her husband's passionate and extended lovemaking. It had been a long time since they had made love like that. Like two lovers who knew they had one last night to be together.

The thought struck Pru as she lay in that fuzzy world between sleep and waking.

One last night.

Quickly, she rolled in her bed to reach for Jack. She was alone.

'Jack?' she called out.

Crawling out of bed, she moved over and picked up Henry. He needed to be dealt with first, so she gave him her breast and sat back on the bed to watch her son feed.

Why on earth would Jack be up so early? she wondered.

Perhaps he had decided to go and milk the goat and let her have a lie-in. Perhaps he'd had trouble sleeping. It had been a frightening night and very late when they had finally fallen into bed. And she had felt him tossing and turning beside her for a good portion of the darkest hours.

When Henry had finally had enough milk, she lay him over her shoulder and walked out into the kitchen to make a pot of tea. Henry finally let out a cute little belch and she chuckled.

'There's my good little man,' she said and put him down on the floor with his favourite toy, a drum Jack had seen in a store in Ballarat. The thing gave her a headache, but Henry loved banging the big wooden stick against the animal skin, and it kept him entertained for hours. 'Now, where is your daddy, do you think?'

Looking about the room she glanced at the bureau, and froze. The gun. Jack had laid it on the bureau the night before after he'd disarmed her.

It wasn't there.

She opened all the drawers in the bureau. Nothing.

She dashed across to the stables. Persephone was gone. Jack was gone. And she knew exactly where.

'Dammit.'

She rushed back into the house and impatiently thought about where he would have gone first in order to find Viktor, all the while trying not to think about Jack killing Viktor, or worse, about Viktor killing him.

She paced the floor. 'When I get my hands on that father of yours, Henry, I'll wring his neck myself.'

Henry looked up at her with big brown eyes and stopped drumming long enough to smile at her. He looked so much like his daddy at that moment she gasped. The same tawny eyes and devilish grin, and the boy was not even a year old yet. If Jack lived to see his son grow up, he'd see a mirror image, she was sure. And just now she wasn't convinced that was a good thing. The last thing she needed was another devil on her hands.

She needed to go after Jack, but how could she with Henry?

She'd just poured tea when she heard horses. Praying it was Jack, she rushed to the door and threw it open. Bobby and Katie dismounted their horses and Katie stepped up onto the porch to kiss Pru's cheeks.

'Good morning. Where's that beautiful boy of yours?' She moved past Pru and into the house.

Pru stayed where she was, watching as Bobby stepped up onto the porch too.

'Where's Jack?' she asked.

He looked conflicted, wouldn't meet her eyes.

'Bobby, I know he's gone after Viktor,' she said. 'Please, tell me he hasn't done anything that can't be undone.'

Bobby hesitated and then gave in. 'Not yet. Not as far as we know anyway. He showed up on our doorstep in the godforsaken wee hours of this morning and asked us to come out and protect you and Henry in case Viktor came back.'

Pru moved quickly into the house. Katie had Henry on her lap and he was gurgling and laughing happily. Her prayers had just been answered.

She disappeared into the bedroom and a moment later came out dressed and shoving a gun into the pocket of her coat. She'd remembered the tiny pistol Jack had popped into her purse one afternoon for protection on the roads.

'Pru, what are you doing?' Bobby asked.

'I'm going after Jack.'

'He told us you should stay here.'

'I told him I didn't want him going after Viktor,' Pru shot back angrily. 'He'll get himself killed.'

She moved to kiss Henry on his soft downy head.

'Take care of Henry for me,' she said to Katie.

'Pru—' Katie started.

'What would you do, Katie?' Pru interrupted. 'If it were Bobby? What would you do?'

Her heart ached as Bobby and Katie exchanged loving and understanding looks.

'Go,' Katie said with a resigned nod. 'We've got Henry. He'll be safe.'

'Take my horse,' Katie offered. 'She's already saddled.'

'I'm going with you,' Bobby insisted.

'No,' Pru said. 'If Viktor comes back, you need to be here for Katie and Henry. Please, Bobby, please do this for me.'

Reluctantly he nodded.

'Where was Jack going?' Pru asked as she headed for the door.

'Duchess of Kent Hotel,' Bobby called after her. 'Viktor stayed there last night, room five. Pru, be careful. Viktor is a dangerous man. You don't know what he'll do.'

'I'm more worried about what Jack will do. I've never seen him so deathly calm in his anger before. He's going to kill Viktor, I know it.'

'Would that be such a shame?' Bobby asked.

Pru didn't answer. She took a last look at her smiling baby, hoping he would get to see his mama and papa again, and closed the door behind her. Mounting Katie's horse with ease, she turned and headed out of the gates, on her way to Ballarat.

All the way to Ballarat, Pru's mind whirled with what she might find when she found Jack. If he'd found Viktor, had he killed him? Or had Viktor killed Jack? Neither scenario was good. She prayed, and willed Jack not to do anything stupid.

Shaking the multitude of unhelpful images from her head, she urged Katie's horse to go faster. Didn't he realise that all he had to do was tell the police where Viktor was and the convict would be tossed back into gaol where he belonged? No, Jack was too angry to think clearly. But then, would Viktor give Jack up as well? Would the police believe Viktor? She couldn't take that chance; she had to get to Jack.

Arriving at the Duchess of Kent, she tied the horse at the rear of the saloon. It would be smarter to remain unseen. Jack had God knows how many hours head start on her. Surely he'd caught up with Viktor by now and … No. She couldn't, she wouldn't, think that way. Perhaps Viktor had been out bushranging, playing cards at another hotel, or maybe he was at Miss Lola's. He'd been in prison for eight years. A man like him would spend time doing all the things he'd missed out on in gaol. He'd need money and he'd want a woman. She hoped the man's basic needs would keep him away from the hotel.

Peering into the rear entrance of the hotel, Pru stopped to listen. It was quiet. Most patrons would still be in bed, she assumed. Taking the back stairs as silently as she could, she moved up to the second floor.

Room five, Bobby had said. Standing at the door, she tried to think of what she would say to Viktor. Not only had she grabbed the gun when she'd left the house, she'd taken the wad of pounds she had hidden away in case of an emergency. It was a lot of money, and if this wasn't an emergency, she didn't know what was. She doubted Jack would pay Viktor what he owed him now, but if she could get him the money, perhaps Viktor would take it and leave them all alone. She'd tell him to take the money and get out of town or she'd tell the police where he was. And if that didn't work, if he threatened to expose Jack ... The gun was cold against her hand in her pocket, but it didn't stop her palms from sweating as nerves overwhelmed her. She hoped she wasn't too late and that Jack hadn't found Viktor already.

Taking a deep, steadying breath, she knocked softly. There was no answer, so she knocked a little louder. When there was still no response, she tried the door handle. It opened and she stepped quickly inside.

The room was dark and smelled like man and liquor, blended with another odour she didn't recognise. Only a thin sliver of dawn light made it through a gap in the heavy curtains. Dust motes danced in the pale light, and as her eyes adjusted she could see the shape of Viktor sprawled across the bed fully clothed. She closed the door behind her with a bang, surprised when he didn't make a move. Still so drunk from the night before, no doubt, that he couldn't move. But she took the pistol from her coat pocket anyway, just in case.

'Viktor, wake up,' she demanded in a voice that didn't waver, despite her fear. 'You need to get out of town before I go to the police.' Not quite how she had rehearsed it, but he'd get the point.

Nothing. The damn man was probably passed out drunk. A pillow across his chest obscured her view, feathers scattered across the bed from a tear in the lining. Stepping a little closer, she tried to make him out in the darkness of the room. Too frightened to stick to her original plan, she pulled the money from her coat pocket and tossed it on the end of the bed.

'Here's the money Jack owed you. Take it and get out of town. And never come back, never threaten me or my family again, or I'll show you just how good a shot I am.' The gun shook in her hand, and she took a deep breath to steady it as she pointed it at his chest.

Still nothing. She kicked his leg where it hung off the side of the bed and tried again.

'Just thank your lucky stars that I got here before Jack.'

Moving closer still, she saw his half-opened eyes. He looked strange. Too relaxed even in his drunken state. Her foot caught in a corner of the blanket that had slid to the floor and she staggered forward, pulling the rest of the blanket down from his body as she fell. She had to put a hand out on the bed to stop herself from landing flat against Viktor's body. Knowing she was far too close to Viktor than was safe, she scrambled to get up and away from him. He was a strong man who could overpower her—even blind drunk. But as she righted herself, the pillow shifted and she saw the dark stain on his white undershirt.

'Oh, dear Lord!' she gasped.

Pushing up off the bed, she gasped again as Viktor's head lolled to the side. The man was dead.

Seventeen

She managed to stifle the scream that threatened, mostly because her mouth had dried up. All that came out was an unnatural squeak. Staggering back away from the bed, her foot caught the blanket again, and as she skidded on the shiny wooden floors, she squeezed too hard on the trigger.

The noise of the gunshot exploded into the room about a second before the noise of the door bursting open.

'Prudence?'

She whirled around.

'Jack!'

He rushed forward and took the pistol she was still waving about, before staring down at the body of Viktor. She began to shake uncontrollably as he checked Viktor for any signs of life.

'Pru. What have you done?'

'What have *I* done? What have *you* done, Jack?'

'You're the one with the gun.'

'He was dead before I got here,' she insisted.

'Then why did you shoot him again?'

Pru frowned at the new bullet wound in Viktor's chest.

'It … it was an accident,' she stammered, horrified that she had shot a man—a dead man, but a man all the same. 'I slipped on the floorboards and the gun went off.'

'Shhh,' he reprimanded. 'We have to get out of here. People will have heard the gunshot.'

He pushed her roughly out of the room and down the back stairs of the hotel, just as they heard people rushing up the front stairs.

Finally outside, they mounted their horses and set off at pace for the scrubby bushland that would hide them.

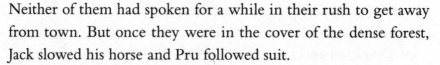

Neither of them had spoken for a while in their rush to get away from town. But once they were in the cover of the dense forest, Jack slowed his horse and Pru followed suit.

'How could you do it, Jack?' Pru asked. Now that her fear had abated, the horror of what she'd seen, what she'd done— unintentionally, of course—hit home.

'What did I do?'

The innocent look in his face would have been funny, if the situation weren't so serious. 'You killed Viktor!'

'I didn't kill him!'

'But you shot him.'

'No, I didn't.'

'So it was just a coincidence that you left our house in the early hours of the morning. That you happened to be in his room. And that now he's dead.'

'You were the one in his room, waving a gun about no less.'

'But I didn't shoot him!' she yelled and then shook her head, trying to clear it. 'That is, I didn't shoot him the first time, and the second was an accident.'

Jack was unusually quiet as they walked the horses, and Pru gasped at his expression.

'Oh Lord, you don't believe me.'

He still didn't say anything.

'Why would I shoot him when I specifically told *you* not to go after him?'

'He wasn't in the hotel when I got there,' Jack threw back. 'I went out looking for him and he must have come back while I was searching all the hotels of Ballarat.'

She gave an unladylike snort. 'Jack, you said you'd given up bushranging. You can hardly be surprised that I don't believe a word you say to me just now.'

'I have given up bushranging!' he yelled at the sky. 'I didn't lie to you about that, Pru, and I'm not lying about this. Why would you believe what Viktor told you? He hasn't seen me in years. Of course he'd assume I'm still working the highways.'

They rode in silence again for a while, both lost in their own thoughts, trying to work through the situation.

'You still went after him when I told you not to?'

'He threatened my family,' Jack said through gritted teeth. 'I didn't shoot him, but I am not unhappy he's dead.'

'What are we going to do now?'

'I'm sure you didn't mean to kill him,' Jack said. 'He pushed you to it.'

'I only came looking for you. To try to stop you.'

'And you found Viktor first. It's okay, Pru. I'm not going to have you arrested. In fact, we should throw a damn party.'

'A party is hardly advisable after you've just killed a man.'

Jack made a grunting noise of frustration.

'Let's just forget about it, alright?' Pru suggested. It was obvious that neither of them believed the other didn't kill Viktor. 'Do you think anyone saw us there?'

'Someone could have seen either one of us going in or out of the hotel,' Jack said thoughtfully. 'We need to get our stories straight.'

'We'll talk about this later. We need to get home to Henry,' Pru said and kicked her horse into a trot.

For two days, Jack and Pru stayed close to the house, trying to remain positive, trying desperately to get on with life, knowing that any minute there could be a knock at the door and the police on the other side of it.

Bobby and Katie promised to let them know if they heard of anyone being arrested or questioned. By Tuesday evening, there'd been no news and they'd started to relax a little. Pru couldn't help but wonder though. If it wasn't Jack who'd killed Viktor, and it certainly wasn't her, then who had?

They were about to sit down to dinner when it came. The hoofbeats of several horses coming towards the house. And when Pru opened the door, her worst fears were confirmed.

'Good evening, Sergeant Carmichael.'

'Evening, ma'am,' the sergeant said, removing his hat. 'Is your husband at home?'

'We were just about to sit down to dinner, Sergeant,' Pru said, trying hard to calm her racing heart. 'You're not here to question him about coaches being attacked again, are you?'

'May we come in?'

Pru glanced from the sergeant to his two constables. His reluctance to tell her why they were there rang alarm bells. Finally, she stepped back and motioned for the three men to enter the house.

'Sweetheart, who is it?' Jack asked, as he stepped in from the kitchen with Henry in his arms. 'Oh, hey Sarge. What can I do for you? Mickey.'

'Mr Fairweather,' Constable Mickey Doyle returned.

'Mr Fairweather?' Jack laughed. 'Come on, Mickey, what's with the formalities? We're mates. I've been beating you at cards since you were fifteen.'

The constable gave an uncomfortable grimace. 'Jack, give over. I'm here on business.'

'Business?' Pru questioned.

The sergeant graced Mickey with a glance that had the constable stepping back. 'We have some questions regarding the death of man at the Duchess of Kent Hotel on Monday morning. Mr Fairweather, where were you yesterday between midnight and eight am?'

'You say a man died?' Pru asked.

'A man named Viktor Petrovic was shot and killed in his bed at the Duchess of Kent in the early hours of Monday morning.'

'Should I know who that is?' Jack tossed Henry in the air and caught him, making the boy giggle.

'He's a convict. Escaped from Pentridge Prison about a month ago. He's been spotted in this area and one of the waitresses at the Duchess said you and he had quite the heated discussion behind your office a few days ago.'

'I don't recall any such heated discussion. I may have perhaps had a passing word with a gentleman about transport to New South Wales. I suppose that may have been him. He's an escaped convict? How has he been in the area for a month now without having been caught?'

The sergeant's jaw went tight; he was not enjoying having the interview turned back on him. His failure to capture an escaped prisoner was clearly a sore point. 'I'll ask you again, Mr Fairweather. Where were you yesterday between midnight and eight in the morning?'

'He was with me, of course,' Pru answered quickly.

The sergeant didn't look convinced. 'Unless you can provide a better alibi than that, I'm afraid you are going to have to come down to the station until we can get this sorted out.'

'Am I under arrest?' Jack asked, handing Henry across to Pru when he grizzled.

'A gentleman saw you leave the Duchess of Kent Hotel that morning,' Carmichael said. 'You need to come to the station and see if the witness recognises you.'

'Plenty of people come and go from that hotel,' Jack said with an easy shrug.

'There must be some mistake,' Pru argued. 'As you just heard, Jack was with me. He couldn't have killed this person.'

'Of course it's a mistake.' Jack waved it off.

'A wife's testimony doesn't hold much sway, ma'am,' Carmichael said.

In a panic now as the men led Jack to the door, Pru blurted, 'He didn't kill anyone. It was me.'

'Pru! Be quiet!'

'It's very noble of you to try to save your husband, Mrs Fairweather. But no witnesses saw you entering the hotel.'

'Can we have a minute, Carmichael?'

The sergeant hesitated. 'Don't run, Mr Fairweather. It only makes you look more guilty.'

Jack snorted out a laugh. 'I have no intention of running. I haven't done anything wrong.'

Sergeant Carmichael and the constable moved outside, but didn't close the front door.

Jack ran his hand over Henry's soft hair and spoke in a low voice to Pru. 'It will be okay. It's just a misunderstanding.'

'Is it possible someone saw you leaving the hotel?'

'It's possible. I was there twice, after all. Don't worry, I'll be back here before you know it. But just in case? Call on Harold Renstein. He's a good lawyer.'

'Lawyer?' Pru asked breathlessly.

Jack kissed Henry's head and then Pru's forehead and lips.

'Please don't worry, love.' He winked. 'They won't come near you.'

She frowned and then gasped. 'You still don't believe I didn't shoot Viktor, do you?'

'I wouldn't go to gaol for anyone else,' he said, and kissed her soundly on the mouth before she could protest anymore.

'Gaol?' Even whispering the word made her feel ill.

'Harold Renstein,' Jack repeated, as he headed for the door. 'You'll find him at widow Barnett's boarding house in Ballarat. Or Miss Lola's.'

Pru screwed up her nose. 'And where will I find you?'

'Ballarat holding I suspect, for now,' he told her. 'Don't worry love, everything will be fine.'

'Everything will be fine,' Pru huffed out a week later, as she sat wringing her hands in the Ballarat courtroom. Everything was not fine. It was far from fine. The witness hadn't hesitated to point out Jack among the miscreants he shared his cell with, and he'd been kept in the holding cells for a week while the police and the prosecution pieced together their case against him for the shooting of Viktor Petrovic.

Despite the courtroom being half filled with people, Pru sat in a row by herself. Alone. She felt so alone. She'd left Henry with Katie, but Bobby had promised he would be in court to support her. As she waited, she let her eyes wander around the building, trying to keep herself calm. The high ceilings, lofty and elaborate with their moulded cornices, gave the room a cavernous feel. A long, dark wooden table, intricately carved, sat at the front of the room and served as the judge's bench. It was quite the opulent set-up for a country courtroom.

Jack had been ordered to stand trial for the murder of Viktor. He was throwing himself on his own sword in a misguided effort to save her. She was sure he still believed she had killed Viktor, and was refusing to give himself an alibi in case they came after her instead.

Bobby dropped down on the wooden chair beside her, making her jump and bringing her attention back to the here and now.

'He's being a stubborn arse,' she murmured to Bobby.

'Stubborn.' Bobby nodded. 'You're a matched pair.'

She glowered at him and his lips curled. 'Want me to break him out of holding?'

'Think you can?' she asked, playing along.

Bobby shrugged a shoulder. 'Easy.'

She smiled for what seemed like the first time in days. He probably could do it, would do it, if she gave him the go ahead.

She exhaled heavily. 'Jack didn't do this. He didn't kill Viktor.'

'You say that like you're not really sure,' Bobby said, studying her closely.

She stayed quiet.

'If you don't believe he's innocent, Pru, what chance does he have? Jack's no killer. He's never so much as shot a gun at anyone.'

'Neither have you, Bobby,' she said, and met his eyes. 'But what would you do if someone came after Katie? Threatened her?'

He had no answer to that, but she knew he'd kill for Katie. Just as she knew Jack would kill for her and Henry.

As the jury members were brought in, she made a study of every single man, trying to determine whether they might be sympathetic towards Jack. Surely they wouldn't judge a man for killing an escaped convict like Viktor. But murder was murder— and Jack had made some enemies in the business world too. She only hoped none of those enemies sat among the jury and held the fate of her husband in their hands.

Overwhelming relief enveloped her when Jack was brought in. He looked tired and a smattering of rusty stubble had grown to shadow his jaw. It reminded her of how he'd looked when he'd been shot and laid up in bed for weeks. She swallowed down the fear at the memory. And here they were again—his life in danger, and her waiting to see if he would live or die. Would their trials never end?

He sat at a table beside Harold and turned back to smile and wink at her. How dare he grin that devil's grin at her now with what he was putting her through? He was refusing to speak. Refusing to give any alibi that might save his own life. Her fear gave way to anger as her mind went over all the 'what ifs'. What if he had simply turned Viktor in to the police? The man was a dangerous prison escapee. Would he have turned Jack in as well though? Would the police believe that Jack Fairweather, Ballarat businessman, had been a bushranger in another life? She couldn't discount it, considering the sergeant's suspicions, and all the accusations that had been flying around about Fairweather Transport and its possible involvement in highway robberies. Oh, why had Jack insisted on going after Viktor?

'All rise,' an officer of the court called. 'Judge James Collins presiding.'

Everyone in the court stood.

James Collins? Prudence frowned. How did she know that name?

She saw Jack slump a little as he sat back down, and she remembered. He was the man who had accused Fairweather Transport all those months ago of being complicit after bushrangers had bailed him up on the Melbourne road and stolen most of his belongings.

'Oh Lord.'

She could see the hint of satisfaction on the judge's face as he looked directly at Jack. He knew exactly who he was. Jack would never get a fair trial now.

'So gentlemen,' the judge began, taking a seat behind the wooden desk. 'Who are we today?'

'Arthur Randall, Crown Prosecutor, Your Honour.' A man as round as a bowling ball stood behind a table on the right side of the courtroom. 'The defendant, Jack Fairweather, is committed to stand trial on the charge of the wilful murder of one Viktor Petrovic.'

'Harold Renstein for Mr Jack Fairweather, Your Honour. I do not wish to waste the court's time with this farcical trial accusing my client, a reputable businessman, of murdering an escaped convict.'

'I assume the prosecution has evidence to support the charge?'

'We do, Your Honour,' Mr Randall answered the judge.

'Then we have reason to continue with this "farcical trial", Mr Renstein.' Judge Collins exchanged glances again with Jack. 'Let's get started, shall we? Mr Randall, call your witness.'

'The Prosecution calls Mr Richard Wellsley.'

Pru watched the man walk to the front of the courtroom and take a seat in the small wooden chair beside the judge's table.

Mr Randall stood and walked around the courtroom, strutting like a peacock. Even if he hadn't been trying to put her husband in prison, Pru would have disliked him immediately.

Taking a deep breath in through his nose, he puffed out his chest, projecting his voice to the rafters. 'Mr Wellsley, you were staying at the Duchess of Kent Hotel on the night of Sunday the fourteenth of September?'

'I was.'

'Please tell the court what occurred on the morning after, the morning of the fifteenth.'

'I was in the dining room with several other gentlemen having breakfast when we heard a gunshot.'

'And what time was this?'

'A little before seven-thirty, I believe.'

'Go on, Mr Wellsley, what did you, and the two gentlemen you were with, do when you heard the gunshot?'

'Nothing.'

'Nothing?' Mr Randall questioned, faux shock in his voice and expression.

'Well, it was the Duchess of Kent, sir,' Mr Wellsley said with a light shrug and a grimace. People in the courtroom chuckled, understanding exactly what he meant. 'I mean, it's not uncommon to hear gunshots in the vicinity. It's hardly a reputable place, and being so close to the Eureka gold-mining leads, well, men fire off shots at claim jumpers and thieves day and night.'

'But you said you saw someone leaving the hotel in haste,' the prosecutor pushed.

'I walked to the window that looks out over the rear of the hotel, thinking I'd perhaps see where the shot came from.' Wellsley nodded.

'And what did you see?'

'I saw a man in a bowler hat, moving quickly away from the rear entrance of the hotel and to the stables. He disappeared inside and I didn't see him again. It didn't seem unusual to me at the time, but when they found the dead man upstairs, I thought perhaps the fleeing man might have had something to do with it.'

'And is the man you saw in court today?'

'He is,' Wellsley said and pointed at Jack. 'That man there.'

'Thank you, Mr Wellsley.' The prosecutor grinned at the judge. 'I am finished with the witness, Your Honour.'

Pru took a deep breath. The prosecution had a good case, but it was hardly conclusive. Just because Mr Wellsley had seen Jack didn't mean he had shot Viktor. Harold was a smart barrister, and knew this too.

'Your cross-examination, Mr Renstein,' the judge instructed.

'Thank you, Your Honour.' Harold stood and walked towards the witness.

'Mr Wellsley, you say you saw a man wearing a hat leaving the Duchess of Kent Hotel at almost half seven in the morning?'

'Yes, sir.'

'You were also wandering about the hotel at that time, so actually it could have been you who shot Viktor Petrovic.'

'As I said, I was in the dining room with three other gentlemen when the gunshot rang out. The men saw me.'

'Men who aren't here today to corroborate your story,' Harold was quick to point out. 'It's your word against my client's, Mr Wellsley.'

He let that hang for moment as he picked up a piece of paper from his table. 'Viktor Petrovic was shot twice. The doctor who examined Mr Petrovic discovered two different types of bullets, from two different guns. You could have shot him earlier that morning and the second shot came from another of Mr Petrovic's enemies. He had quite a lot of them, I understand.'

Feeling ill, Pru swallowed hard. She'd been the one to put that second shot into Viktor. If he hadn't already been dead when she'd accidentally squeezed the trigger, it would be her standing trial for his murder now.

'I never met the man.' Mr Wellsley shrugged. 'I would have no reason to kill him.' Pru noticed he was completely unperturbed by Harold's accusations. She knew that all Harold had to do was discredit this witness and Jack would go free.

'Mr Fairweather had no reason to kill him either,' Harold added. 'But you seem to think he did because you saw a man in a bowler hat leaving the rear of the hotel.'

'He was moving quickly, running from something,' Wellsley said.

'Perhaps he was rushing to get home to his wife,' Harold suggested. 'A gentleman cheating on his wife and fleeing his lover's hotel bed in the early hours of the morning is not a crime.'

There were chuckles about the courtroom from other men and Pru cringed. It wasn't the sweetest form of defence, but she didn't care. As long as it gave Jack an alibi.

Harold walked over to his chair and lifted up a bowler hat. 'Is this the hat you saw the man wearing?'

Pru held her breath. It was Jack's. And, yes, he had been wearing it the morning they had seen Viktor at the Duchess of Kent.

'Yes,' Mr Wellsley said with a nod. 'I recall it was not a hat I had seen many men wear.'

Pru's teeth ground together. *Blast Jack and his insistence on staying at the forefront of fashion.*

'Really?' Harold asked, looking surprised. 'Do you not follow the latest trends, Mr Wellsley?'

'I spend much of my time on the road, Mr Renstein,' Mr Wellsley said.

Harold looked shocked. 'Are you a bushranger, sir?'

The man looked offended. 'No. I am a travelling stock salesman. I don't spend a lot of time in cities.'

'But you do not need to go to the city. Why, these hats are for sale right here in Ballarat, in our own Criterion store,' Harold explained. 'In fact, this is my hat, not Mr Fairweather's.'

There were more murmurs from the crowd.

'Gentlemen in the courtroom,' Harold said, turning to face the gallery. 'Who here owns one of these new bowler-style hats?'

At least five men stood and held up their bowler hats. Pru had never seen anyone other than Jack wear this type of hat and she certainly hadn't seen it for sale in the Criterion store. Although, she'd bet money that when they left the courtroom, the store would mysteriously have changed its window dressing to include the latest in bowler hats out of Melbourne. Harold Renstein may have had a thing for the loose women of Miss Lola's, but he was a magician in the courtroom. Pru began to see light at the end of the dark tunnel she'd been in the past week while she'd awaited Jack's trial.

'So it seems your statement about seeing a man in an unusual hat doesn't hold much water, Mr Wellsley.'

'It was dark, but I did see his face.'

'You just said it was dark. How can you be so sure the man you saw was Mr Jack Fairweather?'

Wellsley shifted awkwardly in his seat. 'I can't be a hundred per cent certain. But I am pretty sure it was him. It was his hat.'

'We've just determined the number of bowler hats currently being worn in Ballarat, sir.'

'But—'

Harold cut him off. 'Thank you. No further questions.'

It wasn't ironclad, but Pru hoped Harold had thrown enough doubt into the witness's story to make the jury think twice, although the looks on their faces didn't fill Pru with much hope.

The judge banged his gavel. 'It's late in the day. I suggest we recess until tomorrow morning. Take the defendant back to holding.'

Pru reached out to take Jack's hand before he was led away. She was exhausted—physically and emotionally. She hadn't slept well since Jack had been arrested. Worry and panic kept her awake half the night, and Henry kept her awake the other half. Which reminded her, she needed to get back to Katie at the hotel and pick him up, but first she needed to see Jack.

The far-off squeak and groan of the main holding-cell gate opening was followed swiftly by whistles and lewd comments from his incarcerated neighbours. But Jack didn't bother to move from his uncomfortable wooden slab, with its thin mattress that served as a bed. He'd slept in worse places in his younger years. The ground usually, back when he'd started bushranging. He thought back to those early days. They'd been hard days. But they'd given him a good life eventually. Until now. Would he do anything differently?

He sighed. How could he wish he'd done things differently, when bushranging had brought him …

'Jack.'

'Pru?' He stood and moved to the bars, reaching through to take her hands. 'How are you? How's Henry?'

'He misses his daddy,' she said, leaning her head against the bars. 'We both miss you.'

He sighed again, closing his eyes. A week now he'd been sequestered in this cell, waiting to hear his fate. No one would touch Pru. Their son needed her. Whether she had killed Viktor or not, Jack still wasn't completely sure. Was she even capable of murder? It didn't matter. A witness had seen *him* at the Duchess of Kent. No one had seen Pru. So he would do everything in his power to keep her from harm. He'd had a lot of time to think about things, alone, in his small box. And he'd come to a hard decision. And it was time to put his plans in motion.

Opening his eyes again, he held her hands tightly in his.

'I need you to do something for me, Pru.'

'Anything, Jack. You know that.' She had that determined look in her eye, but she looked tired, too. This was going to be hard on both of them. 'Anything that will help get you out of here.'

'I won't be getting out of here.'

'Jack, don't be defeatist—'

'You heard that witness today,' he stopped her. 'You saw the looks on the jurors' faces. They didn't believe Harold's attempt to show reasonable doubt. The witness saw me, and no one else. And that judge has already made his mind up about me.'

'You can't give up, Jack.'

'I need you to go.'

'Go? Go where?'

'Take Henry, pack up your things and go to Geelong.'

'Geelong? Why in God's name would I go to Geelong?'

'I have a house there.'

'You have another house? How did I not know this?'

'I've had it for a long time. Before I even met you. I set it up as a safe house, just in case …'

'Just in case?'

'In case something like this ever happened. No one else knows about it. Not even Bobby.' He pulled his hands out of hers and back through the bars. 'At Little Windsor, buried under the back porch steps, there's a metal box with the deed to the Geelong house. You'll find the address on it. When you arrive, there's a loose brick to the left of the back door. The keys are there. Under the mattress in the main bedroom you'll find enough pounds to last you many years. If you're careful—'

'Jack, stop!'

'You have to go tonight.' He continued to talk over her denials.

'No,' she shot back. 'I won't leave you. Not now, not ever.'

'If I go to prison—'

'Then I'll come and visit you. But that's not going to—'

'I won't see you.'

Her hurt gasp had him faltering. The shattered look on her face broke his heart.

'Pru, if I go to prison, you and I …' He had to get this over with and fast. Before he could change his mind. 'I won't have you wasting your life and love on me. You and Henry deserve better than a bushranger who would have hanged eventually. This was my fate, Pru, it always was. You simply delayed it when you came into my life. I can't thank you enough for the time you gave me. But it's over now. You should go. Go home to Henry, pack your bags, and go to Geelong. And never look back.'

Tears tracked down her face, and he bit the inside of his cheek to stop himself from moving back to comfort her.

'No,' she said definitively. 'I won't go. Push me away all you like, but I'll never leave you. Don't you give up on me, Jack Fairweather. If you go to prison, we'll think of something. If Viktor can break out, you can too. I'll talk to Bobby.'

God, she was incredible. A bushranger's wife to the core.

He took in her pretty face, the stubborn set of her jaw. 'They'll be sending me to the new gaol. It's a fortress, impenetrable, they say. No one can escape from there.'

'I'll think of something.'

He shook his head, turned his back. 'Goodbye, Pru.'

'Jack, please—'

'Constable!' Jack called, bringing the guard in from the office. 'We are done here. Please escort the lady out.'

'I'll see you tomorrow in court.' Her voice was a whisper. 'I love you. No matter what happens.'

The clang of the outer gate closing heralded the end of his life. Unless Harold could pull out a miracle in court the next day, he would go to prison. Whatever happened to him after that didn't matter. He would lose his family. His life was over.

Pru was furious.

Tears had filled her evening, and all the while Katie had tried her best to console her. But when Henry had woken for a feed and she'd stared down into his bright eyes, so much like his father's, her sorrow had turned swiftly to anger. He may have given up, but she would never. She was resourceful and she was smart. She was also the wife of a bushranger. And that bushranger had friends.

Putting Henry down to sleep again, she'd made a strong pot of tea and, moving back to the dining room with Bobby and Katie, they'd got to work. The table was covered with maps as they planned. It had been a long night, and none of them had got any sleep.

Now sitting in the courtroom on a hot October morning, exhausted, her plan in place, her need to be calm battled with her righteous fury when Jack was led back into the courtroom. His eyes met hers quickly and narrowed with confusion. If he'd been expecting her to still be crying and simpering like a scorned wife, then perhaps he didn't know her at all.

Taking a deep breath, she rose as the judge entered the court-room and the players took their places. And the breath whooshed out of her, taking all of her fury-inspired strength with it, when Harold called his first witness of the day.

'The defence calls Mrs Deidre Stanforth.'

Eighteen

Pru could only stare, caught between confusion and horrified shock, as her grandmother walked through the doors into the courtroom.

'Close your mouth, Prudence,' Deidre instructed, as she walked down the aisle towards the stand, her walking stick clacking against the hardwood floors with a marching cadence. 'And that's Lady Stanforth to you, boy,' she directed snootily at Harold. 'As the wife of the late Earl of Carrington, I still deserve the title.'

Jack spun in his seat to look wide-eyed and questioning at Prudence. She shrugged and shook her head. She had no idea what her grandmother was doing here. And testifying for the defence? Gran hated Jack. She was up to something. Pru had no idea what that might be, but it terrified her to her core.

She had no doubt it had occurred to her grandmother that putting Jack in prison would mean she and Henry would be forced to go home to Carrington Manor. There was no way in hell that would happen. If Gran's testimony put Jack in gaol, Pru would make sure she never saw her or Henry again. Even if it meant

323

living in squalor. She could get a job to support herself and Henry until Jack came home. If Jack came home. If he was convicted, he'd most likely hang. Tears threatened as she thought of Henry, that he might never know his father.

The Bible was held out and her grandmother swore the oath to tell the truth. What truth? Pru wondered, her mind reeling. Her gran knew nothing about the situation. Pru fidgeted nervously in her seat while Deidre sat still as a statue, her back ramrod straight, her expression unreadable.

'Mrs …' Harold began and then paused. 'I beg your pardon, Lady Stanforth.'

Deidre nodded from her position on the stand, clearly pleased that he had used her title.

'You are Mrs Prudence Fairweather's grandmother, is that correct?'

'It is.'

'And is it true that your granddaughter, Mrs Fairweather, ran away from her family home at Carrington Manor?'

'Yes,' Deidre answered. 'She married that dreadful man over there. The defendant.'

Pru's heart sank. Her grandmother was going to ruin everything. She saw Jack slump in his chair.

'You oppose your granddaughter's marriage to Mr Fairweather?' Harold continued.

What was he doing? Pru stared wide-eyed at Harold. He was their defence lawyer and he was feeding Jack to the wolves.

'I do oppose the match,' Deidre went on. 'It is obvious to anyone with eyes that she married beneath her.'

'So it is safe to say that you hold no love for the man now on trial for murder,' Harold went on.

Pru's stomach roiled with nausea.

'I have no love for a man who would steal an old lady's only granddaughter from her,' Deidre went on, her voice wavering slightly. 'A granddaughter whom I raised from birth and gave all the love and care I knew how.'

Tears welled in Pru's eyes as her grandmother spoke. She looked quite a bit older than when Pru had left Carrington Manor. So much had happened in that time. She was a mother now. Pru hadn't paid much attention when they had run into Deidre in Melbourne. She'd been in too much of a rush to get away, fearing her grandmother would try to take Henry from them. Now, as Pru took a good look at her, she noticed her skin was thinner, translucent almost, and more wrinkled. Her eyes had lost much of their severity, and she looked at Pru with a sort of sadness. The anger she'd held on to for so long towards her grandmother lessened. But it didn't change the fact that she seemed to be there to set fire to her husband's already flimsy defence.

'And do you believe that Jack Fairweather is capable of murder?'

'I believe the man to be capable of many things,' she said and Pru closed her eyes, horrified that her own grandmother was going to be the one to put her husband in prison.

'However, as much as I disapprove of the man,' she began, her voice strong and steady again, 'the only thing criminal about Jack Fairweather is that he cheats at bridge.'

'Bridge, madam?' Harold questioned.

'Yes, it's a card game, Mr Renstein.'

'I know what bridge is.'

'Then why did you ask?' she responded, shifting impatiently on the hard wooden seat.

There were some titters of laughter around the courtroom, but Pru could only stare, dumbfounded at what she was hearing. What was the old woman up to?

'Order,' the judge called, bringing quiet once again to the room.

'Tell me, Lady Stanforth, where were you on the morning of Monday fifteenth of September?'

'I was at home at Carrington Manor.'

'Alone?'

'No, my son's wife, Alicia, was there, as were the staff.' She paused. 'Along with my granddaughter and her card-cheat of a husband.'

More whispers, louder now, filled the court.

'Order!' The judge struggled to bring the court into line, so he banged his gavel on the wooden table. 'Order in the court.'

'Are you saying that there was no way that Jack Fairweather could possibly have shot and killed Viktor Petrovic because he was with you at the time of the murder?' Harold asked. Pru thought his surprised incredulity seemed forced and she suddenly smelled a plot.

'Why else would I be here, you silly man?' Deidre tossed back. 'Do you think I make it a habit to enter courtrooms for the pleasure of it? It is true I dislike my granddaughter's new husband, but it would be against my honour not to speak out in his defence should I have reason to do so.' She huffed with impatience. 'My granddaughter, and that man, arrived at Carrington Manor on the night of the fourteenth of September. We enjoyed a meal of lamb shanks. My son, Robert, raises his own livestock. It was slightly overcooked, but it's hard to find good staff out here in the backwater.'

'Lady Stanforth.' The judge interrupted her monologue. 'The evidence, if you will?'

'Yes, yes.' Deidre gave him a tight smile. 'We played bridge with my son's wife, Alicia, until around ten that night, at which point I retired to my bedchamber and Prudence and that man were shown to the second-floor guest quarters.'

Pru's eyes nearly popped out of her head as the courtroom erupted in astonished discussion. It was a lie. A bald-faced lie. Gran was lying for them? Why? What could she possibly gain by ensuring Jack's freedom?

Jack turned in his seat again to stare at Pru, stupefied, but she was so bewildered herself that all she could do was blink.

She noticed Gran was keeping Robert out of it. Had he decided he didn't want to be part of the fabrication? Or perhaps he had been away in Melbourne on business again and was happily ignorant of the fairy tale her grandmother was weaving.

'What time did Mr and Mrs Fairweather leave Carrington Manor the next day?' Harold asked, holding the lapels of his jacket as he paced the courtroom. Pru thought he looked like the cat that got the cream. She only hoped he could pull it off.

'We enjoyed luncheon on the south-facing patio, before Mr Fairweather took his wife and child back to the bush house where they choose to live.'

Gran knew where they lived? She'd been sure after they had run into her in Melbourne that she would do whatever she could to take Henry from them. The thought had terrified her, and she had known where they lived all along?

The judge rapped his gavel again to halt the murmurs in the courtroom.

'Lady Stanforth,' Judge Collins addressed her. 'Can anyone else corroborate your story?'

'My word is not enough?' Her steely-eyed gaze had the judge sitting back a little in his seat. Pru had seen many a man cower at that look. Deidre sat up straighter, and again Pru could see how old she was looking. Just sitting in the uncomfortable seat was clearly taking its toll on her.

'You may ask any of the staff at the manor. They were excited to see Prudence back home, even for one night.' At this point,

Deidre moved her gaze out across the courtroom and connected with Pru for the first time, her expression softening into one of weary sadness. 'They'd missed her, you see.'

Pru swallowed hard against the lump that formed in her throat. Was Gran saying *she'd* missed her? Was she using the servants as a cover to tell her just how much she'd missed her? Her grandmother had never been very good at showing emotion. Stiff upper lip of the aristocracy, and all that.

'Mr Renstein, we have not yet heard from Mr Fairweather in this case,' the judge said. 'I'm assuming should he be questioned, he would provide the same story?'

'He would, Your Honour.'

'And why did he not explain this story to the arresting officer ...' The judge searched his notes. 'One Sergeant Carmichael?'

Carmichael stood in the gallery behind the prosecutor. 'Your Honour, Mr Fairweather waived his right to speak in his defence. He did not offer an alibi at the time, but was determined to keep quiet on the matter.'

'No wonder you thought him guilty.' The judge frowned. 'Mr Fairweather, stand please.'

Jack stood.

'Is Lady Stanforth telling the truth?'

'Why would I lie?' Deidre interrupted, huffing with irritation.

The judge ignored her. 'Mr Fairweather.'

'She is telling the truth, Your Honour,' Jack answered. 'My grandmother-in-law and I share a rocky relationship and I am sure she would be happy to see me put away in prison for the rest of my life.'

Pru couldn't argue with him on that count.

'I didn't offer Lady Deidre as a witness as I was unsure if she would testify on my behalf, or line up to tighten the noose herself.'

The judge looked to Deidre. 'I believe I understand your hesitation, Mr Fairweather.' His smile dissipated when she turned cold eyes on him. He cleared his throat. 'Members of the court, in light of this evidence from such an esteemed member of the community, I recommend this trial be dismissed. How say you, Crown Prosecutor? Do you have any evidence to conflict with the testimony of Lady Stanforth?'

The prosecutor stood. 'Not at this time, Your Honour.'

Pru felt hope bubble up as the judge banged his gavel one last, glorious time.

'I want to thank the jury for their time in this matter. Case dismissed.'

Noise erupted in the courtroom and Pru rushed down the aisle to where Jack was shaking hands with Harold.

'I don't know how you did it,' she heard Jack say quietly to Harold.

'Well, you'd provided no alibi for yourself, so I knew it couldn't be disputed if I were to find you one.' Harold winked and tapped his nose before moving away so that Pru could embrace Jack.

'Oh, Jack.' She kissed him and squeezed him to her.

They kissed again more fervently, all their fear, their heightened emotions, rolling into relief and passion as they held each other.

'Alright, that's enough of that. A public courtroom is not the place for such debauchery.'

Separating from Jack, Pru met the hard gaze of her grandmother who stood before her.

'How ...? What ...?'

'Speak properly, child,' Deidre scolded and glanced around the courtroom at the many law officers still present. 'And not here.

I need some air. This courtroom is musty. It's not good for my lungs. Shall we take a stroll?'

'Of course, Grandmother,' Pru said, suddenly feeling like a chastised child again. She enfolded her fingers in Jack's and they followed Deidre out of the courtroom.

The day was hot and Deidre's parasol was up before the sun hit her. They walked in silence to a nearby park where Deidre placed a handkerchief on a park bench before sitting.

Pru sat beside her and Jack stood.

'Grandmother, I don't know how to thank you,' Pru said. 'How did you even know about the trial?'

'It was in the paper.'

'I am indebted to you, Lady Deidre,' Jack added, still holding Pru's hand. 'Whether you believe this or not, I did not kill Viktor Petrovic.'

'I don't care if you did or you didn't,' Deidre shot back. 'The world will hardly miss another thieving bushranger.'

Pru and Jack exchanged glances. If only she knew.

'But that's not why I perjured myself on the stand.'

'Then why?' Pru asked, still amazed by her grandmother's extraordinary behaviour.

'Because I want to be able to see my great-grandson,' Deidre admitted, losing some of the harshness in her tone. 'And I knew this was the only way you'd let me close to him.' She hesitated, looked uncomfortable. 'Or let me close enough to say that I am sorry, Prudence, for lying to you all these years. I should never have kept you and your mother apart. I thought I was doing the right thing. I see now, too late, that I was wrong.'

Pru was speechless. It still hurt that she had never had the chance to know her mother. But she could no longer go on punishing her grandmother for mistakes made more than twenty years ago.

She leaned in to kiss Deidre's papery, thin cheek. Her grandmother had always been an old woman, but she was elderly

now. Reconciling with her seemed the kindest and only thing
to do.

'I forgive you,' she whispered.

'Yes, well. I've learned enough about you and your obstinate
ways to know that if Fairweather was convicted, the two of you
would run.'

'Well, I ...' Pru blushed and Jack gave her a questioning look.
'What?'

'Don't be mad,' she begged him, standing and moving him
away from her grandmother's keen ears. 'I wasn't going to live
without you, Jack. And what's the point in having friends who
are, shall we say, wise in the ways of illegal activities, if you can't
ask them to bail someone up for a good cause?'

Jack still didn't seem to understand.

'I told you I wouldn't let you go to prison.'

'Pru, what did you do?'

She bit her lip, knowing he was going to be mad at her. 'If you
were found guilty and sent to prison, Bobby was going to bail up
the prison transport and get you out.'

'What? Prudence! I don't know whether to be angry or proud,'
Jack said with a stunned laugh.

'We would have run with you, Jack. Me and Henry.'

'And I would never see my grandson again,' Deidre added.

How much had her grandmother heard? Pru rushed to sit
beside her again. 'Oh, Gran, I ...'

Deidre raised a hand to stop her. 'I do not care to hear all the
sordid details of your no-doubt nefarious plans to run from the
law. Now I wish to see the child. Where is he, by the way?'

'I left him with friends. Would you like to see Henry, Gran?'

'I would,' she answered, and Pru thought she saw a weak smile
peek out from her grandmother's thin lips. She began to stand
with the aid of her walking stick and Jack moved to take her hand
but she waved him away.

'Alright, alright, I'm not for the knackery yet,' Deidre snapped, pushing herself upright.

'Madam, I was simply going to kiss your hand,' Jack said, taking her hand again and laying his lips lightly to her thin lace glove.

'I see now why you were so taken with him,' Deidre said, surprising Pru with a chuckle. 'He's a smooth one, isn't he?'

Epilogue

The giant Christmas tree in the corner stood like a beacon. A beacon a child couldn't resist, and being a child, Henry made a beeline for it, crawling like a crab towards the pretty ornaments. Luckily, his father was faster.

'No you don't, young man,' Jack said, tossing Henry into the air and catching him. It was Henry's favourite game, only slightly overtaken recently by the 'disassemble the Christmas tree' game.

'We need to put a cage around that thing,' Pru said, sipping cool tea over ice.

'The tree or Henry?' Jack joked.

They lounged around the drawing room, a large pork roast with all the trimmings having been devoured a few hours before sending them all into a contented state of restfulness.

'I'll never get used to these hot Christmases,' Deidre said, waving a fan with one hand while she sipped sherry with the other. 'It just doesn't feel like Christmas.'

'It feels very much like Christmas to me,' Pru said, standing to kiss her husband and baby. Although, he was no longer a baby. One year old already. How the time had flown. Her little boy was growing up. 'I have all I want for Christmas. My husband is not in gaol and my family is reunited.'

She smiled at Deidre and attempted to take Henry and prepare him for his nap. Henry had other ideas and began one of his famous tantrums. He was overtired, Pru realised. Too much excitement for a little boy, too many presents. Most of which had come from none other than Deidre.

'I still say you spoil that child,' Deidre admonished, making Pru shake her head with the irony of it. 'One year old or not, he should have better manners.'

Jack just chuckled and Pru wondered at how he never seemed to get flustered or annoyed at anything her grandmother said. That was almost as infuriating to Pru as her grandmother's constant advice and criticisms about their parenting skills. But Jack took it all on the chin, said something smooth to Deidre to make her laugh, and that was that.

'I should put Henry down for his nap,' she said, fighting the little boy as he squirmed and leaned towards his tin truck abandoned on the floor. She gave in and put him down to play a little longer.

'What is that you're drinking, Jack?' Deidre asked. 'There is condensation on the bottle. It looks cool.'

'It is cool, and refreshing,' he told her. 'It's beer, Lady Carrington. Would you care to try it?'

'Beer,' she repeated. 'Oh, yes, I've heard of it.'

'Much more refreshing than a sherry,' he said. 'Sherry will make your face hot. Beer will cool you to your toes.'

Deidre thought on it for a moment before summoning Gerald, the butler.

'Gerald, bring me a bottle of cold beer please,' she instructed. 'And get one for yourself and the other servants. It's Christmas.'

Gerald nearly tripped over his own shoes with shock at the gesture, before he stepped back out of the drawing room to fetch her beer.

When he began to pour the beer into a glass, Jack stopped him with a shake of his head.

'Out of the bottle, Deidre,' he instructed. 'It's much nicer that way, and stays cooler longer.'

Pru's mouth dropped open when her grandmother put the dark brown bottle to her lips and tipped it back to take a slug of cool, frothy ale.

'Refreshing,' Deidre reviewed when she'd taken a sip.

Jack tapped his bottle to hers and they drank. Pru just shook her head in astonishment. Whoever said people didn't change hadn't met these two.

They all heard the knock at the door and a moment later Gerald returned to the drawing room.

'A telegram,' he announced, but when Deidre held out her hand, he looked to Jack. 'For Mr Fairweather.'

Jack took the telegram and read. 'It's from Harold Renstein.'

'The lawyer?' Deidre asked.

'Yes.'

'Oh, this can't be good,' Pru said, placing a worried hand on Jack's arm. 'Have they found more evidence against you?'

Jack shook his head.

'Then what?' Pru asked as he read on. 'Jack, please, you're scaring me.'

'They caught the real killer.' Jack handed the telegram to her.

She took it and read out loud. 'Paolo Cirrocco arrested Castlemaine yesterday for shooting of Viktor Petrovic stop confessed he shot Viktor over stolen property stop.'

'Seems Viktor finally robbed the wrong person,' Jack said, putting a comforting arm around Pru. It was finally over. Jack had been cleared of all suspicion.

'I never got to ask you what happened when you went to see Viktor,' she said, folding the telegram away.

'I was furious,' he admitted. 'So ready to kill him. But he wasn't there when I arrived and that's when I went out looking for him. I think I went to all the pubs in Ballarat. And when I returned, as I was climbing the stairs of the hotel, I thought of you and Henry. By the time I reached Viktor's room, I knew I couldn't do it. I didn't want Henry to grow up knowing his father was a murderer. I had the money I owed Viktor. I'd intended on leaving it in the room and going home to you and Henry. But I heard the shot and opened the door to see you there.'

Pru smiled. 'So, you really didn't do it?'

'Me?' Jack asked with a huff. 'I still thought it was you.'

'Hah! Wonderful start to marriage,' Deidre tossed in sardonically as she shifted to pick Henry up to bounce on her knee. 'Each believing the other is a murderer. Trust between partners is paramount if you want your marriage to survive. You should work on that.'

'Yes, Gran,' Pru said, and laughing, she threw her arms around her innocent husband. 'We'll work on that.'

Acknowledgements

After *The Girl from Eureka*, I just wasn't ready to let go of the Ballarat goldfields. I had done so much research for that story that it seemed a waste not to use more of it in another book. Before I'd even finished writing *The Girl from Eureka* I had already started Jack the Devil's own story. He was such a fun character and I had to find him a woman who would give him a hard time and be his equal in everything.

Thanks to the fabulous folks at HarperCollins Australia, Harlequin MIRA and Escape for taking on Jack and Pru's story and the editors who worked with me on making *The Bushranger's Wife* the best it could be.

Special thanks as always to Belinda Stevens and a giant thank you to all my readers who have been wonderfully supportive. Writing makes me happy. Being able to share the stories with you makes me blessed.

talk about it

Let's talk about books.

Join the conversation:

 facebook.com/romanceanz

 @romanceanz

romance.com.au

If you love reading and want to know about our
authors and titles, then let's talk about it.